RUN BEFORE THE RAIN

RUN BEFORE THE RAIN

AN ANTEDILUVIAN ADVENTURE

Michael Vetter

iUniverse, Inc.
Bloomington

RUN BEFORE THE RAIN
An Antediluvian Adventure

iUniverse books may be ordered through booksellers or by contacting:

iUniverse
1663 Liberty Drive
Bloomington, IN 47403
www.iuniverse.com
1-800-Authors (1-800-288-4677)

ISBN: 978-1-4759-5150-9 (sc)
ISBN: 978-1-4759-5152-3 (hc)
ISBN: 978-1-4759-5151-6 (ebk)

Library of Congress Control Number: 2012918003

Printed in the United States of America

iUniverse rev. date: 10/11/2012

To Mary—for her love, encouragement,
support, and strength.

To Dr. John Whitcomb—Bible teacher and author of
The Genesis Flood, who sparked my interest in an advanced
antediluvian civilization.

The earth also was corrupt before God,
and the earth was filled with violence.
And God looked upon the earth, and, behold, it was corrupt;
for all flesh had corrupted his way upon the earth.
And God said unto Noah, The end of all flesh is come before me;
for the earth is filled with violence through them;
and, behold, I will destroy them with the earth.

Genesis 6:11-13 (KJV)

Knowing this first, that there shall come in the last days scoffers,
walking after their own lusts,
And saying, Where is the promise of His coming?
for since the fathers fell asleep, all things continue as they were
from the beginning of the creation.
For this they willingly are ignorant of,
that by the word of God the heavens were of old,
and the earth standing out of the water and in the water:
Whereby the world that then was, being overflowed with water, perished.

The Second Epistle of Peter 3:3-6 (KJV)

PREFACE

This book is a work of fiction that uses information in the Bible about the Great Flood of Noah's time to speculate what life was like before Earth was totally destroyed by water.

I believe in the verbal, plenary inspiration of Scripture and a young, divinely created Earth. My goal has been to write a story of what an antediluvian—or pre-Flood—civilization might have been like while remaining consistent with the facts revealed in the Bible. If I have contradicted anything explicitly stated in the Bible, that was not my intent.

I have tried to infuse a fictional story with Biblical principles of faith, godliness, and truth that are valid in any period of time. The epic truths of redemption through Jesus Christ were only foreshadowed in the earliest revelation, but they finally became clear in the New Testament when Christ lived, died, and rose again to pay, once for all, the infinite price of redemption for each human being. People of all ages—back to Adam, Seth, Enoch, Methuselah, Noah, and Japheth—were covered by the blood of the future Promised One, when they put their full confidence in God. We do not know how people before the Flood understood and interpreted the prophetic revelation found in Genesis chapters 2-6. We also do not know if they received detailed divine revelation in addition to what Moses wrote in the book of Genesis. In light of that, my characterization of beliefs and spirituality in the pre-Flood age—however rooted it is in my understanding of fundamental Biblical theology—is entirely speculative.

This story extrapolates the conditions of the sixteen hundred years before the Great Flood from the facts given in the Bible, suggests highly intelligent characters capable of rapid technological progress, and inserts inventions of science and engineering into a plot of mystery and adventure. I believe that untainted human intellect close to the time of creation, combined with individual longevity, could have resulted in an undiminished, accelerated accumulation of knowledge.

ACKNOWLEDGMENTS

Run Before the Rain: An Antediluvian Adventure took shape in my mind over a period of almost ten years. I began writing this story four years ago and now it is my privilege to recognize the people who helped make this published work possible.

My special thanks to Brian Weaver for the cover and interior artwork that helps the reader visualize characters in an antediluvian civilization. Brian immediately appreciated the speculative technologies in the book and how they meshed with the characters and plot. His cover design dramatically captures the excitement and adventure of the story. I am very appreciative of his valuable contribution.

Lauren Fiorelli was a late addition to my "editorial team." She bravely took on the task of unwinding my awkward sentences to make them more intelligible, more brief, and grammatically correct. But most of all, I am grateful for her insightful comments and questions that forced me to reexamine plot lines, characters, and event chronologies. I predict that Lauren has a secure place in the publishing world until her "real" career as a singer and actress takes flight!

Several people spent hours reviewing early versions of the manuscript and making helpful changes and corrections: my sister, Gale Grosso, used her years of newspaper production and technical editing experience to delve into the details; my niece, Terra Vetter, applied her imaginative and inquisitive mind to raise excellent observations about characters and plot; Steve and Kathy Routhier took time to review the manuscript for words and punctuation that escaped earlier reviewers. Thanks also to Nancy Krawczyk, Jen Mitchell, and Lori Gallo for checking the final proofs.

I want to give a special thanks to my friend, Ray Toomey, for engaging me in lively discussions about pre-Flood civilization possibilities. Ray's helpful comments, based on his sound knowledge of the Bible, continue to be an encouragement and a motivation for me to search the Scriptures daily.

Dr. John Whitcomb is a world-famous Bible and creation science teacher without equal. That is not hyperbole. His book, *The Genesis Flood*, coauthored with Dr. Henry Morris, began the creation science movement. I met Dr. Whitcomb when he spoke at a Bible conference in New England in the late 1970s. At a later conference in Middletown, CT, I suggested the plot of a fictional high-technology adventure story set in the advanced antediluvian civilization and his eyes brightened at the idea. We had several good conversations during conference breaks when he encouraged me to continue with my thoughts. I am indebted to him for laying the pioneer groundwork of creation science for our understanding of "*the world that then was . . .*"

The editorial, production, and marketing team at iUniverse have guided me with professionalism through the steps of self-publishing. A special thanks to Hope Davis whose patient, knowledgeable, and timely replies to my many questions could not have been more helpful. I made many mistakes before signing on with iUniverse, but their comprehensive authoring literature turned my earlier detours into valuable learning experiences. Thanks to iUniverse, my next book in this series will move into print faster and with fewer missteps on my part.

Finally, my wife and best friend deserves a gold medal for listening to me talk for years about outlandish story plots and imaginary characters. But Mary did more than listen. She kept me moving forward with encouragement when my writing became sluggish. She was equally ready to suggest I go kayaking on the lake when writing, work, and family demands overwhelmed me. Even after reviewing the manuscript multiple times, her keen eye for detail found hidden typos.

This work of fiction is entirely my responsibility and any errors are mine alone. It has always been my goal to conform the imaginary events and actions of characters to facts and doctrines explicitly revealed in the Bible.

PROLOGUE

The world that our human race has called home for the past one thousand six hundred years is gone. Forty days of inundating rain, screaming winds, and incessant pounding by gigantic waves are finally over. Now we wait in the eerie calm for whatever comes next.

Our family spent more than a century building a wooden ship to preserve us and the diversity of animals needed to repopulate the planet.

This story is a record of what happened leading up to the catastrophe known as the Great Flood. Much of it will be judged so unbelievable by future generations that it will be dismissed as a myth. Maybe this will give you a sense of how terrible the world was back then. Future generations may say that conditions on Earth were not so bad before the Flood, but the condition of mankind was terrible—far more terrible than anyone could have imagined.

No matter how much my father, Noah, warned people about the certainty of God's judgment coming as a worldwide flood, they refused to listen to him. He offered a place on our ship to those who would acknowledge their wickedness and place their faith in the One True God. But when the rains came our family boarded the ship alone. We are the sole remaining believers—remnants of a time when God's people covered the earth and numbered in the millions.

When you read this account, wherever you are, I hope you realize that those who came before you lived through one of the most exciting periods in human history. Yes, it was a time of high cultural achievement and technological advancement, but it degenerated into a primitive civilization saturated with evil. Our average lifespan was eight hundred years and we boldly thought there was no limit to what we could do. We imagined we would someday travel to the stars. But by the end of our era there were only eight people devoted to pleasing God at any cost.

Japheth, son of Noah

BOOK I

NOAH

First Sixty Years
1536-1596 AC (After Creation)

CHAPTER 1

Eden's Promise

What was that light ahead?

In the calm, warm dawn, Noah was checking on a new litter of bobcats born a few weeks earlier in the foothills above his remote estate when the sound of a rushing wind around a bend in the path caught his attention. He didn't smell smoke, but he could clearly see what looked like a flame through the brush. Rounding the bend, he observed a small tree not more than four or five feet high. It was not glowing, exactly, but radiating, as if every leaf and branch were infused with fire. The flame ascended ten feet into the air, but there was no smoke or heat. Bright flames, but no smoke or heat? Radiating light, but with its green leaves still lifted to catch the morning moisture?

"That is strange," Noah uttered aloud.

Approaching the tree, he felt a sinking feeling in the pit of his stomach and his knees gave out under him. This seemed vaguely familiar to him—the brilliant flames rising into the sky, no heat or smoke, green leaves that should have shriveled and fallen off, the sound of a strong wind, but no movement in the trees around him.

When Noah was a child, his grandfather, Methuselah, told him how he would sit beside Adam late into the night to hear what it was like when God spoke to Adam and Eve in the Garden. Noah's great-grandfather, Enoch, related the same captivating experience of when God spoke to him from a flame, but none of these stories prepared Noah for what happened next.

"Noah!"

God spoke his name!

Noah's instant reactions were terror and reverent subjection. He fell to his knees, spread his arms with palms on the ground and lay prostrate with his forehead pressed into the mountain trail.

Noah heard a voice—better yet, he felt a voice—that entered his body from the burning tree. Oddly, though it somehow resembled the intonation of a deep voice, he couldn't distinguish specific words because the sound of rushing wind overpowered his hearing. He tried to concentrate, but the sounds all seemed to run together. He needed to relax, but he couldn't.

Divine instructions—inaudible, but perfectly clear inside his head—came to him in a single thought that flooded his mind and drowned out the sound of the rushing wind. The pulse of information raced from his mind to his heart and into his soul, where he sensed, at first, a profound dread. A vision—again more felt than seen—of what would soon happen to the world and what he should do filled Noah's being and impressed itself upon his memory. Finally, his initial fear was replaced with a calm feeling that all would be well with him and his family.

It was hard to tell how much time passed; it could have been an hour or a second, but Noah's physical sensations slowly returned: the smell of dirt moistened by the morning dew, the feeling of the pebbles pressing against his face, the warm sun on his back. *What was this all about? What have I done?* he questioned. Noah rose to his feet and brushed the dirt from his hands and tunic. His mind reeled with thoughts of what all this might mean. His breathing and heart rate were back to normal, but he had so many questions.

Then he heard a bird singing nearby. From the middle of the path he saw a sparrow perched on the branch in front of him, chirping a beautiful melody. It was as if this little creature knew that God had been there and was naturally lifting his song in praise of his Creator.

Noah cautiously approached the tree. The sparrow flew off to sing in the distance as he stretched out his hand to confirm that the tree was real. The heart-shaped leaves were warm in the sunlight, still moist with the last remnants of morning dew. They had the scent of a plant's natural freshness and held no odor of smoke. Had he been seeing things? Was this real? How could a tree look like it was burning with flames reaching into the sky and yet not be consumed?

The flame ascended ten feet into the air, but there was no smoke or heat.

On his way back home, Noah forgot about the litter of bobcats he had come to check on and stopped several times in mid-trail to think. The experience was so dreamlike and the message from God so fantastic that he doubted anyone would believe him. He sat on a rock by a stream that flowed from the hillside to rehearse what he would tell his wife, Miriam, and his father when he returned home. If what God said to him was real, then this supernatural event would change their lives forever.

Noah's training as an objective scientist led him to carefully outline God's message and reason through each part, but he was having difficulty fully understanding it. God was angry with mankind—that much was clear. Yes, they had obeyed God's early command to multiply and fill the earth with millions of inhabitants. But over the centuries, mankind had grown profoundly evil. Some of this was due to the influence of the appearance of Anakim giants, but it was sin within the heart of each person that caused him or her to act upon every wicked impulse with unrestrained violence. God was grieved in His heart by this rampant, worldwide sin. He was determined to destroy every creature on the face of the earth and start over. Noah had no trouble understanding that part because the trend in the past few centuries was undeniable.

But the fact that Noah and his family had been singled out as the sole recipients of God's saving grace was too astonishing to handle in his mind. This unmerited favor was not due to their "goodness," but it was because God's future plan for the world's redemption involved repopulating the planet from one family. Noah didn't understand it, but his faith compelled him to accept it.

The final part of what Noah "heard" was what caused his inner turmoil. He and his family were told to build a ship—a giant boat that God had called an "ark"—that would be their home while God destroyed the rest of the planet in a global flood of water. God's specifications for the ark were brief, but they described a vessel of immense proportions to protect them during the global deluge. Male and female of every kind of animal on Earth were to be his passengers during the flood. In Noah's mind, this made for an impossible journey, but he knew that it would happen in the next one hundred and twenty years. God had made a covenant promise with Noah to bring it about exactly as He said.

Noah felt a little better after he reasoned this through, but he was no less settled about what lay ahead for him and his family. He had no idea where to start, so he began his walk back home to talk it over with his wife and father.

By the early Earth's timetable, Noah was a middle-aged man of almost five hundred years, showing evidence of slowly advancing age: thinning hair and streaks of gray in what was once a red beard, wrinkles around the eyes, and the usual aches and pains on damp mornings. But Noah spent most of his days outdoors, and his tall, muscular frame was otherwise in good shape. He was a typical specimen of vitality for this era. His wife, Miriam, was also from the line of Adam's son Seth, whose descendants were called Sethians. Rather than fair-skinned and blue-eyed like Noah, she had almond skin, brown eyes, and glistening, black hair. The significant difference in appearance was not unusual; the Sethian family line had always exhibited a diversity of colors, shapes, and sizes. In the beginning, their race was commanded by God to multiply and spread over the earth, and that they did. At one time their numbers reached into the millions. In contrast, the distinct Cainite civilization, descended from Adam's son Cain, remained in urban areas and the Cainite's facial features and body types were less diverse due to intermarriage. Some say you can tell a Cainite just by observing him, but do not be mislead. If you didn't notice the "mark of Cain" on the back of their necks, some Cainites could be mistaken for Sethians from their facial features alone. It was their aberrant lifestyle that usually gave them away. From early times, Cainites were raised to deny the existence of God; this belief in "no God" was reflected in a lifestyle lacking absolutes. Without acknowledging the definitive truths revealed by their Creator, they lived for their own satisfaction according to a code of relativism determined arbitrarily by their feelings and circumstances. This lifestyle led to the steady decay of Cainite civilization and, ultimately, to God's unfavorable judgment.

Cainite population also numbered in the millions, but they were concentrated in a handful of densely populated, high-rise industrial cities. In more recent years, as Sethians became attracted to modern city life, many adopted the atheistic Cainite lifestyle. Civilization as a whole had been in moral decline ever since, and now Cainite and most Sethian life was faced with annihilation at God's hand.

Noah's family estate had existed for a millennium and occupied a half-million acres of wilderness in the valley watered by the Euphrates River, whose origin was half a continent away in unfathomed, deep, underground springs. Noah's ancestors had named their estate "Eden's Promise" because they said it was located near the original Garden of Eden and, although they had tried to replicate the original Garden, they knew Eden would never return to its original form in their lifetimes. A return to the ideal Garden of Eden was just that, a promise for the future. Over the years, they expanded their home into a walled compound that measured almost a half-mile square, with many small laboratories, animal pens, and their home, surrounded by a high stockade fence to keep out the larger, wild, predatory animals, and flesh-eating dinos. What the family called Eden's Promise was technically the Center for Creation Zoology Research—part of the larger Adam Institute—which was the main center of knowledge and learning in their part of the world. Miriam and Noah made zoology their life's work as they continued their family tradition of nature research. They decided to live in the hills, rather than closer to town where the Institute was located, to be near the wildlife, and to have enough room to breed and study animals in their natural habitats. They had been married for more than four hundred years with no children. Animal research had always been their only passion. All that was about to change.

Miriam would be understanding, as she always was, when Noah told her what happened on the mountain. She would weigh the message from God with her usual godly judgment and common sense. Despite the fact that this would change their lives completely, Noah knew she would stand beside him. However, he had no idea how his father might react. His father was in poor health, so he might not handle this dramatic change very well.

As startling and profound as his morning had been, Noah walked confidently and briskly toward his house in the distance. Had he known how much their lives would change from that day forward, he would probably have been more worried.

Miriam greeted him cheerily when he walked into the large kitchen of their home.

"Where have you been? I thought you would be back hours ago," she asked as she took the coffee pot off the stove and poured a steaming cup for Noah who took it gratefully and stood staring out the window at the distant hills. Miriam had turned the kitchen into a large laboratory space so that she could experiment with animal feed. Something was always cooking on the stove, but most of it was not particularly appetizing to humans. Noah almost didn't hear her as he tried to form in his mind what to say.

He told her about the burning tree and tried to explain how he knew it was God that had spoken to him.

"It was a supernatural miracle, without question," he began with conviction. "I am a scientist and have been studying plants and animals all my life, and this was definitely supernatural. I cannot explain how I know that it was God, except that the appearance of the flaming tree resembled what Adam described to our ancestor Enoch many centuries ago. The phenomenon was definitely miraculous." What God actually told Noah would be harder to explain to her. So, he blurted it out all at once.

"I must build a giant wooden ship called an 'ark' that will be large enough to carry our family and two of every kind of animal. God will drown every living thing that is not in the ark in a global deluge of water." Noah paused to form his next words. "Miriam, God said that you and I will be in the ark with our three sons and their wives. We don't have any children!

"Building an ark is one thing," Noah continued, "but for God to wipe out every human being and animal on the face of the earth is a terrifying prospect. God is very angry. He is angry every day with the wickedness He sees in the world and how civilization has been polluted with the selfish desires, intentions, and actions that spew from mankind's evil heart. The Cainites first corrupted world government and commerce many centuries ago; and then a powerful world leader took over with such violence that everyone—Cainite and Sethian alike—were gathered under his brutal domination. The corrupt influence of the empire spread to the extent that there is not a town or city where the original, godly Sethian order survives. We, and the few other Sethians like us, are fortunate to live on isolated farms in the country where we can work and worship as we wish, but it is only a matter of time before the controlling arm of the empire reaches us too.

"What is more amazing is that God has been merciful this long. He has held back His wrath and tolerated the world's wickedness long enough. Now, He has given us one hundred and twenty years in which to repent or face global destruction. It is a task that seems like trying to empty a lake with a teaspoon, but I am supposed to warn about the coming judgment and the world's need to get right with God while our family builds the ark that will save us from the flood. I honestly do not know how we are going to do it. I am a zoologist and a professor—I can barely build a decent tool shed, let alone a five hundred foot boat!" Noah finished, taking a deep breath.

Miriam took all this in stride and nodded knowingly. "You know more than you realize, and God would not have chosen you for this task unless He also gave you the ability to complete it."

Noah appreciated her effort to encourage him, but he remained skeptical. "I am a zoologist and you are an animal nutritionist. Like Adam and all our forefathers, we have spent our lives studying the creatures that God created and placed on Earth for our benefit. I suppose that will come in handy when we have a boatload of them to care for, will it not?"

"Now you are thinking more positively about the circumstances," Miriam chimed in her usual upbeat tone. "We can prepare for their care and build the right habitations inside the ark. With our understanding of animal genetics, breeding methods, hibernation cycles, and eating habits, we can be ready to care for and preserve God's creatures while we are inside."

"But that does not change the fact that I lack the construction skills necessary to build such a large ship that will have to stay afloat for who knows how long when the flood finally comes." Noah stood and began to pace. "I will need help to build it, that is for sure."

Noah's father, Lamech, entered the room as they were finishing their talk, and Miriam wisely excused herself to check on some tests she had underway in the breeding pens. She turned and gave her husband as knowing smile as she went out the kitchen door and closed it quietly behind her. Noah watched her walk across the courtyard and thought how blessed he was to have her as his wife and companion.

"What was that discussion about? You sounded very excited, Noah," his father commented as he walked slowly to the stove and poured coffee into his oversized mug. In the past few years, Lamech tired easily, but he still tried to go outdoors every day to tend the animals as he had for most of his life. His once-healthy body was paying the price of almost eight hundred years of hard, outdoor labor. He eased himself into his favorite chair next to the window where he could watch the animals in the yard. Joining him by the window, Noah thought he should start from the beginning and tell his father what happened that morning. As he emotionally described how God planned to obliterate the earth, Lamech listened impassively. Finishing his story, he anticipated his father's skepticism by asking, "Pretty unbelievable, isn't it?"

"Not really," Lamech replied absentmindedly while he continued to gaze out the window.

"What do you mean, 'Not really'?"

"I need to reflect more on this before we discuss it further," Lamech replied in a slow, calm voice. "When I explain it later, you will understand why your announcement is not a complete surprise to me."

"If it is about the complete annihilation of our civilization, we should talk now!" Noah exclaimed.

"You are emotionally worked up because this is all so new to you, and I want to be sure I explain some things to you very clearly. I do believe God appeared to you as you said, and I might be able to fill in some of the missing gaps." With that he looked at the coffee in his mug, then out the window again, and ignored his son as if in a trance.

Lamech said nothing more, and as the minutes went by he seemed to doze off in his chair. When Noah finally left to join Miriam outside he thought he heard his father whisper under his breath, "*Ah, so that is how it is going to happen . . .*"

CHAPTER 2

Highway to the Adam Institute

Several Days Later

Noah set his pair of commuter quadruped dinos to stay at the speed limit while they lumbered briskly along the well-paved highway to the Adam Institute that was still more than two hours away. He always enjoyed this part of the ride through the fertile countryside because it gave him time to think as fields of golden wheat undulated into the distance. With the breeze in his face, he thought how easy it was to travel great distances now. Newer methods of dino breeding and training had been so successful that the animals were being used for personal and industrial transport throughout the country. Networks of paved highways connected most towns with each other as people and goods moved everywhere around the clock. The recent invention of soft wheels and rubber boots for the quadruped ungulates and high-speed biped dinos had all but eliminated the clatter and jolting that used to make this trip anything but peaceful. Commuter quadruped dinos, also known as "oak lizards," are herbivores, smaller (about nine feet tall at the shoulder), long-legged, and more agile than the massive, muscular breeds like the ugly, but docile, armor-plated or spiked breeds that worked in the fields during planting and harvest time or hauled heavy loads on the highway. Biped, plant-eating breeds are smarter and can be trained to take to a harness, respond to verbal commands, and run upright on their powerful hind legs for hours at a stretch without stopping to rest or drink. But Noah preferred the quiet ride of his slower, paired quadrupeds so he could sit back and think while they moved steadily onward.

Reflecting on what had happened in the past days, Noah thanked God for how blessed Miriam and he had been since they met at the Institute, married, and started their careers. He came from a long line of direct descendants from Seth who made a point of calling themselves Sethians because they were distinct, or at least used to be, from the descendants of their uncle, Cain, who was banished from the family for murder almost two millennia ago. People don't easily forget a brutal murder in the family, so consequently their two genealogical lines had been at odds with each other ever since. Sethian and Cainite families, or tribes, had mostly kept apart, but the distinctive lines between them had blurred in recent centuries; high profile marriages between the two families had, from time to time, heightened tensions. Admittedly, there were things about Sethian history that were kept a mystery. But through it all, the family line—from Seth through Enoch, Methuselah, and Lamech—remained faithful to the original teachings of Adam. Nobody is perfect, but they had tried to obey God as best they could and He had blessed them beyond measure.

Thinking about his family history brought Noah to thinking about the purpose of his trip to the Institute. With Miriam's support, he had decided that the best course of action was for them to leave their faculty positions and spend all of their time building the ark. But he wasn't looking forward to meeting with the president of the Institute to tell him they were resigning their prestigious leadership positions in order to build a boat. The fact that the Institute president, Vanek, was also his father-in-law made it even harder. Before Noah married Miriam, Vanek thought the young student to be something of an intellectual, but he assented to their marriage because Miriam wanted to marry a Sethian believer and Vanek had given his approval at the time. Vanek's other daughters had married Cainites and the resulting squabbles and fighting split his family, ending in the tragic death of one daughter. The thought of having another Cainite as a son-in-law was intolerable to him then. But that was long ago, and since then Vanek had made a complete turnaround.

The Adam Institute was the largest and most prestigious school for advanced learning in the world. Adam had started it in order to preserve knowledge about God's creation and to pass on his scientific methods for discovery and analysis to other Sethian descendants. Adam's life's work—the study of all living organisms, later called "biology"—resulted in books, data, specimens, and laboratories that filled entire buildings. This steady accumulation of knowledge continued through successive generations of eager Sethian students, who used their sharp intellects and extended life spans to explore new areas of God's creation. They found that biology could be extended into an almost indefinite series of natural subdivisions, topics, and disciplines.

Noah's father, Lamech, specialized in the study of animals and founded the field of "zoology," which Miriam and Noah had embraced since they were children. Together they pioneered new areas of animal study and practice. They found that certain animals could be domesticated through breeding and behavioral training. Many mammals like horses, cows, oxen, and goats could be easily domesticated to live closely with humans and perform simple tasks. It was the reptiles—dinos mostly—that fiercely resisted domestication or any form of training. The smaller ones were highly intelligent and seemed to have a natural, inbred independence. One category of biped dino, the carnivores, could be deadly if cornered and had never been fully domesticated. Fortunately, they represented only one percent of all dinos on the earth; they were harmless if left alone in the wild, and they rarely attacked humans unprovoked. But with the right psychological techniques, the herbivores could be domesticated to great advantage for humans. Miriam and Noah spent their lives perfecting these techniques and teaching them to their students. The result was a range of dino sizes and temperaments that served as mankind's helpers in agriculture, transportation, commerce, and industry.

Since its founding, the Institute had been devoted to the Sethian study of biology and its many related branches. Under Vanek's leadership, and despite the strong objections of Sethian faculty, Cainites were admitted to join the faculty and student body. Until then, Sethians had shunned collaborating with Cainites who they viewed as apostates living in rebellion against God's plan for mankind. Cainites in the Institute, whether as students or faculty, would have been unthinkable in Adam's day. But it was Vanek who had changed everything when he reasoned that as long as Cainite students agreed to obey the school's rules they would all benefit from the exchange of new ideas in an open academic environment. Vanek felt that the strong Cainite interest in a commercial and industrial economy would diversify Sethian studies of the "soft sciences" and would create more research options for students, making them better citizens of the world. His inclusion of Cainites in the Institute evolved gradually to the point where the school began offering electives like "Military Training of Dinos" and "Human Genetic Engineering." Compromises at the Institute heralded tectonic shifts in the world's civilization.

CHAPTER 3

Adam Institute, Administrative Building

The Institute president's office was on the top floor of the twenty-two-story glass-faced administrative tower overlooking the complex of academic and research buildings, which resembled a small city more than an academic campus. He gave his destination to the machinery operator, and the glass floating capsule began its steady ascent. Dinos in the cellar, hooked up to a system of cables and pulleys that multiplied their power, easily lifted the capsule slowly higher. Noah, looking across the campus grounds before him, knew he was making the right choice to confront Vanek now. Animal research had been his life—he had grown up in the Adam Institute and on the research farms in the countryside. But the Institute that stretched before him now had become the military-industrial machine of the empire, representing all that had gone dreadfully wrong with their civilization. Severing his ties to the place now was the right thing to do; though, confronting Vanek with reality would be dangerous.

Noah walked from the landing down the thickly carpeted corridor to the foyer of Vanek's corner office where he greeted Vanek's secretary. Though a Cainite, the secretary was always pleasant with Noah, but careful to protect Vanek from anything she knew would upset him. She gave him a nod of recognition as he approached her desk.

"Could you see if Vanek can give me a few minutes?" he asked. "I don't have an appointment, but I won't take much of his time."

"And what is the subject?" she asked dutifully.

"It's personal. He will understand," Noah replied.

She quietly slipped from behind her desk to open the massive iron door that swung silently on oiled hinges, and she closed it carefully behind her. Noah looked at the imposing door and wondered why Vanek had replaced the original, beautifully carved double wooden doors to his office with these hulking iron doors, ornamented with metal rivets and jagged welded seams that wreathed the blasphemous emblem of the empire. What was once a colorful work of art engraved in natural wood that spoke of openness had been changed into a manufactured, industrial, armor-plated monstrosity. The power of the Institute as a force for research and learning had been exploited and distorted to typify the irrepressible, unstoppable might of the new empire.

"Come in, Professor Noah. President Vanek will see you now," said the secretary, emerging from Vanek's office.

Vanek's office had a lofty view through floor-to-ceiling windows, overlooking miles of undulating, forested hills. If the view wasn't obscured by the constant humid haze of tropical heat you might have seen the blue ocean on the horizon fifty miles away.

"Noah, my favorite son-in-law! How are you?" Vanek boomed as he came around his desk and hugged Noah. Gregarious and voluble, Vanek filled the room physically and audibly. Six-and-a-half feet tall and over three hundred pounds, Noah had never heard Vanek speak in anything but a shout. Resting upon his large frame was an equally massive head with a thick black beard and a head of hair that revealed not a touch of gray. His face was always flushed from either exertion or enthusiasm, and his physical energy seemed endless.

"I am well, thank you," Noah replied. "I appreciate your seeing me without an appointment."

"Always so formal. Nonsense, my boy! You can come see me anytime. We're family," Vanek spoke sincerely. "And how is Miriam? Are things with the two of you all right?" Vanek could tell that something was up, and, naturally, his first though was of his daughter.

"Yes, yes, everything is fine with us; great, in fact. I came by to discuss some changes in our plans for the future. I might as well get to the point," Noah began.

"Please, do. You have my full attention." Vanek sat relaxed behind his desk.

"Miriam and I are resigning from the Institute immediately, and I want to explain what has happened. It is rather overwhelming, really, but it is very clear that we have to leave." Noah's mouth was dry, and his head was starting to ache.

"Last week, God appeared to me and told me I must build a large boat because He is going to destroy the world in a global flood."

Vanek's face held a blank expression as if waiting for more. His eyes were unblinking and revealed nothing. This was going better than Noah expected. No shouting . . . yet.

"Say that again," Vanek said with a slight catch in his voice.

"I will try to explain, but it is not easy to say. A few days ago, I was walking in the hills in Eden's Promise, and I thought someone had carelessly started a fire along the trail. When I went closer it seemed that a tree was on fire, but there was no smoke or heat. As I watched, the tree did not burn, but a moving yellow and red flame was intertwined with the branches and leaves, making them look almost alive. When I got to within a few feet of the tree, I heard a voice call my name.

"I fell to the ground on my face. I did not hear, but rather felt the voice coming from the burning tree, and it told me that all life on Earth will end because of the evil and violence that has overrun our civilization. God told me He would destroy everyone on the Earth," Noah said. He trembled nervously as he spoke, sensing Vanek's disbelief, but he continued.

"We both know what has been happening in the world, and this sounded more like a judgment than a warning. God told me to build a large boat—He called it an 'ark,' five hundred feet long—and God said that He will flood the entire earth with water until every breathing thing dies. He promised that those inside the ark—people and animals—would be preserved. When I stood up, I saw a normal tree with not a single leaf or twig singed.

"There is no doubt in my mind that this was God, and His instructions were very clear. So I am here to tell you that Miriam and I are leaving the Institute to devote our lives to this ark, no matter what happens," Noah concluded his brief speech and looked to Vanek for an answer.

Vanek continued to stare at Noah with a blank look of incredulity.

"You need a vacation," Vanek said, finally, in a surprisingly calm tone. "If this was only a few days ago, you obviously haven't had enough time to think this through. Maybe you've been under too much stress lately and need some time off to relax. Go ahead and put in for a sabbatical, and take a year to go fishing, or something. It's time you and Miriam started a family anyway."

"It is not stress," Noah replied calmly. "Things are fine at home, and I love my work. But this is something I cannot ignore. God told me to build an ark, so I need to get started. He even told me when it would happen; one hundred and twenty years from now, the globe will be entirely flooded, and everyone and everything that is not on that ark will die," Noah said emphatically. "God's judgment against evil will be complete and universal, unless the world repents."

Vanek began to raise his voice. "You and I have had this discussion before about what you think of Cainites. If this is another way to stir up problems on campus, I will end this discussion now. I don't want to hear any more about the evil of the Cainites and the Earth being destroyed!" Vanek stated forcefully, his deep voice rising. "Things have been peaceful since the empire began supporting this Institute. The emperor has assured me that everything will continue peacefully as it always has."

"I never said anything about the Cainites or the empire," Noah replied defensively. "But since you brought it up, we both know that the emperor is the reason for the spread of violence across the globe. His lust for world domination has brought out the worst in his followers. Some Sethians openly refused to submit to him and he had them executed. You cannot deny that fact." Noah stood his ground and looked firmly into his father-in-law's eyes.

Vanek's face turned a darker shade of red, his lips parted to reveal tightly clenched teeth, and his massive hands gripped the edge of his desk in barely controlled restraint. "Your claim that you have been chosen by God to save our people from destruction is preposterous! Who are you to come here and lecture me with your sanctimonious attitude?"

"Sir, with all respect, you are misled in your belief that the empire has been beneficial for Sethians, Cainites, or this Institute. I hope some day you will see the truth of what I am saying. Unless the world repents, it will be destroyed."

When Vanek heard that, he jumped to his feet, knocking his chair to the floor. With surprising speed, he rounded his desk at Noah with hands outstretched. Before Noah could evade his grasp, Vanek did something he had never done before: he grabbed his son-in-law's shirt, lifted him off the floor, and, with his face inches away, he screamed, "Your arrogant accusation of the emperor is treasonous! He is the best thing that ever happened to this Institute. I won't have you talking about us being infected with violence because that . . . is . . . a . . . lie!" Vanek dropped Noah to the carpet and shoved him toward the door.

"Get out of my office now, before I . . . before I . . . Get out, now!"

Noah retreated through the vault-like iron door and saw Vanek's secretary's ashen gaze follow him down the hall.

The ride down to the ground floor and the parking lot was silent, except for the creaking of the capsule's gears and cables. Noah wondered if the machinery operator had heard what happened in Vanek's office because the man stared silently at his control panel during the entire ride.

Vanek dropped into his chair as if the weight of his outburst had drained him. Noah was gone, and Vanek wondered if his daughter or son-in-law would ever speak to him again. He had thrown his cause in with the empire long ago. The empire, he convinced himself now, would outlast blood relations and would forever receive his full allegiance.

"Come here!" Vanek yelled to his secretary, bypassing the more civilized intercom system.

His secretary opened the door timidly and peered in.

"Take a memo to Chief Inspector Hin at Imperial Police Headquarters. Have it hand-delivered to him immediately."

CHAPTER 4

Highway to Eden's Promise

On the slow drive home Noah was still shaking. He had not intended to kick over a hornet's nest, but now it was only a matter of time before the empire stung him. Miriam's father was so entangled with the empire's security machinery that he was sure to report Noah's treachery, causing trouble for him in the days ahead. Vanek's uncontrollable rage left no doubt in Noah's mind that Vanek would challenge the warning of God's coming judgment. Vanek had never physically attacked Noah before. The transformation of his personality was symptomatic of the world's widespread violence and hatred.

As Noah drove back to Eden's Promise, he barely needed to concentrate on the road. The dinos were happy to be walking and not running. They knew the way home anyway; their padded hooves' drummed a steady, muffled rhythm on the pavement while Noah calmed from his confrontation with his father-in-law. He wished he had been able to better explain to Vanek what was going to happen in the future and how he could avoid it by repenting and coming on the ark with him and Miriam. God had said that Noah and his wife, plus their three sons and their wives, would be on the ark. That didn't mean others couldn't come with them also. It was confusing to Noah that Miriam could be such a strong believer and yet her father lacked any interest in God and showed no fear of His coming judgment. Vanek's focus was on the here and now—only what he could see and touch with his burly hands. He had compromised with the Cainite philosophy of indulgence in the physical world with no recognition of the spiritual implications. How could he not see what was happening before his eyes in the Institute and in the world?

By now, only the Zoology and Botany Departments were led by Sethians; the rest were headed by Cainites. New departments were formed regularly, as money flowed steadily to the Institute from the empire's Education Ministry. Most distressing were two areas of research that had resulted in fateful changes in their civilization: human genetics and military engineering.

The Human Genetics Department was unapologetically chartered with "improving" human health and minds under the pretense of medical research. But its research was shrouded in secrecy. Word leaked out that one early experiment produced grotesque, cloned mutants of all sizes and shapes that were so defective they had to be destroyed. Women were brought from across the empire to be "volunteer donors" for offspring production. Eventually, one result was heralded as the greatest scientific breakthrough in history—a half-human and half-artificial being. These creatures were called "chimera" by their developers, and in their early years they demonstrated an exaggerated muscular physique and such a brilliant intellect that their creators were convinced these were the "super humans" long-sought as the pinnacle of mankind's technological aspirations. Scientists were so excited about being able to break God's original genetic code for the human being that they quickly bred more, until hundreds resided behind locked doors at the Institute. Only when the early hybrid humans reached maturity did they evidence a critical flaw. The males (there were no viable female products of those experiments) exhibited no moral conscience: no ability to show love, empathy, or concern for others; no personal regret, sorrow, or emotion; not even regard for their own bodily pain or fear of death. Their developers hoped the chimera's superior intellect would overcome any moral deficiencies, but their personality traits of violence, aggression, and domination prevailed.

In an attempt to dampen such failures, the genetic scientists joined their colleagues in the Institute's Military Engineering Department to find some beneficial use for these ruthless creatures. With military training, the chimera had shown themselves to be natural warriors—killing machines without consciences. In a move of arrogant stupidity that would irreversibly change the world, researchers foolishly gave the creatures weapons for training which one day they used to escape from their imprisonment to a remote part of the continent where they organized themselves with one purpose: to wrest control of civilization from human beings and conquer the world for themselves.

There was nothing Noah could do about Vanek and the Institute now. It was time to go home and make plans to start on the ark. They had enough room on their estate for a construction site and they needed to get started. He had to hire people to help, but most of all he needed a plan. God had given him some rough dimensions, but, quite honestly, Noah didn't know where to begin.

I am a zoologist, he kept thinking to himself as dusk approached. *What do I know about building a giant ship?*

CHAPTER 5

Approach to Eden's Promise

The scenic approach to Eden's Promise—riding along the crest of a ridge overlooking the valley below—reminded Noah why he loved this place. He stopped along the way to get glimpses of the winding driveway below as it snaked through thick forest, leading to a traditional mansion of white limestone standing opposite well-kept barns and research buildings. While the dinos quietly munched grass, Noah pondered what it must have been like when his grandfather, Methuselah, and father, Lamech, lived here in more peaceful times. The estate was pleasantly remote, and Noah and Miriam loved the expansive fields and forests enough to spend the rest of their lives here. When he looked at Eden's Promise from here, he knew he was home.

But his mind kept going back to his meeting with Vanek and the violent opposition he should have expected, but which still came as a shock. Ever since he began yielding more control of the Institute to the Cainites, Vanek had grown more frustrated with Sethian objections, and he took it out on those around him. Every family occasion ended in confrontation and belligerent verbal attacks. His children avoided him because it was too painful to endure his overbearing, abusive presence.

Noah needed someone to talk to about what God had told him and why all this was happening to help him sort everything out, and he thought of his father, Lamech.

Lamech had become the patriarch of their Sethian family line when his father, and Noah's grandfather, Methuselah, disappeared more than two hundred years ago. Now, Lamech's health was declining, so he gave

Miriam and Noah all of the family property and access to the Sethian family's accumulated wealth, which was substantial; their fortune was only surpassed by that of the emperor himself. All of Noah's brothers and sisters had moved away; they had no interest in Eden's Promise or the family traditions. That seemed to be the way things went for most people in recent years.

Noah found his father in the library where Lamech now spent most of his time. Lamech was going over animal research textbooks that he had written in years past, reliving those times when his classroom was filled with eager Sethian students hungry to learn about animals and their natural environment. Those days were gone since the Cainite takeover of the Institute, which altered the focus of their research from Adam's early studies of creation to developing new, potentially harmful, technologies. The Cainite philosophy of "new academic morality" justified human genetic experiments, mechanical devices for mass destruction, and exploitation of the natural world. The fast-growing Cainite faction within the Institute, driven by intolerance and violence, forced Sethians, like Lamech, to retreat from the laboratories where they had spent their lives in service of Adam's founding directive.

Noah sat next to Lamech and brought him up to date on his trip to the Institute. "I met with Vanek this morning and told him I was leaving for good to start work on the ark," he said. Lamech looked up from his book and gazed calmly over his glasses.

"His reaction was predictable, I assume?" Lamech asked, knowing the answer already from the pained look on Noah's face.

"Unfortunately, yes," Noah answered. "Vanek accused me of being a traitor to the empire. His response was exceptionally violent, and I think he will report me to the authorities. There will be negative repercussions, I'm sure."

Noah walked across the room before turning back toward his father. "Can I change the subject and ask you something about what God told me?" His serious tone prompted Lamech to put his book down and lean forward in his chair.

"What would you like to know?" Noah's father asked.

"When I first told you what God said, your reaction wasn't what I expected. You didn't seem surprised."

Lamech looked out the window at the hills in the distance. "There is more you need to know about God's plan for the future of the human race."

"More? I do not understand. Do you mean God spoke to you, too?" Noah sounded surprised.

"Not directly. Not as He has to you," Lamech replied. "Our family's oral tradition is based on many firsthand accounts from Adam: how he walked with God in the Garden that He created with His spoken Word; how Adam and Eve sinned and were expelled from the Garden into the world we live in now; how they began a family, but that Abel's tragic murder, committed by his brother, Cain, devastated them.

"When Seth was born, things got better, but Adam was never the same. He was a broken man; he was reminded daily of what happened in the Garden between him and God, and how the consequences would ripple down to affect his children's children for centuries and millennia.

"Adam, Seth, and our forefathers who came after, were sustained by the knowledge that God would someday faithfully provide a Redeemer to finally take away sin. We offer our regular family sacrifices as we wait for the perfect Lamb of God, who will take away the sins of the world," Lamech reminded Noah. "Today, we call upon the Name of the Lord in faith, believing that He will accept our offerings. I have taught these things to you since you were a child, just as my father taught me."

Noah had heard prophecies of the promised One ever since the earliest family sacrifice that he remembered as a small child. At those ceremonies, Lamech rehearsed what it would be like one day in the future to not be continually obliged to offer animal sacrifices to cover sin. He explained to his family how they could have a right relationship with God by faith in what He had revealed about Himself.

"These stories of our family history were memorized and passed on down the family line through Enos and the other patriarchs to my grandfather Enoch, who was God's spokesman to his generation," Lamech continued. "When Adam neared the end of his life he wanted Enoch to record the accounts of his talks with God in the Garden, because he was afraid that the details would eventually be lost or misinterpreted. The resulting text was known as the Book of Adam; even though Enoch wrote it, he transcribed it in the first person based upon Adam's recollections. I can remember vividly much of what I read back then. The Book was about God, His plan for life, and the future of mankind. It was a book of cosmic history, detailing how and why God created the universe, the earth, all the animals and plants. God created man in His own image and likeness. It was also a prophetic book about what God would do in the future. The Book explained why we are who we are today and how God wants us to live by faith in Him. But it was God's prediction of future things that I found most interesting, even though the prophecies were not explained in much detail.

"When you told me what God had spoken to you, Noah, it reminded me of something my grandfather Enoch read to me from the Book long ago," Lamech confessed. "God told Adam that He would someday destroy the world because man's wickedness would eventually saturate the entire fabric of civilization. Society would be so evil that everyone would act upon the most base impulses and there would be no limit to what they would do to one another. The world would come to the brink of self-annihilation. But God promised that He would save a small remnant of His people to continue His plan through history of the future promised One, in spite of what mankind and unseen demonic beings did to deny Him. The leader of the remaining believers would be a voice for God; he would go to the people and tell them of God's righteousness, and warn them to repent before the coming judgment.

"What I didn't know then was 'how,' or 'when,' or 'who.' Now, that is clear. God will fulfill His plan of worldwide judgment with a global flood of water and it will happen in one hundred and twenty years. You, Noah, will be the voice for God in your generation, and your family will survive on the ark. You will fulfill God's prophetic plan for the survival of mankind and the continuation of the family line stretching from Adam to the promised One," Lamech concluded.

Noah had been so puzzled for the past few days about *why* this was happening to him and now things came into focus! He looked down at his trembling hands. Now he understood that God was going to use him and his family—though they didn't have any children yet—to warn civilization of coming judgment and this was happening according to a divine timetable predicted long before Noah was born. His earlier apprehension about building a giant ark was now combined with a sense of complete unworthiness and inadequacy to accomplish what God had chosen him to do. How was he going to get all of this work done? Building an ark seemed an insurmountable task on its own, without the added pressure of acting as the voice for God's righteousness to the people.

"Son, this will be the hardest thing you will ever do in your life. By God's grace, you can do it," his father said, knowing exactly what was going through Noah's mind. "I wish I could be more help to you, but now you know why it is so important that you do exactly what God told you to do. When He commands us, we must obey," Lamech advised.

"Was there anything else in the Book about the future? I am surprised this is the first time you have told me about it. Can I read it for myself?" Noah hoped that the Book contained more information about how to build the ark or something else that might help him.

Lamech, again, had that distant look in his eyes and paused for a while. "I never saw the Book of Adam again after that day Enoch and I read it together. Sadly, it was lost. It was not long after that that my father, Methuselah, left our family to go in search of it." Indicating that their conversation was over, Lamech opened his textbook and thumbed through its worn pages while his mind pondered God's mysterious ways.

CHAPTER 6

Imperial Police Headquarters

Eight Days Later

The courier from the Adam Institute entered the offices of the Imperial Police Headquarters in the city of Enoch after an eight-day highway journey. Chief Inspector Hin raised his eyebrows in surprise when he saw the confidential seal of the Institute president on the envelope. He'd met Vanek once for the opening of a new Police Research Center at the Institute; Hin wondered why he would be sending him a letter. He soon got his answer when he read the tidbit of intelligence supplied by this solicitous servant of the empire.

Hin read the missive several times, memorized its contents, and then placed it back in its original envelope and filed it in his private desk safe. This was fresh information about an individual who might someday present a threat to the empire, as Vanek intimated in his note. He doubted this inconsequential professor that Vanek named would present a real threat to the empire, but one never knew. He would make discrete inquiries about this man, Noah, and maybe, if he leveraged it to his advantage, bring it to the attention of the emperor when the time was right. Better that the emperor found out from him than from anyone else.

The chief inspector rose from his chair and admired his crisp, black suit in the mirror behind his office door. He avoided the traditional uniform of the imperial police in order to distance his image from that of a 'common policeman' and, instead, had a wardrobe of personally tailored black suits, which he always wore with a white shirt and a blood-red tie. If he fit the figure of an undertaker shrouded in mystery, that was exactly his intent. His dark appearance was a daily reminder to his subordinates that—as a figure to be feared—he demanded obedience and loyalty at any cost. When citizens of the empire had the misfortune of meeting with him, they immediately understood his lethal potential.

Hin returned to his plush chair, turned to gaze out the window, leaned back to rest his immaculate black shoes upon his desk, and wondered to himself—but only briefly—what would happen if Noah's prediction came true.

CHAPTER 7

Eden's Promise

God said that three sons would enter into the ark with Noah and Miriam, which was a surprise to them because they had not been able to have children until then. But Miriam gave birth to Shem the following year. Noah was more than five hundred years old and a father! The joy and certainty of knowing that Shem and his future wife would be on the ark was a comfort. In short succession, Ham and then Japheth were born, and God saw fit to end Miriam's childbearing years. They didn't understand why, but they figured it was what God intended all along, for if only their three sons and their wives were prophesied to be with them on the ark, it was best that she bear only three sons; the thought of having to leave any other children behind was too painful to contemplate.

Miriam had her hands full with three little boys in the house, but Noah made some progress on preparing to build the ark. He hired laborers from town to clear a large plot of land at the top of the hill where he would lay the ark's foundation. It took longer than he estimated to clear the land and gather some materials. Finally, he felt it was time to inquire about a master carpenter who knew something about construction in order to lay out the design and help oversee more workers.

"There's a man who's built grain silos up north, and I think he's worked on office buildings in the city too," said one of the merchants at the local farm equipment supply store. "His name's Wazim, and he can probably help you, though he's a funny sort of character, and I can't say he's too reliable."

Wazim's Cabin

Undeterred, Noah obtained directions to Wazim's house and found it at the end of a long road through the dense forest outside town. *If this man knows anything about construction, you cannot tell it from his house,* Noah observed. It hadn't seen a coat of paint in decades, and the roof over his garage sagged precariously. The front porch had half-finished railings and uneven cement blocks for steps. A few crude chairs and a worn bench showed that they were regularly used. *A real handyman,* Noah thought as he carefully stepped on the loose blocks and knocked on the front door.

"Who is it?" growled a voice from the other side of the door. "Whatever you're sellin' I don't want none."

"My name's Noah, and I am looking for Wazim. I need someone to help me build a large ship," Noah called out.

He wondered if he would get any reply, but after a minute the door opened a crack and the voice, less rough this time, inquired, "A ship? What kinda fool's building a ship 'round here?"

"I am," Noah explained. "I need someone to help me build a ship—a large one—and I was told you have construction experience."

The door opened and a pale, thin man in a dirty, rumpled yellow jumpsuit stepped awkwardly onto the porch. Wazim's eyes squinted in the daylight, as if he hadn't been outside in days, and he looked furtively to his right and left like he expected someone to be spying on him from around the corner. His frame was almost skeletal, but if he stood up straight he might have looked more substantial. His yellow jumpsuit made him look like he'd just escaped from a prison, and he smelled like he'd been living in the same clothes for weeks. When he walked, he had a pronounced tilt toward one side, forcing him to instinctively grab a piece of wood on the side of the house that was obviously nailed there to act as a stabilizer. When he reached the porch bench, he eased onto it with a groan.

"All right, tell me 'bout this here ship of yours." Wazim sounded like he was in pain.

Noah had come all this way, so he thought he might as well tell him about the ark and then leave if Wazim couldn't grasp what he was saying. "It is not a ship like any you may have seen. It is called an 'ark' and it is very large. It will be five hundred feet long and forty-five feet high, and it will have three decks to carry a lot of cargo—animals mostly." Noah wasn't sure if any of this registered with Wazim, because he still kept looking back and forth like someone might be eavesdropping on their conversation. Maybe he was thinking about the size of the ark, but then again, maybe he wasn't sober. "Why don't you begin telling me about your experience in building. Have you ever built any ships before?" Noah asked.

Though he still appeared to be in a daze, Wazim told Noah in a clearer voice about his work in the city of Enoch on a number of different construction jobs. Some of the buildings were ten- and twelve-story jobs, with iron frames. The largest buildings he had worked on had dimensions comparable to the ark. Aside from his appearance, Wazim seemed to know construction well enough. Not surprisingly, he had no experience building boats or ships. He had heard of some large oceangoing vessels, but he only knew of them from hearsay and pictures in magazines. That was the case with most people around Eden's Promise, since they were far from the ocean and the only watercraft were river barges. Wazim was the most qualified person he was likely to come across, so Noah figured he'd hire him and see how things worked out. That's when he inquired about his work habits and reliability.

"Well, I likes to be flexible in my schedule, ya see," Wazim replied. "Some days the fish bite, and it's a shame to have to work. 'Course during hunting season I be gone for a while, too. But I do ya good work the rest of the time. Just so happens I got no work right this moment, so when do ya want me to start?"

Noah hadn't offered him the job, exactly, but it seemed Wazim was up to the task, so they set a weekly pay rate and talked for a while about clearing more land and gathering more timber. With Noah's permission to hire a few helpers, Wazim suggested they house workers on site so their wages could be lower, and they could work from sunrise to sunset. This suggestion came as a surprise to Noah since only a short time ago Wazim had hardly seemed to him a quick thinker. They made arrangements for Wazim to move to the compound, and, as Noah extended his hand to close the arrangement, the new hire said, "So's you don't get no ideas, I heard about you and that Sethian preaching you been doing in town. I been raised a Cainite all my life, and I'm not interested in any of that salvation stuff you people give out. Just so you know, Chief, I'm all right and figures we is all going to the same place anyhow, no matter what direction we take."

"I hear you, Wazim, so let us leave that subject open for now, and we can talk about it later. Do we have a deal?" Noah asked.

Without a word Wazim got up, shook Noah's offered hand, and went back into the house.

"See you tomorrow!" Noah said optimistically as he walked away, half expecting that Wazim wouldn't show up and that that was the last he'd see of him.

But Wazim showed up the next day, and that's how they came to have him as the construction boss and designer of the ark. It wasn't the best decision of Noah's life, as it turned out.

CHAPTER 8

Eden's Promise, Family Compound

One Year Later

Wazim proved to be a surprisingly hard, if erratic, worker; he was knowledgeable about construction, even if he sometimes didn't show up for a few days, or a week, at a time. He and his small group of workers built a dormitory building at Eden's Promise, and they moved into the family compound to essentially work full-time. Even after he moved onto the estate, Wazim would disappear for a few days—to go fishing he said—and come back ready to work again. His whereabouts seemed mysterious, but Noah dismissed it as part of his natural shiftiness.

Before they could get started on the ark, Wazim's team needed to expand their construction compound at Eden's Promise; more buildings were constructed from timber that came from clearing trees from the hillside to expose a larger work area. Here, they would soon lay the foundation of the ark, build segments of the structure, and store materials and supplies. Tree stumps were pulled out of the ground with the help of strong, harnessed dinos, and the land was graded level. Using long two-man saws, they made rough planks for buildings, and within one year the compound had grown to include a kitchen and dining hall, open bay construction sheds, and tall storage warehouses for building materials and accumulated ark provisions.

During this time, Noah was praying that the ark's construction would begin soon and that he would see some evidence of the ship's frame take shape. But Wazim liked to construct buildings and storage sheds more than arks.

Noah's frustration got the better of him when one day he cornered his building supervisor in the assembly yard. "Wazim, we need to start on the ark. When will I see a design?" Noah demanded, when Wazim had come back from his latest "fishing" trip and was casually sipping coffee in the dining hall.

"Well, Chief, I been thinkin' 'bout just that and figures we can start gettin' some of that there gopher wood you said we need and gettin' it here to the compound." He wouldn't look his boss in the eye, anticipating Noah would disagree with what he was about to say. "We need more workers though, so I been talkin' to some of my friends from Enoch City 'bout movin' out here to cut trees up river and start shapin' them into planks." He waited for a response from Noah, who was looking at him askance as if there were something else to be said.

Noah waited for more of an explanation, but when there wasn't one he began firmly, "That would depend on how many more men you need and how long you think they will be needed."

"That's the rub, Chief. I was thinkin' that we need about a hundred more men and it might take a couple of years to git all that wood here and cut it into pieces." Wazim still wasn't looking Noah directly in the eye, and now Noah knew why.

"One hundred men for a couple of years?" Noah choked. "Why so many?"

Wazim moved closer and pulled out a dirty piece of paper, and he spread it out on the table. "I've been doing some calculations, using a simple three-deck design for the ark and the overall dimensions you gave me. We will need approximately eight to ten thousand gopher wood trees. There are none nearby, so we will bring them from forests upriver and float them here on barges, because gopher wood logs are so dense they won't float in the water themselves. Then we need to form each plank individually using axes and adzes, because gopher wood is almost as hard as iron. One hundred men might not be enough, but they will be a start."

To Noah's astonishment, Wazim's vocabulary and diction had changed to those of an educated man. So, his bumbling speech and unkempt appearance were all an act! Wazim now looked Noah straight in the eye, since he'd proved his point, and he almost dared Noah to disagree. If Noah argued, he was sure Wazim would recite the schedule again and say that the ark wouldn't be finished in time if he didn't get all the helpers he needed. Noah was baffled by the change in the man's presentation, but he relented and gave Wazim the go ahead to hire one hundred more workers. Wazim showed his stained teeth in what passed for a smile and said, "Good, Chief. I goes and gets me friends from Enoch City, and the rest of them there workers can starts addin' on to the dormitories and chow hall."

Wazim almost skipped out the door leaving Noah feeling like he'd been conned. He could see Wazim's point though: the great size of the ark would require an enormous amount of gopher wood, and the men they had hired already would not be able to harvest that much wood in twenty years, let alone make the planks individually by hand. He still didn't understand how they would actually build the ark itself, but he assumed, based upon his recent performance, that Wazim knew what he was doing. Noah would continue to pray for wisdom because he didn't have a good feeling about their schedule, and now he was more suspicious of Wazim than before. Noah didn't have much choice but to go along with him for now.

One hundred of Wazim's friends from the city of Enoch would become two hundred, and the years would drag on.

CHAPTER 9

Imperial Police Headquarters

Same Day

Chief Inspector Hin started his file on Noah when he first learned from Vanek of the Sethian's wild predictions of a worldwide flood. Over the ensuing years, the chief inspector had received reports from various townspeople about Noah's public announcements that disaster was coming because of the global violence that permeated civilization. Noah never said directly that it was the fault of the empire or blamed the emperor for this supposed calamity, but it was interpreted by those who listened to his preaching that the decline had begun when Anak made himself Emperor.

It was time that Hin found someone inside Noah's family compound whom he could rely on and who could slip him advance information on Noah's plans, especially if they took a more subversive turn. It would take time to find the right person, to suitably motivate him, and to wait for him to supply the inspector with the information he had in mind.

Chief Inspector Hin had the germ of a plan in his sardonic mind that would bring Noah to the attention of the emperor, ingratiate himself with the Fatherland Protection Secretary, and get himself promoted to that same position. *It is simple, really,* he mused. *You only need to appreciate that the emperor lashes out without mercy at anyone who threatens his power.*

CHAPTER 10

Eden's Promise, Family Quarters

Twenty Years Later

"Is something bothering you dear?" Miriam asked her husband as they sat in front of the fireplace after dinner, and the boys were in bed. It had turned into a cool night. A small fire felt good to take the slight chill and moisture out of the air. "You have been very quiet tonight, which is not like you."

"It is nothing I can put my finger on," Noah replied pensively as he inched his chair closer to the warmth. "More than twenty years ago, we started building the ark and there has not been the progress that I expected. I envisioned we would have most of the frame of the ark done by now, given all the laborers we have on site. We have spent all this time gathering timber from the countryside and making planks." He stared into the fire and thought of all the energy—and money—spent thus far and their progress wasn't as satisfying as he thought it should have been.

"Like I teach the boys," Miriam reminded him, "you need to be patient and wait on the Lord for things to take their course. Sometimes things do not happen the way we think they should. I am learning from raising children that God has a schedule for everything, and His timing is perfect."

"I know, but I have an uneasy feeling about how all of this is playing out—or not," Noah persisted. "Have you noticed how the mood of the work crew has changed since we first started? There is a tension that is almost palpable on some days." Noah was frustrated and had his suspicions about what had changed.

"I have little contact with men on the work crew," Miriam observed, "but I have noticed the women in the kitchen do not talk with me as they used to. When we began, they seemed a part of our family, and we talked about things of the Lord and what was going on in their lives while we did our daily chores. We talked about the open invitation to repent and put their trust in the One True God and join us in the ark. Some seemed interested, and they said they would think about it. Of course, they are Sethians by birth, but it seems to me they are only working for the pay and are not concerned with God's coming judgment."

"The men are much the same way," Noah observed. "We spend hours together on the site and have plenty of time to talk. We used to talk about what was happening in the empire, the horrible violence in every town and village, and why people are rebelling against the old peaceful ways. But now they have blindly accepted the philosophy of the empire, going against anything that is honest and true in favor of what materially benefits them or their families. Corruption is ignored by the rest, as if it does not exist. Now, when I talk about why we are building the ark and why God is going to judge this worldwide evil and rebellion, they brush it off as my 'opinion.' Some have even told me that they think the world's problems stem from the Cainites fighting against one another and that it has nothing to do with Sethians. They deny with a straight face that the empire is against Sethians! They chat about the ark's construction, animals, or some trivial subject instead. They consider anything of moral or spiritual substance not worth discussing."

"Do you think they might turn against us?" asked Miriam, with a hint of fear.

"I do not know," Noah replied. "It is clear that they do not believe, or want to believe, in God's coming judgment, but they seem willing enough to continue working on the ark as long as they get paid. I would be more uneasy if they thought my preaching or building the ark was somehow a threat to them. They might do something to stop us. I know they steal supplies from time to time, and maybe I should confront them about that. But with tensions being what they are, I do not want to press the matter right now."

A knock on the door interrupted their conversation, and they looked at each other. "Who could that be at this hour?" Miriam asked.

"We shall see," Noah said as he went to the door and opened it.

"Good evening, sir," said Wazim, standing in the doorway. "May I come in?"

"Of course, come in and sit by the fire."

"Thank you," Wazim replied as he took a chair next to the hearth. He shifted his eyes to Miriam, and then to the fire, and back to her. "Are you feeling well, Mrs. Noah?"

"Yes, I am doing well and the children too. We were just talking about God's timetable for the ark, and how He knows what is best for all of us. Would you like a cup of coffee?"

"No, thank you, Mrs. Noah," he replied politely in his 'educated' voice. "Sir, I must report that we had an . . . accident on the site today." Wazim's voice was cautious. He seemed fearful that Noah would react in anger at what he was about to say.

"Tell me what happened, and we shall see what we can do about it. Was anyone hurt?"

"No, sir," he responded. "Nobody was hurt, thankfully. But I am afraid we have lost the large planking saw."

"What do you mean 'lost'?" Noah asked. "Was it stolen?"

"No. It broke in half while the men were cutting a difficult log. It snapped in the middle for no reason. They tried to weld the pieces together by heating them in the forge and rejoining them, but it only broke again. I'm afraid we will have to have another made, and that will take some time." Wazim didn't sound sufficiently disappointed or contrite, so Noah pursued the matter further.

"How could the large saw have broken? We have been using it for years, and all it needs is regular sharpening. It was made of the best tempered metal in the empire."

Wazim paused and said, "I don't know. The crew told me it broke, and that they tried unsuccessfully to fix it. That is all I know."

"So you weren't there when it broke?"

"No, sir." Wazim replied weakly.

"Where were you?" This sounded like an accusation, but Noah wanted a more direct explanation of why this had happened.

"Sir, I went into town to get supplies, and when I came back this evening I got the news. It was not my fault, I assure you." Wazim's attempt to evade responsibility was grating on Noah. What was he hiding?

"Well," Noah said in exasperation, "we still have a second saw we can use to continue shaping planks, right?"

"I'm afraid that, too, has broken, sir." Wazim cringed further and looked as if he wanted to escape before Noah asked him more embarrassing questions.

Noah took a few deep breaths and tried to keep his temper under control. "And how did that happen? Were you there, or did this also happen while you were away in town?" Sarcasm crept into Noah's voice, and he was close to shouting.

"It wasn't my fault, sir." Wazim tried to explain. "When the workers broke the large saw, they looked for the other one in the tool shed and found that it, too, was broken in half. Someone must have broken it earlier and put it away without telling me. I cannot say whose fault that was." Wazim's act at contrition was not convincing.

Noah was resigned to the loss and tried to think how it could be accommodated. "What is done is done at this point, I suppose. We will need to get another saw and put the crew on other projects until it arrives. You might as well order two saws. How long will that take?"

"Sir, no one can say about these things. I will place the order for the saws and ask that they be sent to us as soon as possible. However, it could take months."

"Months? I suppose, then, we are at the mercy of craftsmen in town to make us two more saws, and we shall see what we can do to keep up the schedule. When we get the new saws, I want you to personally supervise all the planking from now on, is that understood?" Noah hoped to get some commitment from his supervisor, instead of excuses.

"Yes, sir." Wazim stood quickly and almost flew to the door.

He left without saying any more, and Miriam and Noah looked at each other as the door closed quietly behind him.

After a few moments of silence, Noah ventured, "Something's up, and I don't like it. Do you think I was too easy on him? I really felt like letting him have it! I can't believe both saws happened to 'break' while he was in town, and he doesn't know how it happened. There's something else going on here." He was boiling mad as he paced back and forth in front of the fireplace.

"The fact that none of the help wants to hear about God's plan to save them is no coincidence," Miriam sighed. "It is in the heart of mankind to want to earn our deliverance, rather than trust the only One who can give it for free. Neither is it an 'accident' when things break without explanation, or simply 'disappear.'" She looked into the fireplace as the flames died down and the embers gave off their final warmth for the night. "We should ask ourselves: *What does God expect us to do now?*"

Noah also gazed into the glowing coals and thought for a while. "Well, first, He expects us to continue to obey Him, consistent with what He has told us. And second, He told me clearly to preach righteousness to anyone who will listen. His offer of deliverance on the ark is still there if anyone wants to accept it."

"And have we been doing these things?" Miriam asked gently.

"I believe we have. God told me to build the ark according to His dimensions and to warn others about the coming judgment. We have been preparing for the flood for more than twenty years, and we have been telling others how they can be delivered. We have been living our lives according to the commands and promises that God gave to Adam and which our forefathers passed down through the centuries to us."

Noah paused to find the words to say next. "But still, I wonder about the lack of results. If we have been doing what God told us to do, why has there not been more progress on the ark, and why has not a single person responded to my offer of free passage on the ark? I know I am completely inadequate for the task of this building project. I keep saying 'I am just a zoologist,' but it is true. I cannot build this ark myself. It is too much for me—too big, too complicated, too time-consuming. And my speaking abilities cannot possibly change anyone's heart or convince anyone to join us on the ark."

It was a while before Noah could speak again, and when he did, he began to understand the logic of Miriam's complete faith. "So, maybe I can answer my own questions," he began. "It is God who will produce the results, right? So far, I have been working day and night to achieve successful results, when, in fact, it is God who produces the results. All I have to do is remain faithful to what He told me to do."

"Having a baby is a good illustration of that," Miriam reminded him. "We do our part, but it is God who brings a new life into the world. We cannot produce the 'results' of a new life—only God can do that.

"I think that is a good note to end the evening on," Miriam said as she slowly rose from her chair. Noah banked the fire for the night, and they walked down the hall to their bedroom. In spite of the problems that came up that night, they could still look forward to another day of work for the Lord. Noah was ready to place it in God's hands, and sleep peacefully.

CHAPTER 11

Eden's Promise

Years Later

Noah and Miriam's three boys were close in age, but very different in character and abilities. Shem, the firstborn, quickly showed a love for animals and took to spending almost every waking moment outside, trapping wild animals in cages for study. When he grew old enough to go out alone, he spent his days tracking small dinos, sitting quietly, camouflaged in the forest trees documenting their eating and socializing habits.

Ham, their second son, was introspective and quiet. He spent hours by himself reading Lamech's books and discussing them with his grandfather. His insights into creation were more abstract than his brothers' but he was always thinking and asking questions.

The youngest, Japheth, was a unique combination of his older brothers' temperaments. Of course, Japheth grew up wanting to do whatever his brothers did, and that meant that he loved being outdoors tracking dinos, as well as spending time reading and discussing his ideas. The fact that he was such an imitator of his older brothers didn't surprise his parents. But what distinguished him from Shem and Ham was his dogged pursuit of knowledge with intensity and enthusiasm. He was competitive, eager to learn, and had a keen intelligence that, at times, surprised his parents.

The three brothers eventually became full-time partners, building the ark with their father. When the boys had learned everything that

Wazim could teach them about construction, they took on their own projects.

Noah followed their projects as they helped him and worked with each other. Japheth had become their leader, despite being the youngest. There was something familiar about his never-ending curiosity and his drive to solve difficult problems.

"You remind me of my grandfather, Methuselah," Noah remarked to Japheth while they caulked seams inside the ark one day. "He was always inventing something or analyzing how things worked."

"When did he die, Father?" Japheth asked.

"He might still be alive, for all I know," Noah replied. "He left our family more than two hundred years ago, and we haven't heard from him since. Lamech speaks little of him, especially since he and Methuselah had an argument. Methuselah was disgusted with the changes happening at the Institute, and he built his own private laboratory far away from here in the Great Forest. When he told his children and grandchildren that he was heading off to find his brother, Eli, and to retrieve something his father, Enoch, had given him, we thought he was chasing an illusion. It was a foolish thing to leave his family like that, but my grandfather had a mind of his own. He said it was the quest of a lifetime, and something he needed to do before it was too late."

"Too late for what? What was so important?" Japheth sensed something intriguing in his father's tone; he set down his bucket of caulking pitch and leaned forward. "Did he tell you what he went looking for?"

Noah hesitated to continue the story, because, even after all these years, his grandfather's sudden departure was still painful for him and Lamech. If Noah went further with his explanation, he was sure Japheth would press him for more details.

"What did he go in search of? Was it valuable? Did it have to do with you?" Japheth could hardly contain his curiosity.

"He said he had to find the lost Book of Adam. His father, Enoch, had given a copy of the Book to Eli, his eldest son, for safekeeping. But then, Enoch suddenly disappeared without a trace and Eli left home shortly thereafter with his copy of the Book. Methuselah's copy was later burned in a fire and nobody knew where Enoch's original went. Since then, the only record we had of the words in the Book was verbal, and most people eventually lost interest in the subject. But my grandfather never let it go. He had read the original from cover to cover before it was lost, and he would always tell us, 'Anyone who reads it and believes it will be changed forever.'"

"That's amazing!" Japheth exclaimed.

"It is indeed," Noah replied. "Back then, I never appreciated what Methuselah taught me, but I certainly believed the Book to be true, and I still do. Much of what your mother and I have taught you boys over the years is based on what I remember from the Book. I wish Methuselah were still here. You would love learning from him."

CHAPTER 12

Eden's Promise

Twenty Years Later

It was difficult for Noah and Miriam to find Sethian daughters who would make godly wives for their three sons. While most young ladies were nominal believers, Miriam often questioned their family's motives when they showed too much interest in her boys. Was their interest genuine or was it an insurance policy to guarantee them passage on the ark? Were they true believers or, like most Sethians by this time, had they merely learned to say the right things and pretended to be spiritual? In past generations, there had been many young true believers to choose from, but not anymore. Extreme caution was needed when parents arranged marriages for their children.

It took years, but Noah and Miriam eventually found good matches for Shem and Ham, and God blessed their marriages. True, the boys were young—younger than Miriam and Noah had been when they had gotten married—but their parents decided that the perilous times demanded it.

Shem, the oldest, married Taléa, who was from a family well known among Sethians for a consistent testimony of righteousness. Shem's parents had known her from her birth, and Shem and Taléa had even grown up together. They shared similar interests in the outdoors and a love for animals.

But Noah and Miriam were astonished when Ham found a young lady himself. At a Sethian harvest festival, they observed him speaking with a girl whose family they knew but who had been dismissed from consideration because she was so shy and withdrawn in contrast with Noah's outgoing boys; but her reserve seemed to suit Ham's reflective temperament. It wasn't long before Ham asked his parents if they would arrange for him to marry Akima. Noah and Miriam were overwhelmed with joy that Ham had found the one God wanted for him without their help. Ham and Akima were married soon thereafter, and the family gained another daughter. Miriam's focus then turned to finding a wife for Japheth.

But Japheth was not interested in a wife, no matter how much he was prompted by his parents. He knew that he and his brothers were prophesied to take wives into the ark, but he felt there was still so much time, and he had so many other plans before he took that step. Miriam was more concerned than Noah by Japheth's disinterest in marriage. With a mother's understandable, though exaggerated, concern, she had contacted the dwindling number of Sethian families in the region with eligible daughters, but Japheth was not interested.

A few towns away from Eden's Promise, a Sethian family had taken in a homeless girl, named Deva, whose parents had been captured in a daytime imperial police roundup. These abductions were dreaded, but regular, occurrences in vulnerable areas across civilization where Sethians had once lived in godly peace before the empire took over.

Deva, an only child, had avoided her parents' fate by hiding from the imperial troopers and escaping into the countryside. In time, she was hired by a family to take care of their children. Though she did well as a governess, she outgrew her abilities when she became a young woman. Maybe because of her hardship as a child, Deva entertained daydreams of riches and an exciting, luxurious life in the city of Enoch, where she could put the Sethian country ways behind her and enjoy the delights of all the city's attractions. Seeing her restlessness, her foster family had recommended her to Miriam for a position at Eden's Promise, where at least she might learn a skill to better herself. Deva lived in the woman's dormitory with the hired female servants, and Miriam took a liking to her as soon as the young girl began work in the kitchen. Miriam saw potential in her and made it a point to teach her domestic skills as if she were her own daughter.

Deva was a young woman who knew that her beauty made her attractive to young men. Her blond hair and lightly tanned but fair skin made her stand out among the older, dowdy kitchen help. From the start, the help had speculated about Japheth as a match for Deva. But it was years before Miriam began to consider that possibility. Deva was a responsible worker and always eager to help others. With her sunny disposition, she was a pleasure to have at Eden's Promise, and when the thought of Deva as a potential wife for Japheth entered Miriam's mind it became a settled arrangement. Miriam was so eager to see her youngest son married—and subconsciously help move God's plan ahead faster—that it did not occur to her that this young woman's goals for the future and her inner spiritual life might be at odds with those of Japheth.

The young woman had similar designs on Japheth to secure her future. Deva's strategy to win him over was subtle, showing only indirect interest in Japheth until he noticed her. She spent extra time grooming and dressing, hoping that when she served him meals in the dining hall he might take special notice; but Japheth appeared entirely uninterested. He was always too busy talking with the other workers, either about ark construction or ideas he had for labor-saving gadgets. He spoke politely to Deva, but avoided conversation.

Miriam, fully invested in the match, asked Deva if she would be willing to help her in the family kitchen, thinking that having Deva in the family residence might improve her chances of bringing the two together. Deva instantly agreed. The three brothers usually ate breakfast and lunch in the large dining hall with other workers, but it was their practice to eat evening meals together as a family in the main house. Miriam formally introduced Deva to Japheth one evening, and he was polite, but turned the talk quickly to work. Once they were formally introduced, Deva found ways to take him snacks in the work yard and talk for a few minutes. They spent more time together during breaks. Then they began taking walks after dinner.

Miriam observed something about Deva, however, which she shared with Noah one day. "She appears interested in knowing more about why we are building the ark, yet she never brings up spirituality in our conversations. At first, I thought she might make a good wife for Japheth, but now I'm not so sure. She and Japheth spend more time together talking, but I have a feeling they are not discussing their spiritual lives."

Noah looked up from the book he was reading. "He is still young," he said. "I would not worry about it. After all, his future, and the future of the entire family, is in the Lord's hands."

But Miriam had her doubts about Deva; she did not think that her initial plan to pair the beautiful kitchen helper with her son was such a good idea after all.

Japheth and Deva were walking to the river after dinner one evening, when Deva cautiously brought up a topic that Japheth had avoided on many occasions. He always changed the subject, but she hoped this time would be different.

"What future do you see for yourself, Japheth? Your whole life is ahead of you. What plans do you have when the ark is done?" Deva hoped to get him to talk about something other than work on the ark, and to steer the conversation toward their relationship.

"We have years of work left," he began. "I haven't given much thought to my life beyond that. Of course, if there is time when the work is done, I'd like to study at the Institute. But Dad probably won't let me. He's very set against the strong Cainite influence on campus. I'd love to study mathematics and engineering someplace, but that seems out of the question, for now."

Japheth wanted to turn their talk away from himself. "What about you, Deva? I don't know very much about your plans for your life."

"I'm just a kitchen maid, but I would give anything to travel and see the sights of the big city and other parts of the empire before I settle down and have a family—not that I have a husband in mind or anything like that, of course," she assured him coyly. "I've read so much about Enoch City in magazines that I can't wait to go there and see it for myself! Music concerts, shopping, museums, fine restaurants, parks, sporting events, and parties every night. So much to see and do! Have you ever been to the city?" she asked.

"No. I don't have any interest in that stuff. I guess I'm just a down-to-earth country boy, who prefers the simplicity of life here to the flashy city life." Japheth wondered where this conversation was going.

"You can't be serious!" Deva exclaimed. "Why, the concerts and parties alone would be worth traveling there to see. Thousands of people get together in the stadium and the music is loud enough to break your eardrums. Crowds gather for a party in the city square. Doesn't that sound like fun?"

"Honestly, no. I get a headache just thinking about it," Japheth confessed. "If that's what you want to do, that's your business. I'm looking forward to finishing the ark and getting some schooling. After we've completed our journey on the ark, everything we've learned will come with us into the new world. I can't waste my time before then." Japheth was determined.

"Will you be coming on the ark with us?" Japheth asked pointedly.

"I try not to think about that very much," Deva answered lightly. She didn't want to pursue that subject again. Miriam had asked her that same question many times, and Deva always deflected her mistress by changing the subject.

"I think that when the time comes, it will all work out," she said. "Until then I don't see why I shouldn't fulfill my dreams and enjoy my life." Japheth raised his eyebrows in disapproval, but he said nothing.

As they headed back to the house, Deva took his arm and turned him around to face her. "Do you think getting married would be a waste of your time?" she asked with her best smile.

"Not if it was with the right person; somebody who shares my love for the Lord and love for learning. But I haven't met that person yet." With that, he turned abruptly and walked toward the house.

Deva's face flushed with anger at Japheth's implied insult. How could he say that to her and just walk away? She wasn't surprised about his lack of enthusiasm for going to the city and partying, but she didn't expect such a harsh rejection. Her secret thoughts of someday marrying Japheth were shattered.

Japheth was furious with himself for the way he'd answered her. He immediately returned to her to apologize. He saw tears welling in her eyes and felt ashamed for his severity, not realizing they were tears of anger and bitterness.

"Deva, I'm sorry for the way I spoke. I'm often too abrupt in telling people how I feel, and I didn't mean to hurt your feelings. We have different interests, that's all. I know my mother has been trying to get us together. I'm pretty thickheaded most of the time, but her efforts have been hard to ignore. Anyway, we'll be seeing each other every day, so could we at least remain friends?" Japheth hoped this would smooth things over between them.

"Sure, if that's what you want," she replied coolly as she wiped her eyes. "I was hoping it might turn into something else, but if you want to be friends, that's fine with me."

"I think that would be best. Let's go back to the house and see what everyone is doing," Japheth suggested.

Returning to the others at the house, Deva's initial anger calmed only slightly as she turned over in her mind another plan to get everything she wanted.

CHAPTER 13

Eden's Promise, Construction Yard

Next Day

Hoisting planks to the upper deck of the ark was a dangerous job, especially because they used the large three-horned dinos for the crane's lifting power. The mechanism of pulleys, gears, and ropes was built to leverage the brute force of the dinos for lifting, while a ratchet in a geared drum kept the load from falling if the dinos stopped or stumbled suddenly. Japheth and his brothers had built the mechanism themselves, and Shem had trained the huge animals to respond to vocal commands. A human operator on the ground still needed to engage the clutch for driving the gears for lifting, rotating the crane's arm, and lowering loads. The gears were cast bronze—something Japheth learned from the forgers in town so that he could replicate the mechanisms himself. The ropes were braided with many strands overlapping to provide the necessary strength.

One morning, Lamech watched Noah pile planks on the ground and secure a harness of rope around a large bundle, ready to be lifted. They sat down in the shade for a few minutes before they harnessed the dinos.

"Have you noticed anything strange about the work crew lately?" Lamech asked as he sipped water from a drinking ladle.

"What exactly do you mean? That there are some new workers?" Noah responded. "Wazim fired a half-dozen men a few weeks ago because he said they were giving him a hard time. The new workers seem all right."

"They are good workers, I have no complaint there. But they seem *too* good. I wonder if they are overqualified for this type of labor." Lamech sounded hesitant, so Noah asked him to elaborate.

"If you have some reservation about them, you should say something. Maybe we are so used to Wazim and his crew's indolence that we have forgotten what it is like to have motivated people on a crew." He thought that might explain it, but he could tell that wasn't what his father was thinking.

"Maybe, but I cannot help thinking that two of these men stand out as more than common laborers picked up from town. I noticed that the rest defer to these two in Wazim's absence when they think I am not looking; and Wazim gives them orders only tentatively."

Noah, thinking about the two his father described, remarked further, "I think I know what you mean. I have seen them walk through the compound like policemen on patrol. Their eyes sweep back and forth, noticing everyone and everything. Do you think they might be plants or spies?"

"I tried talking to them about God's righteousness, and the responses I received were revealing," Lamech said. "They know all about the coming flood and the reasons behind it. Their answer to me was the usual about the empire not being so bad and how much things had progressed under 'his Royal Highness,' as they called him. Then they smirked and said, 'Things are not always what they appear. Of course, a worldwide flood is not possible. We do not believe there is anything to fear.' The two men I spoke with looked at each other, and then at me, and proceeded to return to their work." The concerned look on Lamech's face was mixed with puzzlement.

"We should watch them and see what they do. It might not be a good idea to fire them just yet if they are good workers. Meanwhile, I will say nothing to Wazim," Noah suggested. "If he knows what is going on but is somehow intimidated by them it will only cause us more trouble."

"We need to move these planks before lunchtime," Lamech observed to Noah as he got up and put on his hat. "I wish I could do more to help you than give hand signals on top of the ark. The sun is getting high, and I do not like looking up into the sky with a load of wood suspended above my head."

While Lamech slowly climbed the ladder to the top deck of the ark, Noah walked to the dino pen next to the crane and roused the beasts from their nap. They wheezed as they lumbered slowly off the ground and stood in their pen. The strength of the pair of three-horned dinos was astonishing. Measuring almost thirty feet from the tip of their center horn to the end of their spiny tail, they were lazy most of the time; but, when yoked together and hooked to the geared crane, they could lift a load weighing thousands of pounds. Noah led them to the side of the crane, away from the ark, and he clipped the yoke and harness to the cross bar fitted over the animal's center horn. One large horn in the center of their forehead and two smaller horns further down on their face above their eyes gave them a fierce look. But the large horn, about three feet in length and almost a foot thick at its base, fit snugly into the yoke so that they could push on the yoke with their neck and shoulder muscles. Their massive legs did most of the heavy work, as they plodded slowly forward and strained the drive rope holding its load of planks.

With the dinos harnessed, Noah received the go-ahead hand signal from Lamech on the top deck of the ark. Noah shouted the command, "Walk!" and the pair trudged forward. Noah hurried to the pile of planks, holding the end of the lifting rope that hung from the top of the crane, and he hooked it to the harness around the planks. "Stop!" he commanded and the dinos halted just in time to put the correct tension on the drive and lifting ropes. With the next command, they would move ahead after he engaged the gears for lifting. "Walk!" Noah shouted, and the harnessed dinos slowly trudged forward, and the tension on the rope increased until the load lifted off the ground. The destination for the pile of planks was over sixty feet above them, and with the gearing, the dinos would have to walk several hundred feet before the planks reached the top. They took to the load easily, and, in a few minutes, the planks were high in the sky and ready to be shifted over to the top of the ark. Noah knew this was the hardest part of maneuvering the crane.

"Stop!" Noah called out and was glad the dinos were so well trained that they responded immediately to his vocal command. He made sure the cog holding the lifting rope was secure and switched the drive over from lifting to turning the top of the crane. When he had done this with another lever, he once again gave the command, "Walk!" and since they were no longer lifting the heavy weight, the crane rotated easily until the pile of planks was high over the top deck and ready to be lowered.

"Be sure you don't stand under the load!" Noah shouted to his father. He couldn't see him, but he figured it was safer to remind him.

When he had switched the drive mechanism into reverse, to lower the load, he again gave the command, "Walk!" so that the dinos once more took on the full weight of the load before it could be lowered slowly. They inched ahead, while taking up the slack and bringing the line taut.

Suddenly, the line snapped and whipped over Noah's head like an angry serpent. As it whooshed by, the wind took his hat off and knocked him to the ground. The line unthreaded itself from the crane drum, whisked through the multiple pulleys, and the bundle of boards smashed through the top deck of the ark to the second deck below. Thankfully, the rope hadn't touched Noah, but the force of the whiplash made it feel like someone had taken a giant swing at him with a hammer. He stood and shook his head to clear the ringing in his ears. "Father!" he yelled as he looked up at the ark. "Are you all right? Say something to me. Are you hurt?"

"I am here," Lamech answered weakly. The pile of splintered wood was scattered around him and he slowly rose to his feet amid the settling dust. "It just missed me."

Noah saw his father's head appear through an opening in the shattered planks of the hull and could tell that he was shaken, but not hurt.

"What happened?" Lamech asked when he climbed out of the hole and looked at the pile of shattered timbers and decking. The dense bundle of gopher wood had acted like a sledgehammer, punching through the top deck and buckling the timbers below before stopping in a jumbled pile. Not only was there extensive damage to the hull and upper deck, but the bundle of carefully shaped planks was now a pile of splinters.

Noah remembered the dinos connected to the drive rope, and he noticed them wandering off in a distant field with the rope still trailing behind them. They had continued walking obediently, and, when he hadn't given the "Stop!" command, they found themselves free to feed in the field, unburdened of their heavy load, until their master came to retrieve them. He was more concerned about the damage sustained by the ark and the mystery of why the rope had broken.

One end of the rope had whipped past him, snaked through the crane mechanism, and flew up onto the ark. He called to Lamech to find this end to see what had caused the break.

When Lamech found the end of the rope, it was immediately obvious that the rope hadn't broken from wear or overloading. Of the ten strands braided into the large rope, five had been cut clean through.

"This is sabotage—no question about it!" Lamech called down to his son. Noah was furious that someone would do this. If the load had dropped on Lamech, it would have killed him. It was a miracle that the rope broke when it did and that nobody was hurt. Nonetheless, the incident cost them months of work on the ark and irredeemable time fashioning countless planks. Whoever did this wanted to severely set back, or even halt, their schedule.

A sudden movement in the bushes nearby caught Noah's attention, and he looked straight into the face of one of the workers he had been discussing with his father just minutes before. Their eyes locked, and the worker turned and broke into a full run toward the front gate. Noah ran after him, deftly avoiding piles of planks and tools on the ground. The chase took him toward the front gate and onto the road, where he gained steadily on the worker, who was obviously the culprit behind the accident. But when Noah got just beyond the gate, it was only to see the rascal and his accomplice jump onto two biped dinos that had been hidden in the brush for their escape.

Noah ran toward the two men settling into their saddles before their could get away. "Wait! Who are you and why did you try to harm us?" Noah was breathing hard, but demanded an answer.

"Keep away old man," warned the one whom Noah had chased. "Come any closer and you'll regret it."

"Who sent you to do this?" Noah was desperate to know.

"If you value your life and the lives of your wife and children, you'll stop building that silly boat of yours," threatened the other. "You've irritated some mighty powerful folks with your stories about the end of the world. You'll keep quiet if you value your life."

Noah stood helplessly as they kicked their steeds and raced away. He returned to the compound in a slow walk.

"I do not know how much more of this I can take," Noah said to Lamech when he returned to the scene of the accident. He sat and cradled his head in his hands. "We have so little to show for all of our years of work; I am not even sure this design will hold together—or if it will even float—when it is finished. I expected that my preaching would face opposition, but I did not think that people would go out of their way to harm us or destroy what we are trying to build for ourselves." This personal attack on him and his family had caught him off guard.

"Wazim will have some explaining to do for this," Noah muttered angrily. "Those two snuck onto the work crew to do damage to our project, and the rest of the crew knew it. The sabotage was calculated, and timed so that the rope would break straining under the heavy load directly above the deck of the ark to cause the maximum amount of damage—to possibly even kill someone. I mean to get to the bottom of this!" Noah exclaimed.

Later that evening, Noah found Wazim in the bunkhouse, and he held nothing back in confronting him. "Where were you this afternoon?" he asked pointedly as he stood inches from Wazim's face. "My father or I could have been killed with what happened today!"

"Mister Noah, I heard about it when I came back from town, and I am glad nobody was hurt. Believe me when I say that this was a most unfortunate accident, and I am thankful it was not worse." He sounded sincere enough, but Noah wasn't going to leave it there.

"It was no 'unfortunate accident'! That rope was purposely cut so that it would fail under a heavy load. The damage was done by two men *you* hired. They threatened me and my family before escaping. What do you have to say?"

Wazim paled noticeably at Noah's direct accusation and stepped back. "Sir, I had nothing to do with it, honestly. I was in town all afternoon."

"But you hired those two, did you not?"

"They came with good recommendations from other workers, and their previous employment checked out. I apologize, but what more am I supposed to do? You wanted work to progress faster, and that is what I have tried to do," Wazim pleaded.

"What about the other workers? Nobody's been working all afternoon. Why?" Noah demanded.

"They asked for the afternoon off because they had been working hard for the past week. They will all be back tomorrow morning, and we can ask them then if they know anything. What more can I do?" he pleaded further. It was clear that Noah wasn't going to get any more from Wazim tonight, so it would have to wait until they could investigate tomorrow.

Needless to say, Wazim and Noah discovered no further information the next day when they questioned the other workers. No one knew anything, or if they did, they weren't telling. At least Noah knew about the two who had sabotaged the crane. But were there other saboteurs working in the crew undercover? Noah had obviously attracted the attention of someone high up in the empire who did not want the ark built. Could Vanek be behind this? His violent reaction to Noah's explanation of the coming judgment of mankind had triggered a violence in Vanek that Noah had never witnessed before. Whatever the reason, Noah was sure that whoever was behind this latest "accident" would be back.

CHAPTER 14

Adam Institute, Faculty Meeting

Months Later

Trying to speak one-on-one with neighbors and townspeople about the coming judgment, while still spending full days building the ark, was time-consuming, and so far it had proved completely fruitless. Noah decided it would be more efficient to speak to a larger group, so he sent a formal request to the Institute asking to speak to a gathering of his former colleagues. He was surprised when his request was approved, but the letter of approval indicated that his father-in-law would not be in attendance due to a prior engagement. That was probably for the better.

Noah arrived early on the date of the Institute faculty meeting and was received coolly by those who had once been his friends and coworkers. It was clear that, though they had granted him an opportunity to speak, they were skeptical and in no mood to listen patiently. The crowd of several hundred professors was not gathered exclusively to hear Noah's plea for their repentance; a number of regular faculty business issues were scheduled first on the agenda. They listened to recent successes in areas of research sponsored by the empire, and they cheered when they heard of new funding grants. Generous research money from the empire was allotted for the development of advanced chemical weapons to be used against some unspecified enemy.

Noah was granted twenty minutes on the agenda to explain to the Institute why he was building the ark. This was his opportunity to tell his peers that God had warned of a terrible future for an unrepentant world. He looked around at the audience of once-friendly researchers, who now met him with looks of stony opposition. They were not going to like what he had to tell them. When the flood came, he didn't want anyone saying that they hadn't been warned.

"Thank you for coming here today and . . . allowing me to explain a few things about my ark project and . . . why I began its construction," Noah began hesitatingly. This was not easy, but he pressed ahead as he sensed the icy atmosphere in the auditorium.

"I have told a few of you about how God spoke to me from a burning tree and how the tree shined with an intense flame, but the leaves did not burn." He raised his hands to silence the murmuring that immediately swept across the audience. "Now, before you get all worked up thinking that I must have been hallucinating, I want you to remember that I am a scientist, just like each of you. I have been trained to approach the world with an open and questioning mind, observing phenomena with all of my senses. And, even though this tree appeared to burn, with flames shooting high into the sky, there wasn't even the smell of smoke on its branches, nor were its leaves singed.

"But the main thing is not what I saw, but what I heard," Noah continued nervously. "And the message was not encouraging. It was terrifying, and it should be terrifying to you, too, when you hear it." As he went on, it seemed he at least had their attention, skeptical though they were. "First, God told me to build an ark. And before you attribute this task to the flighty imagination of an eccentric old man—building a large boat in a landlocked town—let me explain why. God told me He is not pleased with the direction our civilization is going. The righteousness that began with our forefather Adam, the founder of this Institute, has been steadily eroded to the point where violence and corruption have warped our society. In fact, God is so angry with us that He swore to completely destroy everyone on the face of the planet if we do not change our ways and return to the righteousness that is found only in Him. He plans to inundate the planet with a deluge of water that will cover the mountains and kill every person and animal if they are not on the ark. So, I have come here today to tell you all that there is plenty of room on the ark for anyone who would come with my family and me, if you will only repent and believe what God has said."

The meeting moderator pounded his gavel on the table furiously to quiet the crowd that had jumped to its feet as one with screaming and cursing at Noah's offer of salvation. "Calm down everyone, calm down please," the moderator yelled to no effect, his sweating face becoming redder as he pounded his gavel again and again.

"Get that crackpot out of here!" one professor yelled.

"Why is he at this meeting? We don't want to hear any more of his mindless babbling!"

"A worldwide flood? Covering the mountains? What a stupid, impossible thing to say!"

"We're decent, law-abiding people—nothing is going to happen to us!"

"He's trying to incite a panic and overthrow the empire!" shouted someone in a booming voice. This loud cry was picked up by others, who chanted, "Traitor to the empire! Traitor to the empire!"

The cries became more threatening, and Noah rushed out of the auditorium as books and chairs were hurled in his direction. The accusation that he was trying to overthrow the empire was initiated by an official-looking monitor who Noah did not recognize. After the incident with the saboteurs on the work site, Noah had become more suspicious. He wanted to refute the charge of treason and explain that building the ark was not seditious and that he posed no threat, but instead he was forced to flee from the violent mob.

This encounter marked a turning point in Noah's warning ministry, from which there would be no turning back. What he feared most had happened: someone had planted the thought that he posed a threat to the Anakim Empire. Word would soon reach more powerful authorities, who would not tolerate any opposition to the emperor, real or imagined. If the emperor himself became involved things would turn very violent indeed.

CHAPTER 15

Eden's Promise, Construction Yard

By the sixtieth year of construction most of the hull was fully planked and caulked. It wasn't pretty, but it looked solid enough. Wazim had given Noah his assurance that its box-like shape, more resembling a large four-story, window-less building than a ship, maximized the space inside and was easier to build than a sleek, oceangoing ship. But they had spent almost sixty years getting the structure to its present condition, and considerably more work remained to be done to finish the inside. Noah was nagged by the thought that something about the ark didn't feel right. The design was simple enough, but he had doubts about its long-term seaworthiness as a ship. The overall dimensions conformed to God's instructions, and there was certainly enough room inside. But was he relying too much on the expertise of someone in whom he placed little trust? Or was it a case of not trusting enough to God's care to see that the ark was eventually built properly? His anxiety wouldn't go away.

The cry of "Fire!" rang through the compound while Noah was repairing a tool in the workshop. He ran from the shop, with other workers following closely behind him, to see clouds of black smoke billowing from a door in the side of the ark. Shem, Ham, and Japheth raced toward the ark and more workers appeared, coming from all directions. Women spilled from the house and dormitories to see what was happening and to lend their help.

There was a large water tank built uphill from the work site specifically for use in case of a fire. Thick, oily, black smoke told Noah that burning pitch, and not burning wood, fueled the fire. Water might not be effective against this type of fire, because burning pitch could not be quenched unless it was completely submerged in water. But they had to try. Workers connected hoses to the standpipe on site, while someone ran up the hill to open the valve at the tank. When the valve was opened, the pressure from that height would feed water through the hoses in a full-forced gush. Noah grabbed the end of a hose and dragged it toward the door where the smoke was emanating from; the passageway inside the ark was thick with smoke. Noah fell to the floor to avoid suffocating. The black smoke from the pitch interspersed with gray wood smoke caused others to cough and cover their faces with their shirts. The hose started to shake, so Noah knew the pressurized water was on its way, and that he'd have to stop crawling in order to aim the torrent down the passageway toward the source of the fire.

Even with a workman helping him to stabilize the nozzle, the two were almost knocked off their feet when the pressure hit. They supported their backs against a beam as they sent the spray toward the smoke. After a few seconds, they could slowly crawl forward down the passageway holding the nozzle. The spray hissed as it hit the flames and molten pitch. It seemed to be having some effect, but they had to stop moving forward or the smoke would overwhelm them. Water streamed down from overhead as others directed their hoses on the fire from above. Maybe together they could put enough water into the blazing compartment to extinguish the burning pitch.

After ten minutes, it appeared that the torrential stream from above had doused the hottest part of the fire, and that the black smoke had diminished. Noah handed the end of his hose to another workman who had come up behind him, and he crawled closer to see where the fire had blazed most intensely. In about twenty feet, he came across someone lying on the floor, who had apparently been overcome by the smoke.

Noah suddenly realized who it was.

"Father!" he cried when he saw the familiar face blackened with soot. "Someone come here and help me! We need to get Lamech out of here!" Noah pried a charred bucket from his father's fingers and struggled to pull him along the floor out of the passageway. Lamech had tried to put the fire out with a bucket of water. Noah clenched his father's legs and made his way back toward the door in the ark, toward fresh air. The heat and smoke were still stifling, and the only place Noah could breathe was close to the floor. Soon, hands grabbed them. It was Shem and Ham who quickly moved their father and grandfather to fresh air.

The boys pulled Noah and Lamech to the grass outside and immediately began to tend to Lamech, but there was no pulse, and he didn't respond to their attempts to restart his breathing. Lamech, covered in black soot but with no visible burn marks, had escaped the flames, but the smoke he inhaled in the passageway had suffocated him. Noah could only stare numbly at his father's lifeless body and wonder if all this was worth it. After almost sixty years of building an ark they had been rejected by their friends, endured years of endless days of labor, and now suffered Lamech's tragic death. Shem and Ham went back into the ark to look for others and make sure the flames were entirely extinguished. Even though wisps of smoke still drifted from openings in the upper deck, it was clear that the worst of the fire was over.

The family mourned Lamech's death for several days and put off any contemplation of what to do next. As Noah reflected on his father's long life, he tried to find some comfort in Lamech's good example and optimism about life. Lamech saw much suffering in his seven hundred seventy-seven years on this cursed earth. It had been difficult for him and his wife to raise their many children, and yet, he had maintained a determined faith that had kept him going. As a devout Sethian, he had trusted the One True God and looked forward to the promised Savior who Adam said would one day conquer death for all mankind. He had taught his children right from wrong, and even when his father, Methuselah, left him, he had remained faithful. The sin that first brought death into the world had only temporary victory over his body, and Noah knew that he would see his father again. Meanwhile, they mourned him, and the emptiness that Noah felt with his passing was crushing. He was now at the "head of the line" of his family and probably the last generation of faithful Sethians. Where should he go from here?

"Do we have any idea how the fire started?" Noah asked his sons as they picked their way through the charred shell of the lower deck.

Though the fire had been extinguished days ago, the acrid smell of burnt pitch was still sickening.

"It definitely started down in this compartment on the lowest deck," observed Shem as he stepped over what remained of the door to the compartment and entered into a room about twenty feet square. Dim sunlight illuminated the room now, since the fire had destroyed the upper deck timbers and planks. "The door must have been closed, allowing pitch fumes to build up inside. It wouldn't take much of a flame to ignite volatile fumes in an enclosed space," Shem explained.

"But what could have started the fire in the first place?" asked Japheth. "We caulk the seams with hemp soaked in pitch, but we remove excess material on the side of the hull."

"I can't be sure, but, like I said, it wouldn't take much to ignite fumes in a closed room," replied Shem as he began moving timbers that had fallen from the upper deck. "I want to go through this room carefully and see if we can find evidence of how it started."

Ham was picking through the charred remains, when he said, "The thing that bothers me is that nobody should have been down here anyway. This part of the ark was essentially finished and the door was closed so nobody would come in. It wasn't locked, but all the workers knew it was finished and not to be used for storage. I could understand if pitch-soaked rags caught fire spontaneously, but we always make it a point to keep finished rooms clean of anything."

"Right, that's what's so puzzling about the whole thing," Shem said, still moving around the sides of the room. The sunlight didn't illuminate much in the recessed corners of the room, since the deck and sides of the compartment were black from charred wood.

"Sadly, what killed grandfather was toxic smoke and not burning wood. When he first came upon the fire, it had probably just started and he thought he could put it out with a bucket of water." Shem continued moving around and stooped to pick up a piece of wood from the floor. "This is where the pitch came from," he observed grimly, holding up a blackened shell.

"That's a pitch bucket!" Japheth exclaimed. "You can tell because it's smaller than the ones we use for water. But how did it get in here?"

"Look at this," Ham called from the other side of the room. He held a melted lump of brass in his hand. The lump, with what remained of a handle still intact, had been an oil lamp.

Shem held the fragments of charred wood and melted brass in his hands. "A full bucket of pitch next to the hull and a lit lamp at the other end of the compartment. It would only take a few hours for the fumes to build up in this closed space and for the small flame from the lamp to start a fire in the bucket of flammable material across the room. The instant ignition would blow the door open and oxygen would immediately rush into the compartment to feed the flame."

After carefully sifting through the rest of the room, they climbed over fallen timbers and planks back to the entrance and gathered on the grass where they had lain Lamech a week earlier.

The piece of charred bucket and the lump of brass were silent witnesses to what remained unsaid. After a few minutes, Japheth asked out loud what they were all thinking, "Does this mean what I think it means?"

"We've suffered setbacks before from accidents and the unexplained disappearance or breakage of valuable tools and other materials," Noah began, staring at the ground. "But this murderous sabotage has gone too far. We have had close calls from mysterious falling timbers, and that accident with the crane was a warning to us. But this is too much to take. I never thought that obeying God would result in my father being murdered." With that, Noah turned and walked to the house with a slow pace and slumped shoulders. He had never felt so empty and hopeless.

The ark sustained serious damage to its hull and decks from the fire. The hull planking would need to be replaced and any charred wood had to be taken out; new timbers and planks had to be fashioned. There was no telling yet how extensive the damage actually was, and it could mean a setback of years, as opposed to the days or months lost due to previous "accidents." On top of that, it meant that someone was still determined to keep the ark from being finished. The death of Lamech meant that whoever was behind this sabotage was ruthless in their methods. One murder would lead to more, if these accidents continued.

The three brothers stayed outside and talked among themselves about what to do next, but they couldn't help but be moved by how hard their father had taken this latest catastrophe. His slumped shoulders and slow walk across the yard to the house spoke of a defeated heart.

CHAPTER 16

Eden's Promise, Noah's Study

That Night

Noah locked the door to his study at the back of the house, where he knew it would be quiet and he would be free from interruption. It was during dark times like this that he needed to pour out his heart to the Lord. He knelt on the rug in front of his desk and held his face in his hands.

Lord, I do not know what to do any more. The opposition to your message of deliverance is almost unbearable. Now, I have lost my father to those who hate you. What more is ahead? I know you are loving and kind, and you have blessed us abundantly in many ways. But I am even beginning to doubt if I can bear up under this heavy load you have placed upon my shoulders. You told me what you want me to do, and I have done my best. You have given Miriam and me three boys, who love you sincerely. We desire to obey you by setting examples for the Sethians and Cainites around us. But how much more can we take?

Dear Heavenly Father, I know that you have a purpose in all that you do, and I wish I knew what your purpose was for testing us with so many setbacks in building the ark, and now with my father's death. Nobody listens to me when I speak of your coming judgment, and nobody has yet accepted your offer of deliverance on the ark. Now, the empire seems to have targeted us with their wrath. I do not know what more I can do, Noah confessed.

I acknowledge my sinfulness and I ask Lord, that you offer me some encouragement and lift me up from the dust of the earth at this time. Please Lord, take pity on my weakness and insufficiency for the tasks that you have put in front of me. I believe you want us to finish the ark, so that, when the time is right, we can enter it with a clear conscience, knowing that we have done all we could to offer others salvation through you and our coming Savior.

Noah remained praying in his study until late into the night as the house became quiet after the day's activity. As he prayed, he was overcome with peace, knowing that God would deliver him and his family from the calamity that was sure to follow in the next sixty years. God was good and would always be faithful to His promise.

Unknown to Noah, a violent struggle was taking shape between invisible powers of darkness and spiritual guardians at the gates of Heaven. A battle was forming on two fronts: on planet Earth between the empire and Noah's family, and in Heaven between supernatural forces of evil and good. God was firmly in control of the battle's outcome.

CHAPTER 17

Imperial District Court

Two Weeks Later

After the fire in the ark and his father's death, Noah was reenergized by his communion with God. He had a new determination to finish the ark and bear witness to those around him. In response to trumped-up reports that he had accused the empire as the reason for coming judgment, Noah had been formally summoned to the nearest Imperial District Court to answer for these accusations. He always welcomed an opportunity to explain his motives and message. But now he was having second thoughts about whether this was such a good idea so soon after his father's death and his assumption that work on the ark was still being subverted. The last thing he wanted was to become so emotional in his presentation that he openly accused the emperor of sabotage and murder in front of government witnesses.

When he arrived at the court, a large crowd had already filled the gallery, while a group of press and local police were conspicuous in the back of the room. The crowd made him anxious, but he could see some of his neighbors in the audience, and he hoped they would at least defend his character, if not his message of righteousness. Causing a great disturbance on government property was far from his intention, but he had to tell the truth, even if it meant being arrested. He was glad he had left Miriam and the boys at home so they wouldn't have to see this spectacle.

He did not have to wait long for the judge to enter and the prosecutor to take his place next to him. Noah's name was immediately called, and he walked to the front of the courtroom where the bailiff motioned him to take his place in the witness box.

"The court will hear from the Imperial Prosecutor, who will be questioning citizen Noah concerning statements allegedly made against the empire." The judge turned to the energetic young prosecutor.

"Thank you, Your Honor. Mr. Noah, you have talked around town about a terrible disaster that you say awaits our empire in a few years because we are such . . . wicked people." A smattering of snickers emerged from the crowd, and the Imperial Prosecutor broke into a sarcastic grin. "In a public arena at the Adam Institute—an organization largely sponsored by the empire—you made wild claims about a worldwide flood. You have been charged with speaking treacherously against the empire. Now, you will be given the opportunity to speak in your own defense, but if your defense disrupts the peace and these proceedings get out of hand, you will be removed from this court by police escort and held in custody until a sentence for provoking this disruption is determined at a later date. So, Mr. Noah, please explain to the court why you do not pose a threat to this community."

Noah stood in the witness box and looked over the room packed with his neighbors before he spoke. He knew most of the people in the room, except for the police and press. He noticed four muscular thugs standing casually at the back of the room next to one local police officer.

"I know most of you, and you all know me. My wife, Miriam, and I have been in this town for most of our adult lives. We have never caused anyone any trouble, and we have helped in community projects for years. We always support our town government and have been law-abiding citizens. In fact, I received all the requisite town permits for clearing the work site to build the ship, which we call an 'ark.' Moreover, my project has employed hundreds of people from this town, and other nearby towns, since I started it. So, I can only assume that the opposition to my building the ark stems from my reason for building it," Noah boldly assessed.

"That brings me to the heart of the matter," he continued. "When our forefather, Adam, was created in the Garden seventeen centuries ago, he sinned, and that sin was passed down through all generations in his line ever since. Each of us in this room can trace our family tree back to Adam. We are all sinners in the sight of God—by thought and deed.

Now, before you jump up and say that doesn't mean you, think about your own life and whether you ever did anything that violated your conscience and made you feel guilt. If we are honest, that has happened to all of us more than once. Whether you are Sethian or Cainite, you know you have sinned at one time or another, and that sin needs to be dealt with somehow. It cannot be dismissed and left to fester. Back in the old days, as some of you still remember, families would offer animal sacrifices to cover past sins in anticipation of the promised Lamb of God. Our family still does that every year. But most of the world has moved away from the old traditions and forgotten what it means to be right with God. The entire world has slid into a cycle of violence and corruption." Glancing over at the four thugs at the back of the room, Noah saw them rocking on their heels and snickering, but he pressed on. "Now, God has given an ultimatum to the world. Repent and get right with God, or He will destroy the world and everything in it with a global flood of water. My generous offer—God's generous offer—to each of you still stands: Whoever will repent of their sin and trust God to save them from the coming annihilation of the human race can live if they come with us onto the ark. It's that simple and it's your choice."

Noah waited anxiously for an eruption in the courtroom. But, aside from a few murmurs, there was no shouting, yelling, or throwing of chairs.

The prosecutor and the judge exchanged glances before the prosecutor turned to Noah and assumed a formal stance before the witness box amid a rising rumble of voices from the audience. "The witness has made himself clear. I have no more to say, Your Honor." The prosecutor sat and looked to the judge.

The judge raised his hand to silence the crowd. He proceeded to read what appeared to be a prepared statement: "I find the accused's statements heretical and disturbing to the general peace of this community and the empire. His hateful bigotry has no place in public discourse and—having heard his accusations of the empire from his own mouth in front of a courtroom of witnesses—we need not proceed further. Mr. Noah, you must now answer to the empire for your actions."

The judge pointed to a man in the back of the room who had slipped in just as Noah concluded his testimony. He was neatly dressed in an expensive black suit that was finely tailored to fit his tall, thin frame, and he carried himself like a prosperous businessman or attorney.

"Chief Inspector Hin of the imperial police, please come forward," the judge intoned solemnly.

Hin strode confidently up the center aisle, pausing to look over the courtroom and then toward the witness box with a cold stare he'd practiced many times to freeze people's attention. When he spoke, it was in the deep, authoritative tone of a person of great power who was accustomed to being heard and obeyed.

"Citizens, let me be very clear. Incendiary statements like those we have heard today will not be tolerated. I assure you, on behalf of our Beloved Emperor, that this man means to intentionally disrupt the peace of this fine community and promote bigotry and prejudice against our chosen way of life. This man," he exclaimed as he turned and pointed at Noah, "is imposing his intolerant views on an innocent public that has done nothing wrong!"

Hin spoke to the audience in a commanding voice, while staring at his subject unblinkingly. "Let me make this clear," he repeated. "The idea that there could *ever* be a flood to cover the whole world is so unbelievable that it can only be interpreted as a sick scheme to panic the population for this man's twisted purposes. I am convinced, as should you be, that his is a deranged mind. Mr. Noah is a menace to this community, spreading his false ideas of a supposed future catastrophe and attempting to gather a troublesome following to intimidate your peaceful community.

"Our Beloved Emperor has authorized me to 'examine' this traitor to determine his true intentions and place him under imperial order to not spread his message of bias and hatred. Using his own statements tonight as evidence, I can assure you that he will be charged and punished for his crimes. You are all dismissed to return quietly to your homes, knowing that your government will deal with this matter firmly and fairly." With that, two of the ruffians at the back of the room came forward and grabbed Noah's arms in vice-like grips. They were followed out of the door by the other two men, with the grim chief inspector bringing up the rear.

"Don't give us no trouble now," one of the escorts growled at Noah. "Come with us and we'll have us a little chat." They dragged Noah into the parking lot, where their black-scaled high-speed dinos were parked in a row next to a polished police coach; their "chat" was over in less than ten minutes. When they were finished, Noah was bleeding from a half-dozen different places, his eyes were swollen closed, teeth were missing, and he was sure ribs had been broken by their sharp, well-aimed kicks.

Their leader, in his perfectly tailored black jacket and razor-creased black pants, watched from a distance as his men pummeled Noah with apparent gusto. He walked up to Noah's prone body and kicked him once with his spotlessly polished shoe. He bent down and hissed, "Listen to me carefully. I don't want to hear from you again—ever. If I do, you and your family will be killed and your little boat will go up in flames again, and this time there won't be anything left of it." Hin straightened, and his goons followed him leaving Noah slumped in the parking lot.

That threat was clear enough, groaned Noah as he brushed bloody sand from his battered face.

The chief inspector paused to look back at Noah's crumpled form before stepping into his imperial coach. His glare was more threatening than the blows of his brutal flunkies. Hin closed the coach door and the vehicle immediately accelerated, kicking rocks and dirt back into Noah's face as he and his mounted escort sped into the night. Chief Inspector Hin commanded his driver to press the mounts hard, change them at police stations along the way to maintain a fast pace around the clock, and reach the city of Enoch and police headquarters within days.

When Noah had recovered enough to walk, he found his dinos lying motionless on their sides in a deep pool of blood. It looked like Noah had a long, painful walk home ahead of him. He was silently thankful that Miriam and the boys hadn't come with him. Who knew what the police might have done to them. His body would eventually mend, and in a way, he considered it a blessing to suffer for what he knew was right. He didn't hold a grudge against the judge or the townspeople; they were intimidated by the empire and its power. The fact that the emperor himself had taken notice of Noah's preaching was worrisome. The empire was an unstoppable force. But God wanted Noah to stand up and obey Him, so he had to continue to trust that He would somehow protect his family and the ark to the very end. In the meantime, he would *not* stop construction on the ark, and he would *not* be silent.

CHAPTER 18

Imperial Palace, Throne Room

Five Days Later

The Emperor Anak was a physically imposing figure over nine feet tall with heavily muscled features. His face was a mask of pock-marked flesh with deep-set coal-black eyes. Those who dared look at him directly said that his double eyelids, closing from top and bottom, were almost reptilian.

The initial goal of scientists back in the early days of genetic research was to make human beings healthier and somehow reverse the curse of sickness and death, which had plagued humankind since the sin of Adam and Eve. No one could remember—or they refused to admit—how the first misguided experiments had begun. When officials at the Institute discovered that human subjects were being used in unauthorized experiments, they simply looked the other way and allowed them to continue. The "products," as they called the human-like creatures, were larger and more physically powerful than natural-born humans. But it wasn't long before their research turned into a national project to produce these half-humans in greater numbers because it was believed they would give the Cainites an advantage in future warfare. It mattered little that there were no known enemies against the rapidly expanding Cainite civilization. Sethians never sought world domination or warfare, but Cainites were unscrupulously ambitious and the Sethians feared—rightly so, as it turned out—that these new creatures would some day be used against them. Many women—Cainites at first, and most of them unwitting—were implanted with genetically developed embryos and they gave birth to monstrous offspring. The size of the newborns inevitably resulted in the death of their "mothers." The unviable babies were casually destroyed when results did not meet expectations, while others were kept alive for further experiments. Those whose outward features met the desired physical specifications of size and health were allowed to grow to maturity. But each of the half-human creatures developed erratic mental and emotional traits.

When experimenters used enslaved Sethian women as hosts, scientists discovered they could achieve predictable and viable results for mass production. The offspring grew large and were physically healthy, but they lacked a conscience or a sense of morality. Scientists pursued this method of breeding further and generated hundreds of warrior beings who would follow commands blindly. These human-like warriors were called Anakim. They were a corrupted mixture of natural human and artificial genetic materials. What their developers did not anticipate was their subjects' increasing independence as they grew in age and education. Behind their coal-black eyes was a mind fueled by hateful resentment of the scientists and civilization that brought them to life and anyone else who tried to restrain their raw impulses. This hatred focused on anyone who was not like them.

One Anakim at the Institute stood out for his superior intelligence and ambition. It was he who one day broke out of the laboratory and, with the help of his cohorts, destroyed the laboratory and all the scientists in it. The formula for genetic breeding was lost in the rubble and a race of unrestrained Anakim was unleashed upon the world.

The Anakim warriors organized under this dominant leader, who called himself Anak, who led them to confront the cowering human population. Within a few years the Anakim brutalized those who openly resisted them, taking control of every city and town. Anak proclaimed himself Emperor, and Enoch City became home to his palace. It was this creature and his similarly altered warrior kin who systematically imposed their evil domination upon the world. Emperor Anak was the singular embodiment of the hate and violence that came to characterize life for those who swore allegiance to him. Those who opposed him were systematically crushed.

So it was that life at the Imperial Palace revolved around the Emperor Anak who had ascended to his throne over the bodies of hundreds of thousands of humans who dared to oppose his rule. The Imperial

Palace was the seat of the worldwide government that answered to the emperor. Life in the palace was in constant turmoil.

"I want a full report within the hour about what happened with this man Noah," the emperor barked to the nearest messenger. "I expect to hear from my chief inspector directly. Go!"

"Yes, Beloved Emperor. It shall be done immediately for the glory of the empire." The Cainite messenger scurried down the marble hallway to deliver the emperor's order to the palace scribe. He was glad to be out of the emperor's presence when Anak was in a foul mood, which was all of the time.

The messenger stood before the scribe, who regarded him with the contempt every palace scribe had for mere messengers. "The Beloved Emperor wishes a report from the chief inspector within the hour about his meeting with Noah," repeated the emperor's messenger to the scribe.

The scribe wrote the message into the log and turned to his assistant to summon Chief Inspector Hin. He dismissed the messenger to return to the emperor and await further instructions. Such was the life of a Sethian messenger who had taken the oath of the emperor. He was like a trained hamster on a treadmill running back and forth all day between the emperor and the palace scribe. It didn't matter that his feet were running on beautifully polished marble. It was a treadmill nonetheless. And he was forced to witness things that gave him nightmares.

Within a half hour the messenger announced Chief Inspector Hin, who reverently entered into the emperor's presence. The chief inspector was dressed in his customary crisp, black suit. He assumed an appropriate attitude of submission and confidence when he stood before the emperor. He was a Cainite who had pledged his loyalty to the emperor long ago and received compensatory rewards for his continued loyalty and competence. But he knew those rewards only lasted as long as the emperor was pleased with his work. If he failed to please the emperor his good fortune would end abruptly and painfully. But that was life for a loyal Cainite in the service of the emperor. You lived in constant fear, but you enjoyed extraordinary benefits while they lasted.

Hin stood at the foot of the raised dais while the emperor sat on his padded velvet and gold-inlayed marble throne and stared at him. Anak looked like a tightly wound spring, coiled and ready to release at any instant. Those who had never been in his presence before were terrified that he could unleash his angry energy upon them at any second, and they often shook and stammered the entire time they stood before him. It was enough that they heard stories of his ability to fling a knife through a petitioner's heart before he even realized the weapon had been drawn. But Hin had stood before Anak's imposing presence many times and was still alive. He knew that the emperor grudgingly respected those who were not afraid to die could stand before him without flinching.

"Give me your report chief inspector," the emperor demanded flatly.

"Yes, Beloved Emperor. I am always at your service." Hin began to relate what Noah had said at the meeting, but he was immediately cut off.

"That is not what I want to hear!" the emperor interrupted. "This nonsense about a worldwide flood will not be tolerated. I do not want to hear of Noah's babbling! My science advisors assure me there is no possible way there is enough water in the world to cover it completely. It is simply impossible. Now tell me, chief inspector, what you did to silence this man." Any audience with the emperor had the risk of turning ugly, and Anak was becoming agitated.

"I assure you, Beloved Emperor," the chief inspector replied calmly, "he will not be a problem in the future. My men dealt with him severely. He will not speak any more about repentance or global floods. I can report that I consider the matter closed, and I give you my word that he will no longer be speaking publicly about it." Hin waited confidently for the emperor's reaction to his report.

"Good," acknowledged the emperor, "so your men killed him?"

"Well, no, Beloved Emperor," replied the chief inspector as his confidence disappeared and his mouth suddenly dried. "His death was not in my orders from your scribe." Deflection to the scribe always worked for him in the past when orders were unclear.

"I explicitly said that he was to be 'silenced,'" the emperor shouted as he descended the stairs from his throne toward the inspector. "Chief Inspector Hin, do you not understand how a person is to be 'silenced' in this empire? When I say 'silenced' I mean that they are to be permanently and irreversibly stopped from ever speaking again. Now, tell me that you understand!"

"Beloved Emperor, I understand perfectly."

"Good. Now I want you to personally take charge of a police squad, go to this man's home, and 'silence' him and his family. That is my direct order! I expect that it will be obeyed swiftly and completely without any confusion about my meaning. You will give me a report—a very brief and positive report—as soon as humanly possible. You are dismissed." With that, the emperor flicked his hand toward the door and returned to his throne.

Chief Inspector Hin bowed and walked toward the door as calmly as he could. He didn't feel a knife in his back although he felt the emperor's eyes boring into him as surely as if they were knives. He would return with the proper report or face certain death.

As soon as he reached Imperial Police Headquarters, Hin summoned his deputy and a trusted officer from his personal special tactics squad. The squad was made up of young, ambitious men who could put together a team at a moment's notice to quickly and efficiently carry out the emperor's deadly instructions.

Deputy Chief Inspector Baaki and Lieutenant Lasou stood before their superior minutes later to receive his instructions. Baaki appeared to be a clone of the chief inspector in his physical appearance, except he was younger, more fit, and if it were possible, more ambitious. He dressed and acted like his superior, who was so flattered by this that he encouraged the imitation to further boost his ego. Lieutenant Lasou was the product of the elite Imperial Police Academy who had been carefully selected to perform "special projects" for Chief Inspector Hin. He was unflinchingly loyal and would not hesitate to kill for Hin and the emperor.

"Here is what I want you to do," the chief inspector began, with no introduction or explanation. "The emperor has ordered the killing of this man Noah and his entire family. You will assemble a team of your most loyal troopers and draw up a plan to enter the compound and kill everyone there. You will report back to me in one hour with your plan for my approval. I do not expect any resistance from this group of Sethian traitors, but we will take no chances of surprise. I want the assault to be fast, overwhelming, and decisive.

"I have someone on the inside," Hin continued, "who supplied me with a detailed map of the compound and assured me you can enter the compound quietly any time from a hidden gap in the fence." He withdrew a drawing from his desk safe and handed it to Lieutenant Lasou.

"That is all the background information you need. No dossier or pictures of the targets. Get in, complete the mission, and get out. We will depart for this man's home as soon as the plan is approved, essential supplies are gathered from the depot, and weapons of your choice are drawn from the armory."

"Sir," asked the lieutenant, "do you wish to spare the informant? If so, we will have to incorporate that into our plan. Also, what about any servants or workers living in the compound?"

"I am not concerned about any of them. A successful mission means no survivors, and losing an informant or other collaterals means nothing to me." They had received Hin's ruthlessness tasking before, but it still chilled them the way he issued orders to kill with such lack of emotion.

Hin's deputy and the lieutenant walked down the hall from the chief inspector's office to the squad's mission briefing room and called a dozen black-clad men together to go over the sketch of the compound. "Men," began Lieutenant Lasou in a measured voice, "this special job will be easy. Our targets are twenty to thirty unarmed civilians—fifty at the most. Surprise and overwhelming firepower will ensure success. We will be back in no time."

CHAPTER 19

Eden's Promise, Family Residence

Five Days Later

"You made my favorite biscuits tonight Mom!" Japheth always looked forward to dinner.

Noah looked over his family gathered around the table, and he was proud of how hard they had been working on the ark these past weeks. He still ached from the beating at the courthouse, but he managed to get out of bed to sit at the dinner table and relish this daily time with his family.

Noah began with this prayer, "Our dear God and Heavenly Father, you are our wonderful Creator and Sustainer. We ask your blessing on our meal tonight. We also ask for your special protection of us in the days ahead as we face perilous times. You are our Protector, and we trust in your hand to give us all that we need to walk in obedience to you. We look forward with expectation to what you will do in the future and how you will deliver this family, and all who trust in you, from judgment to come. We ask this in your Wonderful Name, Amen." He looked around the table at his boys and their wives. Shem and Ham had married godly Sethian girls, and it was a comfort to see them all serving God. Japheth was growing in the Lord, and Noah hoped they would soon find a wife for him.

"Oh, I forgot to lock the front gate!" Japheth pushed away from the table and headed for the door.

"Come right back," said his mother. "You don't want your biscuits getting cold."

"No chance of that Mom. Back in a minute." He left the dining room, went out the front door, and ran toward the front gate.

It's strange that there's ground fog this early in the evening, Japheth thought. *Usually the air turns to a light fog near dawn when it's cooler. This fog is thick tonight and blankets the ground up to my knees,* he observed as he walked quickly across the estate grounds. By the time he reached the gate, he was walking in fog up to his chest. Fortunately, the gate bar was easy to find in the dark, and he closed both sides of the gate in darkness so dense that he had to do so by touch. Walking back to the house, he emerged from the fog and looked behind him.

That's really strange, he thought again. The air didn't feel that cool and yet the fog had risen high enough to cover a person's head. The fog settled along the stockade fence as far as he could see in either direction, but the house and ark were clear. He trotted back to the dining hall, looking back a few times to wonder at how tightly the fog hugged the fence all around the compound.

Outside the Compound Fence

Chief Inspector Hin ordered his deputy to remain at the palace while he joined Lieutenant Lasou and his squad to make sure nothing went wrong. The lieutenant didn't like the chief inspector tagging along for such a simple mission, instead of Deputy Inspector Baaki, but how could he object? This mission had better be textbook or they'd both lose their jobs, or maybe their lives.

They drove the dinos hard for five days to reach their objective as soon as possible and a few animals died from exhaustion along the way. It was after dusk when they arrived, as planned, to rest for an hour before forming up for the assault. A single lookout stayed with their dinos in a large clearing a half mile from the stockade fence and near the river. After marching silently through a thin forest they thought they saw the roof of a tall storage building next to the fence in the dim light of a quarter moon. The top half of the high compound fence rose above a dense fog that crept up around the walls of the wooden structure. There was something eerie about the fog that Lasou didn't like.

The lieutenant turned to his sergeant and whispered, "I want you and two men to go to where the fence meets the tall storage building. You should find some boards loose in the fence. Push them aside and quietly enter the compound there. Look around the interior for a minute and report back what you see." Lasou was uneasy about the fog because it was difficult to see where the fence met the building from where they stood.

"Are you sure this is where we'll find the loose boards in the fence?" Lasou asked the chief inspector in a hushed tone.

"Of course!" Hin hissed.

The lieutenant was cautious from experience. "If your informant double-crosses us and there's an ambush, we'll lose men. In this fog, I can't ensure what awaits my officers on the other side of that fence." But, despite the danger presented by this low visibility, it was better to send a few men ahead to be sure.

"Report back when you've made it through the fence and confirmed that the immediate area inside is clear," Lasou instructed his men.

The sergeant and two black-clad commandos stepped quietly through the low brush toward the fence and slipped into the fog. They made it as far as the fence. Lasou heard a "thud" as if one of the men had bumped against the fence. He waited for some signal from the men that it was clear to follow, but it never came.

He turned to the officer next to him in the dark and said, "I didn't hear any loud noises so there isn't an ambush. Maybe they can't find the entrance in this fog. Go see what happened."

The lone commando entered the fog without a sound. It wasn't long before Lasou heard a muffled cry, followed by silence.

"Listen up!" The lieutenant spoke with anxious authority and gathered the remaining men in the shadows around him. He looked pointedly at the chief inspector. "Four men have gone in and we have received no report back as to the conditions inside, so I want everyone to have their weapons at the ready. We're all going in with full force. Don't hesitate to fire first if you're met by any opposition. We'll end this mission successfully, but in case we become separated, I authorize you to continue on individually and complete it to the best of your ability. No enemy survivors, understood?" Lasou's men nodded in reply.

"Are you coming with us sir?" Lasou asked the chief inspector.

"Of course," his chief smiled as he removed his weapon from its holster. "I wouldn't miss this fun for anything."

Hin and the others followed the lieutenant's lead as he advanced in a crouch into the fog. The soldiers moved forward in a tight formation with all their senses on alert. Lasou knew instinctively that this mission would not end as he originally planned. Making his way toward the opening in the fence, he came across one body and then the others, all lying faceup. As he examined each body, he detected no obvious wounds. In the fog-diffused moonlight their faces were contorted, as if silently screaming. They were all dead, but how had they died so silently?

While searching for the opening in the fence in the consuming darkness, the rest of the squad dispersed, lost in the fog which muffled all sound and seemed to envelope each man in its grip. The chief inspector immediately became disoriented in the mist and tried in vain to determine the direction to the fence. He felt himself enshrouded by a chilled cocoon of moisture. He was completely alone.

For the first time in his life Hin experienced inescapable terror. The thick fog was like an odorless gel that tightened around his body. Numbness moved slowly up his body as the fog, like a giant cold hand, gripped his feet, legs, and torso and squeezed his life from him. His last thought, when the tightening mist eventually reached his throat, was that this was better than reporting a failed mission to the emperor.

The soldiers moved forward in a tight formation.

Family Residence

While the family finished their dinner and talked over the day's activities, Noah noticed a bright light shining through the windows at the front of the house that looked out at the work site. Maybe it was a last glimpse of a brilliant sunset shining through the front windows. But a second later it registered with Noah that this was another fire set in the ark!

"Fire!" he shouted as he spilled his drink and pointed out the window. Shem, Ham, and Japheth leapt out of their chairs and, followed by Taléa and Akima, scrambled through the doorway.

Noah followed at a fast hobble, clenching his teeth in pain. How could this be happening again?

When Miriam helped him through the door, they bumped into the three boys standing transfixed on the porch.

"Hurry!" Noah shouted. "Get the hose hooked up to the water tower! What are you standing there for?"

Noah shifted his gaze upward at the brilliant light that came from a giant pillar of fire. The image mesmerized everyone.

A column of fire was suspended in midair, undulating in slow motion. The base of the flame rested on the roof of the ark and extended as high into the sky as the length of the ark itself—almost five hundred feet. They felt no heat from the flames and the wood of the ark appeared unmarred. Accompanying the brilliant light was a loud rushing noise like a waterfall or windstorm. The fire's colors flickered through a spectrum of bright colors. Like autumn leaves in a vast forest of different colored trees illuminated in bright sunlight, the flickering was made of individual, distinct flashes of color that pulsed.

Without taking his eyes off of the majestic light, Noah asked no one in particular, "What is it?"

Japheth ventured to describe out loud what they saw before them in terms that seemed wholly inadequate. Whatever it was, the flashing colors seemed to obscure the view of something enveloped within the elongated pillar of fire.

"It's like the fire is transparent—almost like crystal glass. I think I see something moving inside!" Japheth exclaimed.

An obscure shape, that was impossible to distinguish clearly, was veiled behind the shiny surface of the flame. Then the rushing noise took on a more recognizable sound; not a natural sound, but it was like thousands of voices speaking at once, yet not a single word could be discerned.

The fiery pillar slowly rotated, and Japheth saw someone, or something, appear inside the flames: a large creature, almost as tall as the flame itself, with wings that extended up to the top of the flame and down to its feet. Flashes of light rose up over the creature's body, as it slowly moved in a circle within the flame. The creature, Japheth could see now, stood on a rotating base driven by glistening metallic wheels and gears. As the creature rotated, it turned to face the silent spectators. The flame ascended from the ark into the sky.

When they had first looked at the flame, it had been so brilliant that it pained their eyes to look at it directly. When the flame stopped ascending—reaching high into the sky above the ark—its light took on the soft brightness of a full moon and was easy to gaze upon without blinking. The sound of many voices tapered to silence when the flame stopped ascending and a cloud of smoke flowed out the top of the pillar to spread like a thin veil across the sky in all directions. The spreading cloud layer reflected the glow from the flame below it, bathing the surrounding darkness in a soothing light.

All of this happened in only a few moments, but it seemed longer. They couldn't take their eyes off the object in the sky. The pillar of fire flickered motionless and silent, suspended like a brilliant star.

"I've seen something like this before," Noah finally said. "When God spoke to me years ago about building the ark. It was a much smaller flame, but just as amazing." Everyone on the porch turned to look at him, ungluing their eyes from the spectacle before them.

"But what does this mean now?" asked Japheth.

"God has always been with us, but I think we have not seen Him," replied Noah. "No man can actually see God in all His glory, but He sometimes takes on different figures and shapes. When He does, there is no doubt that it is God Himself making His presence known. Nobody who sees it can say it is merely an illusion or a natural phenomenon. I believe He is assuring us that He is with us, in spite of all of the problems we have had building the ark and the opposition we face from the empire. My sense is that He will remain above us from now until we enter the ark for the last time. That cloud going out from the flame in all directions is protection that will remind us every day that we are under His care."

Noah resumed after a long pause. "I vaguely remember Enoch telling of this long ago. He called it the 'Shekinah' of God. I don't know exactly what that word means, but he said it somehow represents God in a physical form that goes back to Adam and Eve in the Garden." The family members, less anxious now, brought chairs from the front porch and sat in the yard for a long time, drawing comfort and peace from the brilliant star-like light high above their small home. When they reluctantly filed into the house around midnight, they glanced back repeatedly at the object that cast a glow on their yard and on the shell of the ark. As Miriam and Noah lay in bed unable to sleep, Noah saw the light in the sky through their window like a bright, guarding sentinel. Drifting off to sleep, he wondered about changes to come. Whatever happened, he knew they were safely held in God's hands.

CHAPTER 20

Imperial Atmospheric Agency: Weather Outpost #22

Same Time

From a hilltop observatory platform more than a hundred miles away, three student interns gathered with mouths agape to stare at the distant fire in the sky. Akmed was a senior co-op student, who had been monitoring the weather from this outpost for six months, while the others, Mobi and Karaa, had arrived at the observatory only a week ago to begin their tour.

"Maybe it's some sort of sunset phenomenon," commented Mobi.

"I don't know what they've been teaching you at school, Mobi, but the sun set a few hours ago on the opposite side of the hill behind us. Maybe it's an early sunrise?" The senior intern's sarcasm was intended to put his junior in his place.

"It's nothing like I've ever seen in my textbooks," said Karaa. "I wonder if it's man-made or natural. Maybe a forest fire? Or a rocket test?" She was as uncertain as the others, but she asked her questions with an air of genuine inquiry.

Still looking at the bright glowing flame, Akmed spoke over his shoulder to the others, "Go get Mr. Tuuki. He needs to see this."

Mobi dutifully ran into the cement block building behind the observatory to get the station manager. Tuuki was a professional who had adapted completely to the solitude of the remote observatory and its routine. He didn't have to shave or bathe every day; he ate whenever he wanted; and he did anything else he wanted, as long as the twice-daily weather observation reports were sent back to headquarters on time.

But when they sent interns from the university he had to pretend to conform to a more orderly lifestyle and set an example for the students. He tried to teach them the practical side of meteorology by assigning projects for them to apply what they had learned in school. Above all, he taught them the importance of taking accurate instrument readings, keeping a detailed logbook of their observations, and reasoning carefully about everything they observed. These three were more inquisitive than some of the others he'd had, and he was constantly bombarded with questions and breaking up arguments amongst them.

"What is it this time?" Tuuki was hesitant to leave the warmth of the station to answer yet another question. But when Mobi sputtered, unable to explain the flaming phenomenon he had seen in the distance, Tuuki decided he'd have to see for himself. He followed Mobi along the worn path from the station to the observation platform.

He stood next to the trio and looked at the distant object in the sky. From this distance, it appeared the size and color of a large candle flame about twenty degrees above the tree line. The single flame dimly illuminated a flat cloud layer above it.

"Burning swamp gas. It'll go away soon." Tuuki proclaimed and headed back into the station. He was only a few steps up the path when Karaa pleaded for him to return.

"Wait. Don't go. That can't be swamp gas."

"And why not?" he asked, walking slowly back to look more closely. He knew it wasn't swamp gas, but he wanted to hear what Karaa had to say.

"Well, I saw it appear on the horizon more than thirty minutes ago, and it ascended into the sky and then stopped where you see it now. It hasn't moved or changed in intensity since then." She paused and added, "Burning swamp gas would have a blue flame, while this is red and orange."

"Thirty minutes is a long time for burning swamp gas," Tuuki observed. He was proud of her keen observation and logic. "Well, whatever caused it, it will eventually either burn out or move. It's getting late, and you have to launch a measurement probe before dawn. If that thing is still there tomorrow, I'll put it in my morning report as an unexplained phenomena. We won't speculate about it until we've had a chance to study it more and discuss it as a group. Now, everyone, come inside where it's warm."

The team returned to the station to prepare their instruments for morning measurements and to catch some sleep before dawn. Akmed chuckled at Tuuki's "burning swamp gas" explanation.

Karaa was convinced this was a unique atmospheric phenomenon never seen before, and she wanted to study it. Maybe she could publish a paper and become a famous meteorologist! She watched the glow out the window from her bed late into the night. It never moved or dimmed. The flame remained anchored in the sky well after she drifted off to dreams of becoming a world-renowned scientist.

BOOK II

METHUSELAH

LAST SIXTY YEARS

1596-1656 AC (After Creation)

CHAPTER 21

Eden's Promise, Ark Compound

More than one week after the blazing star-like flame had appeared over the compound, Noah was sharpening an adz at the forge grindstone when he saw a man in the distance walking through the front gate of the dusty compound. The gate was usually left open during the day because of the traffic in and out of workmen bringing more supplies. The family had already become used to the Lord's constant protection from above, and they didn't think too much about leaving the gate open during the day.

Noah could almost distinguish the lone figure from a distance. At first, he looked like any other drifting laborer seeking work, but something was familiar about his gait; he was an older man from the way he walked, steadily pacing himself, like a traveler used to being on his feet all day, who used his walking stick to propel himself forward. He was dressed in baggy long pants of the old style, leather boots almost to his knees, a black cloak, and a wide-brimmed hat that hid his face from the heat and glare of the sun. As he approached, his long gray hair and unkempt beard further accentuated his age. He probably hadn't had a bath in a while either. As the man walked slowly up the long driveway he kept his eyes focused on Noah.

When he was about fifty feet from where Noah stood with the adz suspended in midair over the stone, the old man stopped and peered at him through clear gray eyes. The visitor removed his hat and broke into a wide smile. "Noah," he said in a clear voice—not a question but a statement.

He knew that voice! "Grandfather?" Noah asked hesitatingly. "Is that you?" he asked again, not sure what else to say.

"One and the same," the gray man said, speaking through his smile.

Noah walked closer to gaze directly into his eyes and was sure it was him—his grandfather, Methuselah! Years of memories overwhelmed him, and Noah hugged him like he did when he was a child. The familiar smells of leather, dirt, and sweat surrounded him.

They held each other without speaking, until Noah stepped back and looked at him at arm's length from head to toe through teary eyes. He looked older than when he had last seen him. He had more wrinkles, his skin was darker from living outdoors, and he didn't seem as tall as Noah remembered. The long hair and the beard almost to his waist gave him the classic look of an aged patriarch.

"I have so many questions. Come inside and let us get you something to drink and eat. You appear to have been walking all day." Noah took him by the arm and led him inside to the cool dining hall.

"Actually," Methuselah replied as they walked side-by-side, "I have been walking for two months, ever since I saw that star appear. I concluded that you would need my help building your ark."

His statement brought Noah up short. "What do you mean? How did you even know I was building an ark? How could you have started walking two months ago when the star only appeared last week?"

"I can explain everything, but first I will take you up on that refreshment."

In the dining room, they found Miriam, Deva, and a few other women preparing lunch. After hugs and warm greetings, Miriam insisted that Methuselah be served immediately, and the servants offered to clean his clothes later while he bathed. Methuselah loved the attention from the women and smiled at them between generous servings of food and drink.

Noah watched his grandfather eat like a man who had not had a decent meal in months, and he thought about his grandfather's legacy, descended from a long line of patriarchs of the entire human race. Methuselah was the first son of Enoch, in the long family line of descendants from Seth, the third son of Adam. After he became the patriarch of the Sethian line, he distinguished himself at the Adam Institute with so many discoveries and inventions that he impacted the advancement of civilization more profoundly than anyone else, before or since.

When Cainite scientists began applying his genetic discoveries to animals and humans, Methuselah had abandoned that field of study and had spent the rest of his energies on inventing mechanical devices. He told his colleagues that he worked better with mechanisms because they were free from sin, and they didn't fight back against their inventor. He articulated the fundamental laws and equations of mechanics that govern the motion of all objects. His many mechanical devices found their way into daily life and were noted for their usefulness, precision, and elegant craftsmanship.

Methuselah also studied the atmosphere and objects in outer space using his telescopes. He studied the heavens that God had created to function like a celestial clock, whose movement could be predicted using universal, mathematical formulas. He explained the thick, transparent vapor canopy that surrounded the earth at a very high altitude, which kept the earth's climate within a steady, beneficial temperature range.

Noah was always in awe of his grandfather's brilliant mind that could be so skilled in so many areas from studying a tiny plant, or taming a monstrous animal, to pondering a distant star, or fashioning a piece of brass into a beautiful and practical instrument. His concentrated focus to gain knowledge was inspiring.

Unlike when Enoch was taken up to heaven by God Himself, Methuselah's disappearance was not by the same means as Enoch's, nor for the same purpose. Noah had never known the exact reason, but, more than two centuries ago, after Methuselah and Lamech had had a loud argument, his grandfather walked out and hadn't been seen again, until now.

"You appear to have married wisely," Methuselah commented, after observing Miriam during the meal. He sat back with a satisfied sigh. "As I recall, you married her before I left. I was very pleased that you married a believer."

"Yes, she is from the line of Mahalaleel and a true daughter of Seth by faith," Noah replied proudly, continuing to look into his grandfather's familiar gray eyes. "She has been my life partner and friend since we first met. She is all the blessing a man could ever want for a wife."

"That is as it should be. You have indeed been blessed by God, and you have my blessing as well. I am happy for you both."

He seemed to have more to say, but he looked around at the furnishings of the dining hall appraising their construction instead. "Whoever built this place knew what he was doing."

"That would be the work of Wazim, our construction overseer. He knows what he is doing when it comes to buildings. I have my doubts about the ark however . . ." Noah's voice trailed off in uncertainty.

"There will be time to talk about that later." Methuselah then wondered to himself if Noah realized how much trouble his project was in.

"Wait, you said that you have been traveling for two months, but the star just appeared overhead a week ago. That can't be," Noah observed.

"Maybe the star was overhead all this time, only you did not see it until now," Methuselah replied with a twinkle in his eye. "You do look up from time to time, do you not?"

"Not lately . . . So many things have been going wrong with the ark," Noah admitted. "But you said we would get caught up on things after lunch. So, where have you been, and what have you been doing all these years?"

It appeared that Methuselah was ready to answer, but then a sad change passed over his face. "Where is Lamech?"

Noah suspected Methuselah already knew the answer, and he carefully related how Lamech died trying to extinguish a fire in the ark set by saboteurs intent on destroying the ship. Methuselah listened without expression, except his eyes glistened with tears.

Methuselah spoke gently, "I suspected he was no longer alive, even before I set off on my journey. I confess that, when I arrived, I was afraid to ask because of the conditions under which we parted ways long ago. I am so sorry I did not return earlier to see him. He was the best son I had, and I truly regret not seeing him in his later years. At my age, you accumulate many regrets about opportunities lost forever. Leaving Lamech when he needed me is my greatest regret. I still hope to one day make it up to your father, to honor his memory and to secure your family's future."

Facing the reality of Lamech's death dampened Methuselah's interest in talking further that day. He slowly rose from the table and unsteadily balanced himself against the chair.

The visitor removed his hat and broke into a wide smile.

"I wish to mourn my son's passing privately, but I promise I will give you and your family a full explanation tomorrow. Do you mind if I retire to bed now? This day has tired me more than usual."

"Of course! Miriam will show you to our guest room, where you can stay as long as you like."

Noah watched Miriam show Methuselah up the stairs to his room. So many questions filled his mind: *Why had my grandfather arrived now? How did he know that the ark project was in trouble? Where had he been all these years? Would he help us finish the ark? Or would he stay briefly, only to leave again suddenly?*

CHAPTER 22

Eden's Promise, Family Residence

Next Morning

Methuselah descended the stairs to find Noah's entire family assembled in the dining room for breakfast. The patriarch took an immediate liking to Shem and Ham, and their wives, but he took a particular interest in young Japheth, who responded in kind by peppering him with questions during breakfast about his many scientific exploits. Methuselah paused after each bite to expound at length on every topic Japheth brought up.

Finally, Noah asked Japheth to let Methuselah finish eating. "Your great-grandfather will be with us for some time; there will be plenty of time to ask your questions later. For now, let him be," Noah chided gently.

Methuselah poured himself another cup of coffee and sat back in his chair.

"Bear with me as I try to explain why I left my family and what I have been doing these many years since. As Noah may have told you, many years ago my father, Enoch, was given the unique charge of spending a year with Adam to record Adam's recollections of his life with God in the Garden. Even in his last days, Adam's mind and memory were sharp. The resulting memoir was a massive collection of handwritten pages that documented verbatim many of Adam's conversations with God, both before and after he and Eve left the Garden of Eden. My father learned things about the past and predictions of the future that Adam had passed on verbally to all of his descendants; but it wasn't until much later, after the written word was invented, that Enoch recorded Adam's knowledge in a book. Before Adam died, he charged Enoch with keeping the writings safe within our Sethian family line. Enoch fully appreciated that what he had written was the only accurate revelation from God remaining that would survive through the generations, and it needed to remain complete and unchanged. He carefully transcribed two exact reproductions of the Book. He kept the original for himself and he gave the copies to me and to my brother Eli. When my father was unexpectedly taken to heaven by God, we could not find where he kept the original. He probably put it somewhere he thought was safe, but he never told anyone where it was.

"I can tell from the look on your faces that you do not believe this story to be of much importance." Methuselah had thought his tale about the Book was profound, and its significance self-evident, but he was apparently mistaken.

"It is not that," answered Noah. "But I learned about the Book and its teachings from my father. He believed that the traditions originated in the Garden were faithfully passed down by Adam through the Sethian line to us. I have taught these traditions to Shem, Ham, and Japheth, and they will teach them to their children like Sethians have for centuries. I am wondering if you have not made more of this Book than you should have. We have upheld the beliefs of our forefathers well without it. And I do not see what it has to do with you suddenly and mysteriously leaving our family. From what my father told me, the Book is a collection of Adam's reminiscences about the Garden of Eden. I don't see why its loss should have torn the two of you apart when we have continued to live by Adam's traditions regardless."

Methuselah paused thoughtfully for a few moments, and resumed his story. "Over the years, my brother and I lost touch with each other as he moved his large family to another part of the world where they had more land. One day, a fire destroyed my private laboratory, and I lost everything. I assumed that my copy of the Book—what I had begun calling the Book of Adam—was safe in my fireproof vault, where I kept my manuscripts. However, the vault was located next to a chemical storeroom, and the chemicals intensified the fire so much that the vault melted, and its contents were destroyed. With my copy of the Book gone, the only surviving copy was with my brother, and I did not know where he was.

"The more I thought about it, the stronger I felt that I needed to find that last copy and reproduce it for future generations before it was lost forever. You see, the written record is much more accurate and complete than verbal traditions. We cannot assume that a verbal tradition will persist for thousands of years without natural, unintended alterations. So, I had to drop everything immediately and find my brother before it was too late. I figured, 'Why not go now, since my wife—your grandmother, Noah—had died and all of our sons were grown up?' I had reached a point in my life when I had few responsibilities, so I thought that I could simply leave to search for my brother. Your father didn't see it quite that way, and we had some harsh words—foolish words as I look back on them now—about my leaving my family on what he called a 'fool's errand.' We said things we should not have said to each other. But now he is gone." It was, again, obvious that he regretted being unable to apologize to his son, but he looked at Noah and did the next best thing. "I'm sorry about leaving the family when I did. I told you last night that I hope to somehow make it up to you."

Noah was uncomfortable with his grandfather's confession, especially since his memories of his departure were vague in his mind.

"But what have you been doing all these years? Did you think you'd be gone this long?" Japheth asked, puzzled about why it took Methuselah so long to find his brother.

"Of course not," his grandfather replied. "I found my brother Eli easily enough, but he did not have the Book. Eli never fully appreciated the value of the Book, and he thought, as you do now, that it was only a collection of Adam's reminiscences. He carried it around for years, but he sold it for a high price when someone admired its leather binding, gold clasps, and ornamental script. That the Book was a written revelation from God was not important, in his mind."

Puzzled looks around the table showed that his attempt to explain his absence and the importance of his quest for the Book were still not satisfying. Noah folded his arms. The others waited for more.

"You need to know more about the contents of the Book to appreciate the importance of what I am saying. I will try to be very clear: I read my father's copy of the Book from beginning to end more than once; it was almost a hundred carefully written pages in all, and portions of it were lengthy, direct quotes of what God said to Adam.

One prophetic passage told of the future when the world would 'grow worse and worse' and God would bring total destruction on the planet because of mankind's wickedness. I saw that reality developing all around me in the evil brought on by the Cainites and Sethians battling against each other, and then the pollution of the human race by the Anakim. Don't you see? That is what God has confirmed to you, Noah, in his warning about the coming flood. God told Adam that the human race would eventually descend to such depths of wickedness that He would destroy all but a few of them."

"We certainly see that in today's world," observed Noah. "But what else did it predict of the future? What did it say about turning the world around?"

"Besides speaking of judgment on a corrupt world, the Book explains in a firsthand narrative what God will do one day to change what is wrong in the heart of mankind. My brother did not like it when he read the parts of the Book that said we are all sinners, that we fall short of the glory of God, and that He is not willing that any should perish. Eli closed his heart and mind at that time to those words, and so he missed the promise about the coming One who will someday be the final sacrifice for the forgiveness of sin. The Book speaks clearly of one called the 'Lamb of God,' explaining who He is and what He will be like. So you see, I couldn't just let that revelation get lost because people like my brother could not appreciate the difficult truths it contained. I had to keep looking for the Book with all the energy I still had left in this old body to preserve the words of God."

Understanding was beginning to show in Noah's face, though Methuselah still had so many things he wanted to explain to his grandson. The others were spellbound waiting to hear what else he had to say.

"I broke down in despair when my brother told me that he had sold the only remaining copy of the Book. When he told me who he'd sold it to, I determined then and there that I would track it down to my last breath. If it still existed, I would find it. That is when my search for the Book of Adam became an all-consuming obsession, and I have been tracking down leads—unsuccessfully, so far—ever since. Every time I would get close to finding it, the trail would vanish. I have searched all over the world for it, but only recently has the trail warmed again. I know generally where the Book is now located, but that is all.

My many sources are making inquiries for me, and I hope someday to find it and bring it to you."

Methuselah waited for a reaction from those around the table. Noah spoke first. "I can see now why you have poured your life into the search. What a tragedy it would be to lose the last copy of God's written word. I've always wondered if there was more revelation from God than what we have in our oral tradition. Now that I know your motivation, I apologize for my many years of resentment."

It was Japheth, of course, who had many more questions.

"Now, about your role in all this," Methuselah went on, nodding toward Noah and regaining some energy when he remembered that the Book had been so close at hand. "A few years ago, my quest for the Book had to be curtailed. I was forced to go underground to avoid capture when Sethians were being arrested and executed in the city. I formed a kind of 'resistance' group with some other Sethians to help believers smuggle others into the safety of the wilderness. But still, many Sethians were systematically picked up on the streets by imperial vigilantes—both Cainites and Sethians, who had sold their souls to the emperor. We could not understand the reason for this brutality, until we captured a Cainite soldier who revealed Anak's motives to us.

"Anak was outraged about faithful Sethians refusing to obey his edicts when those commands went against God's moral law. If there is anything Anak cannot stand, it is the slightest hint of opposition. But, when he heard Sethians mention your name, he became irate. He learned that you are building a gigantic ark to save humanity before God destroys the world. Your ark has come to the attention of powerful, ruthless people who will try anything to destroy you and the ark. So, the supreme ruler, immoral to his core, has decided to eliminate all believers. But God, in His gracious sovereignty, is more powerful than Anak and all his armies. God has obviously put His protective hands over this compound and your ark construction. You are safe as long as the Presence of God, in the form of that pillar of fire, remains overhead.

"When I remembered the prophecy written in the Book about the coming destruction and heard from my sources that God had actually told you to build an ark, that is when I decided you would need my help. The ark must be finished in time for God's people to use it. We *must* accelerate work on the ark and finish it as soon as we can!"

Noah now understood why those imperial saboteurs had infiltrated his compound and why the court had charged him as a traitor to the empire. He felt that spreading God's message was an act of kindness, but it was much more than that. He saw now that he could not expect the empire to let him do God's work without starting a fight. God's message of salvation was more than a kindness; it was a mission. After Methuselah's explanation, Noah felt reenergized and determined; there was so much work to be done!

The rest of the family needed time for all this new information to sink in. Japheth, especially, had many questions which he uncharacteristically held to himself, for now. His questions were mostly about the Book and what else was in it that Methuselah had not mentioned. From his description, it would seem he had only scratched the surface of its many revelations.

"Boys, why don't you give your great-grandfather a quick tour of the compound and the ark?" Noah suggested. As they went outside he stayed behind with Miriam.

Methuselah was arguably the greatest engineer the world had ever seen, and he, more than anyone, understood what needed to be done to finish the ark. Noah prayed that his grandfather would take over the ark construction and turn around what had seemed to him a futile endeavor.

"I now see that God brought him here for a special purpose," Noah said to Miriam as she cleared the table.

"Well, I'm glad he's here," she added. "If he is one tenth the genius you say he is, the ark will be finished in time."

Methuselah was God's answer to Noah's prayer.

CHAPTER 23

Imperial Palace, Throne Room

Same Day

"Beloved Emperor, there is a policeman awaiting your audience who has a report concerning Chief Inspector Hin," the scribe announced emotionlessly. He was not looking forward to having to clean up after this meeting. Life for a servant in the presence of Emperor Anak involved constantly cleaning up after him.

"And why isn't the chief inspector himself reporting?" the emperor snarled. "Never mind. Bring him in."

The police commando had never been in the emperor's presence before and, though he was a hardened, trained professional, he couldn't stop shaking.

"Beloved Emperor, I have a report concerning a mission more than a week ago, which I was told you had personally ordered."

"I said I wanted an immediate report and it has taken more than a week? First, tell me that Noah and his family have all been permanently eliminated," he shouted, throwing the police commando off balance.

"That, Beloved Emperor, I cannot report," said the shaking man, cringing. "The force of twenty men in four squads, including the chief inspector and my lieutenant, never returned from their mission. I was left as a lookout and the chief inspector and squad did not return by dawn. I searched for them all day and could not find them. I began my journey back to the palace a week ago and came directly here to give my report to you." He had done everything he could, and he was gaining some slight confidence that he might walk out of the room alive. It wasn't his fault the team never returned from their mission.

"Is that it? They just didn't return? Do you expect me to believe that?" The emperor screamed. He bounded down the steps from his elevated platform toward the policeman.

"A squad of veteran police commandos led by my top policeman were sent to silence a handful of civilians and you expect me to believe that they simply disappeared?" The emperor stopped a foot from the policeman and stared down with gleaming eyes while saliva ringed his mouth. His breath was hot and putrid.

"Do you think I am an imbecile?" Anak bellowed.

Before the man could answer, the hulking Anakim demanded, "Are you Sethian or Cainite?"

"Sssethian, sir. I have tttaken the oooath, Bbbeloved Emperor, sir," he cried.

"Ah, I thought so. You are a Sethian traitor. You vermin are all the same—oath or not. Well, you obviously tipped off that fool and his family and they set a trap for my men. That's what happened, isn't it?" In an instant, he had a knife in one hand and raised the other in a massive fist. The blade inched down silently.

"Nnno, sir." He fell to his knees. "Ppplease . . ."

"Yes, that's what happened. And here's how the empire deals with traitors."

It was over in less than two seconds.

Anak glared at the cowering servant against the far wall. "You there! Clean up this mess."

The angry emperor returned to his throne to ponder his next step in dealing with that pest, Noah.

“Are you Sethian or Cainite?”

CHAPTER 24

Eden's Promise, Ark Compound

When Noah joined up with the tour, the group was on a path to the riverbank, almost half a mile from the ark construction site.

"Grandfather, will you supervise building the ark for us?" Noah asked.

"Yes, but on one condition," Methuselah replied quickly.

Methuselah paused for dramatic effect. "Would you like to know what my one stipulation is? I take from your looks that you do," he observed, like a professor about to launch into a lecture.

"It is clear to me that I am probably the only person who can lead this project to a successful conclusion before the judgment arrives. I know you meant well and have been diligent," he said turning to Noah, "but you simply lacked the skills to design a survivable floating structure on such a massive scale. I am not telling you anything new. Your hired Cainite supervisor has been fleecing you from the start, and it is time to step in and put construction of the ark on a realistic schedule.

"My one condition is that you allow me to finish the ark's construction ahead of schedule and use several years of the remaining time to teach Shem, Ham, and Japheth what I know, so they can take some of my scientific knowledge with them into the new world."

Noah was as puzzled as the others by Methuselah's explanation of his one condition. "Of course, grandfather, finishing the ark ahead of schedule is beyond anything I envisioned—if you think it can be done. But you sound like you are not planning to go on the ark with us. You realize, of course, that there will be plenty of room."

"Let us not discuss that now, but suffice it to say that I hope to contribute as much to building the ark and training your boys as time allows. If things work out, and the flood has still not yet happened, I would like to spend my last year locating the Book so that you can take it with you onto the ark."

From the day he arrived, Methuselah's presence and energy galvanized Noah's family into the ark construction with a new sense of urgency. He was a natural leader, and his drive and knowledge focused everyone's attentions.

Within days of his arrival, he brought Noah and his three sons together to walk through the ark's shell where he pointed out things he thought needed more work or demolition and rebuilding. As usual, he went straight to the point and focused on the shortcomings of Wazim's design that he thought would prove disastrous. He asked Japheth to take notes while he dictated his observations and instructions.

"Let us start with the shape of the ark itself," Methuselah began as they stood in the yard and looked up the side of the massive structure. They could see the length of the box-like shape through the scaffolding that surrounded it from the ground up, past the height of the top deck. From the disapproving look on Methuselah's face, Noah knew that there was little he saw that met his satisfaction. He steeled himself to expect harsh criticism.

Walking closer to the side of the ark, Methuselah placed his hand on the corner where the bottom met the sides. "Notice this edge here? A corner like this would work well for a house or some other land structure. The bottom is heavily reinforced, which is good. But when you attach two surfaces to each other at a ninety-degree angle, the corner is where forces in opposition to each other produce high stresses that can snap the structure. Usually, this is not a problem with a building like a house because the major force is the weight of the building down on the foundation, due to gravity. High pressure put on building structures from wind is minimal since we never receive strong winds anyway. So the walls sit on the floor or foundation and are not subjected to strong sideways forces." Methuselah picked up a small wooden model of a long, narrow box he had assembled and set it on the ground while he pressed on its top to show how the sides supported the top and rested on the bottom. But then he picked it up and held it in his hands.

"When this box is floating free, the sides do not have a solid foundation to rest on. The sides must do more than support the weight of the box and rest that weight on the bottom. They must hold the top and bottom together against forces in all directions." With that, Methuselah held the box in one hand and pressed on the side which caused the top to move when the bottom remained still. As he pressed, the sides bent at the corners until they separated from the bottom, and the box broke into pieces. Having made his point, he dramatically threw the pieces to the ground and hurried up the ramp to the door of the ark with his apprentices following at his heels, trying to keep up.

"I like the large door on the side," Methuselah gestured with his hands spread wide. "Placing it at a midpoint in the side makes for a single access to all three inner decks. What I see, though, is that there is no watertight seal around the door. How had you planned to keep the water from leaking in?"

"We figured we would keep a barrel of pitch near the door, and, when the door was closed, we would pitch the seams, and it would become watertight." That was the explanation Wazim had given Noah when he had raised that very subject, but it was clear that Methuselah disagreed.

"That might work for a barn door, but it will not work for a ship working against the forces of large waves and heavy winds. I have a solution we can talk about later," he said.

"I am concentrating on these important design flaws because I want you and the animals to survive for a long time in this vessel," Methuselah reassured his grandson. "God gave you the overall dimensions, but He did not give you exact specifications or a shape. There must be a reason for that, which I do not believe any of us knows yet; so, we must assume for now that we have the freedom to build the ark in a shape that conforms to common engineering sense and our limited knowledge. I have solutions in mind for improving these weak points in the structure, so you don't need to look so downhearted, Noah. All your work has not been for nothing. Relax. We can do this. Things are not as bad as you think they are."

With this reassurance, Noah and his sons followed Methuselah around the ark for the rest of the day as Methuselah pointed out things that needed to be changed or rebuilt, and Japheth wrote his great-grandfather's rapid-fire instructions in a notebook. From time to time, Methuselah took the notebook from him and quickly sketched and annotated his ideas for changes in his precise handwriting, and he had Japheth mark sub-projects by their priority.

After a walk-through that consumed an entire day—except for a lunch break—they gathered in a workshop where Methuselah, looking over the notebook, reviewed the day's list. It was over fifty pages in length, but he seemed upbeat about all the things he had seen. He was excited about having a project to manage.

"We have talked about the overall shape of the ark, and there is not much you can do about that in the timeframe we have. I must develop new hull plans right away that make the most of what you have already done. I will not sugarcoat this; there is considerable work to be done to make the ark into a shape that can handle the pressure of high winds and large waves. The good news is that the interior spaces are well-built and organized in a way that makes it easy to care for so many animals. Clearly, the God-given dimensions accommodate an interior volume more than adequate for all the animals, water, and feed you will carry. We 'simply' need to modify your box to be more like a seaworthy ship, rounding out the hull as much as possible. That will involve removing large portions of the outer walls to shape it into a survivable ship's frame design.

"The rest of the changes are ones that we can make without assistance from your hired work crew; I have plans for them that will move them off-site for a considerable time—more on that later. Some of the modifications are larger jobs, but we can implement them ourselves, without outside help. These include changes to the side door seal, no-maintenance ventilation, illumination by changing the skylights around the top deck, fresh water tanks, food and water distribution, waste removal, safer cooking facilities, and some other conveniences you will want on a long voyage.

"I will need a few months to prepare detailed drawings of the more complicated designs," Methuselah concluded, "but you can start on changes to the feed bins, chutes, and troughs that I sketched in the notebook. With all the bins you have already constructed, it should still take you several years to finish."

"Does anyone have any questions?" Tired faces silently looked back at him. Noah and his family had spent sixty years building what they thought was a reasonable structure for an ark, but it was clear they had fallen short. Methuselah sounded optimistic about the alterations needed, but the others wondered how much of their work would need to be redone.

Japheth was the only one who seemed to be warming to the tasks ahead and brought up again an idea he had suggested earlier. "What about using large crystal prisms in the top deck to diffuse light into the interior? I've thought that opening windows for light and ventilation would be risky if heavy waves came over the top. If even one or two windows broke loose, they could let in tons of water before we could cover the openings. If we had another ventilation method and only a few openings in the top deck, it would be a lot safer."

"That's a great idea, Japheth!" Methuselah beamed. "I'll include that idea in my drawings. Let me know if any of you have other ideas like that. Does anyone else have any other suggestions to add?"

"There is something that has been bothering me ever since God first spoke to me," Noah said hesitantly. "I do not know how long we will have to stay on the ark before the flood waters abate and we can exit the ark to repopulate the earth. How much food should we store for ourselves and for the animals? This has been on my mind for a long time, and God has seen fit to not give me an answer."

"Ah, that is critical information, is it not?" Methuselah replied. "I have pondered those questions also, because the answers will determine the ark design and the amount of preparation you will need to do. God did not say anything about the duration of the voyage at all?"

"Only that it would rain for forty days and forty nights. That was the extent of the revelation about the voyage duration," Noah said.

"So, allow me to think out loud about that for a minute," Methuselah suggested. "To cover the entire earth with rain in forty days means a very heavy downpour of water—more than anyone on earth has ever experienced. My sense is that the protective vapor canopy surrounding the earth will be the primary source of that water. A continuous deluge at a rapid rate for forty days means that it will take longer than forty days—maybe two or three times longer—for the water to disperse naturally and give you enough dry land to live on. If the floodwater alters the earth's topography, it will take even longer. I am not sure where the water will all go, but assuming it does recede considerably, you might have to live in the ark for about a year or more before you can safely open the side door of the ark and return to land. Of course, the new land will be bare of all useful vegetation, having been scoured clean by the floodwater, so you will need food for yourselves and the animals for maybe six to twelve more months, until a season of new crops can be harvested. Yes, I would say you will need a minimum of two years of stored food to sustain you until you can cultivate the land again and see your first harvest. Assuming that you can easily find drinkable water after you land, which I believe to be a good assumption, you should be able to live on the ark by storing about one year of fresh water in tanks."

"That means almost two years of feed for the domesticated animals?" Noah exclaimed with eyes bulging. "The amount of hay alone will fill almost the entire ark itself. How can we possibly store all that and enough food for us too?"

"Oh, I have a plan for that," Methuselah replied with a wry smile. He stared at Noah for a moment, waiting for him to say something. When Noah looked at him hopelessly, Methuselah placed his hands on Noah's shoulders, and his gray eyes twinkled. "I have a mechanism in mind that will bind the hay into tight, square bundles and reduce the volume by more than a factor of ten. You can efficiently stack the bundles in your storage bins and only remove bundles as you need them." Methuselah waved his hands in the air and proclaimed, "See? Problem solved!"

God had miraculously answered Noah's prayer by sending Methuselah, who had a design or mechanism for everything. Noah could only wonder in amazement at this man, who had withdrawn from Noah's life when he was young, never to enter his life again, or so Noah had thought. And now, here his grandfather was, enthusiastic to help Noah in his time of greatest need and with answers to every question. He was convinced that Methuselah could solve any problem.

CHAPTER 25

Eden's Promise, Ark Compound

Six Months Later

Methuselah worked tirelessly in a large space above one of the workshops on the compound, where workmen built a large table in the center of the loft and a drafting table with a slanted surface beside it, and a tall chair. He made customized drawing instruments in the shop downstairs and bought oversized sheets of heavy paper, which he hurriedly rolled up whenever someone came up to the loft to see how he was progressing with his designs. The cooks brought his meals to the room, and he slept in a bunk next to his drawing table. In the early morning, he walked purposefully through the ark, talking to himself while scribbling in a notebook. In the evenings, at sunset, he retreated alone to the solitude of the Euphrates River, where he stared at the serene expanse of flowing water.

Noah and his sons left Methuselah alone while they built interior feed bins, chutes, and troughs from the sketches he had given them. Methuselah would let them know when he was finished with his drawings, so it was best to not bother him while he was working.

One day, after he'd eaten his breakfast, Methuselah sent one of the cooks to summon the men to his loft. They hurried to see the work he had done after their long wait. The table in the center of the room was piled with paper rolls, and a large wooden model occupied the far end of the expansive surface. Noah and the three boys gathered around him.

"Well, here it is!" Methuselah gestured to the model that hardly resembled the box shape in the yard outside the window. "This is the new ark that you will be living in for two years. How do you like it?" he asked proudly.

"It looks . . . ah . . . different," observed Japheth. The original rectangular, almost cubic, box design now had pointed ends; the sides met the bottom in a sloping curve, and there was a large structure above the deck at one end. Japheth looked at the model skeptically, but he observed, "I'm sure you have good reasons for these odd changes; so, please, stop the suspense, and tell us what this is!"

"Of course," Methuselah began as the other men made themselves comfortable in preparation for a long lecture. "What we have here is a very strong, seaworthy, comfortable shape that will withstand large waves and very strong winds." The model was almost six feet long. Methuselah tugged it across the table top for a closer look and picked up a pencil as a pointer. They could tell he was enthusiastic about the design, because his voice rose in pitch with excitement.

"First, let us begin with the rounded sides of the hull. It's rounded to eliminate those stresses I mentioned when we took our first tour." He pointed to a gradual slope on the model that would replace the straight sidewall of the original box design. The bottom of the model boat was not flat, nor parallel to the ground, in the new design, but it angled down to a very thick piece of wood that ran the entire length of the bottom of the structure. "And the ends are not square, but pointed, for the same reason that you cannot have edges on the sides, and for another reason that will become obvious in a minute."

"I can see why you wouldn't want flat ends or sides, but why isn't the bottom flat?" Japheth asked.

"For a couple of reasons," Methuselah replied quickly, in his element, speaking with barely pent-up enthusiasm. "It gives us room for additional hull strengtheners and divided, but interconnected, bottom compartments, called a bilge, that will keep waste and any water leakage away from the animals, provisions, and water tanks on the bottom deck. Also, tying the length of the hull into that long, heavy structure along the bottom, called a keel, strengthens the overall structure. These features, the curved hull, the pointed ends, and the reinforced keel, will give the ark the strength it needs to keep from breaking in half in large waves.

"Waves—especially large waves produced by very high winds—are also handled by another feature in the design." Methuselah pointed to the structure that rose above the top deck at one end of the model. "The ark is different from a conventional boat or ship you might see on the river or ocean today in that it has no propulsion or steering mechanism. While God never said it could not have propulsion or steerage, it seems impractical and overly complex to build any of those capabilities into the design if you do not have a specific destination you are steering toward. The ark is built only for survival in the worst possible conditions, not to propel you from one place to another. Also, for simplicity, durability, and safety, we definitely do not want the ark to turn sideways and capsize. High winds and large waves need to work in your favor and not against you while riding out the tempest that could last months."

"So, what does that thing do?" asked Japheth, pointing to the structure on top of the ark's deck.

"That, son, is my totally unique design—a rigid sail to keep the front of the ark aimed into the wind," Methuselah grinned proudly.

Until now, they had never thought of the ark as having a "front" or "back" because, in Wazim's design, both ends were flat like a box. In Methuselah's design, the large wooden structure on the top deck marked the front of the ship. This was the rigid sail that would aim the ark into the wind.

"So, what's that long underwater structure extending behind the hull?" asked Japheth, warming to the details of Methuselah's lecture.

"Right! You noticed that the keel reaches about thirty feet behind the back of the ark hull, and that is for directional stability also. The rigid sail points the ark into the wind, while the keel out the back helps steady it, and, like a fixed rudder, it keeps the ship from making sharp turns in case the wind or waves change direction suddenly. The last thing you want is for the ark to turn quickly and tip over.

"Finally, you see that the ends have a flared shape—rather than the flat front of Wazim's boxy design—that will push waves aside more easily and deflect some of the water away from the hull sides. Inevitably, and I suspect quite regularly, high winds and waves will result in large amounts of water coming over the front of the ark, and this will run off the top deck along deep troughs. Oh, I have also sloped the top deck toward the sides and put your crystal windows at regular intervals along both sides of a narrow deckhouse that runs along the center of the deck. This structure is about three feet high with a slightly sloped roof to help the deluge of rainwater run off faster. Having the windows in the sides of the deckhouse will make them less likely to leak than if the windows were placed directly into the top deck.

"I assure you, Noah," Methuselah proclaimed confidently, "the hull shape meets all of the divine specifications you were given. I have applied my informed judgment as an experienced engineer to make the ark as strong and seaworthy as possible. You understand, of course, that it is entirely up to God to get the ark and its contents through this coming deluge. He will see you through, or else why have you built an ark in the first place? All we can do is perform our best, and trust Him for the outcome.

"Now, let us look at the interior features that will make your life on the ark easier as you take care of the animals until the flood has dissipated and you can leave the ark for your life in the new world. Ham and Japheth, put the model over there out of the way, and I will show you the interior designs in the drawings I have made."

It took both boys' strength to lift the heavy model off the table and set it on a shelf near the window. Meanwhile, Methuselah unrolled the scrolled drawings and spread them on the table.

"Here, gather around this one, and let me show you how the crystal 'skylights' will work."

Before he could continue, Japheth raised his hand like an overeager schoolboy, curious with another question. "How will we find crystals that big? They don't exist, as far as I know."

Methuselah nodded and explained. "So, I will show you how to grow crystals—pure crystals from fine sand—that will focus the sunlight into a concentrated beam!" He looked at Japheth and continued. "We will use the crystals to focus light down into the interior spaces from either side of the deckhouse. You will also be able to open a few of the windows in the side of the deckhouse for fresh air after the rain has stopped, or on days when the waves subside. Wait until you see what else I have come up with for inside illumination!" Methuselah exclaimed.

He retrieved his pencil and showed them how the crystal skylights aimed the light down to mirrors positioned along the inside cabin walls and into the center openings in the decks. They would have to experiment with the mirrors, but it seemed there would be enough focused light reflected inside to brighten lower decks for feeding and other chores along the bins, stalls, and passageways that lined the hull on the lower decks, leaving the interior of the ark open. It might not be as bright as direct sunlight, but it would be sufficient to see the animals and move around. The problem was getting light deeper into the outer compartments and the bottom-most food and storage bins.

Japheth recognized this problem and noted it to his great-grandfather. "We will eventually need oil lamps when working on the inside of the hull," he said, "and I don't like the thought of using open-flame lamps inside the ship with hay and bedding all around. That seems very dangerous to me. We've already had a fire in the ark, and we don't want another." There was an awkward silence as they inevitably thought of Lamech.

"Sorry to bring that up, but it's just that any danger of fire should be avoided," Japheth observed.

"That is true," replied Methuselah. "I have an idea for a 'flameless lamp' that I will explain later, but suffice it to say for now that this is a problem that still has to be solved. Carrying an open flame in a moving vessel filled with hay and sawdust is indeed a recipe for disaster. We must solve that problem, for sure. And we will."

They looked over drawings for a self-bailing bilge while Methuselah explained how it automatically directed water and waste out the rear of the ark through a one-way flapper valve. Also, he illustrated how a few shaped funnels in the top deckhouse would always bring fresh air in—keeping water out—and exhaust stale air without attention or maintenance. The feeding chutes he designed allowed most of the heavy feed on the middle deck to be distributed by gravity to the larger animals on the bottom deck. Also, the fresh water tanks on the bottom deck were connected to watering troughs by copper pipes. A human-operated hand pump filled the troughs through a series of valves that let the pump operator direct water wherever needed. A second, independent system of pipes with one-way valves was used to pump outside water into the stalls to wash waste into the bilge where it would be voided out the back.

Finally, Methuselah showed his design for living spaces and the kitchen. One of the boys went to get Miriam to see Methuselah's kitchen mechanism. When Miriam arrived and saw the drawing, she was skeptical.

"This, my dear," Methuselah began, "is a cooking stove that will stay flat even when the ark is bouncing around in the wind and waves." He gestured proudly as he directed her attention to the drawing of a massive round object that looked like a barrel surrounded by metal rings.

"You hardly expect me to cook dinner in that contraption, do you?" she asked with a frown. "Why can I not bring my stove with me and nail it to the floor?"

"Ah, that would not do, would it? Your pots would fall off the top of the stove as soon as the ark tipped! The contents would slop out onto the floor and you would be scalded! No, that would not work at all. Believe me, this may look like a monstrosity, but my mechanical kitchen will be much safer, and you will learn to appreciate its convenience."

"I am not so sure about its 'convenience' and the thought of cooking food in a 'mechanical kitchen' sounds disgusting, but I am willing to give it a try."

Undaunted, Methuselah tried to reassure Miriam by offering to rename his invention a "gyroscopic airtight oven," which, though it was a valiant attempt to earn her praise, did not enhance his credibility with her.

Gyroscopic airtight oven indeed! she exclaimed in mock horror.

Noah had no misgivings about having his grandfather take over the ark's construction. What an answer to his prayer! He thought back to the night when the pillar of flame became a sentinel over the compound, and how he had prayed in desperation for help to finish the ark. Miraculously, Methuselah had seen the star, recognized its significance, and was approaching to help him even before he had uttered his prayer. All would turn out well. Nothing could harm them now.

CHAPTER 26

Imperial Palace, Fatherland Protection Council

While the members of the Fatherland Protection Council waited for arrival of the emperor, they spoke nervously amongst themselves in hushed tones. Meetings with the self-proclaimed Supreme Leader could be announced suddenly, at any hour, and they often led to violence. Every meeting was fueled by the emperor's inbred anger, and one or more members could end up victims of the imperial dagger. Membership required a mixture of bravery and pliability to react to Anak's every command. The Council's sole function was to carry out the emperor's wishes immediately and without objection. To defy him meant certain death. Those who survived his meetings had proven their abilities to bring up new information that cast the emperor in a favorable light, or had agreed with him while offering alternatives that could benefit him further. The emperor manipulated the Council because he was Anakim and those on the Council were mere, subjugated Cainites. No Sethians were on the Council for obvious reasons: Anak hated them with such a passion that he chose two Sethian members for his Council, and then, at their first meeting, brutally murdered them in front of the others as an example of his absolute ruthlessness. From then on, each meeting—and there had been many since he assumed the throne—took on the air of an inquisition. He gave the orders, and they carried them out. Other members of the Council had their lives ended in similar fashion, and this guaranteed total submission. Opposition was unthinkable.

"Why are we meeting at such a late hour, Mr. Secretary?" The timid question from one of the members was directed at Council Secretary

U'ungu, a proud and vain man who kept his position in the empire by being almost as brutally ruthless as the emperor himself. He was Cainite by birth, and it was rumored that U'ungu had some Anakim blood in his family background, though that was genetically impossible. The secretary kept his own ambition in check in front of the emperor and carried out imperial orders with enthusiasm.

"I fail to see why that should be of any concern of yours," U'ungu replied without looking up. "Do your job, and you will have nothing to fear. We can always find someone to replace you."

Hushed conversations amongst the members ended abruptly when the emperor burst into the chamber, crossed the room in long strides, and occupied the elevated throne at the head of the table. His raw, primeval physical presence dominated the room. Across the table's expanse of dull, scarred wood, Anak stared at each of his underlings through coal-black eyes. Thirty cowering faces looked at him furtively, and then lowered their eyes in submission rather than meet his piercing glare. Even U'ungu averted his practiced eyes to not appear to challenge his leader. He could stare back just as intently, but this was not the time or place. The emperor could grudgingly acknowledge someone who held his ground. Nobody could stand against the physical power of Anakim warriors, but in the case of Anak, his look was enough to make the toughest Cainite cringe.

His first words made his authority clear, although there could be no doubt he was their superior. "You are here at my command to listen and obey. Is that understood?"

"Yes, Emperor," they replied quickly, in unison and with enthusiasm, lest there be some perceived hesitation or lack of conviction in their voices.

"There is a Sethian named Noah who presents a threat to my empire. Some of you have listened to his criticism of me and his prediction that our way of life will end in a worldwide catastrophe. I am here to tell you that he is a liar, and what he says will not—*cannot*—take place." He looked around the table slowly to see if any faces revealed doubt or uncertainty. The Council members were practiced at facing this intimidation, and their faces wore masks of assent.

"You will take notes on the following points." Each subordinate immediately opened his notebook, took out his pen, and began making notes of Anak's every word.

"First, our global program of eradicating Sethians has been progressing too slowly. Instruct my Department of Cleansing to redouble its efforts to herd them into the camps and carry out my orders. Is that understood?"

"Yes, Emperor," replied the Minister of Moral Correctness, who began sweating as soon as the emperor mentioned one of his departments. "Your Excellency, we will need more resources if a doubling of results is to be accomplished." This was given as a statement of fact and not a challenge of his emperor's orders. "We estimate that there are approximately two million Sethians remaining across the globe, and their systematic eradication will take many more years because they are no longer passively following our instructions."

"You will have what you need. In addition, the imperial police will assume a greater role in the gathering phase of your operation. That is why Chief Inspector Baaki is now part of this Council. His network of informants is skilled at identifying deviant Sethians among the population and tracking down any resistance. This will allow you to focus your existing resources on the extermination process, which I expect to be done efficiently and without delay."

"Emperor, my department stands ready to happily carry out your every wish," injected Chief Inspector Baaki solicitously.

"Of course it is!" Anak snapped. He met Baaki's look with one of satisfaction at having human toads jump at his commands. But this one needed careful watching lest he overstep his portfolio and show too much self-initiative.

"Second, I wish this meddlesome Sethian, Noah, to be held up as an example to others who think they can speak out against me and not be crushed as enemies of the empire. Our local leaders have been too lenient in their dealings with him, and the previous chief inspector paid for his failure. I wish this so-called prophet taken alive and publicly dealt with to discredit once and for all his efforts to sway the population with his warnings and false predictions. Only when he and his 'ark' lifeboat are destroyed will his influence cease. Then I will move forward with my other programs."

"Again, Excellency, this matter will be taken care of immediately and completely," Chief Inspector Baaki responded dutifully. "May I request that your imperial troops at the palace be put at my disposal, so you can take personal credit for making an example of this troublemaker?"

The emperor's lips formed a primal sneer that exposed perfectly white, razor-sharp teeth. "Indeed, what an excellent suggestion! You will find my personal troops most eager to take action against any Sethian."

Anak had one more thing to say, but, in the silence that ensued, he looked around the table to see that everyone was attentive.

"Finally, I hear that some of you believe this heretical Sethian may be right."

Anak was carefully attuned to changes in sounds, facial expressions, or body movements that could signal a person's weakness. He had a Council member in mind, but he waited to see if the suspect gave a visible indication of discomfort or guilt. When one of the men at the far end of the table shifted in his chair, Anak forced a sickening grimace of satisfaction.

"Doctor, you seem uncomfortable with something I have said. Are you a believer?" Anak directed his hooded eyes toward his Minister of Nature and Science, whose seat was positioned as far from the raised throne as possible. Anak waited motionlessly to sense the tone of the doctor's answer for any sign of deceit.

"Your Excellency, my devotion is entirely to you and your programs. By your own statement, this man's prediction will not—indeed *cannot*—come to pass." The minister's careful answer was devoid of emotion.

"Have you not said, however, that this Sethian's prediction *could* take place? This would be contrary to what I have proclaimed." Anak was keeping the intensity of his voice momentarily in check for the desired effect.

"I believe science fully backs up your statements, Excellency. The vapor canopy of water that surrounds the upper atmosphere has been stable for over sixteen hundred years and will continue to be so for all time. It *cannot* fall to earth as this fool has suggested. His predictions are false." The minister held his eyes on his notes and hoped that he would not be called upon to elaborate. If he continued further, it could prove fatal.

But his technically correct answer was not sufficient to keep the emperor's voice from rising in volume. "Doctor, have you not previously hypothesized—no, maybe even *confirmed*—that this naysayer's prophecy of global destruction has some, shall we say, scientific validity?"

"My statements were purely academic in nature, your Excellency. In a private conversation with my colleagues, I shared my calculations of the volume of water in the high-level vapor canopy and my measurements of the earth's terrain. As a hypothetical exercise, I concluded that *if* there were a total collapse it *could* cover the earth. But I hasten to add that this was a theory only, and, of course, it was rejected since it could never actually happen." Was this enough to stop the questioning and save his life?

"Well, Doctor, here is my problem; you obviously did consider this traitor's warning seriously. You spent enough of your valuable time, and my imperial resources, pursuing the treasonous statements of this fanatic. It is enough that you conducted extensive calculations and thought them important enough to discuss. Are you not mincing words with me and trying to have it both ways?" Anak was now toying with the man for the sick pleasure of seeing him squirm in terror.

"Please, forgive me if I have given that impression, Excellency. You appointed me to this position as a man of science to advise you on factual matters related to physical nature and our environment. I deal in facts and wish to give you the best advice possible. If I pursued theories and claims, it was only to see if they had any basis in fact. When I became aware of this man's statements, I tested them against the facts and concluded that they *cannot* be true. The water canopy in the upper atmosphere around our globe is as unshakable as the ground we stand upon. It has never, and I repeat, *never*, given any indication of movement or instability. If it were to collapse, which it will not, the amount of water might be sufficient to engulf the surface of the globe itself." The scientist fought to keep his voice from breaking into a pitiful whine.

"That is all I said, and the facts of science bear that out. Again, my apologies if my work has given the appearance of disagreement with your proclamations."

The silence that ensued seemed like an eternity.

"Doctor, you were only doing your job. That is all." Anak stood and strode out of the Council chambers.

There was an empty stillness in the room, and no one mistook the emperor's swift departure to indicate his satisfaction with what had just taken place.

"You are a brave man, Doctor," Chief Inspector Baaki said cheerfully as he walked behind the scientist, who trembled with his head bowed over his notes. "You are the only person I know of who exchanged that many words with our emperor and is still alive. I admire your bravery."

The doctor looked up with moist eyes and whispered, "I did calculations one night at home on a piece of paper and mentioned them in passing to a few of my closest colleagues. What is so wrong with that?"

"What is wrong with that, Doctor, is that you think too much and then talk too freely. You'd have done better to keep your ideas to yourself. I'm afraid, however, that the seed of doubt has been sown in the emperor's mind, and your life is now hanging in the balance. If that seed so much as germinates, I might be obligated to nip it in the bud, so to speak." The chief put his hand on the man's shoulder, and squeezed firmly. "I'll have my eye on you, doctor. You'll be careful, won't you?" When he released his grip, the aged scientist lowered his head to the table with a sob.

Chief Inspector Baaki hurried down the corridor after Secretary U'ungu as he hurried to his office. "Sir, may I have a word with you?"

"What do you want? Ah . . . Baaki, isn't it?" the secretary asked without stopping, and the policeman struggled to keep pace.

"Yes, sir. I have an idea that the emperor may like that I would appreciate hearing your advice about first. Do you have time to hear it?"

"I can only spare a few minutes. We can talk along the way."

"With respect, sir, I would prefer that we speak in private, if that is all right."

"Very well. Come."

They reached Secretary U'ungu's office and swept past the official's functionaries and bodyguards without pausing. One of the guards hurriedly opened the office door and the secretary walked directly to his desk while waving to Baaki to sit across from him. He leafed through papers on his desk for several minutes, ignoring the policeman.

The secretary's office was larger than the quarters occupied by Baaki's entire department. Ancient Cainite artifacts, imperial awards, and framed pictures decorated all the walls. The furniture was the finest Baaki had ever seen, and he guessed each chair would cost him a year's pay. Of course, all the pictures were of U'ungu and the emperor in various poses while nothing in the room carried a hint of the secretary's past, except for a large painting of the secretary in a finely tailored military uniform that he did not recognize. Trying not to stare, Baaki concluded it was probably a uniform of the secretary's own design—complete with colorful ribbons, medals, and a sash—invented to satisfy his own vanity. He knew U'ungu had never been a military man, so Baaki concluded that he enjoyed giving visitors that impression.

"What is it?" The secretary's question broke the policeman's dangerous train of thought. "I have five minutes before my next appointment."

"Mr. Secretary, I did not mention this directly at our meeting for fear of appearing to challenge the emperor. However, I have an idea that might benefit him greatly, and, incidentally, us as well, regarding this fellow, Noah. I have a reliable source inside his compound, who sends me highly accurate and timely intelligence about Noah's activities, and I am told the famous inventor, Methuselah, Noah's grandfather, has joined them and taken over construction of the ark. This, combined with some type of protective field around the compound, means our future attempts to impede construction will likely be repulsed, and the ark will probably be finished and ready for use in a matter of years. What I propose is a direct contradiction of the emperor's orders that were just given in the Council chamber; I appreciate that this is a very dangerous thing to even contemplate. However, I feel the benefits of persuading the emperor to change his orders outweigh the risks, so I need your advice on how to introduce my idea to him in the best possible light. I am willing to present it to him at the risk of death, if you will advise me from your vast experience in dealing with him."

Baaki outlined his plan to Secretary U'ungu, but was careful to withhold key facts. An hour later, he left the secretary's office with a smile of satisfaction. U'ungu liked the plan so much that he offered to suggest it to the emperor himself, and Baaki eagerly and generously agreed that the secretary should take full credit for the idea. Chief Inspector Baaki congratulated himself as he walked slowly along the polished marble corridor that might one day lead to his own office. His plan cleverly offered all the benefits and none of the risks to himself and his career!

CHAPTER 27

Eden's Promise, Ark Compound

Noah might have anticipated how construction of the ark would bog down when he had hired Wazim, a man who had no experience building ships. It was equally clear to Methuselah that Wazim either didn't know what he was doing, or he had intentionally wasted time and sabotaged the project to drain the family's wealth for the benefit of himself and his cronies. A darker thought was the possibility that Wazim was also guaranteeing failure so that the emperor could mock Noah's message as fiction and portray God's judgment as a farce. In Anak's sin-twisted mind, he probably thought that if he stopped the ark from being built, God's judgment could be avoided or delayed. If judgment really were to come, Anak would at least take Noah and his family down with him.

At one time, Noah had employed two hundred workers gathering materials and assembling the ark, though he relied on Wazim so much that he didn't have a good grasp of what they were doing most of the time. Methuselah had changed all that and brought a long-range vision and disciplined order to building the ark.

An immediate benefit of Methuselah's leadership and thoughtful planning resolved a problem that had plagued the ark construction from the beginning: the regular disruptions and "accidents" that had drained resources and discouraged Noah and his family, seeing their progress pushed back time and again. Methuselah established a schedule of timber harvesting and stone quarrying that would keep Wazim and most of his unruly crew busy in the distant forests and mountains for many years. He gave them a long list of what he wanted and sent them far up the Euphrates River. They had to cut large trees from the dense forest, drag them to the river and float them down to the sawmill that was under construction. They were under strict orders to cut and shape stone blocks as ballast for the keel at the quarry site, where they would be taken to the Euphrates River and transported to the compound according to a set schedule. Methuselah didn't want to see trees or stone blocks appear on site until they were needed. He also set up their wages so that they were paid for the delivery of needed timber and stones upon arrival and not for simply putting in hours. If the materials didn't meet his demanding standards and arrive on schedule, the workers didn't get paid. Wazim and his crew protested initially, but, eventually, they grudgingly agreed.

"Don't worry about them," Methuselah told Noah. "If they deliver what I have on my list, they will make more in wages than when they worked at the estate. At least we will have less commotion in the compound, and we can get on with the work. Now the housekeeping staff can cut back on taking care of the large crew, and they can spend their time preparing food and provisions for the ark. Nobody will lose their jobs. This way, everyone will be more productive."

CHAPTER 28

Weather Outpost #22

The hypothesis that a water vapor blanket collapse could cover the world in water was examined and discussed quietly within the specialized group of those who monitored the atmosphere. Word of possible collapse of the watery canopy spread faster among scientists than anything Noah had said, in spite of efforts by the Ministry of Nature and Science to quash it. Weather scientists discussed amongst themselves different ways to test the collapse theory further to see if the vapor blanket was as stable as the politicians and the emperor were so vociferously insisting. Scientists agreed that it was a career-ending topic to pursue openly, but, on the other hand, the consequences of the theory being true were frightening. Eventually, the conclusion of most experts was to bury any vapor canopy speculation and concentrate their research in safer areas.

But meteorology students—not yet having invested their lives in comfortable, lucrative government positions—considered the theory of a natural disaster with global cataclysmic implications exciting. The trio of interns who gathered one morning at Weather Outpost #22 on a remote mountain far from imperial oversight thought they were in a safe position to test the theory.

"Suppose there were some instability in the vapor shell. How would we first observe it? Do you think it would be visible?" The questions were posed by Akmed, the senior co-op student, assigned with his classmates Mobi and Karaa to take measurements every other day using weather balloons launched from the outpost and then recovered from fields and forests around the observatory mountain. "We know a lot about the vapor blanket from regular measurements of temperature and altitude using our balloons. The temperature of the air increases with altitude and then at the atmosphere-vapor layer boundary—around one hundred thousand feet—the temperature reverses and declines. I wonder what would happen if the layer became unstable?" He speculated further, "We might not see much change by sampling only once every couple of days, would we?" As Akmed thought out loud, his fellow students weren't following him, but his supervisor Mr. Tuuki listened in the background to this exchange as he prepared his breakfast in the coffee break room. He saw an opportunity to keep his eager young students occupied to avoid being bombarded with their endless questions.

"Sounds to me like a project for some students," said Tuuki as he set his coffee down and looked at charts spread on the chart table in the center of the room. "You three put your heads together and come back with a way to measure that, and we'll see what the data looks like."

Akmed quickly took charge of the group and outlined his plan. "In order to measure a rapidly changing activity, we need to take sample measurements faster than changes in the activity that we want to measure. If our sample is too slow, the measurements may or may not capture the event as it is happening."

Akmed, Mobi, and Karaa rigged a paper recorder with a clock gear feed in an instrument box or "pod" hung under one of the measuring balloons to take moisture and temperature samples while the balloon hovered at the bottom of the vapor layer—rather than sending out many balloons at more frequent intervals—to get the most accurate readings. Each measurement would be tagged with the time and altitude. With several hundred good data points from one long excursion, they ought to see a fairly flat line of temperature and moisture if the bottom of the layer was stable. With Tuuki's permission, they filled a large observation balloon with hydrogen gas and anchored it while they prepared the instrument pod for launch. The students attached the pod and released the balloon toward the water vapor layer.

It took them several days to retrieve the balloon after it finally came down. All the farmers for miles around knew what their balloons looked like and were eager to receive a reward for bringing a pod back to the outpost.

"We ought to be able to see the results right away. Go ahead, open the case and let's see," said Akmed eagerly. Mobi unscrewed the pod's outer protective case and Karaa lifted the recorder drum out carefully so the paper chart could be unrolled. As Karaa and Mobi laid the paper out on the chart table surface, the results could not have been more obvious. The trace showed cycles of an oscillating wave stretched across the length of the paper. The amplitude of the wave showed the balloon bobbing up and down at the bottom of the layer by plus and minus a thousand feet and the spacing between peaks of the wave were clearly fifteen minutes. "That looks like almost a one hundred feet altitude shift per minute. Not a small movement, from what I can see," concluded Akmed proudly, not realizing the implication of what he was seeing.

"Well, that doesn't really prove anything," countered the station supervisor. "It could be some instrument noise or just a daytime temperature shift. I think you're wasting your time."

"I don't think so, sir," Akmed replied. "The temperature measurements are unchanging with time, as are the moisture measurements, so it looks like it was definitely riding the bottom of the layer. It's got to be that the layer altitude is moving up and down faster than the normal diurnal change." Akmed wasn't backing down, even if this meant going against his more experienced supervisor. The data looked convincing, at least to him, so why back down? "Don't you think we should report this?" he asked, prompting Tuuki to do something about what they found.

"Not yet. I want more evidence than just one trace of a paper recorder," Tuuki replied cautiously. "If you come up with confirming measurements from an independent source, I'll consider sending this up the chain to headquarters." With that tone of finality, he left them alone to discuss what to do next.

"We could take another chart reading over the course of a few days, loading as much paper as possible on the drum to capture data over an even longer period of time. We should launch another balloon tonight to at least confirm this reading and show it wasn't instrument error or some random anomaly. Or, we could try to think of another way to detect layer oscillation," Karaa suggested.

Akmed pondered this for a while and thought out loud. "We know the layer is there, even though it's transparent to the human eye. But really, the vapor layer isn't perfectly transparent. When we look at stars at night, they seem to twinkle because of slight variations in the atmosphere that bend their light rays. Since the variations take place quickly—like in fractions of seconds—we easily notice them. But if the brightness of stars varied every fifteen minutes, for example, our eyes wouldn't notice that. Our visual attention span isn't long enough to notice slight variations over long periods of time. But, on the other hand, if we had a telescope rigged with light-sensitive film to take photos of stars over a longer period of time, we might capture some variation of their intensity over longer periods. It would filter out the higher frequency twinkling and show gradual oscillation."

"That sounds like it might work, but we don't have a telescope," Mobi observed.

"True, we don't have one here, but I have a cousin who is an astronomy intern. I think she'd be willing to help us," mused Akmed.

Imperial Space Agency, Observatory #3

Two Months Later

The request came to the astronomical observatory innocently enough through informal channels that bypassed the government's atmospheric or space agencies. Akmed's cousin, Mahaa, held a prized internship at Observatory #3, which was funded by the government to catalog stars for navigation charts. Although she was only a junior "number cruncher," she had access to some telescope time and knew exactly what this request from Akmed was about. She, too, had been thinking about the vapor blanket collapse theory that was circulating quietly among the astronomy interns. It sounded catastrophic, if true, and attempts by the politicians to cover it up only intrigued her more. Akmed's data made further astronomical measurements seem worthwhile.

I think I can do this by advancing the camera to the next frame precisely every minute and taking an entire roll of snapshots, Mahaa thought to herself. *A roll of film is expensive, but, if I develop it myself, maybe I can pay for it out of my personal account. If it shows what I think it will show, I'll be famous and get all the telescope time and rolls of film I need!* The dramatic consequences such a discovery would produce did not yet enter Mahaa's mind.

It was two weeks before she found time to capture thirty continuous one-minute timed frames on film. That was all Mahaa could afford, but, with shots every minute, she should be able to see the cycles if they were there to be seen. When she had developed all thirty frames, she spent another week bent over a low-power microscope tediously measuring starlight intensity from each frame and plotting it on a graph. She even selected several different stars in the frame to make sure it wasn't oscillation of an individual star. The resulting chart was exactly as Akmed told her in his request. Success! She and Akmed would become famous!

When she discussed her findings with her fellow interns, they pointed out that her findings ran against the official position of the emperor. For an intern to contradict the emperor was suicide, they warned.

Mahaa took their caution seriously and realized the data was dangerous. If the vapor layer wasn't as stable as they had been telling everyone, it meant the prophet's warning about the end of the world might be true. Scientific data was truth no matter what the authorities said. In the face of the imperial authorities' continued insistence that the vapor layer was stable, Mahaa had to pass the results to Akmed quietly and urge him to be careful.

CHAPTER 29

Eden's Promise, Sawmill on the Euphrates River

Three Months Later

After he sent Wazim and his workers upriver, Methuselah taught Noah, his family, and a few newly hired workers how to read his detailed, annotated construction drawings. The large sheets were tacked to boards and placed in strategic locations inside the ark for easy reference as the interior was built. Within the God-given parameters, Methuselah had come up with a reliable design to weather the most catastrophic deluge of water imaginable. More than any other ship built before, the ark design was impeccable in both the strength of its structure and the careful fitting of its materials to make sure it remained intact under the harshest conditions. True to his reputation for clever mechanical innovations, Methuselah also designed practical features inside to help the family care for the thousands of animals that would fill the interior decks and stalls.

A major project necessary to prepare for the many trees that would float down the river from Wazim's team was to build a mechanized sawmill to shape large curved "ribs" for the hull, and to cut straight, finished exterior planks to attach to them. A sawmill like this had never been built before. Small mills beside rivers used the power of moving water to grind corn and wheat into flour, but this sawmill would be much larger, and it would use the river's continuous energy to drive two saws at high speed through a system of gears, leather belts, and pulleys. Access to water to power the mill came from the Euphrates River that flowed half a mile from the compound. The high stockade fence around the compound was extended to the river to envelope the sawmill within the compound's perimeter. Between the mill and the ark, Methuselah built a twin-rail pathway so that the large finished planks, weighing hundreds of pounds each, could be transferred to the ark site using wheeled carts. Next, he erected a high platform next to the mill where a winch, powered by the large sawmill wheel, hoisted planks up to a waiting cart, which, when its brake was released, coasted on the downhill grade with the help of gravity toward the ark, and a brake brought it to a stop in front of the ark's ramp. This one efficient mechanism alone saved man-years of labor.

Shaping timbers for months on end in the sawmill was slow and boring work. If not for the animated conversations he had with his great-grandfather, Japheth would have rather spent his time studying Methuselah's textbooks on mathematics and mechanics. He valued their time together, talking about the countless subjects that intrigued his young and energetic mind. Japheth could see, hear, and feel the massive sawmill gears as they meshed in perfect unison to drive the blades that cut precisely finished timbers. During this time working beside Methuselah, Japheth's interest in machines deepened, and they spoke of the countless mechanisms he dreamed of one day building.

But recently, he had become more curious about the Book that Noah and Methuselah spoke about quietly when they were alone. Noah gave Japheth only cursory answers about the Book that did not satisfy his inquisitive mind.

One day, Methuselah overheard Japheth question why they were spending years on the ark just because his father thought he heard a voice telling him to do it. Years and years of hard work and countless setbacks had begun to shake Japheth's faith in his father's mission. He had begun to think the world situation was not all that bad and saw work on an ark was a waste of time. Japheth and his father had been through this time and again. But Methuselah was more patient and waited for an opportunity to give Japheth more satisfying answers to his questions.

They took a break at the sawmill one day from bagging shavings for animal bedding. They had sawdust in their hair and sticking to their clothes, when Japheth broached the questions that had been kicking around in his mind all day.

"I don't see why we need to build this ship just because Dad says so. So, he saw a vision and heard a voice. How do we know it was from God? Maybe this is all pointless. I could be doing something more productive with my time." Japheth sat down with a scowl; he was in a foul mood.

"There are other reasons," Methuselah began. "Just look up in the sky and ask yourself why that pillar of fire is over us day and night and has not moved. That is clearly a divine sign of God's protection, but also an encouraging sign of His approval of what we are doing. I am convinced this is what we should be doing with our time. You are young and anxious to make progress with your life and accomplish great things. I understand that. But you have other questions about life that I cannot satisfy—only God can do that." When Japheth didn't respond, Methuselah felt the boy needed more encouragement.

"I can give you another reason," intoned Methuselah in his measured, reasoning voice. Japheth was all for hearing a new reason. He had been arguing with his father too much lately and all he ever got now was the usual "because-I-said-so" response. If this was something new, he wanted to hear it.

"Let me guess. It has to do with the Book of Adam, right?" Japheth asked eagerly.

Methuselah nodded.

"The Book is unique," Methuselah said, "and you know a little about my long search for it. It is more than a history of Adam and Eve's time with God in the Garden, their Fall, the early lives of their children, and the spread of civilization on the earth. Some passages are very specific predictions about what will happen to you and your family in the future. Interested in knowing what they are?"

Japheth was obviously intrigued to hear something new, so he nodded encouragingly. He was ready to put his bad mood aside.

Methuselah motioned to his great-grandson to come with him. "Let us sit outside where it is cooler, because I believe this will hold your interest more than cutting planks." They sat on a bench in the shade, dipped their cups in a barrel of fresh water, and the aging patriarch began his longest explanation yet about the Book of Adam.

"One of the reasons Adam developed the written word early in our history was so that we would have a more permanent record of events and ideas that could be preserved and passed on to future generations. Ultimately, he wanted us to understand what it was like to walk with God every day and to experience the unbroken love that Adam and Eve enjoyed in the Garden with Him. Sure, things were very different later when God expelled them from the Garden, but the memories were still very real, and God's promises and predictions took on a new meaning." Methuselah was speaking with a quiet intensity and Japheth forgot all about their work, already engrossed in Methuselah's story.

"One of the sections in the Book, besides God's promises of a coming One who would ransom us from sin, is a prophetic section about events that will come next and permanently mark a change in earth's history. Adam did not know the exact time in years when this would happen, but God revealed to him that human civilization would experience an unprecedented period of growth in fertility, knowledge and prosperity, followed by a sudden, global collapse caused by unrestrained, violent wickedness. God predicted that He would judge and destroy the entire world through a globe-covering deluge of water, and only a handful of people from one family and a large number of animals would survive in a floating vessel. Signs of a rapidly degenerating civilization during the past few centuries have been a clear fulfillment of that prediction. That prophecy and recent world events fit exactly with what your father was told about needing to build an ark."

"I've heard all of that before," Japheth objected. "What else did God say?"

Methuselah continued, "Adam's recollection of future events included more information about life after the worldwide flood: your family line will grow in numbers through good times and bad; a land will be given to them for a permanent dwelling; dispersion will result when God's people disobey; there will be a regathering when they repent; and finally the prophesied Lamb of God will come in bodily form to pay the penalty for the sins of the whole world. After a miraculous physical resurrection, the anointed One will go to heaven and return later to make everything right and set up a Kingdom that will be better than the Garden of Eden. Adam's writing is unclear about many details, especially the exact times of these events, but in a few pages it sets forth the sequence of God's program for the future of mankind.

"So you see, it is not just your dad's 'opinion' that motivates him to build the ark, but a promise from God that even though the entire surface of the planet will be destroyed by water, there will remain descendants of Adam, through you and your brothers, who need to be preserved for the future. That is why he works so tirelessly to finish the ark."

Methuselah paused for a full minute before he spoke again. "One more thing that I hope will set your mind at ease. The revelation given to your father contained a detail that I think you have ignored. You will have a wife when you enter the ark—whenever that event takes place. I know you have resisted efforts by your parents to find a wife for you. You should not be anxious or in a hurry to find one, but you can be sure that you *will* have a wife on the ark. God will provide the perfect wife for you in His time. Of that you can be certain."

He looked at Japheth with gray, sad eyes, almost as if he had himself relived the history of the world in this telling.

"I don't know what to say . . ." Japheth said as he stared into the distance. "That's the first time I've considered how all those predictions fit together. I hadn't thought of God's revelation as being that absolute and reliable. I suppose I should have, but I wasn't thinking. Promises from God . . . You'd think everyone would want to know about them." Then he remembered that the Book was lost and Methuselah had spent almost two centuries looking for it without success.

"Why don't you go find the Book now?" Japheth asked abruptly. "I'll go with you."

"For one thing, I am an old man. And you are still a young man with more growing up to do before you head off on an adventure like that." Japheth thought Methuselah was trying to discourage him, but the thought of going on a search into the unknown completely gripped his imagination.

"Someday, I'd like to find it," Japheth announced as he leapt to his feet and paced back and forth. "You and me together. If it's everything you say it is, it sounds like it could be life-transforming," he thought out loud. "What would I have to do besides get older for you to take me to look for it?"

Methuselah chuckled at his outburst. "Most importantly, we need to finish this ark. One of my conditions for helping build it was to finish in time to train you and your brothers so you will have the knowledge you will need to start a new civilization after the flood. When your training is done, if there is time, we can ask your father for permission to go to the city of Enoch where I think the Book is safely hidden and then we can return it to the ark. There are a lot of 'ifs' in that statement and I doubt we will have time to see all of them fulfilled. Meanwhile, young man, we need to get back to work on your future home," Methuselah chided.

Japheth was excited about the idea of going on a quest when they finished the ark and he completed his education. "I've already been studying those books you lent me. The math isn't that difficult, but the mechanics books are harder to follow."

"That is because you need practice in a laboratory to see firsthand how mechanisms work according to basic principles of nature in those books. We will also continue our math tutoring, which you will need for astronomy. You are anxious to get going, and that is a good thing. But you need to learn much more about how mechanisms work in the real world. We have only scratched the surface with this sawmill and other inventions inside the ark. The modern mechanized world of our seventeenth century is many times more complex than what you have been exposed to here. I want to teach you about tiny calculating machines, mineral chemistry, optical and light science, and animal and plant designs. It would take many years for you to learn all that, and I do not know if there will be time."

Japheth was undeterred by the need for more study. "But if we finish the ark ahead of schedule, why couldn't I do that? We've accomplished a lot on the ark already, and you said we're making good progress. You've always been my mentor, and I'd love nothing better than for you to teach me about those things. But most of all, I want to know what the Book says. I'm not going to be able to sleep tonight just thinking about it!" Japheth's excitement was overflowing.

"Well, I can tell you are serious about that. You have that look in your eyes and strength in your voice like I did when I was younger. Why not sleep on it, and see if we can move the ark schedule ahead enough for us to go to my underground laboratory to further your studies? I think if you spend a few years in a well-appointed workshop, you will be surprised how many things you can achieve with a solid education."

"You have an underground laboratory? A workshop? Where is it?" Japheth was exploding with excitement.

"Why not save that for another time, so we can get today's work done?" Methuselah regretted mentioning his laboratory. He had not been there in years, but knew it was safely concealed and awaiting his return. Japheth would be his last student, and he knew the future of mankind depended on teaching him all he could.

The dinner bell rang in the distance, and they looked at each other in surprise. "You see, Japheth, we wasted all afternoon talking and neglected our work." Methuselah said this with no regret. It had been a wonderful afternoon that drew him and his great-grandson closer together. As they walked toward the house, the old man felt young again inside.

Japheth's mind was spinning. The smell of sawdust was still on his clothes and his hands as he strained inside with a desire to learn more so he could join Methuselah on what he envisioned as the journey of a lifetime. But more than that, deep inside and unknown to anyone else, there grew in Japheth a yearning for a relationship with God, which his parents and brothers seemed to have, but which, until now, he did not. *What was it like to pray to God and have prayers answered? What was it like to have an inner peace with God?* There had been an emptiness inside him ever since he could remember, and he knew it wasn't going to go away until he found out for himself what God said in the Book. Japheth determined that nothing would stop him from finding it.

CHAPTER 30

Imperial Security Command, Rephaim Military Base, Armory

One Year Later

The two men who called the meeting at the largest military base outside the city of Enoch represented a dangerous combination of bureaucratic ambition and ruthless violence. U'ungu had the emperor's confidential ear, while Chief Inspector Baaki was a hardened police commander with his department's commandos and the elite Imperial Guard under his command. The two stood before their carefully selected troops to brief them on the emperor's latest plan.

The men assembled before them numbered less than one hundred and represented the best in their chosen fields of expertise. Many were trained security commandos with experience in every form of combat from silent, covert operations to the employment of high-powered weaponry. Others in the group were doctors, agriculturists, scientists, administrators, drivers, and cooks. Some had skills that could not be readily identified, but carried themselves with such confidence it was obvious they could be counted upon to accomplish any task with steely determination. This diverse gathering of talent hushed immediately when Secretary U'ungu began to speak.

"Men, you are here today to take part in an imperial contingency operation that has been approved by our Beloved Emperor. I stress that this operation has the daily, personal attention of His Excellency, and I need not remind you what that means. The purpose of this group is to ensure the continuation of the emperor's rule in the event of a natural disaster that endangers the palace and government functions needed to guarantee the smooth operation of His Excellency's dominion. This royal exercise is code named Operation GOLDEN DAWN. Each of you has a top security clearance. You may not discuss details of this operation with anyone outside this room. This base will be our headquarters, and whatever you need to accomplish your specific missions will be made available to you from military or police resources. Now, Chief Inspector Baaki will explain the operation in more detail."

"Thank you, Mr. Secretary. It should be obvious that, with the attention this operation has drawn from the highest level of our government, it is imperative that you do not fail in your tasks. GOLDEN DAWN is a contingency operation to test our ability to move the seat of government from the palace to a remote area approximately seven days journey to the south near the Euphrates River. The word 'contingency' is used intentionally to stress that there is no current threat and no expectation that the emperor, his staff, and his consorts will need to move in the foreseeable future. Our initial objective is to test our ability to move a large group of people quickly if a natural disaster were to render the palace non-functional. In the event GOLDEN DAWN were initiated, your responsibilities will be to provide transportation, security protection, provisioning, and administration for approximately one thousand designated personnel. This will be a live exercise and not a mock or paper exercise in that you will prepare all the required support on this base and strategic supply locations and make them ready to be put into action instantly at the emperor's directive. He will be advised when GOLDEN DAWN is ready, and he may choose to test you at any time with a full-scale deployment. The timetable for initial operational capability is demanding, and, after that, we will maintain a high state of readiness for an extended period. Do not disappoint our emperor. I am counting on you to be vigilant until His Excellency terminates the exercise.

"Each of you has been assigned to teams, where you will be organized by rank and given operational orders detailing responsibilities in your areas of expertise. Team meetings begin in this building in twenty minutes. Dismissed!"

U'ungu and Baaki walked away from the bustling crowd of troops and motioned their assistants to leave them.

"Do you think they suspect the operation is more than a simple exercise? What if the true purpose is made known?" U'ungu worried.

"It doesn't matter. They are all professionals with jobs to do, and, even if they suspect anything other than an exercise, they will keep their mouths shut. The important thing is that the logistics for large-scale movement such as this must be put in place with people standing ready to implement the plan, whenever it is initiated. My men and the Imperial Guards are loyal to the emperor and will do whatever is necessary."

"I must say," Secretary U'ungu observed, "your idea struck a sharp chord with the emperor—a good one, fortunately for us. I think he saw the underlying purpose of the plan even though it was carefully left unsaid. He could not help but notice that the location of the alternate government site coincides with Noah's compound. When I told him the entire contingent would be ready to deploy without notice or reason, he gestured for me to continue. When I explained that the force would be always ready in the event of some hypothetical natural disaster, he stiffened as if I had suggested agreement with Noah's outrageous prophecies. But just as quickly, when I repeated that the madman's forecasts of destruction could *never* happen, he speculated that it wouldn't hurt to have a plan for survival in case some 'unforeseen accident' took place."

Baaki nodded in satisfaction when he heard U'ungu's account. His clever idea was taking substance and would be available to him and U'ungu if the disaster foretold by Noah actually happened. Baaki's agents were intercepting reports from the empire's global atmospheric monitoring stations looking for any indication of impending danger, and, although there were none for now, if any signs of drastic climate change became known, he would increase the alert level for GOLDEN DAWN and set the next phase in motion. Allowing Noah to finish the ark meant that the giant ship could be commandeered by GOLDEN DAWN troops when the time came. The ark would easily hold the emperor and all of his entourage, but, most importantly, Baaki would have a cabin in the ark for himself if Noah's prediction was right. All they needed was seven days to reach the compound when the final word was given. Half the GOLDEN DAWN complement of personnel was uniformed police commandos or Imperial Guards with the latest in heavy weaponry, so they should have no problem overtaking the compound and commandeering the ark for themselves when the time came.

Baaki dared not reveal what he believed and feared: GOLDEN DAWN *would* be implemented some day, and getting inside the ark before the vapor canopy collapsed would be his only chance to avoid the coming global catastrophe.

CHAPTER 31

Eden's Promise, Ark Compound

Next Fifty Years

Construction on the ark progressed steadily and without significant incident. Methuselah's new ark design that used the existing structure had resulted in the need for more materials, including thousands of new timbers shaped individually so that the three layers of side and end sections could fit together tightly. Most of the previous work on the hull was useless because the hand-shaped timbers and planks had such large gaps between them. They overlapped to some rough extent, but they required so much pitch in the joints that calling them "sealed" was a joke. Methuselah said they would last a few minutes submerged in water before they leaked profusely. Not exactly comforting for those who would be on the inside counting on those seams to last for at least a year!

The volume of space inside the ark was so large that, even with thousands of animals, animal feed, and provisions for Noah and his family, the ark would float high in the water, bouncing violently in the waves like a cork on the surface. It needed heavy ballast—something Wazim's design had not considered—so that the ship would ride with its center of gravity deep below the water. Construction of the newly fashioned hull and deck would take at least fifty years, according to Methuselah's calculations, because their curved shapes and carefully fashioned joints had to fit together tightly, and their assembly required attentive workmanship. Detailed drawings and a project plan to guide them meant their progress could be measured, and builders could see the completed shape of a usable ark.

Methuselah made large drawings of each deck and called out the special features he wanted built into the walls and floors. He also developed formulas to figure out the sizes of supports and planks necessary to strengthen spans that would withstand the pressure of giant waves. After his many calculations, and tests with a scale model in the pond, he determined that they needed to fit almost six hundred large stones in the bottom of the ark for ballast as a counterweight inside the structure to keep it from overturning.

The keel that Methuselah designed was unique because it was built upon a single, unified wood structure almost five hundred feet long. It was formed from interlocking slabs of gopher wood soaked in water and banded with metal hoops every three feet to form a long, monolithic structure five feet high. This formed the base to which other parts of the ark's framework could be attached. Masons shaped thousand-pound ballast blocks with interlocking "tongue and groove" edges so that they could be locked together, set inside the hull along the top of the gopher wood keel, and fitted inside notches in the structure to keep them from shifting.

The amount of work required to fashion the keel, ballast blocks, hull, and top deck was enormous. Manpower to gather the materials and form them into the desired sizes and shapes before they could be used was something that Methuselah had addressed earlier. This "front end" work, as he called it, was crucial for a consistent shape and quality to the hull structure. He argued that, if they skimped on the materials, they would pay for it later in leaks and, worse, failures in the hull structure when the high wind and waves swept across the earth. Noah thanked God for Methuselah's careful approach to building the ark and his tireless consideration of the myriad details.

Methuselah's strategy proved accurate because they found they accomplished more work with fewer people. They were left with a working crew of twenty-five laborers, and, without Wazim to stir up discontent, they immediately saw the kind of steady progress on the ark they hadn't seen before. It took years to lay the keel under the core boxed structure and put the curved ribs into place, but it was clear that the resulting ship was stronger than Wazim's structure.

Methuselah also made tools that advanced the construction process and resulted in a better quality hull. They made iron drills to bore perfectly round holes in the planks for the pegs that would join adjacent, grooved planks and attached them to layers beneath. The excess material of the pegs were then shaved off with a sharp iron chisel that made the plank smooth and ready for the next layer on top of it. By overlapping planks, staggering seams, and filling each seam with a thin layer of pitch-soaked oakum, they finally understood how this structure could last a long time underwater.

The family's dino-powered cranes for lifting the large ballast blocks into place were improved upon so that their progress was smoother. As the hull took shape, the interior details of feeding chutes, water pipes, and drainage ducts were roughed in to make sure they fit into the spaces allowed. When the upper deck was ready, the ventilation and shafts for the lighting mirrors could also be fitted. The water tanks and feed storerooms were constructed to keep the center of gravity low but close to the animals. Finally, animal pens, cages, and coops were fitted into their designated spaces. There was still an abundance of undesignated space available for more animals and low-density feed, if they were needed.

"We need to talk," Deva insisted, cornering Japheth on his way out the door after breakfast one day. He was preoccupied with a new project and looked momentarily surprised.

"Now?" he asked, faking interest, yet continuing out the door.

"Yes, now!" She looked angry, and he tried to think of what he had done to upset her.

She took him by the arm, and they walked away from the dining hall to sit on a bench near the vacant workers dormitory that had been converted to a storage warehouse. She sat with her hands nervously clenched in her lap and composed herself to speak.

"What's going on between us?" she blurted. "You've hardly spoken to me in who knows how long. I thought we would still be friends, but, ever since that old man came here, you've been absorbed in another world. What's happened?"

Japheth answered back quickly, "First of all, that 'old man' is my great-grandfather whom I love dearly. He's turned the ark's construction completely around, in case you haven't noticed, and, thanks to him, we have a hope of finishing it in time. And on top of that, I've been very busy." Japheth tried to contain his own anger. "Whatever was between us was something you and my mother tried to fabricate when you first came here, but I never agreed to marry you. I thought I'd made that clear."

"But what about us going to Enoch to see the city?" Deva pleaded. "Why don't we go there to do some shopping and take in some concerts? That's something I've always wanted to do. Maybe you and I could go there for a few weeks, just as friends."

"We've had this conversation before, too." Japheth's disappointment with Deva was beginning to show. "The two of us can't go alone on a trip if we're not husband and wife. It wouldn't be right. Besides, I don't share those dreams of yours for the so-called art, fashion, music, and entertainment of the city. They're of no interest to me. My life is here, where I want to spend my last years in this world investing in the start of a new civilization after the flood."

Deva stood in tears with a look of contempt that made Japheth flinch.

"You are such a fool!" she shouted. "Can't you see that this world is all there is, or ever will be? Your whole family is obsessed with this idea that the world is evil, and God is going to destroy everyone and everything around us. Well, I don't believe any of it!"

Deva ran sobbing back to the dining hall as Japheth slumped and wondered what had just happened between them. Had he somehow misled her to think they could go off like that without being married? He thought he'd made it clear that she was fun to be with and he liked talking with her, but only as a friend. If there was an obsession, it was her consuming desire to see the glitter of the city and the "sophisticated" Cainite way of life. If that's what was motivating her, he could only conclude that she wasn't the girl for him. He walked toward the ark as his mind forgot Deva and his thoughts turned to his next project.

CHAPTER 32

Eden's Promise, Ark Compound

Months Later

One challenge that Noah had mentioned to Methuselah only in passing was still not resolved. Besides the task of planning for a voyage of yet unspecified duration, he hadn't been able to come up with a count of the number of animals that would be on the ark.

Noah's continued concern became evident one day, when he and Methuselah were discussing the layout of the animal and feed spaces. "It is impossible to estimate the type and amount of animal feed to bring on the ark without knowing how many animals you will have and how long they will be kept inside. There is a large amount of room in the ark, but limiting the animals to two of each category or 'kind' is still almost an unbounded number," Methuselah observed.

"Not really," replied Noah. "From studies we have conducted of animal procreation over the years, we know there are only variations in appearance among some animals that have been breeding among their same 'kind' for the past sixteen hundred years. If we bring two from each category we might have twenty or thirty thousand different animals. But before we get too carried away, remember that most of these are very small animals, and they will not require large quantities of food or attention during a year. The larger animals we bring, like dinos and the horned mammals, can be juveniles who will grow during the year aboard the ark. If they are barely weaned when we bring them in, they will be easy enough to handle and feed as long as we give them plenty of space to grow. My biggest concern is getting them all rounded up and into the ark."

Noah and Miriam had given this considerable thought ever since God had revealed His initial instructions. "We see it as an impossible task to gather all the animals ourselves. Certainly, we can bring the few additional animals identified for later sacrifices, but it's the twenty or thirty thousand different types—double that number in all since there will be one male and one female each—that I see as daunting. Even if we started gathering them now, it would take us many years before they are loaded, and by then they would be full-grown and we would have to keep them caged, fed, and healthy for who knows how long before finally getting them into the ark. We would be busy doing nothing else but caring for animals, and we would have no time for finishing the ark."

Noah continued as he looked up at the ark structure towering over the yard. "I have to wonder which of God's instructions are commands, which are general guidelines, and how much are prophetic predictions?" he asked rhetorically. "From the beginning, it was obvious that God would bring to pass all that He said, but how? Did he *command* us to have three sons and get wives for them? Or did He *predict* that would happen someday? Don't get me wrong, I'm not trying to negate what He said. I believe it will all happen exactly the way He said and when He said. I'm just trying to reconcile a seemingly impossible task with my desire to obey Him. How do I do that?" Noah entreated.

"Take the ark as an example," began Methuselah. "You admitted that you did not know how to build an ark at the first, but you started by faith to construct one as best you knew. You ran into roadblocks along the way, but it was not for nothing. God brought you to the place where you realized you could not finish the ark yourself. You prayed, and God answered your prayer, and here we are with an ark nearly finished within the time allowed." Methuselah stopped for a moment to let this sink in.

"Now, let us translate that same approach of walking by faith to a need to gather twenty to thirty thousand animals. It is indeed an impossible task, even for experienced zoologists like you and Miriam. There apparently are not enough days or years to gather the number of animals that need to survive to repopulate a new world. Nonetheless, we know it will happen because God said it would. So, let us divide the problem into manageable pieces, and see if you can start now on something that will result in as many animals as possible. If you take God's revelation as a *prediction*, there will be enough animal pairs in the ark when the time comes. From that perspective, if you did nothing at all, God would somehow bring animals into the ark to fulfill His will. But if, as I believe, it was a *commandment* that you bring those animals into the ark, you need to step out by faith to accomplish that task as best you can. Having done your best, God will see to it that His perfect will is accomplished and that all the animals are where He wants them to be when the time comes."

"Of course, grandfather, you are right. Again, I was discouraged, and you have put it all in perspective," Noah answered sheepishly. "We will divide the categories of animals and begin gathering as many creatures as we can take care of. It may only be about two thousand, but we will do our best with the time and resources we have."

As the family members went their separate ways, Miriam caught up with Japheth on his way back to the dining hall.

"Japheth, have you spoken with Deva lately?"

"No, not recently." Japheth replied. "Why?"

"Oh, that poor girl," she replied. "Since she returned from her visit to the city two months ago, she has kept to herself. She has been avoiding you ever since your argument, and I do not think she wants to face you again." Miriam hoped that telling Japheth of Deva's despair would convince him to at least speak to Deva to cheer her up.

"Well, she's not the right girl for me," Japheth said abruptly. "She's in love with the city's bright lights, and spiritual things have no value to her. I think she fooled us into thinking she was a believer so that you'd encourage us to get married. But she cares nothing for the things we believe in. You realize that now, don't you, Mom?"

"Yes, but she is still a nice girl, and she has been asking me about what you are doing on the ark. She takes an interest in what is going on around here, but when she sees you coming she turns the other way. She is an emotionally hurt young woman, and I wish there was something I could say that would change her mind about the ways of the Lord." Miriam's concern for Deva remained on her face.

"You couldn't say anything she hasn't already heard," Japheth assured his mother. "She's so captivated by her dream of a life of luxury and entertainment that I'm surprised she even came here. There's nothing she wouldn't do to get what she wants."

Japheth's opinion was much closer to fact than he realized.

CHAPTER 33

Eden's Promise, Ark Compound

"What will you do now that the ark structure is essentially completed?" Methuselah asked Noah as they stood on a rise overlooking the ark. "We have finished the exterior and inside shell almost five years before the deadline. But you still have much work to do on the interior furnishings."

"We can handle it from here, thanks to your drawings and our considerable progress gathering animals and provisions," Noah replied with satisfaction.

"Good. Now, regarding my original request about teaching your sons before the time comes, you will not be too enthusiastic about what I am going to ask," began Methuselah, "but I would like to take Japheth with me for some training at my laboratory. Shem and Ham wish to stay here with their wives; they are not interested in becoming mechanics. But Japheth has both the interest and ability. In the few years remaining before the judgment, he has much to learn, and some maturing to do as well, before he is ready to take my knowledge into the new world."

"You are right," Noah replied stiffly. "I do not favor that idea. And besides, we need him here to help provision the ark and prepare the animals."

"I do not disagree that he could be of help here. But if it is a matter of provisioning and animal husbandry, that is something any hired workman could do. Japheth is special; we both know that. He has a keen mind and absorbs knowledge quickly. I have tried to teach him basic mathematics and scientific theory, but he lacks practical knowledge that can only come by applying what he has learned from books and seeing the results firsthand. It would be a shame to leave these skills behind when you start over again in the new world."

Noah pondered this as he and Methuselah continued back to the house. "Miriam and I always knew Japheth was special. Of our three sons, he was always the fastest learner and the most inquisitive. Shem and Ham are good, faithful sons. They are as solid in character as any father could want, and their wives are perfect for them. Japheth is like his brothers in most respects, but with a touch of wildness in his blood and a quickness that runs on ahead when everyone else wants to walk." Noah stopped in the path, placed his hand on his grandfather's shoulder, and looked into his gray eyes. "He is like you in many ways, grandfather, and that is probably why you and he get along so well. I suppose it would be a shame to keep him here to farm and tend animals. Miriam will miss him the most, but I give my permission for him to go to the lab with you," Noah consented.

"But you must promise me," Noah added, "that you will have him back here well before it is time for us to go into the ark. Miriam will be frantic with motherly worry and I will be a nervous wreck if the time draws near and you do not have him back here. Do you promise me that?"

Methuselah agreed. "I will do all in my power to have him back with you when it is time to close the door to the ark. No matter what it takes, even if I have to give my own life, I will have him back in time."

CHAPTER 34

Weather Outpost #22

Akmed leaned back in his chair and read the letter from his cousin again. As excited as he was to be proven right and to hold irrefutable astronomical evidence confirming his data, he understood that possession of this knowledge put him and his friends in great danger. If the government could squash the casual hypothesis of their most prominent scientist, what would they do to a couple of students who had confirmed that forbidden hypothesis and contradicted imperial edict? The implications of the data he and his team had collected, plus the astronomical data from his cousin, could not only impact their careers, but it could cost them their lives. That prophet predicting the end of civilization by a worldwide flood couldn't possibly have known about this data, which made what he held in his hands all the more significant. The data revealed that the high-altitude vapor layer was oscillating. It didn't mean that it was about to fall to the ground right away. But, if the collapse eventually did happen, he was convinced there was probably enough water in the layer to cause a worldwide flood.

He must take some time to think this through before he did anything with the results. He'd wait to see if there were any changes in the data gathered from occasional balloon flights. If he could convince Tuuki that it was still worth making the longer measurements, he might give his approval, especially if new data refuted these dangerous results and it meant that no official reports would have to go up the chain that would get them in trouble. Akmed would quietly accumulate data and see where it led them.

CHAPTER 35

The Great Forest

Seven Days Later

Methuselah was enjoying himself, traversing a straight path through the forest and whistling while he made his way easily, but slowly, through the undergrowth. Japheth was less sanguine as he tripped over tree roots and was slapped in the face by tree branches in Methuselah's wake. He already felt a mixture of homesickness and excitement, though they had only been gone a week. He had never been away from the compound overnight. This was definitely a new experience, and he already had some regrets. Sure, he would be learning more about all the things he had been dreaming about his whole life—intricate mechanisms, powerful machines, astronomy, training animals. He never knew anyone like his great-grandfather who had the slightest interest in celestial mechanics, for example—something that fascinated Japheth since he had first lain on their roof at night and studied God's heavens. Still, it would be a lot of work, and he would miss his family.

The underground workshop was more than a seven-day journey from the family compound, deep in what was called the Great Forest, but its exact underground location had always been a secret. Methuselah had taken Lamech, and then Noah, there when they were growing up while he was constructing the facility. At the time, they showed little interest in the large cavern that housed a library, experimentation rooms, and machine shops. It was the farm that hooked Methuselah's son and grandson on zoology.

As Methuselah and Japheth made their way through the forest, they discussed what Japheth would do in the coming years. Japheth was excited to be spending all of this time with Methuselah, but, at the same time, he was apprehensive that he might not live up to his great-grandfather's expectations. He was further intimidated by the reputation of the place where most of the world's engineering developments had originated. After Methuselah left the Adam Institute, he had reproduced the inventions he left behind and over time came up with countless others. Fortunately, he had managed to bring most of his books from the Institute, many of which he had authored, and Japheth would be able to use them for reference. Methuselah's library alone was going to be a bigger treat than his mother's cooking!

During their journey, Japheth came to understand why it was called the Great Forest. The sunlight barely reached the ground through the tree canopy three hundred feet above. The trunks of the oldest trees were fifteen to twenty feet in diameter. Smaller trees among the giants made more canopy layers, crowded with vines and bushes capturing any sunlight in between the larger trees. On the forest floor was a perpetual twilight of filtered sunrays from above and constant mist rising from moss and ground-hugging vines underfoot. Methuselah said there was an old path that came near the workshop, but he didn't want to take it in case there were imperial patrols that could follow them. Japheth was lost within a day of leaving the compound and knew he could never find his way back on his own.

A unique outcropping of trees that did not normally grow together was the first reference point for the laboratory's entrance. Methuselah had planted these trees near the hillside entrance as the only indicator of its location. Widely dispersed pine and evergreen trees towered over stunted orange and lime bushes that grew in their shade. Anyone who happened upon the small citrus plants might note their unique placement deep in the forest, but they would not likely attach any great significance to them, thinking they probably grew because a random bird dropped a seed there or it was once a cultivated grove a thousand years ago. The laboratory entrance was on the south side of a large hill. The giant trees thinned around the hill, and the top of the hill was bare of trees altogether, but was covered with tall grass. An outcropping of rock shielded a small indentation in the side of the hill, not more than three feet in and about the height of a man. The protection it offered from the elements was minimal, and it didn't extend into the hill far enough to encourage animals to make it their home.

Methuselah and Japheth paused outside the indentation, while Japheth memorized the surrounding topography and tree line. If he came across the citrus grove again, he hoped he would remember how to find the entrance. The small opening was only partially obstructed by moss and bushes. The bare stone outcropping above the opening was sturdy and in no danger of collapsing. Only one person could fit inside, if they hunched over.

Methuselah pointed to a flat rock at eye level that he removed from the wall to reveal a row of five dull metallic buttons with the numerals one through five engraved on them. It was a mechanical combination lock that opened the entrance when the buttons on the keypad were pressed in the proper sequence. The mechanical device, when triggered with the right code, released a weight that swung the rock door into the hillside and gave entrance to the interior.

Methuselah's Underground Laboratory

Methuselah pressed the buttons in the coded sequence and was rewarded with the solid but muffled sound of a falling counterweight somewhere inside. The door cracked open about two inches. When he pressed against the door, it swung further inward to reveal a black void. Knowing the layout inside, Methuselah motioned for Japheth to wait at the door while he confidently stepped forward to descend what sounded like a flight of steps. During this time, Japheth had observed the door's combination, and, from the echo of Methuselah's footsteps, he could tell he was walking across a stone floor into a large room. When Methuselah turned a handle on the wall, a diffuse glow from gas jets above revealed the faint details of a vast room and indistinct objects inside. Japheth stuck his head through the entrance to see the steps leading inside; he entered cautiously. The cavern had the smell of oil and an unidentifiable chemical, but lacked the musty, damp smell of a natural cave. This cavern was obviously man-made, using stone and other durable materials to line its walls. The light appeared to grow brighter as his eyes adjusted, and gradually his eyes took in more of the workshop that would be his home for the next five years.

Japheth could tell why Methuselah was very proud of his gigantic facility when he stood in the middle of the large room. This was his great-grandfather's element: surrounded by gleaming machinery, expansive workbenches with neatly arranged tools, rows of books in easy-to-reach nooks, and shelves stacked from floor to ceiling with odd jars, bottles, vials, and boxes in neatly labeled cubbyholes and containing who knows what. Methuselah looked anxious to get started with a tour.

"Before you start showing me around, can we get something to eat?" Japheth pleaded. They had eaten all the food packed by Japheth's mother, and he wondered what they would eat now that they had arrived. He hoped they wouldn't have to hunt for their food or dig up strange things growing in the forest. In fact, his homesickness increased in proportion to his hunger as he contemplated whether Methuselah even knew how to cook.

"Ah, yes! Come with me, and I will show you the kitchen." Methuselah moved quickly down a hallway to a room that had its own indirect light from the ceiling and was as spotless as the rest of the laboratory. He opened an adjoining door and pointed to rows of stocked shelves. The air inside the kitchen was noticeably cooler and dryer.

"Here is everything we need. An abundance of meals preserved using my special technique. All we do is add the package to boiling water, and there we are!" Methuselah walked inside and picked out a package in a shiny metallic wrapping.

"Preserved in seconds to kill all the bacteria, and then vacuum sealed in this special package. 'Vegetable and Cheese Omelet' sound good to you?" Not waiting for an answer, Methuselah grabbed a pot from an overhead rack and put it under a curved brass pipe extending over a sink.

"Stand back in case pressure has built up in the pipe," he cautioned. He reached out and gingerly opened a valve next to the sink. Steam instantly billowed from the pipe with a loud hiss. After a few seconds, water gushed to fill the pot. Methuselah placed the package in the pot and jumped back as scalding water covered the package.

"See that? Boiling water! Leave the package in there for a few minutes, and it will be warmed and ready to eat." After waiting, he removed the package with tongs and carefully opened it with scissors.

He slid a large omelet onto a plate and handed it to Japheth, who gaped in amazement. It had an odd yellowish color, but otherwise, after tasting it, he had to agree it was fairly good. Not quite like his mother's home cooking, but good, considering it was an instant packaged meal warmed with this boiling water.

"Dare I ask how old this is?" Japheth inquired as he stuffed the last forkful into his mouth. It had a slight metallic aftertaste, but the addition of some spices would overcome that.

"Let me see," Methuselah said looking at the label. "It is less than one hundred years old. A nice flavor, don't you think?" He laughed, while Japheth put his plate in the sink. "I hope you enjoyed that, because packaged food is all we have while we are here. I spent years preparing it, but now we will not waste any time cooking. We can use all of our time for study and work!" Methuselah clapped his hands. Studying and working instead of eating was something Japheth would never become used to. Meanwhile, he rinsed his plate in cold water while he kept clear of the brass pipe that was still hissing.

"The boiling water comes from a geothermal vent," Methuselah explained as he waved in the direction of the sink while they walked back to the workshop. "The natural vent is about a mile from here, where I tapped it and ran the pipe underground for hot kitchen and bath water. Cold water comes from an underground spring. I also made a brass valve to mix the two, so we won't have to take boiling or freezing showers. But I never had time to install one in the kitchen. Maybe you can do that someday. But enough of that. Let's start our tour!"

CHAPTER 36

Methuselah's Underground Laboratory

The two walked at a rapid pace back into the main laboratory area, where Methuselah eagerly began his orientation speech.

"The cavern is divided into four laboratories, each outfitted for special research. Plus a central library in an upper level. I want you to finish a project in each of the four disciplines before you return to the ark."

They made their way into a room where the oily smell was the strongest, and mysterious gray metal objects lined the walls.

"The mechanical lab is a machine shop with power- and hand-operated tools. Think of it as a place where mechanisms construct other mechanisms as small as miniature chronometers and on up in size from that. You'll start with the smaller tools, mostly used for working soft metals such as copper, bronze, silver, and gold. You can progress to fashioning devices from stronger metals such as iron and iron alloys. Those are more difficult to manipulate; you'll have a chance to work with those metals later. In back is a forge that can soften and melt almost any metal. You can also use the forge to mix special alloys for castings. Castings—in sand molds for the most part—can reduce the amount of machine cutting needed, if the castings are done with sufficient precision," Methuselah explained.

"You are probably wondering where the power comes from to run the machine tools," he continued. "Just like the sawmill we built, I have my own water-driven power source. I routed a spring from higher up in the hill to create a head of water in a large pond that drives a turbine located entirely underground. When the main clutch is engaged, it turns a master gearbox for power takeoff drives extending into each of the workshops. Pulleys in the ceiling over each machine can be engaged individually as you need to run a machine, exhaust fan, hydraulic lift, or whatever.

"This is the lab where I came up with the designs for the glass prisms and reflecting mirrors we built for illuminating the inside of the ark. The soft ambient light you see coming from the ceiling is from daylight focused through prisms strategically placed in the hillside and directed down to us using polished mirrors. We supplement that light with gas lamps and some interesting concentrated lights, which I will show you in a few minutes."

They ascended a short flight of stairs to a room higher in the hillside and almost directly above the machine shop. Methuselah moved a lever in the wall inside the door, and, when he switched another lever, Japheth heard the hum of fans spinning up. He felt a slight breeze that sucked the door shut behind him.

"The chemical laboratory," Methuselah introduced the second workshop, "is located higher in the hill because it needs better ventilation of toxic gasses. It has taken me a long time to gather samples of every known chemical reagent, catalog them, and put them in glass containers for use in my experiments. When you learn how different chemicals react with each other, there are an unlimited number of things you can do with them.

"Certain chemicals can be mixed safely to produce light, instead of using an open flame lantern. I put the two chemicals inside their respective glass vials and put one smaller sealed vial inside the other. They can stay this way indefinitely without reacting as long as the two chemicals remain separated. But when the inside vial is broken and the container is shaken to mix the chemicals, the light glows brightly for about four hours. Slightly different chemicals make different colors of light. If you want to concentrate the light, you can clamp the glowing vial in the center of a parabolic mirror and produce a rather intense beam. I will tell you how I discovered these chemicals when we get to the last laboratory.

"I have some ideas for a chemical light that works differently, without needing to break a vial. That would make a good project for you in this lab. You can use those lights in the ark, too." Methuselah then walked to the end of the chemistry lab and entered another room that contained what looked like a large tube inside a cage in the center of the room.

The cavern was divided into four laboratories, each outfitted for special research.

"The astronomy lab consists of this instrument, which is the largest and most powerful telescope ever built. Even the imperial service doesn't have one like this. When the sun goes down, we'll spend many nights here. We are far from the city lights, so there is excellent visibility. We also have a master timekeeping device, which will need to be reset periodically for astronomical observations. Once we do that, it will keep time to within one second per month."

"But can't the telescope be seen from outside and give away the lab's location?" Japheth asked.

"The roof is closed now, and the telescope is entirely contained inside the hill. At night we will open the roof and raise the telescope in its cage on a hydraulic pedestal so that it extends past the top of the hill. The doors in the roof are well hidden from the outside and we only open them in the dark. But if someone were standing on top of them, they would get a real surprise! All I have ever done is startle some deer grazing in the grass," Methuselah assured him.

"This is also where the star charts are kept that students carefully assembled from the early time of Adam," he continued. "In fact, one of Adam's great interests was in figuring out what God had intended when He said that He gave us the sun, moon, and stars for signs, and for seasons, and for days, and years. The chronometric purpose of these celestial objects was figured out early in his investigations of the seasons, days and years, but the 'signs' part was hard to understand. Eventually, Adam, with his students at the Institute, concluded that the signs meant 'purposes' when they discovered a way to use the constant, reliable movement of celestial objects to precisely locate a position on the face of the earth. Investigators also found that some objects in the sky are highly reliable and useful in the short term, while others seemed to follow almost random, constantly changing paths. Anyway, the result of almost a thousand years of observation was a library of mathematical formulas for the location of the sun, moon, and major stars at any point in time. The calculations, using multiple angular measurements, take several hours to derive a location. It is accurate to a few hundred yards. I was able to program these formulas and tables inside a mechanical calculating device that can give a location on the earth in minutes instead of hours. I call it an astrolabe, or solar geolocator. It weighs almost eighty pounds. I want you to make a smaller one that fits in your pocket. Another project!" Methuselah exclaimed excitedly.

"I've saved my favorite laboratory for last," he said finally. "I call it my biomimicry laboratory because it combines the study of animals with the construction of different mechanical or chemical devices. When God created the animals, He gave some of them fantastic abilities. As you know, Adam was first and foremost a zoologist. The joy of his life was to study animals and understand their unique gifts. He spent his whole life doing that. Your father is very much like him in his love of studying animals. My interest is in understanding them enough to reproduce their unique functions in man-made devices. That chemical light is a good example. I studied fireflies to understand how the light in a firefly's tail worked and how it could so easily turn on and off. It was obviously some sort of biochemical reaction, and I was able to isolate the specific chemicals. Then, I reproduced those chemicals in the lab and eventually came up with the right proportions to generate light. After years, I was able to do what God, the Master Inventor, built naturally into every firefly at the time of creation. Later, I will show you some other devices that came from studying wonderful creatures in our world. Maybe you can come up with some new things yourself!"

They spent the rest of the evening discussing what interested Japheth the most in the lab and what projects he wanted to tackle. The list became long as Japheth was overcome with wonder and enthusiasm. Methuselah reminded him that the time would pass quickly, and it was best to pick a few things to explore in depth so that he could master the arts behind them. With his whole life ahead of him after the flood, Japheth would have time to extend his knowledge and skills if he already had the basic theory and principles of science to work with. His work in the next few years would simply open up his imagination to all that could be accomplished.

Methuselah assured Japheth that he would one day become a great inventor in his own right and that he need not follow exactly in his great-grandfather's footsteps by imitating or reinventing discoveries of the past. His goal, as a scientist and inventor, would be to stand on the shoulders of those like Methuselah and others who came before. Japheth would have many opportunities to build his dreams in the new world.

While that seemed in the far distant future to Japheth and his youthful mind, Methuselah was sure that it would be Japheth and his descendants who rebuilt civilization. What shape that new civilization took would depend on how God used them in the few years after the flood.

CHAPTER 37

Animal Training Facility: "The Farm"

Next Day

After breakfast, Japheth and Methuselah left the underground cavern to see the animal training facility that Methuselah simply called "The Farm." It complemented the secret underground workshop with innovations and discoveries about the myriad living creatures in the world. It was here that mankind extended his knowledge of animals and made strides in obedience to God's original mandate to "subdue" the earth. Adam rightly understood that this was his task—to understand animal species so that he could use animals for the benefit of mankind. With this mandate came a responsibility to treat animals with understanding, to coax them to submit to man's commands and not to exploit or mistreat them. When certain animals were raised for use in family sacrifices, they were to be given special care since their substitutionary death on the altar was a figurative picture of a spiritual redemption. God had been very clear that, while man was created in the image and likeness of God and was only a little lower than the angels, this did not give him license for wonton destruction or careless abuse of animals. Cainites did not observe this care for animals and, as a result, they found that few beasts submitted willingly to them, and they often resorted to cruel measures to force animals into submission. This was, in part, what further encouraged brutality among their youth and propagated a culture of abuse among adults. It was no wonder that God was disgusted with the violence He found on the earth in these last days.

When Japheth stepped out of the shadows of the dense forest half a mile from the laboratory and gazed upon the farm complex extending before him, he was amazed at how closely it resembled where he grew up. He and Methuselah paused to admire open fields that extended toward the distant forested hills.

"These open fields in the middle of the Great Forest are a surprise. Are they natural, or did you clear the forest to make them?" asked Japheth.

"Some of each," replied Methuselah proudly. "Your father and grandfather thought they needed more open space to work with the animals, and so one of their first projects was to harness teams of the larger dinos to do the clearing. The large herbivores spend all their waking hours foraging for food and nobody thought they could be trained to do useful work. But your father tried raising them from infancy—incubating the eggs, hatching them, feeding them high protein foods, and teaching them to respond to simple voice commands. Now this method is used all over the world. I suppose nobody had as much patience with them as your father. By the time his animals reached adulthood, he could put a harness on them, climb on their shoulders, and move them around by speaking to them. He and his father felled the largest trees around the edges of the natural clearing and the first dino pulled the logs to the first experimental sawmill I had built on the river and we made piles of timbers for building construction. Noah taught other species of dino to clear trees and plow, and they planted fields of grain to feed the other animals. In fact, the tri-horned dinos we used in Eden's Promise to run the cranes are distant offspring of that first generation."

They walked to some of the outbuildings, and Japheth noticed that there were no animals in sight. It was strangely quiet for a farm, and he wondered why this was.

"I suppose there are no animals here because you haven't been to the laboratory in a while, right?"

"That's partly the case. When your father and grandfather moved to build your home, we essentially abandoned the farm here. I never felt comfortable hiring people to run this place, since it is wide open and it would be too easy for Cainites or dishonest Sethians to take the animals for themselves. While you and I are here we will bring in some animals to study, but we will release them when we leave. Let us go look at the other facilities, and I will show you some of the things I think you might work on."

Japheth had another question that was bothering him: "All of the farm buildings are obviously in the open, but you keep the underground laboratory hidden. Why is that?"

"That is a good question." Methuselah replied. "Of course, the obvious reason is that the animals need open space for growth and exercise so we could not easily hide them or the large farm buildings underground. The most important reason for keeping the farm in the open is that there is no technology here that anyone could benefit from. The underground laboratory holds the accumulated knowledge and equipment from more than one thousand years of scientific research and invention. If those fell into the wrong hands they would be used for unspeakable evil. The location of the laboratory must be protected at all costs."

With that said, they entered a large building built from beams three or four feet in thickness and wall planks almost a foot thick. This was more than a barn for domesticated farm animals. The barns at Eden's Promise for sheep, cows, and horses were smaller and nowhere near as sturdy.

"Is this a dino barn?" Japheth asked.

"Yes. This is where your father raised dinos from babies and trained them."

They stood in the center of what would otherwise be simply an open space for exercising, except it was ten times larger than any Japheth had seen. The roof was more than fifty feet above their heads. Open skylights ran the length of the peak. Roof trusses extended more than one hundred feet across and rows of trusses repeated for almost three hundred feet the length of the barn. He had never seen anything like this. At the far end of the open arena, wide doors ran from floor to ceiling and hung on rollers.

"Impressive, isn't it?" Methuselah commented with pride as he craned his neck to look up to the skylights. "I designed it, and we built it using the first dino your father trained. He trained others inside this building, until they were ready to go outside and work. Once trained, he no longer kept them cooped up inside because there was no need; they came back whenever he called them. You could tell they were very attached to him and he to them. It was scary when they came running in response to his call. We ran for cover because we were sure they would trample us in their rush to greet him. But he stood fearlessly still, while the ground shook from their feet pounding until they skidded to a halt in front of him and bent down to carefully eat the treat he held out in his hand. It was a terrifying sight I could never get used to."

From the dino barn, they walked around some other buildings that were used for feed storage and smaller barns—at least, small by comparison to the largest structure—that would hold domesticated mammals raised for wool and milk. There were separate barns for training animals for different tasks such as for riding and cultivation of smaller fields.

At the edge of the clearing, about a half mile from the largest buildings, were a number of trees that were isolated from others in the forest. The top of the largest tree, a redwood, reached upward more than five hundred feet. The trunk was thirty feet across at the ground and its bark consisted of overlapping slabs two and three feet in size like oversized wooden shingles on a roof. Near the top of the tree, or at least as far as they could see, large branches spread like the brim of a gigantic hat. Looking up made Japheth dizzy.

Methuselah walked around the trunk and found a rope looped conveniently around a piece of bark. He untied it and shook it hard against the trunk to make sure it was free from tangles. As far as Japheth could tell, it hung straight down, though the exact branch it hung from was obscured in mist, high up in the tree.

Having made sure it would bear his weight, Methuselah turned to Japheth. "You follow me, and we'll see if the platform is still there." He pointed directly above and began climbing hand over hand, using the rough bark for footholds. With no large branches visible for several hundred feet, Japheth stared up in amazement. It was inconceivable that anyone could climb the tree at all, least of all his ancient great-grandfather. After mustering his courage, he pulled himself slowly up the side of the redwood.

Japheth rested gratefully halfway up on a small branch that bent when he put his weight on it. But the limb held while he caught his breath. Forcing himself to not look down or up, he stared at the bark next to his face and held tightly to the rope. He wondered what the rope was made of, not recognizing the material. *Probably something Methuselah invented in his spare time*, he thought to himself.

When Japheth reached what he figured was their destination, he rolled onto a large wooden platform and lay on his back looking at the branches and the sky above him to catch his breath. Here he was almost five hundred feet above the ground, lying in what felt like an overgrown tree house. He and his brothers had built a tree house once back at home to play on, but this was no toy. He didn't even like going up into the one at home. When he sat up, he took stock of the structure and was amazed at its size. The platform encircled the trunk and extended more than thirty feet out from it in every direction. It was constructed from large beams like those in the dino barn, which looked tiny in the distance below. Fortunately, there was a low, very solid-looking wall around the edge of the platform. If it were a flimsy railing, you wouldn't get him anywhere near the edge. But, when he hesitatingly stood up, he felt safe from falling off the edge of the platform. At least the tree wasn't swaying in the wind. Japheth had never told anyone how much he hated heights.

Methuselah came into view from the other side of the trunk. He had a box in his arms that he set on the platform and opened up to reveal what looked like brass musical instruments.

"What are those?"

"These are whistles that mimic calls of certain dinos. We used these to get them to come here for us to study. The biggest ones are the Quetzas, with wing spans over forty feet across and weighing more than five hundred pounds. Your father tried to find nests to see if he could raise one from infancy, but they were too carefully protected. Quetzas do not like humans."

Methuselah held one of the tubes in his hands and blew into the end, while covering the top air hole with his finger. It emitted a low-pitched cry or moan that sent chills up Japheth's spine. He made the sound several times before placing the instrument back in its box.

"These whistles call small reptile flyers that are not afraid of us; your father trained them to be messengers. The big Quetzas sometimes flew by the platform out of curiosity, and he would watch them for hours. One time, when he and I climbed up to a Quetza nest high in a redwood tree like this, the protective mother and father beat us back and we couldn't get near their babies. Your father's dream was to train a Quetza and fly on it."

Japheth had seen Quetzas flying high above the ark compound, but he never realized his father had studied them. He wondered what it would be like to examine them up close and determined he would spend time up here and call some in for closer study. He'd first have to overcome his fear of heights if he were to do that, but it might be worth it. More than just studying them, he wondered what it would be like if he could train one to carry him on its back and go where he wanted.

Their descent from the treetop platform was faster than their ascent, using a smooth metal clip in the shape of an "S" with a handle on its side. The rope made two sharp bends through the metal device and their descent could be slowed by twisting the handle and increasing the friction between the metal and the rope. Although the metal became hot, it kept them from being burned by the rope passing through their hands. Each was able to control his descent easily by pushing out from the trunk of the tree and simultaneously releasing tension on the clip as he dropped twenty or thirty feet in a single jump. In short order, they were on the ground, where they left the clips in a box and looped the rope around a peg in the tree.

On their walk back to the workshops, Japheth wondered what it would be like to fly on the back of a giant reptile and guide it wherever he wanted to go. That thought stuck with him all the way back to the laboratory. He lay in his new bed that night and thought of the things he would build in the next few years. But being able to fly was something he continued thinking about as he drifted off to sleep.

CHAPTER 38

Weather Outpost #22

When Akmed gathered his fellow students and supervisor Tuuki around the chart table and spread his evidence before them, a grim look replaced his earlier excitement about making a new discovery and becoming famous.

"We've been tracking this anomaly for several years now," Akmed began, "and there's been significant change in the regular oscillations from our first measurements. There is still a peak in the altitude of the vapor barrier layer every fifteen minutes, but there has been an amplitude increased from one thousand feet of variation back then to extremes of more than five thousand feet of variation now." Akmed laid the charts in front of Tuuki with a slight hesitation of anxiety, while Mobi and Karaa looked on with interest.

"Well, that settles it then. We can stop making the measurements, since nothing much has really changed," Tuuki stated flatly. All the students looked at him in surprise. "We can wrap this up and not make any more measurements." The pursuit of truth indicated by the data was too much for him to acknowledge and he struggled to deny it.

"Wait until you see this," Akmed followed quickly. "Like you asked, I received independent confirmation of the oscillation, and I can prove that the measurements we made are accurate. An astronomical observatory made starlight measurements, and they are oscillating at exactly the same frequency we measured here."

"Who authorized those measurements?" Tuuki exclaimed defensively. "I gave you no permission to go through outside channels!"

"I know, and you can relax. This was all done informally, and nobody knows the request came from this outpost. My cousin at Observatory #3 did it as a favor to me. I wanted to wait and tell you when that and other data could be compiled for a final report."

Tuuki's face remained expressionless, so Akmed continued. "There is another piece of data that has changed significantly since we began measuring the layer. The bottom of the layer, where the balloon is bobbing, is at least ten thousand feet lower than it was when we began. We've never seen the vapor boundary layer that low before. So, not only is it oscillating more, but it's base is getting lower, too. All we know is what we see from our lone observatory, but I would bet you this is happening all around the world, and the canopy is getting lower than it has ever been in earth's history."

The students turned to Tuuki for his reaction, but, before he could say anything, Akmed continued. "Also, with the lowering of the bottom of the layer by ten thousand feet, we see a decrease in the temperature at the boundary." Akmed plowed ahead as he saw he had Tuuki's full attention—his supervisor leaned forward in his chair to catch each word. "Most people think temperature drops continuously, or linearly, as you go up in altitude from the warm surface of the earth, through the nitrogen-oxygen atmosphere and water vapor layer surrounding the earth, into the cold vacuum of outer space. But this is not the case. The high altitude vapor layer is made of water molecules in a gaseous state, and because they are exposed directly to the sun's rays they are therefore heated slightly. It's true that most of the solar infrared or heat rays pass straight through the transparent gas to the earth's surface, but some of the sun's energy excites the water vapor molecules, causing them to heat up by a degree or two, and that's what causes the warmer water vapor layer to float over the colder layer of the atmosphere below. In fact, that's what's made the layer so stable and has kept our weather virtually unchanged for the past sixteen hundred years. Until now, that is—and for reasons that nobody can explain."

Akmed leaned back to indicate he was finished and looked Tuuki straight in the eye. "We need to tell somebody about this, and soon. We have enough data to predict when the layer will reach a critically low level and risk condensation, causing a monumental torrential downpour. We're talking maybe five or ten years, which might just be enough time for the government to do something about it."

Tuuki was obviously uncomfortable with this suggestion, and he shifted uneasily in his chair. Although it appeared earlier that he took exception to what his student had reported, he was now more pensive. Expecting to hear more questions or denials, the young interns were surprised when Tuuki stated in a quiet voice, "This is absolutely unbelievable. It's much worse than I ever thought." They had never seen him this pale before. He looked like he might be sick to his stomach. He spoke as if he was in a faraway dream.

"You know, I've worked at remote weather outposts like this all my life. It's boring and quiet on the top of mountains in the middle of nowhere, and that's the way I like it. Surrounded by nature, nobody bothers you. This data profoundly changes everything we have known or assumed about the upper atmosphere." He looked into the eyes of each of the three students and continued. "Listen to me carefully. I want you to make copies of all your data, charts, and notes, and hide the originals someplace safe. Do not tell anyone else that you have performed these experiments or gathered this data. Akmed, you need to warn your cousin also. I will take these copies by hand to the regional office and see that they get the attention they deserve." As he nervously licked his dry lips, he looked at each of them again. "This is very good scientific work, and I'm proud of each of you. Now, hold down the station until I get back, and remember to keep your original materials hidden. If someone comes asking questions, you play dumb and wait to hear from me. Your lives could be in danger, so whatever you do, do not confirm or even acknowledge involvement in any of this until you hear from me. Do you understand?"

Each nodded slowly. Akmed spoke for the three of them. "Right. Nothing gets out until we hear back from you."

They spent the rest of the day copying all the notes and removing all references to themselves and Akmed's cousin. Tuuki would take full responsibility for the data and conclusions, and the frightened students had no objection to him taking their names off the results. They wrapped the originals in an oilskin bag and buried it far from the main building. Tuuki gathered the copies into a heavy envelope. He put it in his backpack, shook hands with each of them and headed out the door. "Goodbye, and don't forget to be careful."

"Mr. Tuuki," Akmed called as their supervisor crossed the threshold. "What if we don't hear from you?"

He stopped and turned. "My advice would be to lock up the station, go home to your families, and pretend this never happened. If what we think is happening really does happen, you might want to find another mountaintop and wait there for a while. But then again, if that old prophet is right, the mountains will draw more crowds than they can hold and none of us will be safe."

Tuuki ambled down the mountain trail with his backpack slung over his shoulder.

Weather Outpost #22

Three Months Later

The three students ate dinner on the front porch of the outpost building. "Will we ever see him again?" Karaa asked.

They all knew who "he" was. Tuuki had been gone for so long that they'd given up hope that he would return. They needed to figure out what they were going to do next.

"I've decided to stay here at the post and see what happens," said Akmed. "Whatever's going on with the vapor layer is the most fascinating development in atmospheric science we'll ever experience, and I want a front seat when history is made. What about you guys?"

"We want to stay together," Mobi said as he took Karaa's hand in his. "And we've agreed that we'd like to remain here with you, if you don't mind."

"I welcome the company! It can get very lonely on this mountain and we've know each other for a long time now. We make a good team."

They made plans to continue gathering vapor layer data as long as their supply of balloons, hydrogen, and charts held out. And they had plenty of food supplies to last them for a couple of years. They also had funds to buy food from farmers, if that became necessary.

Akmed made his first executive decision as the most senior person at the post: "I think we should continue to send our standard reports to headquarters by mail from the village, so the empire has no reason to send someone to replace Tuuki, or worse, shut us down. It's clear he isn't coming back, and we can all imagine why. Maybe they'll leave us alone and not send anyone to investigate."

CHAPTER 39

Methuselah's Underground Laboratory

Five Years Later

The years passed like blurred pictures in Japheth's mind as he and Methuselah came up with new ideas, ran experiments, and built devices that the young student never thought possible. The time spent in the forest laboratory was more than an education. Methuselah was teaching him how to develop his imagination to access new levels of creativity. Working with Japheth, Methuselah asked questions and pushed him to come up with answers, and then urged him to prove his answers by writing out an equation, citing a reference from the library, conducting an experiment, or building scale models of machines.

They studied animals of all kinds, from the smallest to the largest, with new understanding as Japheth learned their behaviors and uncovered their God-given abilities. Japheth built a microscope with pure glass lenses from molten sand, and machined brass for the frame with fine adjustment gears. He magnified living cells to figure out how they worked and concluded each time that they functioned as tiny machines themselves, each reliably performing its designated function, each created by God for a specific purpose. Even the smallest insects gave him new insight into life when he then tried to build something to mimic their form and function. Even if he didn't succeed, he was able to gain a new appreciation for the design built into every living thing. His goal was not to create life itself—only God could do that—but to see if he could understand the functions of a living being or one of its parts enough to mimic it on a mechanical or chemical level.

Methuselah called this inventive process "biomimicry," because it was the best they could do to make a mechanism *appear* to imitate life on a simple, functional level.

When the time neared for Japheth's graduation from his studies and their return to the compound at Eden's Promise, they discussed the things they had accomplished since their arrival five years earlier. It was bittersweet to think that someday they would be leaving the workshop and farm where Japheth had spent such fruitful and happy years. He had learned enough to be able to solve complex quantitative, logical problems, and then turn his ideas into tangible devices. Time at the farm seemed more like a hobby than like actual labor in its tranquility as he developed relationships with different animals, especially those that had never before been tamed. Those that until then had been considered too ferocious or aggressive were acting the only way they knew how when encountering humans. They expected mankind to threaten their existence and reacted accordingly. But Japheth befriended them, and sometimes he thought he preferred them to the friendships of other human beings. When he got to know them and they understood him, they could be trained to perform simple tasks consistent with their abilities. Humans needed to come to them at their level, understand their motivations, and appeal to their natural instincts, which were for the most part not intended to harm others.

It was the biomimicry that resulted in the most marvelous discoveries and advancements. One example of dramatic progress in the field was with chameleons. Japheth and Methuselah had made a photosensitive compound that replicated the ability of the reptile's skin to change colors. It took them months of testing to find out how to make a thin coating of this compound for inanimate objects so that they could be rendered essentially invisible against their immediate background. After much testing, they coated a small wooden model of a horse and put it outside in the grass. They only found it later by combing through the undergrowth on their hands and knees, feeling around for it. It had taken on the color and texture of the grass so well that they thought they'd never find it. And that's how it went, day after exciting day. Never a day went by without having an idea or making a discovery of some sort that nobody had ever thought of before.

One of Japheth's first projects was a great source of pride for him, and he had continued refining, rebuilding, and testing it while he worked on other tasks. Methuselah had challenged him to disassemble a large astrolabe device and understand its operation solely by deducing the functions of its individual parts and their interactions. Having done that successfully, his assignment was to build another, but of a size that would fit into his pocket. Japheth spent much time in the library learning celestial mechanics from the ancient charts and formulas built up over the centuries, and then confirmed these in the observatory. He made exacting measurements of the brass gears, levers, and counter drums to compare them with the assembled charts. He then spent days reproducing the components in miniature. He added some new features as well, and, when he was ready to show Methuselah his finished work, they walked outside for a demonstration.

When Japheth removed the shiny case from his pocket Methuselah's eyes widened in surprise.

"That is smaller than I thought you would make it," he exclaimed. "When I said make it so it could fit into your pocket, I thought you'd make it fit into a larger pants pocket. That fits so easily into your shirt pocket!"

Japheth walked into the partial direct sunlight of a clearing and unclasped the face of the device, which fit neatly in his hand. It measured three inches by six inches and was a little more than an inch thick. The two flat covers on each side opened on opposing hinges, and half of the internal mechanism unfolded to expose a tiny optical tube.

"The covers open up to form a stand, so it sets on level ground. The more level it is, the more accurate the readings. The telescope in the middle can then have an unobstructed view of the sun."

Methuselah interrupted him. "That is a telescope?"

"Yes, though it isn't one you would want to look through, since it magnifies an image of the sun and focuses it onto the calibrated target underneath. The idea is to adjust the telescope with these small dials until the image of the sun rests exactly on the center crosshairs of the receptors. You don't need a perfectly clear day or direct sunlight for this to work. As long as you can get an image to register for a few seconds, it will give you a result."

"But what does that give you? Don't you need to do some calculations?" Methuselah thought he could see where this was going, but he was incredulous that such a small device could do it.

"So, once you get the sun to register in the center of the target, you press this first button and the calculations begin. The azimuth and declination angles between the sun and the earth are taken from the telescope, and, with the time from the chronometer, the formula built into the calculator on one side of the cover comes up with an arc of possible locations on the earth. Then, you need to wait a few minutes and take a second sun measurement. When you press this second button, it does another arc calculation and compares it to the first to give an exact location read-out here on this counter. Oh, and the location is stored in a small memory drum inside the other cover, so you can retrieve it later, if needed." Japheth looked to Methuselah proudly and could tell from his great-grandfather's face that he still had questions. Japheth wondered if he would want to check the output for accuracy.

"How did you get my astrolabe to fit into such a small folding device?" Methuselah asked. "I can see how you miniaturized the telescope, but most of my astrolabe was for memory to store all the possible sun angle calculations. Where are you storing them?"

"I don't store those, because I don't use look-up tables at all. In my research of the sun charts, I found reference to a study that used formulas with assumptions that approximated the tables to a reasonable level of accuracy. I built a computing system of precisely sized gears and levers to replicate the formulas. When I inserted the angle measurements and the chronometer reading for time and day of the year, it quickly gave the arc I needed. The hard part was figuring out how to make a third order approximation using only mechanical pieces." Japheth had, of course, oversimplified what he had done, but he thought it would satisfy Methuselah for now.

"You said you had come up with additional features. I'm excited to see what else this little thing does!"

"It does two other things," Japheth explained. "First, giving you a set of location numbers is probably not too useful unless you have a frame of reference for the numbers. So, I gave this the ability to guide you to a destination from where you are now. You can pre-save the coordinates of up to three destinations, so that later it will tell you how to get from your present computed location to your selected, pre-saved destination. It seemed that might be useful some day."

Japheth picked up the astrolabe, folded it closed, and pointed to recessed dials on the cover. "This dial gives the magnetic heading to the first destination put into the memory. The Farm is our first destination, and this indicates its direction is one hundred ninety degrees from North. Turn it over and there is a magnetic compass in the other cover. So, the Farm is in that direction," he pointed toward the trees. The second dial says it is less than one mile from here. We can use the compass to walk directly there through the woods. The case and all the mechanisms are made from non-magnetic brass, so the compass is quite accurate. Like I said, you need to pre-calibrate your destinations by making sun measurements at that location, so you can't navigate to someplace you've never been. But at least this means you will always be able to find your way home."

Japheth handed the shiny case to Methuselah, who held it carefully and examined the dials and compass embedded in the covers.

"Japheth, this is the most elegant mechanism I have ever seen. It is worthy of the finest craftsmanship. I'd like to use it for a while and see how accurate it is. May I use it?"

"Of course. Just be careful. I don't think I could build another in less than a year!"

Methuselah put the object in his pocket and they made the familiar trip to the Farm complex. As they walked along, Japheth rehearsed his explanations of some of the other projects he had recently completed.

"You wanted me to spend some time in the chemistry workshop," he said to Methuselah, "and though that wasn't my favorite discipline, I came up with a few little things that will be useful. First, I made special sticks that you can carry in your pocket for lighting fires without using flint. Some phosphorous, sulfur, and glass powder are mixed with a little water and put on the end of a splinter. You rub it on any abrasive surface and the splinter will ignite. Coat the stick with wax and it'll be entirely waterproof, in case they accidentally become wet.

"I also worked with the explosive black powder I found in a container in the lab. I ground a measure of that coarse powder into fine dust and added white metal powder dust, and I packaged them inside in a tight parchment tube. The tighter they're packed, the better. A fuse on one end of the tube can be lit with a fire stick. When the tube ignites, it makes a brilliant flash and loud bang that will stun anyone near it for a few seconds. By the way, I took that can of black powder outside to a covered shed, because it made me nervous keeping it next to all the other chemicals in the lab.

"You'll like this, too," he went on. "I studied a peculiar species of spider that paralyzes its prey with a gas emitted from a gland in its forehead, rendering larger insects completely helpless. I was able to concoct a replica of this gas using two chemical liquids that made a cloud of stun gas when they are mixed. I strapped two glass vials together and threw them against the wall to see if they worked. I guess they did, because I woke up on the floor an hour later. I probably should have had the vent fans on then, right?"

CHAPTER 40

Weather Outpost #22

"Akmed, you need to come see this!" Mobi was uncharacteristically excited and out of breath when he ran past Akmed's bunkroom and shouted his news. He and Karaa had been out all day looking for the instrument from the latest balloon flight, which now made special measurements each time they were flown. Although they hadn't been submitting reports to headquarters about these special tests, they continued to send more probes up to the vapor layer, and the results showed continued oscillations. Akmed figured the results would simply show more of the same.

When he entered the chart room, Mobi and Karaa had already rolled out the chart and he settled in his chair to examine the usual oscillation. But instead of a gradual undulation, he saw an irregular up and down motion punctuated by abrupt changes in the probe's altitude. There was no question that the instrument was riding along the bottom boundary of the layer, but it was jerking in a manner that was almost unnatural.

"This does not look good," he observed.

"That's what we thought, too. Karaa and I peeked at the paper on our way back from the landing site and were really shocked. What does it mean?"

"What it means," Akmed replied, "is that the layer is more unstable than we've ever seen. Within the past five years, it hasn't changed much, but now it's suddenly exhibiting a new type of motion. All I can think is that we are getting closer to an instability that could eventually tear or rupture the balance between the lower atmospheric air and the higher invisible water vapor in the canopy.

"What we need to do," Akmed told them, "is look for other changes in the atmosphere or natural phenomena that haven't happened before. Let's run up all of our instruments in the next few days to see if anything else has changed. We'll make a list of all the instruments and sensors we have here at the station and plan on exercising them first thing tomorrow."

"That makes sense, I suppose," Mobi replied carefully. "I'm not sure I want to know about other changes—that would only spell more bad news."

Mobi was right. Things in nature were changing, and those changes only made the students more unsettled.

"Something as simple as a compass has been acting weird." Mobi put it on the table in front of the other two. "Watch, and see what it does."

Sure enough, the point of the needle held steady for about five minutes, and then shifted ninety degrees before it returned to its usual northerly direction.

"How long has it been doing that?" Akmed asked.

"Since I thought of checking it this morning. I watched it long enough to be sure it wasn't the table shaking, or something magnetic causing it to move, but then I couldn't watch it any more. If the instrument is right, it seems the earth's magnetic field is *moving*."

"What else have you found?" Akmed asked, changing the subject.

"Last night, I looked at that shining star in the east that's been there for the last sixty years or so," reported Karaa, "and I noticed it had a new milky-colored halo around it. So, I used my 10X monoscope to look at a whole lot of stars, in case it was just that one that had the halo. I looked at dozens until I got a headache, and each had a milky, circular halo around it." Her face wrinkled with a worried expression. "If I had to guess, I'd say the invisible canopy is starting to condense."

"That's two new phenomena. Anything else?" Akmed asked, ignoring her comment.

"No. Nothing else," Mobi replied. "Except for those two things, everything else is normal as far as our instruments can tell. Nobody else would notice, unless they were looking for these changes specifically. I think we should only be concerned if there were some phenomena that the average citizen might take notice of and that the government couldn't ignore."

No sooner had he spoken than the building shook slightly and the windows rattled for five seconds. Their bodies felt the seismic wave move through the building, and no sooner did they sense its powerful effects than it was over. For the first time in human history, the earth's crust had shifted, and they were too stunned to know what to make of the new sensation.

"What in the world was that?" Mobi exclaimed.

"Not sure," Akmed said as he regained his balance and tried to keep his voice from shaking. "Maybe that was the new phenomenon that nobody can ignore."

"I'm scared," Karaa cried softly, moving closer to Mobi as if he could shield her from the terrifying thoughts that raced through her imagination.

CHAPTER 41

The Farm

The microtremor went unnoticed by Japheth and Methuselah as they walked to the Farm where Japheth planned to surprise his grandfather with a flying demonstration. But, before heading to the redwood tree platform, they stopped at the dino barn to see Methuselah's new transporter. Japheth had worked with this particular dino to tame it to carry the weight of a human with a harness and saddle. Methuselah had given him the project of finding and training an animal that could carry a single human at high speeds for long distances. For that objective, Japheth had selected an herbivore that walked upright on strong hind legs and stood fifteen feet high. There was no doubt it could carry the weight of a human at high speed for long distances; the question was, did it have a temperament that would allow it to be controlled easily and not bolt for its freedom? Up until now, their experience with horses was that they could move quickly on roads for short periods of time, but they had difficulty making time in the forest or through dense underbrush. The large dino quadrupeds were too lumbering and not able to make much speed. They could barrel their way through just about anything and were easy enough to train, but when it came to speed and endurance, they were not suitable for all-day traveling. Unfortunately, most upright bipeds were carnivores and much too aggressive to reliably carry a human without turning on him without warning.

Japheth's assignment was to train a large, bipedal herbivore, but he had had to find and capture one first. Many others had trained bipeds for transportation, but this was a new experience for Japheth.

He and Methuselah searched the library for references to the types of food these animals ate and the characteristics of their habitation. The herbivores normally shunned human contact, so it was unlikely they would come across one in the forest. After a systematic search for miles around the farm, they narrowed down their possible habitats and laid out food they knew the species would be attracted to. After waiting for many days in a tree blind, they saw one eating the fruits left out in a clearing. It had a classical form, and its height of almost fifteen feet indicated it was a full-grown adult. They waited until it moved out of the clearing to track it quietly. Their patience was rewarded an hour later, when they came upon the adult feeding three newly hatched juveniles in a mud and branch nest in the reeds near a stream. The adult, apparently the mother of the babies, was upwind of them and hadn't heard or smelled their approach. The two observers waited in the brush for hours until the mother left to gather more food for the ravenous infants. Quickly, Methuselah and Japheth walked to the nest and removed one of the small animals—the size of a large turkey—and wrapped it in a blanket they had brought for that purpose. Not sure what would happen to them if the mother returned now, they took off in the opposite direction at a run and muffled the cries of the little dino.

They reached the dino barn at dusk and locked the baby in a stall with food and wood shavings for bedding. They hoped the mother wouldn't find it or she would probably stop at nothing to tear into the barn and rescue her baby. To their relief, within days, the infant dino had adopted Japheth as its new mother, and he fed it and cared for it five times a day. As it grew, Japheth took it for walks inside the large dino training area and eventually allowed it to run at top speed from one end of the arena to the other. Within six months, the animal had grown to three quarters its full size, and Japheth had it wearing a training harness and saddle. Soon, he could climb onto its back and walk it for short distances, responding to commands with a set of reins. Finally, he tried letting it run with him inside the arena, and it was all he could do to hold on when it accelerated to top speed. Its ability to go from standing still to racing speed was literally breathtaking. When he finally took the animal for a run outside, he was barely able to stay on. When he returned to the barn, he was out of breath and the dino was puffing and snorting for more. Japheth decided to name him Lively, because he had the temperament and energy of a youngster who gave his all in whatever he did. He was sure Lively could run all day until he dropped, he loved to run that much.

Later, when Japheth taught Methuselah how to ride Lively, they took turns riding the huge reptile through the forest for hours. They both loved the tamed animal that ran with all his heart.

As much as Japheth loved Lively's competitive temperament and the fun he had training him, the challenge of his life was to train a flying dino. There were many more redwoods besides the one they had climbed when they first arrived at the farm. Japheth had spent many quiet days on the platform in the mist, overcoming his fear of heights and slowly scanning the sky within his field of view, looking for Quetzas. One pair had a nest about a mile from his tree, but all he observed was their coming and going. He couldn't detect the exact tree or nest they were using as a home. He wanted to see if he could observe the nest from the ground, so he walked in that direction one day. There were so many trees in the grove of redwoods that he strained his neck looking directly up in hopes of seeing a nest or one of the adults flying by. He never saw any evidence of the adults or their nest during his walk among the trees, but then the most amazing thing happened: a large brown egg bounced in the thick moss at the base of one of the trees and rolled into a clearing. Japheth turned quickly and ran toward the sound. The egg was more than two feet in length and appeared to be dented. The shell was the consistency of tough leather, and, after running his hands all around it, Japheth concluded it had sustained a strong blow when it hit the ground, but it had not cracked or broken. He looked up and half-expected to see an enraged adult Quetza boring down on him from above like a diving bomb. He walked away and waited to see what would happen, and after a while he concluded the egg was either not missed or had been kicked out of the nest intentionally. In any event, he picked it up in both arms—it was as heavy as a full bag of grain—and carried it back to the dino barn.

Avoiding the end of the barn where Lively was stabled, he put the egg into an empty stall, cushioned it in straw, and locked the door. All he could do was let events take their natural course and hope that the egg would hatch and that he would one day be the proud father of a baby Quetza. He had nursed Lively into adulthood and trained him for human transportation. Could a flying reptile be trained to respond to human commands and actually carry a human as well?

The egg hatched a few days later, and, like all reptiles, the baby immediately attached itself to the first creature it saw and assumed it was its mother. In this case, the baby was a she, and she loved Japheth as much as a leathery, bony, cold-blooded reptile could. She ate anything and everything Japheth brought to her and grew much faster than Lively had in his first six months. The leathery reptile had to be moved to a double stall, and eventually to a specially constructed stall with a thirty-foot sliding door that she could walk through to the training ring. Japheth spent weeks trying to get her to fly inside the open arena, but it didn't seem like she knew how. She would extend her wings, stretch up and down on her legs, and flap so hard that the wind she created almost knocked Japheth over. He concluded that since Quetzas lived in the upper branches of tall redwoods that they didn't know how, or simply couldn't, take off from the ground. Unlike birds, they lacked strength in their legs to leap high enough off the ground to take flight. If they had to become airborne by jumping from a height to gain speed before they could fly, that meant eventually he would have to take his charge up to the platform and push her off. The thought of that was terrifying to him, but it might be perfectly natural for her when the time came. But he wasn't ready for that yet, and he didn't know if she was ready either.

Meanwhile, he began training her to respond to spoken commands that permitted him to put a harness and saddle on her while she stood still. She took to the harness and saddle easily enough, but she didn't like it when he tried to climb into the saddle. She immediately shook him off and flapped her wings in protest. It was a long time before he could climb on her back without falling off, and she always skipped, shook, and squawked. Japheth hoped she would like to fly with a passenger, because the last thing he needed was for her to get high into the air and shake him off.

Unlike the whistle his great-grandfather had showed him when they first climbed to the redwood platform, Japheth had perfected one that was silent for humans, but evidently annoying to Quetzas. Whenever he blew into the metal tube, she would jerk her head in the direction of the sound, even though Japheth could hear nothing but the sound of wind in the tube. Using rewards of her favorite fruits and nuts, he trained her to come to him when he blew on the whistle. He hoped this would work when the time came for her to be let loose into the wild.

That day arrived soon enough, and Japheth was apprehensive about taking his baby on her first flight from the platform. Japheth and Methuselah led her on a line to the base of the platform tree and gently tied her wings next to her body with a strong rope and put her feet in a mesh bag so she wouldn't scratch them when she thrashed about. Her mouth was tied shut and a canvas harness placed around her body. Japheth climbed to the platform, now a trivial task after all his practice, and, using a block and tackle, he lifted the animal high into the tree. When she was safely settled on the platform, but still with her wings tied, Methuselah joined him. They had agreed earlier that if she didn't fly off the platform of her own will, they would leave her there rather than force her off. Maybe a mother Quetza could have forced her to learn to fly that way, but Japheth couldn't find the heart to do it.

Either way, they didn't have to wait long. When they untied her feet, beak, and wings, she walked awkwardly to the end of the platform and jumped up onto the edge of the low railing. She balanced there for a moment, looking at the trees in the distance. She looked back at Japheth as if to say, *I'm ready. Goodbye.* And she jumped off.

They quickly ran to the railing to see her plunging toward the ground. Halfway down she opened her wings to their full forty-foot expanse, gave a strong thrust, and shot off into the open air. A few more flaps and she rose up level with the platform and circled around to fly within a few feet of their heads. When she flew by them, Japheth yelled, "Good girl!"

The giant winged reptile headed for the trees in the distance, where Japheth had found her.

"She couldn't possibly remember that, could she?" uttered Japheth. "She was still in her egg when I found her on the ground."

"Probably not," commented Methuselah. "She is just looking around at high trees where she would be comfortable. They are her natural habitat, and that's how God made her. One day, she will build a nest in a high tree somewhere and have her own babies. That is how she is genetically programmed. And someday, you will have to let her go."

"I hope she comes back when I call her. Did you see how she hopped up on that railing and jumped right off? She didn't even hesitate. Just took to the air like it was nothing. Wow!"

They waited more than an hour, and Japheth became as concerned as if she were his own child out past her curfew. He was pacing the platform and muttering to himself, "Where is she? When is she coming home?" Methuselah laughed at his maternal fretting.

"What are you going to name her?" Methuselah asked. They had discussed this earlier, and Japheth wanted to wait and see if she would fly today. "I assumed you would give her a more affectionate name, since you act like she is your daughter," Methuselah chuckled.

"I suppose I do," Japheth replied. "It feels like I've spent the last year constantly teaching and training her. She's so ugly that only her mother would love her anyway. I will call her 'Brave Baby' or 'BB' for short, since she took to the air from her perch without fear.

"She *is* your 'baby,'" replied Methuselah. "I hope she does not take it to heart and expect me to dote on her like you do."

Japheth returned to his worrying and pacing while he searched for her in the sky.

Tiring of Japheth's ceaseless fretting, Methuselah said, "Go ahead, blow the thing and see if she comes back."

Japheth blew the whistle and continued searching the trees in the distance for a glimpse of BB to show herself.

While he and Methuselah leaned on the railing looking for her to appear, they heard a rushing wind and snapping branches above their heads. They looked up to see the winged animal dropping toward them. The two men dove to the safety of the tree trunk.

BB landed, if you could call it a landing, with a less-than-graceful crash on the platform. She stood up and shook her head a few times, pecked at her foot to remove a branch, and then squawked at Japheth as if to say, *"Here I am!"*

Japheth went to her immediately and gave her a hug.

"We need to work on your landings there, girl."

"Not bad for a first flight, I would say," commented Methuselah. "Shall we leave her here with some food and get back on solid ground? I don't think she will go far, and we know she will come when called. Besides, all this flying is making me hungry." They left BB in her new home and descended to the ground.

In the days that followed, Methuselah was proven right as BB easily adopted the platform as her new home, and Japheth could always find her there or call her to him with the whistle. He had accepted that some day she would build her own nest and leave the platform for good. But until then, he had to teach her to fly with him on her back. That would be his crowning achievement as a dino trainer.

When that day came, he faced it with the same trepidation he had when she went on her first solo flight. By now, BB was comfortable taking off and landing from the platform. She would go off for days at a time, and he would see her flying high above the farm searching for food and probably for a place to nest. Maybe she was searching for a mate. Japheth wasn't ready for dating yet.

But after she became used to flying with an empty saddle, he figured the day for him to fly with her couldn't be put off any longer. He had Methuselah stand on the ground with a medical kit handy in case his weight was too much for her and they fell straight to the ground. He climbed the tree to the platform, hyperventilating more from the anxiety than from the exertion of the ascent. He found BB waiting for him eagerly, and he put the saddle on her, all the while talking to her in a soothing voice. Of course, she had no idea what was going to happen, so the soothing talk was really for his benefit and not hers. *Talk about a blind leap of faith*, he thought to himself.

He climbed into the saddle and the animal flinched. He avoided her bony forehead as she twisted her head around to look at him, clung to the harness and tried to put his feet in the stirrups. At that point, she looked as incredulous as he felt. He hadn't considered what he would do to coax her to the edge of the platform for takeoff, since she had always flown off her perch of her own volition. Now that he wanted her to fly, he was having second thoughts.

"Let's go, girl," he said in a commanding voice.

As if they had practiced this together a thousand times, she jumped onto the railing and without hesitation dropped over the side. Japheth clung to the harness, and one foot flew out of its stirrup. This was it, and his stomach rose to his mouth as he saw the ground coming up at them fast. They were heading straight for Methuselah, and he could see his great-grandfather's eyes bulge as he backed quickly away from what he imagined would be the impact point. But just like she had done on her first flight, BB spread her wings, gave a strong surge, and leveled off. A few more flaps and she climbed toward the treetops. With a half dozen more strenuous flaps of her long wings, she was out of Methuselah's sight.

"I don't know who's more foolish, that boy or that bird," Methuselah exclaimed.

Japheth had closed his eyes when he was certain they would hit the ground, but still held his death grip on the harness. That proved to be a good idea since both his feet were now dangling out of their stirrups, and the wind was rushing by. He crouched closer to his animal's back to reduce the force of the wind and opened his eyes. By now the large dino barn was in the distance, and he couldn't pick the platform out from the other redwoods near the farm. It seemed that she had her own ideas about where to go with him, so he hadn't planned for where they were going or if they would make it back to the platform. Both his hands were cramping from his iron grip on the harness. He wasn't about to ease up on the reins.

He reminded himself he should be enjoying the view. But he was still terrified; simply enjoying the ride would require more relaxation than he could muster at the moment. But he did manage to look out rather than down, and he marveled at how far he could see. Even with mist and haze, he could see for miles. The Great Forest covered rolling hills to the horizon. Here and there he saw patches of huge trees, probably more giant redwoods, and open areas of meadow or swamp. As they turned and lost altitude, he held on tighter and looked straight down at a large grassy area, where a herd of more than fifty herbivores dined on the long grass, totally oblivious to them flying overhead. Giant quadrupeds that had necks and legs the size of trees stood half-submerged in a swamp, contentedly munching on water plants.

As much as Japheth was enjoying the view, he felt they should return since he didn't want BB to tire and settle down somewhere miles away from the farm; especially if, for some reason, she landed on the ground. He knew that if she couldn't take off from the ground with him, he'd have to walk back.

Wondering how to get her to go back, he began talking to her. "I've had enough, BB. Let's go back home. Let's turn around and go back. Now. Turn."

Maybe she understood, though he doubted it. Whatever it was, she somehow sensed that it was time to go back to the platform. At least that's what he hoped.

He could tell they were going back in the general direction of the farm, and in a few minutes he spotted the large barn and then the platform. He was concerned about her landing, but figured she had mastered that maneuver herself already and would do the same thing, only landing a little heavier. Sure enough, she flew toward the landing spot, pivoted about twenty feet above the platform, and dropped onto it with a thud. He gratefully climbed off and stretched stiff hands and shaking legs.

"You're a good girl," he crooned in her ear. He kissed her neck and was rewarded with an affectionate glance and playful nudge of her bony forehead.

When he reached the ground, Methuselah was there to give him a long hug.

"That was like nothing I have ever seen, my boy. Congratulations on another first!"

"It was unbelievable, wasn't it? I'm still shaking. How did it look from the ground?"

"It was as I had imagined, but I never believed it possible. You are the first man in history to fly, and I am privileged to have seen it with my own eyes. I believe I am almost in tears." He hugged Japheth again and they walked back to the workshop.

Japheth put his arm around his great-grandfather's shoulders and wondered what else could possibly happen to top all the things they had done in these past five years. During that span, they had often lost all track of time and sometimes forgot to eat or sleep. They had reached new heights of achievement in science and engineering, beyond what even Methuselah had expected. It was the best time of Japheth's life. His enjoyment was only interrupted by the thought that an ominous deadline loomed in the near future that he would have to eventually face.

CHAPTER 42

City of Enoch, Resistance Safe House

Same Day

The small apartment was dark, decaying, and rat-infested, but at least, for now, it was safe. Eli rose from the moldy couch in the living room to make sure the curtains were closed and turned to survey what might be the last cell of the Sethian Resistance. The two men and one young woman were all who remained of a large network that had offered assistance to Sethians who fled imperial patrols hounding down the last remnants of their race. How could humankind have fallen so low that it exterminated more than half of its own population? Cainites couldn't blame it entirely on the Anakim, since they went along with, and willingly implemented, the emperor's bloodthirsty designs out of a combination of their own revenge, hatred, fear, and greed. Believers among the Sethians had gone from meek passivity to active resistance when they saw their families torn from their homes and sent to camps where they were never heard from again. But by the time an organized Resistance had formed, it was too late.

This dank apartment had been their safe house for the past two weeks, and it might be their last place of refuge. They had to be careful when they moved, even in the cover of darkness, to make sure they were not followed. Fear of discovery by patrols or betrayal by neighbors was constant. Eli had sent one of the men out earlier to look for another empty apartment in the many abandoned buildings, but he could tell his small team was exhausted from being on the run. Their numbers were down to Eli, who was the cell leader, and the three others. The two men, Aktek and Reliant, had become hardened by years of sleeping wherever they could in the urban ghettos, navigating the sewers, and eating what garbage they could find. The dumpsters were empty now as the city had been swept of most Sethians, and few Cainite civilians remained. There were still Sethians and Cainite officials in the city who had sworn allegiance to Anak and were permitted, for now, to move about with imperial passes. At first, the Resistance had forged temporary passes, but then their expert forger had been captured and all their good passes had by now expired. Eli knew he could count on his two men to lay down their lives for the Resistance, and for him personally, but he also knew that time was running out.

The young woman, Hannah, complicated matters.

Eli and Aktek had found her years ago hiding in a high-rise apartment building when they were searching for food. She was a terrified child, and it was obvious her parents had hidden her before they had been violently taken away. She couldn't speak when they came across her, and to calm her, they had remained in the abandoned apartment until the food was gone. They had taken her with them as they scurried each night from one hiding hole to the next. It seemed odd that her parents had been taken because she had the mark of Cain on the back of her neck, and that was at a time when most Cainites were immune from the imperial dragnets in the city. Eli concluded that she and her family were Cainite by birth, but had been secret believers betrayed by their neighbors. In any event, Eli raised her as his daughter and she became a valuable asset to the Resistance cell. She had sharpened "street smarts" that were unrivaled among the Sethian men. With the mark on her neck she could pass in public as a Cainite, if needed, but Eli taught her about the Lord and prayed she might one day become a believer. It was unfair to a young girl, he knew, that they lived such a life of secrecy, guile, and deception, hiding among the filth of the city, trying to avoid capture and save those that they could.

It was a fervent concern for their continued survival that caused Eli to gather his "family" to make plans for what might be their final operation.

"Aktek, were you able to find a suitable alternative location to hide?"

"Maybe," his closest friend replied uncertainly. "It's a few blocks away and seems to be deserted, except for the building's superintendent living in the basement. He was passed out from liquor when I entered last night and searched all twenty floors of the structure. Most of the apartments were trashed and none had food that was edible. We could go to one of the upper floors and barricade the stairwell below. We've stayed in worse places."

Eli gave a nod of agreement "We will keep that as an option, though I would rather stay here for now, if it is safe. We need the rest."

He paused to change the subject. "Have you noticed anything strange happening lately?"

"Like what?" asked the one they knew by his code name, "Reliant."

"Do you mean the floor shaking every ten or fifteen minutes?" Hannah asked pointedly.

"Yes." Eli explained, "I am concerned that the end is finally upon us and that everything Noah predicted is finally taking shape." His seriousness was characteristic of an old man, but this time he was more somber than usual. "If that is truly the case, we need to implement the final phase of our purpose. At this point, it matters little what happens to us. We have faced death many times, and this final test will come as a relief. We know we are in the final year, so it could come at any time now."

Eli turned to Reliant and asked, "Can you send the message to my brother, Methuselah?"

"Yes, sir. I can contact him whenever you wish."

"It is time. Do it as soon as you can. He has not been here in many years but he knows the secret procedure for contacting us. He will understand that this final contact is urgent, and he will come to the aid of the surviving remnant no matter what the danger or cost."

Before Reliant departed, Eli added, "Address the message to 'Meta' so he knows it truly is from me." When Reliant had closed the door to the apartment, Eli turned to Aktek and Hannah with a somber look.

"It has been a privilege for us to be part of this final phase of the Sethian Resistance. We do not know how many of us are left, but we will remain faithful to the end. Our solemn duty now is to see that the Book of Adam is taken onto the ark. Each of you has risked your life countless times in the past, and I am asking you to do so again this last time. Are you willing?"

"Yes, of course," replied Aktek. "I have followed you all these years and will do so to the end. My life is in the Lord's hands." He bowed his head.

"And you, my dear Hannah—is it too much to ask of you? It pains my heart to lead you into such danger because you are so young."

Her smile revealed not a trace of fear or concern. "I owe you my life, Eli. Don't worry yourself with concern about me. My faith is also in the Lord who made heaven and earth—nothing will happen to me that He does not allow."

Eli choked up with pride and reached out to grasp her hands in his. He had done his best to raise her in their hard, disciplined Resistance ways. She had learned to survive in the streets of their decaying civilization, and yet she had grown into a mature Sethian woman possessing calm self-awareness, confidence, sincerity, and selflessness. This little girl was now a grown woman, ready to face the biggest test of her life.

CHAPTER 43

Methuselah's Underground Laboratory

Two Days Later

The routine of inventing, testing, and manufacturing new mechanisms in the lab was interrupted by a bell ringing in the distance. Judging from the high pitch sound, it was a very small bell and the ringing came from high in the ceiling. Japheth found Methuselah in the machine shop using a cutting lathe with one of the belts humming loudly. He was wearing his earplugs, so of course he didn't hear the bell. When he saw Japheth standing in front of the lathe, he turned it off and took out the earplugs.

"What is it? Is something wrong?" he asked, concerned.

"No, nothing's wrong. I just heard a bell ringing somewhere in the ceiling and wanted to ask you what it was. I don't know how long it's been ringing and can't quite locate it."

"Ah, I've been wondering when we might receive a message from my contacts and hoped we would be hearing from them soon. Let us see what it says."

"You've been expecting a message? I didn't know you were still in contact with anyone in the city. Is it about the Book?" Japheth overflowed with questions.

They went back into the main lab area, climbed a set of stairs to the ceiling, and opened a trap door. A ladder led up to a dark attic containing cages of birds. Sunlight filtered into each cage through an opening to the outside. A small bird pecked eagerly on a shiny piece of metal levered to a string attached to a small bell. Methuselah put bird feed into the cage and lifted the animal out with both hands.

"This is one of the birds from the city. I left some of them with my contact there long ago. I wonder what he has to say." Methuselah carefully removed the paper from the bird's leg. They descended back to the lab, where he unrolled the small scrap of paper.

It contained urgent news:

META

WE NEED YOUR HELP TO RECOVER THE BOOK AND TAKE IT TO THE ARK.

WE ARE IN GREAT DANGER. COME QUICKLY—THERE IS LITTLE TIME.

RELIANT

"We have ignored the outside world for too long," lamented Methuselah. "It seems that the Sethian extermination has progressed with more efficiency than I thought possible. I must go to the city of Enoch immediately to recover the Book." Methuselah paced the floor in his characteristically deliberate manner as he pondered all the possible courses of action. He would pace nonstop until he figured out the best plan. Japheth had learned that it was best to be quiet and let his great-grandfather think in his own inimitable way.

"I think it would be best if you stayed here, while I go to Enoch and find out what is happening. I can travel alone faster, and, if the Book is nearby, I will get it and come back here. We can then return to the ark together with the Book. That is our highest priority now."

"But I want to go with you. What if you run into trouble and get captured?" Japheth said with concern.

"Please do not take this the wrong way, Japheth, but you would not be much help to me in the city, since you are not familiar with its Cainite ways. And if Sethians are being rounded up, it means that speed and stealth are all the more essential. I have some special methods of protection, knowledge of the city, and do not forget that I have had experience dealing with imperialists. I hope you understand this. You would slow me down if I had to make a quick escape."

Methuselah rushed around the lab throwing things into a backpack and came to Japheth with more concern registered in his face than Japheth had ever seen. Methuselah was always in complete control, but now he was almost in a panic.

He paused at the door and turned abruptly, like he had forgotten something, and looked at Japheth standing speechless and alone in the middle of the lab.

"You will be safe as long as you do not leave the lab," he assured his great-grandson. "I will send you a message in code as soon as I find out what is happening. Use the decoding machine I showed you with the settings untouched. The message will be brief and it should not take you long to decipher it. Always listen for the bell in the attic." With those terse instructions, Methuselah's mind shifted immediately to his contact with the Resistance as he exited the large main door and closed it with a firm thud that echoed through the lab.

Methuselah ran to the farm to harness Lively for the ride. He knew they could make it to Enoch in less than the seven days it took to travel there by foot; the energetic dino could run through forest underbrush, race across open fields, and jump fences with little trouble. He commanded the beast to kneel while he put the leather saddle on its back and strapped it on tightly around the animal's shoulders and under its small arms. It was going to be a hard ride. He climbed up into the saddle and, after he checked that it was firmly cinched, the beast quickly rose on its hind legs. The animal knew it was time to run, and it was anxious to go. With his bag secure, Methuselah said, "Run!" and gripped the reins tightly as he was nearly jerked out of the saddle. They accelerated out of the yard and began their journey toward the city of Enoch, bounding over shrubs, fallen trees, and rocks in their way on the forest floor. The surefooted animal was eager to run, and they left the farm behind in a soft rumble of padded feet.

CHAPTER 44

City of Enoch, Abandoned Warehouse

Five Days Later

The city was quiet when Methuselah arrived past midnight. He tethered Lively in a park to eat grass while he made his way to an industrial area where he and Reliant had held clandestine meetings before. Methuselah waited in the shadows across the street to see if anyone was inside. He had no other way to contact Reliant, so all he could do was wait with his senses keen to any presence and approach the building when he felt it was safe. His contact was trustworthy, and his note had said it was urgent, so Methuselah knew his contact would be waiting for him every night as their prearranged contact plan required.

A muffled cough in the distance immediately put him on alert that someone was in or near the building. It might be a signal for him to approach, but, when he heard a shush from a different direction, he became apprehensive that his contact had been compromised. Confident that he was still undetected, Methuselah stayed hidden in the dark. He would have to find better cover before dawn, but for now he wanted to see who was out there.

An hour later, still well before dawn, Methuselah noticed that the sky became slightly brighter. He checked his pocket chronometer to see if it had stopped, but he concluded that it was working properly. Why was it getting light so early? Soon he had the answer, when what looked like a luminescent sheet brightened the sky with a pale-green light. This light softly illuminated the ground around him, and when he pulled his special chameleon cape over him it took on this same dark green, and

Methuselah disappeared into the artificial background. Hoping he was still concealed, he peered through his cape at the building more intently and thought he saw two men at each end of the structure, crouched where they should have been concealed in shadow, but now the green lights in the sky revealed their positions. They were police commandos in black gear with weapons at the ready. *Where was Reliant? Were they waiting for him, or had they set this trap for someone else?*

Finally, there was movement as two more commandos came out of the building's entrance and looked around with their weapons at the ready. They were followed by two more men, dragging what looked like a body. They went behind the building and soon returned empty-handed to join the others, and the group walked down the street talking and laughing amongst themselves. Methuselah could hear them in the distance even after they disappeared around the corner. He waited a few minutes and ran to the building. He reached the front entrance without a shout of discovery and slowly walked around the corner to find the body facedown in a pile of trash. When he felt no pulse and saw the clothes saturated with blood from the man's brutal death, he finally turned the body over to see the face of his contact staring into the brightening green sky.

Reliant was dead, and now Methuselah had no way of responding to the message from the Resistance without placing himself in greater danger. He also lacked the resources he might need to make a more concerted attempt to find their cell, because he had planned to be away only a short time. He determined to go back to the lab, pack the additional materials needed to survive in the city on his own for a lengthy time, and return to the center of the city as quickly as possible. His prayer, as he gently closed Reliant's eyes, was that he had not revealed anything about the Resistance cell to his interrogators before he died.

Before he returned to his lab, Methuselah rose to search for Reliant's bird cages, probably hidden somewhere high in the rafters of the old warehouse, to send Japheth a message.

Weather Outpost #22

Same Day

The sky had changed color from its usual blue during the day to a darker purple, masking a dimming sun. At night, colorful lights in the northern sky moved slowly across the entire expanse of the heavens, only to repeat again in an unending cycle. Nobody had ever seen these lights before. They obviously meant something, but what? And when the daylight went away, the night stars were masked by clouds that appeared and moved quickly from west to east against a backdrop of green sheets of light high to the north. Clouds moving this fast were unprecedented. The sunsets and sunrises would become dark shades of red, whose resemblance to blood was ominous.

It wasn't just these events in the sky that had caught the three students' attention. The earth tremors had become stronger and more frequent—enough to wake them in the middle of the night. The shakings came at random times, but they occurred several times per hour.

"Do you think we should report these events? After all, we're supposed to be a weather observatory." Karaa looked to Akmed as the most senior of the team, even though he was still only a student himself. She was more frightened now than she was at first, unsettled by the frequent earth tremors and dramatic changes in the sky.

"I don't think it would do any good, and, besides, don't you think the authorities at headquarters see and feel the same things we do? My guess is most of the population is terrified by now, and anything the emperor says to calm them will fall on deaf ears."

"You're right, it's just that I don't feel secure here any more. Can't we find someplace safer?" she asked.

"No, this still seems like the safest place for us to be until we see if the phenomena get better or worse. If conditions get worse, no place on earth will be safe."

Rephaim Military Base, Armory

Next Day

U'ungu tried without success to get the attention of the team members amidst the din of the assembly of troops, who were still arriving after the recall order that had been issued that morning. His voice didn't carry over the sound of everyone talking at once. Finally, Chief Inspector Baaki arrived and shouted the familiar military command: "Attention!"

The room quieted gradually as conversations ceased, and all turned to the two leaders at the front of the room. Baaki knew what the meeting was about and didn't wait to introduce Secretary U'ungu.

"We have received our official orders from the emperor to initiate Operation GOLDEN DAWN. By now, this should be no surprise to any of you, as a simple look outside will confirm a severe change in conditions. Although the earth disturbances are believed to be only temporary, we have recommended, and the emperor has approved, our movement orders as palace buildings have been structurally weakened and could be in danger of collapse. GOLDEN DAWN will commence immediately, and all of you will gather your respective teams and begin to assemble your charges from the imperial government staff and the emperor's consorts. All personnel and equipment will be marshaled here within the next seventy-two hours, when we will move to the temporary palace to the south."

Baaki looked around the room for signs of fear on people's faces and, seeing none, signaled the end of the meeting, setting everyone in motion with the command, "Dismissed!"

Secretary U'ungu moved to his side immediately and spoke quietly, so only Baaki could hear him, "What about our plan to reach the destination ahead of the emperor?"

"It is all in place, Mr. Secretary," Baaki assured him. "Once the assembly of government officials and the emperor's entourage leave the palace, we can move ahead of them on the main road and travel with my personal bodyguard. I assure you that nothing can stop us now."

CHAPTER 45

Methuselah's Underground Laboratory

While Japheth waited for Methuselah to return, he worked on making slight adjustments to his pocket astrolabe and imagined what might be coming in the next few days. Either Methuselah would return with the Book and they would make their way safely to the ark, or . . . what? What if Methuselah couldn't find the Book and came back empty-handed? What if he couldn't reach his contact and he lost the trail of the Book forever? The uncertainty was killing him as he evaluated of all the things that could go wrong and how everything pointed to not being able to recover the Book.

And what about finding a wife? Japheth had put that thought out of his mind since he'd come to the lab, but, now that the time to enter the ark was approaching, he wondered how God would make His prophecy come true. He chuckled inside, wondering if Methuselah would bring a wife back with him from Enoch. *Would you rather he bring back the Book or a wife for you to enter the ark with? Ha! What a choice!*

On the eleventh day of Methuselah's absence, the bell rang in the attic indicating that a message had arrived. It was in code, of course: a handwritten list of seemingly random letters, in groups of five characters with a space between each group. It meant nothing if anyone intercepted it. The complex decoding process would take Japheth an hour using a mechanism that Methuselah had shown Japheth before he left.

The device was housed in a simple, unmarked wooden box resembling a small suitcase with a metal handle and hinges. Its heavy weight hinted at its densely packed contents of intricate brass drums, wheels, gears, levers, dials, and buttons. Japheth set the box on a table, opened its cover, and made sure that the indications on each of five dials at the top of the machine corresponded to the five-letter secret cipher that Methuselah had set in the decoding wheels before he left for the city. Six rows of brass buttons with a letter embossed on each button were inlaid in a wood covering that hid a mechanism inside. Three rows of buttons were for coding a new message and three rows were for decoding an existing message. Japheth began the decoding process by carefully pressing individual polished buttons in sequence to match the first five-letter "word" in the handwritten dispatch. When he finished the five letters, he depressed a lever on the side of the machine, and he heard gears and wheels whirl unseen for several seconds. When the sound ceased, Japheth noticed that five new letters had appeared on the dials. These five letters were the first five letters of the decoded message, which he wrote down. He continued the process of carefully typing the next five letters in Methuselah's message, depressing the lever, and waiting for a new sequence of letters to appear on the dials. Japheth had no idea how the machine worked, but Methuselah assured him that it worked every time—provided he made no mistakes typing the buttons in exactly the same order he read in the original message.

Eventually, after figuring out where spaces between words belonged in his transcribed letters, he could read the plaintext communication, which Methuselah had signed with his boyhood nickname for authentication:

JAPHETH

UNABLE TO RECOVER BOOK. PERSON WHO KNOWS THE LOCATION IS DEAD. RETURNING NOW FOR MORE SUPPLIES.

META

Methuselah was returning to the lab. Surely, he would need Japheth's help to retrieve the book—if only as a lookout and packhorse for supplies—now that the circumstances in the city had changed. Japheth was heated with excitement at the thought of going there with Methuselah. No question, his great-grandfather knew his way around the imperial forces there. Japheth began packing for the trip immediately, realizing he had little time to get ready. If Methuselah had departed Enoch soon after sending the message that meant he could be arriving at any time. Japheth readied his pack with some spare clothes and preserved meals. He took his pocket astrolabe along with some chem lights, several multi-knives, and a canteen. He figured Methuselah already knew what he needed, so he didn't prepare anything for his great-grandfather. By the time he returned, he would already have a list in his mind.

When Methuselah arrived late that night, he fell exhausted onto the couch without taking his traveling cloak off. "We went at full speed through the forest for days with only short stops for rest and food," he sighed. "I feel almost dead."

He lay there while Japheth took off his boots and cloak and prepared a hot drink and a sandwich for him. Methuselah hesitated to tell Japheth too much about what had happened in the city of Enoch. "The imperial patrols are now positioned all throughout the city—day and night—and all of the roads leading out of it have checkpoints. I had to stay clear of patrols because I don't have the necessary imperial identification. They arrest anyone who even looks Sethian and take them away to a central 'processing facility' on a military base; what happens after that, we can only speculate. If the rumors are true and Sethians are being exterminated at these locations in large numbers, we have very little time indeed.

"I passed some deserted farms on the way back; it was apparent that the Sethian occupants had been taken by force against their will. Their empty homes were ransacked and in ruins. The fact that the countryside, and even parts of the city, is so deserted confirms that the imperial plan must be nearing completion. With the emperor conducting such widespread dragnets, you will need to be very careful when you make your journey back to the ark."

"Wait. Won't I be going with you to the city?" Japheth asked in surprise.

Methuselah answered firmly. "I would feel better if you were back on the ark compound with your family. There is no telling how far the imperial forces will go in their search for Sethians. The compound is the only place where I can be certain you will be safe and that you will make it onto the ark in time to be with your mother and father."

"But what about the Book? I can't get on the ark without it! I have to go with you to Enoch to get it!"

Methuselah understood Japheth's intense emotion about finding the Book, but he remained firm. "This is my quest, not yours. Besides, your father would never let you go with me to Enoch, especially this close to the time." Methuselah turned around and started for the supply room, opening his backpack.

"Father can't stop me from going," Japheth insisted.

Methuselah turned and searched Japheth's face.

"Do you really mean that? I know you think you are almost an adult, but going against your father's wishes, especially at a time such as this, would cause your parents great anxiety. And the risk is so great. I do not think this is a good idea."

"But this is more important than him wanting to keep me safe at home. You've said so yourself that the Book of Adam is the most important book ever written. You said we need to do everything possible to find the Book so it can go with us on the ark and into the new world. After everything you've told me about the Book, have you changed your mind about that now?"

"No, I haven't changed my mind about that." Methuselah eased himself into a nearby chair with a groan.

"And besides," Japheth said, crossing his arms in determination, "didn't God say my wife and I will be on the ark together? That's what He told my father, and you said it was confirmed in the Book. So let's trust in God to get me on the ark in time, and let's go together to get the Book while there's still time!"

"You do have a point there, young man."

Methuselah finished his meal and said finally, "Let me sleep for a few hours, and then wake me. We will need to prepare some essentials and leave by daybreak. Lively cannot carry both of us and we would be too conspicuous traveling by dino. It will take us at least seven days to reach the city on foot. Now is not the time to be racing across the countryside to be captured by an overzealous police patrol." With that observation, Methuselah fell back in his chair, immediately asleep.

Japheth set the alarm on his wrist chronometer and lay back to think about the dangers ahead of them. The next moment, he awoke to the annoying buzz from his wrist. He looked at the empty couch and noticed Methuselah was already up and hunched intently over a workbench in the next room.

"Ah, you are awake," Methuselah said as Japheth rubbed the sleep from his eyes and approached the worktable.

"What are you doing?" Japheth asked.

"Creating some travel documents for us in case we get stopped. My hope is that they will at least slow down any officials we might come across long enough for us to break away and continue our journey. I was able to bypass all the highways and side roads between here and the city last time, but, with the new checkpoints and border patrols, the main roads may be unavoidable once we near the city."

As Methuselah placed official seals on the papers, he explained more about his trip. He had found the meeting place soon enough, but it had already been compromised by the police, who had killed Reliant. The imperial forces had all but wiped out the Sethian Resistance in Enoch and the last remaining cells were being rounded up. The waning Resistance confirmed the rumors of the extermination of Sethians all over the empire. Anak, with Cainite support, had unleashed his Anakim warriors on the peaceful Sethians and many were murdered in their homes. That their numbers were now so few was demoralizing. The righteous had been systematically annihilated, and the humans who remained were the most vile of humanity. All of this served to confirm God's judgment: it was time to start over and rid the planet of their curse.

"I have sent a messenger bird to your father telling him about our plans to retrieve the Book. I know he will not be happy about you going to the city of Enoch with me instead of returning immediately to the ark. I have apologized to him for doing this without first seeking his approval, and I hope he will understand how important it is that we do everything we can to send the Book into the new world with you."

Methuselah continued to pack as he spoke to Japheth. "Now, we must focus on the tasks at hand. First, we need to reach Enoch safely and make contact with whoever is left of the Resistance. The message from Reliant intimated that his leader knew the exact location of the Book. He, or whoever is left, will help us retrieve it. Second, once we have retrieved the book, we need to get you back safely to the ark. When you see how drastically the situation has changed in the world outside, you will understand why it is critical that we not waste any time in finding the Book and getting you back to the ark." Methuselah stopped packing suddenly to address his great-grandson with the utmost gravity.

"Finally, I need you to know that, having firsthand knowledge of what the circumstances are like in Enoch, I am ready to give my life to make sure that you make it back to the ark safely. Once we retrieve the Book, my sole purpose in life will be to see that you do not come to any harm before you are able to enter the ark. Now, we must get our things together and move out," Methuselah said, turning back to his packing.

Japheth was momentarily stunned by Methuselah's unreserved willingness to sacrifice his life and he couldn't think of a reply. He had learned that his great-grandfather never exaggerated, and he hoped Methuselah would not have to give his life to get him back to the ark.

They gathered a few remaining items and closed down the lab. Japheth looked around at what had been his home for the past five years, and he wondered if he could build a laboratory like it in the new world some day. Maybe not, but its memory would live with him forever.

They left the lab to visit the Farm one last time and release all the animals. It was only humane that they have freedom in their last days on earth.

After letting all the animals free, they set off toward their destination. Japheth understood what Methuselah had said about why it was now so urgent that they recover the Book and return to the ark swiftly. The night sky, normally lit only by stars, was bright with waves of pastel colors moving slowly across the domed expanse. And it appeared to be closing in. Japheth stared in wonder at the soft, undulating pallet of changing colors. Methuselah nudged him, and they began walking through the forest toward Enoch, planning to stop at the nearest farm, which they should reach by daybreak.

"Can I ask you a question about something that has been puzzling me?" Japheth said as they walked along a partially obscured path. "That message you sent in code took me nearly an hour to decipher with the code mechanism in the lab. I can't imagine all the mathematical calculations that must have been done inside that box to unscramble your message. Did you find another machine in the city to encode it? Did Reliant have one?"

"No," his great-grandfather replied.

"So how did you encode it?" Japheth asked. Before Methuselah could answer, Japheth halted in the middle of the trail.

"Wait. Did you encode it . . . in your head?" he asked.

"Of course," Methuselah replied casually. "Let's go. We have a long trip ahead of us."

Japheth shook his head in disbelief and hurried after his great-grandfather, who was already out of sight along the path.

The two made their way silently through the brush toward the city of Enoch while the colorful lights in the sky faded in and out, casting ominous shadows on the forest floor.

BOOK III

JAPHETH

Final Ten Days
1656 AC (After Creation)

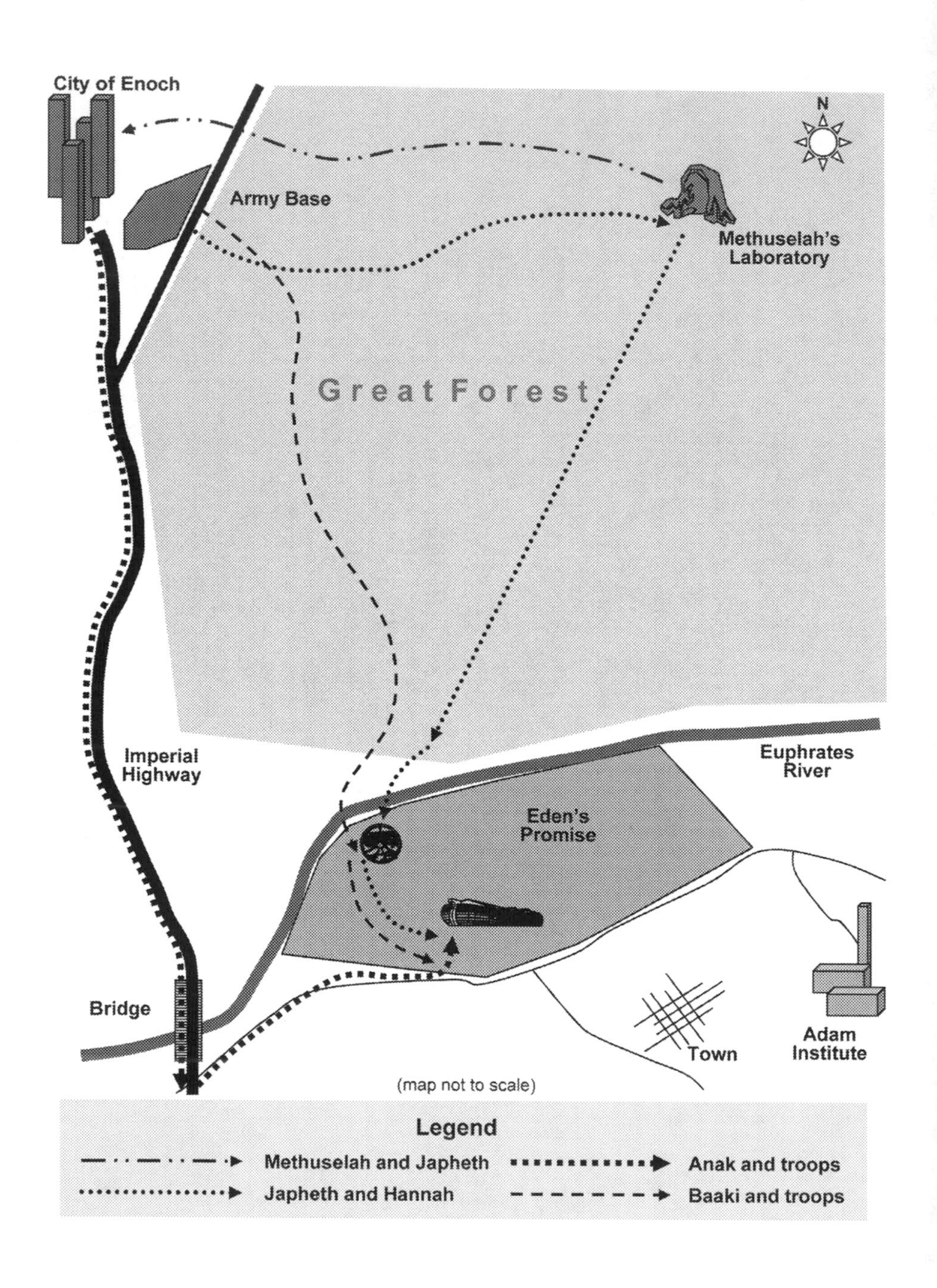

Map of journeys in Book III

CHAPTER 46

Outskirts of the City of Enoch

Six Days Later

The city of Enoch was nothing like Japheth expected. Everything he knew about the city had come from Deva, who had told him tales of its shining skyscrapers, large parks, and friendly people. What he saw before him looked more like the decaying ruins of a vandalized metropolis.

Why was he surprised? Why did he think he would find something beautiful after everything his great-grandfather had told him about the corrupt Cainites who lived there, the increasingly violent imperial presence, and the internment and execution of any and all believers by the empire? He knew better than to take Deva's words to heart. She had been so enamored of the imagined luxury of the Cainite lifestyle that she believed what she wanted to believe, refusing to acknowledge the much harder truth. But as Methuselah and Japheth stood on a hill in the outskirts of the city, looking down on its streets in the distance, Enoch seemed the most uninviting place he had ever seen. He could see some abandoned dinos, still alive, harnessed to wagon fragments or foraging for food. More distressing were the dead dino carcasses that were scattered everywhere. Some buildings smoldered, the fires that destroyed them having burned out on their own with no apparent attempt to extinguish them. There were still a number of people on the streets who moved furtively about their business, looking over their shoulder at each turn.

"How do you expect to find your contact in this place?" Japheth asked as they made their way through the remains of a foundry factory with its five-story furnace peeled back from an apparent recent explosion. The path through the industrial complex was smoky and eerily quiet as they walked through what had once been towering, black smokestacks and recently active machines.

"Not now," Methuselah snapped, ignoring Japheth's question. The curt response warned Japheth that Methuselah was alertly sensing their surroundings while they walked further into the former industrial area. Methuselah looked vigilantly from side to side, as if expecting an attack from the shadows. Japheth was not prepared when a ragged figure stepped out into their way from behind a giant hydraulic press and brought them to a sudden halt. Japheth, distracted by the remains of the towering machinery, bumped into Methuselah.

"Halt! Identify yourselves!" the tall man in front of them shouted. Though he shouted the order with authority, the man did not present a very commanding presence. He looked like a skinny, filthy vagrant who hadn't eaten in days. His voice was a deep baritone, indicating that he had once been a larger man, but now he looked like he barely had the strength to stop them, should they put up a determined fight. But this no longer factored into the equation when he pulled a foot-long blade from under his tattered jacket.

"Don't move, or you'll regret it!" the ragged man barked, stepping closer.

Methuselah calmly looked him in the eye and said, "Let us pass. We mean you no harm. We are going into the city to meet some friends, and, if you let us go, you will not get hurt."

"*I* won't get hurt? Who do you think is going to do any hurting around here? *You*, old man? Or maybe this boy who looks scared out of his wits? I don't think so."

He continued to menace them by waving his knife. "You look Sethian to me, so I doubt you still have any friends in the city." He stepped closer to Methuselah and eyed his iridescent cloak that glistened even in the shadows of the blackened towers.

"Give me that cloak and you can go. Or don't give it to me, and I'll take it from you just the same. Which will it be, old man?"

Methuselah calmly reached into his cloak and slowly withdrew a silver gas canister that immediately caught the eye of the hostile figure. "How about taking this instead of the cloak," Methuselah offered. "You could get better money for it, if clothing or food are what you wanted. However, from your smell, I would suggest a bath instead." Japheth could not believe that his great-grandfather was deliberately provoking this armed attacker! Under the pretense of offering it to the man for closer examination, he held the canister right up to his face. And, just as the filthy vagrant reached out to grab it from him, Methuselah called to Japheth to cover his eyes and hold his breath. Before the man had time to do the same, Methuselah squeezed the canister trigger. The puff of gas went straight into their assailant's face, and he dropped to the ground without uttering a sound. Methuselah stepped back and waited ten seconds before opening his eyes and exhaling. The figure in front of them merely looked like he was asleep.

"A little stun gas from your synthesized spider venom has that immediate effect. You know what it feels like, Japheth, since you tested it on yourself. I assume it is not entirely unpleasant—except, of course, when you fall down. He should be unconscious for about an hour." Methuselah walked carefully to the body, took the knife from the vagrant's hand, and flung it far into the jumbled pile of machinery.

"Let us remove ourselves from here and reach the center of the city. We must look for the signal that our contact is in the area." The two walked faster as they approached the city street, and Methuselah gave his great-grandson instructions on how to behave in case they were stopped.

"Now, we must remember that we cannot look like two farmers in town for the first time. We must walk confidently and with purpose, so that we do not attract attention and become targets for the dragnet patrols left in the city. If we look and act like we have someplace to go, anyone who sees us will think we belong here. The authorities are arresting anyone who has not taken the imperial oath and registered with the police, so take this card and be ready to show it to a policeman if he asks you for it. But let me do the talking." Japheth had never seen Methuselah this tense. He was always so confident and relaxed, but now he was making Japheth nervous.

The puff of gas went straight into their assailant's face.

Methuselah's next comment did little to calm him. "I cannot stress enough how important it is for us to keep moving while I look for the urban tag that is the sign of the Resistance. You must have a lot of questions, but I cannot explain more to you now in case we are captured and you are forced to give up information."

"But if we get separated," Japheth objected, "shouldn't I know what the sign is, so I can look for it, too? That way, at least one of us can make contact with the Resistance."

"That is a reasonable suggestion, and, if it appears that we might become separated, I will tell you what the sign is. But for now, let's keep moving and cover as much ground as we can before dark."

After walking for a half hour, and encountering no checkpoints, they reached what could have once been the center of the city, lined with tall buildings on either side. They walked along the sidewalk as Methuselah examined the walls of buildings along the way. They were all large, imposing structures that had obviously been shops, apartments and offices at one time. They were mostly all abandoned and in ruins now. On the ground level they were either boarded up, burned out, or looted. Broken glass was everywhere, and anything of value had been stripped from the abandoned buildings. Signs, window displays, even metal window frames had been torn out.

"The vandals have taken anything metal they could find to the imperial recycling centers for use by the military," Methuselah observed, answering the question forming in Japheth's mind. "All the pipes have been ripped out for shell casings; iron is melted to make weapons and vehicle parts."

"What about all that iron machinery in the foundry complex we came through? Why didn't they take that too?" Japheth asked.

"I am sure they will come back for it in due time. Nothing will be left behind now that the empire has determined to concentrate their forces and carry out a full-scale attack upon all believers everywhere to wipe us out once and for all. The city is nothing but a graveyard, and any leftover metal is merely food for their military machines."

Just then, Methuselah noticed two police officers coming from the opposite direction; the leader of the two walked with a swagger, and his rumpled uniform bulged over his belt. His partner was a thin youngster, no older than Japheth. When the policemen spotted the two visitors, they immediately crossed the street toward them.

"As I expected, here come the police. Let me do the talking," Methuselah insisted, continuing along the sidewalk as the two policemen approached them with scowls.

"Stop, Sethians! Give us your IDs." The leader looked the part of the tough policeman: squinted eyes, snarling lips, and an intimidating growl. Japheth thought the officers would enjoy beating him and Methuselah for their own amusement before sending them away in a police wagon. He shuddered to think about what would happen if they were arrested.

After handing over their ID cards without a word, they waited while the chubby one examined their documents closely.

"These are forgeries," the policeman stated emphatically, stuffing them into his shirt pocket. "Come with us!"

Methuselah noticed the name on the man's badge. "Before you take us in, Officer . . . Krupp, is it? Maybe you should also look at this," he spoke casually, withdrawing another folded piece of paper from his cloak. "It may serve to keep you out of jail yourself." He handed him the imperial pass and waited as he read it.

It didn't take long and Krupp shifted his feet back and forth nervously. He showed the paper to the younger policeman. "Why didn't you give this to me first?" he asked gruffly.

"Because, you were in such a hurry to arrest us, you only asked us for our IDs, officer."

Japheth was stunned again. What in the world was his great-grandfather doing? This was the second time Methuselah had deliberately antagonized someone who obviously meant them harm. Was he trying to provoke a beating from these two goons?

"Your imperial pass is only sufficient for the next two days, Sethian. If we find you around here after that, and you run off your smart mouth again, you'll be fair game for our patrols, and you'll end up in the pens with the rest of your filthy kind. Now move on!" Krupp handed him the imperial pass with a snarl, hitched up his belt, and tried to maintain his tough appearance.

As the officials walked away, Methuselah called after them, "Wait a minute! What about our IDs?"

The two policemen, increasingly annoyed, walked slowly back and stopped about six feet away. Krupp took the IDs from his shirt pocket, threw them on the sidewalk, and stepped on them with his boot. As he ground them into the pavement, he glared at the two and walked away. His partner looked back over his shoulder and smiled, as if nothing would please him more than to come across them again soon.

"Did you have to do that?" Japheth groaned. "Now what do we do if we run into them again?"

"Do not worry. We will make contact before they become a problem." Methuselah seemed more confident than Japheth.

They walked for the remainder of the day up and down what seemed like every street in the city. Japheth was aching all over. They were stopped twice more by different police patrols, but the forged imperial pass let them continue without another encounter like the first one, which was fine with Japheth. He was beginning to hate this place, and the sooner they made contact with the Resistance, the better.

"What does a basic mathematical symbol look like?" Methuselah asked casually as they came to an intersection and stood watching dino wagons go by carrying human Sethian cargo.

"Is this really time for a math lesson?" Japheth asked, wondering why this question had suddenly come up.

"We could be walking for a few more hours so I thought I could keep you alert with a quiz. Just keep watching the traffic, and tell me what the fundamental mathematical symbols are. Or have you forgotten those already?"

"Fine. How about signs for integrals or differentials? How about zero or infinity symbols? Numbers? What are you getting at?" Japheth was in no mood for a quiz with danger around any corner.

"Here is a hint: the contact sign of the Resistance is a '*mathematical symbol*.' I want you to figure it out without my telling you. But to start with, it should be a fairly simple symbol, right? Not everyone knows more abstract mathematical symbology, and a more obscure symbol would look out of place if it were scrawled on a wall in a public area. So, the sign has to be something fairly mundane, so anyone not specifically looking for it might overlook it completely." Methuselah was trying to get his great-grandson to come up with the right answer for himself.

"If it's supposed to be simple, I guess the basic symbols for addition, subtraction, multiplication, and division would be obvious choices," Japheth said. Finally, he felt like he was making some contribution to the search.

Thinking out loud, Japheth continued. "The subtraction symbol could occur too coincidentally as a random dash or scratch mark, so that probably wouldn't be it. On the other hand, the division symbol might stand out too much as a mathematical symbol and attract unwanted attention. So, I would conclude that a '+' or an 'x' is what we should look for, since it would look intentional, but would not seem too odd or out of place."

"Exactly, my boy!" Methuselah beamed, slapping Japheth on the back. "That's good thinking!"

Japheth felt good until his teacher asked his next question. "Now, what about the 'countersign'?"

"What is a countersign?" That had Japheth puzzled. "I thought if we found the sign, we would then make contact with the Resistance?"

"It is not that easy," Methuselah replied. "For operational security, here is how the sign/countersign system works: The sign is posted in a public area by the group you want to contact. They initiate the sign to say, in effect, 'We are in the area, but need to be sure it is safe before making ourselves known to you.' Remember, the Resistance has been hunted for years, and tight operational security is what has kept them alive to fight the empire. When we make the proper countersign, they will know that another cell wishes to contact them and they will watch for us. At dusk, by which time we will return to see if their scout has seen our counter-sign mark, we will wait for them to approach us. Remember, I do not know who they are, and they do not know us. They must still make sure we are not imposters trying to infiltrate their cell. When they meet us, we will have to give them convincing information of our loyalty to their cause before they fully reveal themselves."

"That sounds awfully complicated. Can't they just see that we are Sethians and approach us in daylight? This whole thing seems like a waste of time, when we have so little time to find the Book and return to Eden's Promise." Japheth was impatient.

"Not, if our lives depend on it," Methuselah explained. "We might look like Sethians, but that doesn't mean we haven't sworn loyalty to the other side. Even after we make contact, we will be treated with suspicion until they are satisfied that we are who we claim to be. Do not be surprised if they rough us up a bit at first. Let them go through their security routine and judge us for themselves. Now, I think I might have noticed their sign a few doors back, chalked on a storefront wall."

The two retraced their steps back along the sidewalk to take a better look.

Soon enough, Japheth noticed a roughly drawn plus mark chalked about eye level on a wall. It was definitely not random, and the chalk mark appeared fresh.

"That is it." Methuselah said, "But keep walking, and do not stare at the mark. We do not know what kind of surveillance they have in this area, or if the sign/countersign system has been compromised and it is a Cainite trap." Methuselah's senses were heightened as they continued walking.

"So, what's the countersign?" The impatient youngster was nervous again with all the secrecy about signs, countersigns, and hidden surveillance. The situation was getting scarier.

"The mathematical symbol needs to be '*raised higher,*' whatever that means." Now, even Methuselah seemed stumped.

Japheth, trying to help, suggested, "Maybe squared or cubed is what they mean, since they're into mathematical symbols?"

Methuselah was doubtful. "I suppose that is a possibility, but, remember, they are keeping this simple, so someone ought to be able to respond without knowing advanced mathematics."

"That's good, because I'm running out of ideas." And besides, Japheth was getting tired of wandering around the city, and he was especially nervous walking back and forth down the same street in plain view of police patrols. He prayed they wouldn't run into Officer Krupp and his sidekick again.

"All right, I know what it is," Methuselah suddenly announced. "Let us turn around here and walk back past the sign. As we near it, I will slow down, and you will run ahead and create a diversion. I want you to throw a brick or rock through a glass storefront and make as much noise as you can. Anyone watching us will turn their attention to you, while I quickly make the countersign and then catch up to you. My hope is that anyone who sees you will be distracted long enough for me to make the mark without being noticed. Oh, and before you break the window, check that no policemen are in view."

"Great. I've never smashed a glass window on purpose before. I'll do it if it means I can finally be of some help."

They progressed down the street, and, as they passed the mark, Japheth ran ahead, picked up a large piece of broken pavement, and heaved it through a store window with a wild holler. While he jumped up and down, laughing hysterically, Methuselah chalked the countersign with a surreptitious sweep of his hand without even breaking his stride. He was certain that anyone watching them was focused on Japheth and had not noticed him make the mark.

"Thank you for that excellent and most effective demonstration of vandalism," Methuselah said to Japheth as he patted his back in congratulations. "Now, we will not know until tonight if the Resistance will make contact with us, so let us find some dinner and hope we do not run into those two horrible policemen again." As they walked around the corner in search of a meal, Japheth wondered how long it would take the Resistance to notice Methuselah's nondescript mark on the wall.

CHAPTER 47

The City of Enoch

Later That Day

It was growing dark when they finished their soup at what must have once been a restaurant, but was now merely an open kitchen with a stove and a few tables. As Methuselah and Japheth walked back to where they had left the mark, they looked around for anyone who might be their contact. Japheth still couldn't figure out how they would actually make contact, since they didn't know what their contacts looked like, and the Resistance didn't know them. The two took a roundabout way back to the block where Methuselah had made the countersign mark.

"Are we in the right place?" Japheth asked after they walked the length of the block. "I'm positive that's the window I broke. But where's the mark?"

"It has been erased, so they know we are here. Now, all we can do is wait for them to approach us," Methuselah replied confidently. "You can call it the counter-countersign. The countersign mark alerted them to our request to make contact, and sometime later they erased it to acknowledge receipt of our signal. They are probably watching us right now." Methuselah walked to the end of the block, and they crossed the street and began to walk slowly back. Nobody was out on the street now that dusk had fallen. Maybe it was past curfew time, and Japheth hoped no police patrols came along, because even their imperial pass might not help explain why they were wandering around after dark.

They walked to the end of the block again and turned to retrace their steps, when a voice spoke in a low tone from the shadows behind them.

"Keep walking, and don't turn around. Go to the end of the block, and turn left. You'll see an open doorway on your left. Walk in and close the door behind you. Do it now!"

Methuselah and Japheth walked at a leisurely pace until they reached the corner, and, as they turned left, Japheth peeked behind him, but nobody was there. Methuselah seemed calm, and when he came to the doorway, he entered the wooden three-story apartment building.

Abandoned Apartment Building

They stood in the dark for only a few minutes before a voice from the stairway above called out, "Come up to the top floor. The door's open."

The stairway of the old building was littered with trash, and the steps creaked as they walked up. Japheth held the handrail in the dark, but soon decided that wasn't a good idea when it almost came off in his hand. He wondered if the stairs would even hold their weight. When they reached the top floor, they saw a dim light through the door left ajar to the apartment on the left. Methuselah and Japheth stepped into a small, dirty living room that had been abandoned for some time. They heard the apartment door across the hall open, and within seconds each was knocked to the floor from behind by someone who obviously knew how to handle himself. Before they could react, their faces were pressed into the floor and their arms were expertly pinned behind them. Quickly, a thin cord bound their wrists and they lay immobilized on the floor with nothing to look at but the worn, dirty carpet.

"Who are you? Why were you walking around on the street? Who were you waiting for?" The deep voice belonged to the same person who had given them directions in the street, and it sounded vaguely familiar. Whoever he was, he was holding Methuselah down so that he couldn't get up. The other had immobilized Japheth with a knee in his back so he couldn't budge either.

"I will answer all of your questions, if you let us loose. Holding us like this will not get either of you anywhere." Methuselah's pained voice revealed his age. Japheth had almost forgotten that his great-grandfather was over nine hundred years old. He was still pretty tough.

"What are your names?" Japheth was thankful that at least they were down to one simple question, and he hoped when they answered it the knee in his back would ease up. He felt pressure from the knee in his back ease up slightly.

"My name is Methuselah, son of Enoch, and this is my great-grandson, Japheth, son of Noah. Now, will you please get off me so we can have a more civil, and pain free conversation?"

After a stillness that seemed to last a long time, another voice quietly said, "Let them stand."

Their captors removed the cords, lifted them to their feet, and spun them around so they could face the person who had ordered their release. Their captors quickly moved to remain unseen behind them. They could tell now that the disembodied voice came from a man in the shadows, just behind the glare of a bright lamp.

"Please, sit down and make yourselves as comfortable as possible, under the circumstances. I must ask you a few more questions before I can give you information about us. My apologies for tying you up briefly, but we cannot afford to be lax in our security. I am sure you understand that security can mean life and death for us." The voice spoke again, and Japheth wondered who it could be.

Their captors, still unseen, led them to chairs and stood behind them. Methuselah was now more comfortable sitting down and calmly looked in the direction of the voice. His face was serene as he waited for the voice to ask another question. Japheth speculated about how much Methuselah would tell them. *What if this is a police trap to get inside the Resistance? What if they were tortured to reveal the sign and countersign?* Japheth's mind raced in near panic.

But Methuselah obviously wanted to get straight to the point. "You now know who we are, so I will dispense with the formalities of any further introduction. We came to contact the Resistance, which obviously we have done, to locate something of immense value to the Sethian civilization. As you know, Noah has finished an ark in which his family seeks to be saved from the global destruction that will come to the earth in a very short time. We wish to find and recover the Book of Adam so that Japheth can take it with him into the new world. If you know where the Book is, we would like to recover it as soon as possible so we can be on our way." That revealed everything about them in a few sentences.

At least now Japheth would find out if this was a trap, or if this was really the Resistance. The captor standing behind Methuselah cleared his throat and exclaimed, "You sure are a crafty one, aren't you, old man?" Japheth's stomach flipped when he recognized that voice. Their attacker from the foundry, whom Methuselah had gassed when they first arrived!

"I am not certain about the crafty part," replied Methuselah, "but I am in a hurry to get Japheth and the Book to the ark, because I believe the destruction of the earth will come in a few days. My apologies for our abrupt encounter at the foundry this morning. Even if you did not seem like a great threat, your knife did give me pause. You will understand why I felt I had to resort to violence to stop you."

"That's all right," replied the voice behind the lamp. "Aktek is our watchman, and he can do a convincing imitation of a nasty Cainite, when necessary. I assure you, he is a loyal Sethian whose bark is worse than his bite." Their inquisitor sounded like a congenial host as he moved the lamp aside and stepped forward. He was a very old man, maybe almost Methuselah's age, of medium height and his face resembled Methuselah's somewhat, though he was bent over from arthritis and his beard and hair were thinned. He came up close to Methuselah and looked into his face from about six inches away.

"Yes, that is you, Meta, is it not? I recognized your voice right away." The man's own voice was quivering, and his eyes shone. "How have you been all these years?"

"I have been well brother, and you?"

That's why his voice sounded familiar! This was Methuselah's brother, Eli; the one who had helped transcribe copies of the Book of Adam for his father, Enoch. God had led them to exactly the person who might take them to the Book, if it still existed.

"We will talk more later, but, since you have already met Aktek, I want to introduce you to your other captor." A figure stepped from behind Japheth to take Eli's extended hand. "May I introduce my ward, Hannah. She is one of our most valuable Resistance fighters and a blessing to me in my old age." Eli beamed with pride as Hannah shook Japheth's hand and smiled shyly. Nobody seemed to notice that she ignored Methuselah.

Hannah radiated an inner strength and beauty that overwhelmed Japheth. Her dark hair surrounded her open face. Brown eyes and full lips expressed a thousand thoughts in one smile. The room became fuzzy for a few seconds, and Japheth wasn't following what Methuselah and Eli were saying. Hannah looked amused with Japheth's bewilderment.

The five sat in the room and spoke quietly through much of the night about Noah's predictions being fulfilled and how God was orchestrating everything according to His will. Eli told them that, at first, the Resistance was able to effectively counter the cruel attacks of the empire. But when Anak's extermination plan gained strength, millions of Sethians were systematically eradicated, and what little the Resistance could do to save them was not enough. The increasing determination of the emperor and his Cainite followers to eliminate the entirety of the Sethian line signaled a severe degradation of their civilization, such as was foretold in the Book of Adam. It was clear that God's program for the end of the world was moving closer. News of Noah's faithful preaching reached the Resistance, and they drew encouragement from it because it confirmed their faith in the teachings and prophecies passed down from the patriarchs. But they suffered more intensely at the hands of imperial troops as God's judgment drew near. According to Eli's earlier estimate, there was only a remnant of believers still alive. His mission, in the little time left, was to preserve those remaining and give comfort to those few children they had saved who had lost families to the empire's eradication program. The Resistance made occasional contact with individuals seeking aid, and they hid them as best they could. But somehow, their network was always compromised, and within days the Sethians were captured and taken away.

Methuselah's enthusiasm to recover the Book of Adam peaked when he heard the good news that Eli knew where it was. Unfortunately, its recovery appeared impossible in the short time left before the flood rains descended upon the world. When Eli had finally realized the importance of the Book, he had tracked it down many years ago and secretly purchased it back. To keep it safe, he had it hidden where the

Cainites would never think to look for it: in a weapons bunker on the Rephaim Military Base.

"It seemed like a good idea at the time," Eli observed mournfully. "All homes, apartments, and businesses were being searched, and when they arrested Sethians they confiscated their belongings. It wasn't that they were looking for the Book, specifically, but they took anything of value and destroyed the rest. At the time, one of our undercover operatives had access to the weapons bunkers where the Cainites stored their most powerful munitions. I gave him the Book with instructions to hide it in the most secure bunker on the base. He told me he'd hidden it at the far end of bunker 400-C, where their deadliest chemical shells were stored. He was killed shortly thereafter and we have no other agents inside the military base. I wish I could tell you more."

Methuselah listened carefully to this information and made sure he understood it. "So, we merely need to find a way to get into the base, find the correct chemical weapons bunker, pick up the Book, and take it back to the ark. Does that sound right?"

"When you say it that way, it sounds easy," said Aktek wryly. "That base is the most secure in the empire. It is nearly impossible to get past the sentries at the gate, to say nothing of getting into a top security bunker and then out alive with the Book."

"I propose that we have the police drive us through the front gate," Methuselah replied casually. "From there, it should be a simple matter to find the correct bunker and get the Book."

Methuselah became more serious and motioned them closer together. "I admit, it has its elements of risk, but we are at the end of the road, quite literally. We must face the fact that there are only a few days left, and, when the time comes, some of us will be on the ark and the rest will die. Whatever our fate, we must do all that is in our power to preserve the Book for future generations of Sethians, if that is possible."

"Danger of death is nothing new for us. Each member of the Resistance has been prepared to die for our cause," said Eli. "We have dedicated our lives to resisting evil and comforting the remaining believers with our last breath. What do you suggest we do now?"

"You yourself have suggested that the people in this room may be the last members of the Resistance, so I propose that we join forces—that the recovery of the Book be our final mission. We will dedicate our lives to making sure that Japheth, at least, returns to the ark safely, taking the Book with him into the new world. If that can be done, our lives will have been sacrificed for a worthy cause."

"But couldn't we all try to get to the ark?" asked Aktek. "Why is it only Japheth who gets to take the Book back to the ark?"

"I am not suggesting that we should not try to reach the ark, if we can. But I know for a fact that Japheth *will* be on the ark when the time comes, because Noah was told this by God when he instructed him to build the ark. Of that I am certain. God did not preclude there being others on the ark who are believers in the One True God. But I spoke of Japheth because I know for certain that he will make it on the ark."

"I am in favor of a wholehearted attempt to retrieve the book. And if some of us make it to the ark as well, so be it," decided Eli.

"I'm in," said Aktek.

"Count me in, too," Hannah responded quickly. She looked at Japheth and then turned to face Eli. "When can we get moving?" she asked.

"It seems Methuselah already has a plan, so we will follow his lead from here on. Brother, what would you like us to do?" Eli asked.

"Before we get into that, I have something I want to say," interrupted Japheth. He hoped that he could contain his emotion as he thought about what they were sacrificing to recover the Book and return him to the ark. "My head is still spinning from everything that has happened in the last few hours. We've only just met, and yet you have just pledged to give your lives so I can reach the ark. Whatever happens in the next few days, I want you to know that you will live in my memory forever. What you are willing to do for me, and for God's Word, is beyond my ability to thank you." With that, Japheth sat down before he lost his composure entirely.

The last cell of the Sethian Resistance spent the remainder of the night developing a plan that was totally outrageous and certain to result in a number of the team being killed. But the team members, including Hannah, calmly made suggestions and proposed alternatives such that the plan had taken full shape by the time the sun came up. Methuselah told everyone to get a few hours of sleep before they implemented the plan that would carry into the following night, maybe their last.

"I need to talk to you," Japheth whispered to his great-grandfather after the others had moved into other rooms to sleep.

"What is it? Having second thoughts?" Methuselah asked as he reclined on the couch.

"It's true that God said I would be on the ark. I believe that somehow that will happen, though I can't begin to know how. But God also said my wife would be on the ark with me. How can that possibly come true in the next few days?"

"That, my boy, is something you must figure out for yourself," Methuselah said as he wrapped himself in his cloak and closed his eyes. "This old man needs his rest."

CHAPTER 48

Abandoned Apartment Building

Next Day

By noon they had slept enough that they were eager to put Methuselah's daring plan into action. Though it seemed counterintuitive, his plan required that they allow themselves to be arrested and transported to the military base, where they would be processed for execution. Once they were in custody there, they would somehow escape from jail, find the Book, get off the base without being killed, and head to the ark. There were parts of this plan that didn't seem like they could ever work—especially the part about escaping from the holding cells on the base after they were locked up. You would think those cells would be strong enough to keep desperate people in, wouldn't you? But getting locked up was preferable to being lead straight to execution! They were counting on being arrested at night and processed so late that the jailers would put them in holding cells until the morning, when they usually lined up their captives for execution. They were counting on their timing and the jailers' routine to ensure this delay.

Japheth had to be honest—he was terrified about all of this. He didn't think of himself as an adventurous sort, and this was more than he'd bargained for. The stories he'd heard about the Resistance always sounded more romantic than dangerous. But this plan seemed like suicide. The only positive thing was having Hannah on the team. Being with a beautiful girl like her on the mission was something he never dreamed would happen. She was experienced in Resistance tactics and seemed to know a lot about police patrols in the city. Japheth sat next to her during their planning session as an excuse to ask her how she knew so much about what went on in the city.

She told him that her parents had been killed when she was a small child. When Eli found her in an abandoned apartment, he promised that he would take care of her as long as he could. He taught her how to survive in the city. Japheth was embarrassed by how little he knew about Cainite life in the city, having spent all his years on a farm and helping his father build the ark. He was good with his hands and knew a lot about machines and animals, but why other people did what they did was usually a mystery to him. How the empire and its military police worked was beyond his comprehension.

Hannah and Japheth talked about the police patrols while they waited in the apartment that afternoon. "We were stopped by two policemen after we ran into Aktek, and they looked like they would be glad to arrest us with the slightest excuse," he commented, sitting close to her on the floor.

"They don't have much to do these days," she told him. "So they've stepped up their patrols in order to round up every last Sethian remaining in the city. I'm amazed Methuselah's imperial pass held up under their scrutiny, since I didn't think those types of passes were issued any more." It turned out that she was very familiar with the intricacies of imperial IDs and passes. She had helped their forger make IDs before he was killed, and she even had a realistic ID that cited her Cainite loyalty so she could courier messages to other parts of the Resistance without being detained.

"When I had to travel under my Cainite identity, I was scared to death," she confessed. "Most Cainite girls my age are very loose with their appearance and use their bodies to entice men. I had to dress provocatively to avoid suspicion, but I hated acting like I would ever be interested in a Cainite. If somebody showed interest in me, I told them I was on official imperial business and hurried to my meeting. Fortunately, I acted confidently enough that nobody ever tried to take advantage of me, though heaven knows a lot of that happened with others."

Japheth looked at her as she spoke and sensed that she liked having someone her own age to talk with. He could listen to her talk all day.

"You know all about me now—the Resistance has been my life for as long as I can remember. Everyone knows about Noah and the ark, but how come you're here with Methuselah looking for the Book of Adam?" She was sincerely interested in knowing more about him, so he gave her as short a summary as he could, since he really would rather listen to her voice over his own.

He told her how Methuselah had appeared at their compound one day when his father had run out of ideas and energy to finish the ark. "I never knew much about Methuselah before then, but he is the most amazing person when it comes to science and technology. He designed the ark, got workmen to buckle down on construction, and worked with my father and me and my brothers to finish the ark in just under sixty years. Given the size of the ark, that was a phenomenal accomplishment. I went to 'school,' where Methuselah taught me all he could about mechanics, chemistry, and animal training. When he told me stories about his quest to find the Book, they captured my imagination. My dad was totally set against our leaving to study in Methuselah's underground laboratory, because he knew the time was rapidly approaching when we would have to enter the ark before the flood came. But we promised we'd be back in time because we felt it was important that, if it still existed, the Book should be taken on the ark and preserved for future generations of Sethians. How much do you know about the Book of Adam?" Japheth asked her.

"Eli talked about it all the time when I was younger. I held it in my hands once and read some of it, though I was too young to really understand it. I know enough about what is in it to be willing to give my life to see it preserved." Her eyes shone when she spoke of the Book, and Japheth asked her if it was as good as people said it was and if it had the power to change your life.

"It is the most life-transforming book ever written," Hannah exclaimed. "Eli had it long enough to memorize entire passages, so that we could still talk about them if the Book was ever lost or captured. We would sit around in the evening, and he'd tell us how God walked with Adam in the Garden, and how much Adam suffered after he sinned and they had to leave the natural lushness of Eden to work the hard ground. But the best part was where God told him to look forward to a Redeemer, who would come one day to pay for Adam's sins and the sins of all those who came after him. Because of God's love for each one of us, He made a provision to pay for our sin. The Promised One would be God Himself in man's flesh, who would one day die in our place so that God could accept us into Eternity forever. Trust in that hope alone was enough to keep Adam going for his entire life, in spite of family tragedy and the constant pain of knowing that he had disobeyed God and that, as a result, all of us would have to suffer for his disobedience." Hannah was excited about the prospect of this hope, and Japheth could see how much it meant to her.

"Is that why you're willing to give your life so I can take the Book with me to the ark?" Japheth asked with expectancy. "You seem to have a peace that I find unbelievable in a dangerous situation like this."

"That's part of it, yes. But also, I want others to hear what God has to say, so they can have that peace, too. Because of my trust in the Promised One, I know I will see Him someday. Everyone, Sethian or Cainite, should hear the truth about God's love for them and what He has promised to do to pay the penalty of their sin."

At that instant something astounding fell into place in Japheth's mind. When he pondered it afterward, he thought it must have been obvious to everyone but him.

"Hannah, this may sound crazy, but, just suppose . . . I mean . . . I can't even believe I'm saying this without analyzing it thoroughly." He knew he wasn't making much sense and broke into a sweat. But Hannah held her gentle eyes on him and waited for him to finish.

"What I mean to say is, just suppose . . . Suppose God has arranged for us—you and me—to be together like this because He has something planned for the two of us. Does that make any sense? I mean, we hardly know each other." He didn't entirely know what he was saying, but it came out sounding almost as he intended.

"When you say 'planned for the two of us,' do you mean, like, 'married'?" she asked. She was still looking at him intently, so Japheth took that as a good sign. *How could she be so calm at a moment like this?*

"Uh, yes. I guess so. That's what I was thinking, but it seems ridiculous when I think more about it. I just met you last night. How can I even be suggesting such a thing? I'm sorry. It was silly of me to even bring it up. You must think I'm a total idiot. Maybe we should take some time to think about this." He felt like it might take a couple of weeks to weigh all the implications of what he was suggesting. This had come on way too fast for his over-analytical mind to fully grasp.

Hannah took Japheth's hands in hers. His pulse skyrocketed. "We live in a time when death can come at any moment. The imperial police could come through that door right now and arrest us or kill us. By this time tomorrow, I might be dead. Yes, normally this would be rushing things. But these are not normal times. This may be difficult for an analytical person like you to fully comprehend, but listen to your heart. When I first saw you," she continued, "I was excited to meet a Sethian my own age. Then, when I heard that you were Noah's son and that God promised you would be on the ark, I felt sad that you would be alone after the flood and that we would never see each other again. But, if God wants us together on the ark, He will work out the circumstances to make it happen. I've trusted God for everything up to now, so I know He will work this out, too."

What she said made a lot of sense. Japheth suggested something that surprised even him. "Let's pray about this during the rest of today and see how Methuselah's crazy plan works out. We'll be together for the next few hours, so we can get to know each other more. If this is something God wants to happen, things will work out in that direction. I'm afraid to think about the implications of Him 'closing the door' when we've only just met. It has a ring of finality to it, but we both know that's possible." They talked quietly for the next few hours until Methuselah interrupted them in the early evening.

"It is time for Japheth and I to be arrested. Given our encounter with the two policemen yesterday, that shouldn't be too difficult. Are you ready, Japheth?"

"More ready than I've ever been in my life!" he replied, looking back at Hannah and giving her a grin. "See you in the dino wagon in a little while!"

Hannah took Japheth's hands in hers. His pulse skyrocketed.

The City of Enoch Late That Night

Eli told them the schedule of the police patrols, so it wasn't hard for Methuselah and Japheth to come across officer Krupp and his young partner shortly after they left the apartment.

"You two—stop right there!" Krupp called out when he noticed them loitering under the glow of a streetlight. "I told you two I didn't want to see you around here again. Are you looking for trouble, or what?" He practiced his growl, and his skinny young partner attempted to look tough, too, but without success.

"Do you want to see our IDs, officer? Of course you do. I have them right here." Methuselah was intent on making the arrest happen quickly. He knew exactly what buttons to push with the rough-talking officer.

"Your smart mouth is going to get you arrested, even with your imperial pass. Let me see your IDs again," he demanded.

"I know I must have mine here somewhere," Methuselah fumbled clumsily through his pants and shirt pockets. "Do you have my ID, Japheth?"

"No, you must have lost it." Japheth searched his pockets, too. "I can't seem to find mine either. What about that imperial pass?"

"Oh dear, I think I misplaced that, too. It seems to be lost."

"That's it!" Krupp had enough of their bumbling. "You two are under arrest. Up against the wall so we can cuff you and call a wagon. What do you have in your pockets? Let me see." Krupp roughly frisked them and found nothing in their pants pockets. Methuselah wore his cape, but for some reason the policemen didn't seem interested in it and thus never found the contents to its many hidden pockets and compartments. Clumsily overlooking the cape, as Methuselah somehow knew they would, the officers handcuffed the two. The junior officer left to summon a dino wagon. Within minutes it pulled up to the curb, just as Eli, Aktek, and Hannah rounded the corner. They approached the policeman and began arguing with him immediately.

"You can't just arrest him, he's our friend and he has an imperial pass. You're going to get in a lot of trouble." Eli was making quite a show of it.

"And who do you think you are, Sethian? Get over there, and shut up. For your information, this one doesn't have an ID or an imperial pass. Let me see yours."

None of them happened to have their IDs either, so they, too, were cuffed and put into the wagon with Methuselah and Japheth. The two officers were pleased with themselves—they had netted five Sethians without even trying. As they sent them off in the dino-drawn wagon, Hannah laughed, "They are so pathetic!"

Japheth was amazed. *How could she laugh at a time like this? We've been arrested by imperial police and are off to jail and then our execution. What's so funny about that?*

CHAPTER 49

Rephaim Military Base, Prison

Later That Night

It was past midnight when their wagon arrived at the gate of the Rephaim Military Base. People ran in and out of the gate, and heavy vehicles filled with soldiers rumbled by at top speed. "What's going on here?" the police wagon driver asked the guard.

"Haven't you heard? The base was put on alert. The emperor is coming here with hundreds of other people. He and his family are moving south because the shaking of the earth has weakened the palace buildings. There's some news about the water vapor canopy breaking apart, and everyone on the base, the city, and the suburbs is evacuating to the south where they think the ground is higher. If you look up, you'll see those streaks across the sky. Supposedly those are tears in the canopy. Doesn't make much sense to me. It's probably just a passing cloud. That vapor canopy isn't going anywhere, if you ask me." The guard motioned the driver forward.

The prisoners were put into one cell together, and the prison seemed empty otherwise. A guard locked the cell door, and they heard him run down the hall to catch the latest news about the emperor's arrival.

Methuselah, Eli, and Aktek deftly removed their handcuffs and laid down at the far side of the cell to rest. Japheth wondered how they could relax peacefully if this might be their last night on earth?

"I know what you're thinking," said Hannah while she removed Japheth's handcuffs. "Eli and Aktek have faced death countless times. God has protected them all this time, and He will protect them even now. If it is His will for them to die, they give their lives willingly. I would do the same thing myself." Hannah seemed so sure of herself. That was something Japheth couldn't get over. She was so different from Deva.

"Have you been praying about us during the day?" he whispered as they sat close to each other.

"About nothing else. And you?"

"Me, too. This morning, the idea of being married seemed crazy. But now, it seems like you and I were made for each other. I've watched you during the day, and you are so trusting in what God will do in your life. I wish I had that confidence. But I also know that God wants me on that ark, and somehow I feel that we will both be on it. Seems almost impossible, doesn't it?"

"Nothing is impossible with God," she replied softly.

"So, will you marry me?" The question came out naturally and effortlessly. No stuttering, no sweaty palms, no hesitation or uncertainty. He had never been more certain about anything in his life.

"Yes, Japheth. I will gladly marry you and spend the rest of my life with you, however long that is." Her face glowed!

Methuselah looked across the room at the couple whispering to each other. Eli and Aktek stared at them too.

"What?" Japheth asked.

The three men continued staring at him. He realized that they knew exactly what had happened. There are no secrets in a jail cell.

Methuselah walked to Japheth and put his hands on his shoulders. "You have been like a son to me all these years. I have been praying for a wife for you since we met. Your father and mother have been praying for you and your wife even before you were born. Now, is there something you want to ask Eli?" He stared into Japheth's eyes, and the young man choked back tears.

Japheth looked at Eli and asked, "Would you be willing to give me Hannah to be my wife?"

"Of course, my boy," he smiled warmly. "If she will have you on such short notice."

"Of course I will!" Hannah instantly exclaimed.

Turning to Methuselah, Japheth asked, "As the remaining patriarch of all Sethians, would you witness marriage vows between me and Hannah?"

"Nothing would give me greater joy, my boy." He thought he saw his great-grandfather's eyes filling.

While Hannah and Japheth held hands and looked into each other's eyes, Methuselah prayed to God for His blessing as they promised to remain together as husband and wife for the remainder of their lives. He reminded them of their duties to put God first in their lives, to love each other with their whole hearts, and to raise godly children to walk with the Lord. It was brief because this was probably the last time the five of them would stand together. They hugged, and cried, and praised God for how He had worked this out in twenty-four brief hours.

Methuselah handed his cape to Japheth and told him what he had put in its secret pockets for any eventuality. He had prepared for this moment even before they left the underground lab what seemed months ago—but in reality was only a few days—and Japheth was honored that he would give him his most prized possession. Methuselah knew he wouldn't need it any more, but, still, Japheth was deeply touched that Methuselah had given him something that he had treasured so much.

The plan was for Japheth and Hannah to hide in the cell when the jailer came for them in the morning. Methuselah, Eli, and Aktek would break away from the jailer on their way out of the cell. They prayed that he would be too surprised to lock the cell door behind him.

It was not long before they heard the sound of keys jangling outside the door. Japheth and Hannah pressed together in a far corner of the cell and spread Methuselah's cape over them. In moments, the corner of the cell appeared empty; the synthetic chameleon skin had quickly adapted to the varied colors of the cell wall's cement and dirt.

"Come with me, you all. Time's up for you," the jailer commanded tiredly. "Hey, there's supposed to be five of you. Where are the other two?" The guard looked around the cell and then at the three prisoners.

"You must be mistaken," Methuselah remarked coolly. "There are only three standing in front of you. Does it look like five to you?"

"I guess not. Let's go, now. And no funny business." The guard pushed them ahead. As he turned to close the cell door, Methuselah yelled their prearranged signal: "Leaping dinos!" and ran down the corridor with Eli and Aktek on his heels. The surprised guard turned immediately to run after them, leaving the door open to what he thought was an empty cell.

After ten minutes, the newlyweds peered out from the cape and stood in the cell, alone. "I'm going to miss them, Hannah. There is no greater love than for a man to lay down his life for his friends," Japheth proclaimed somberly. They walked hand-in-hand away from the cell with sad, heavy hearts as they clung to the fresh memories of those who loved them enough to die for them.

CHAPTER 50

Rephaim Military Base, Ammunition Storage Area

Getting out of the prison was even quicker than getting in. There was nobody from the prison in evidence—guards or prisoners—so they walked right out onto the street of the military base. It was supposed to be morning, but the dark vaulted ceiling of the sky was dingy and oppressive. The overcast appearance was punctuated by sudden bright flashes that highlighted something happening above the cloud layer. Each clash revealed a different color and lasted for five to ten seconds, followed by a deep rumble. The sound from the sky was echoed by rumbling from below as the earth trembled slightly. Japheth and Hannah stood at the threshold of the prison entrance, taking in the rush of people still leaving the base through the main gate. Guards had abandoned their posts—nobody was trying to enter the base—and nobody was stopping the mass evacuation.

Screams of terror and shouts of defiance followed each rumble from the sky and ground. One man stopped in the middle of the street, shook his fist at the sky, and shouted, "I hate you! How could you do this to us?" as if finally realizing that divine judgment was approaching. Japheth and Hannah used the chaos to their advantage to move across the base to the ammunition storage area, though it was difficult to push against the flow of departing evacuees. They jostled their way past families with crying children and troops pushing their way ahead. One trooper tried to stop them because they looked Sethian, but he was carried away from their sight by the momentum of the crowd. Nobody else cared who they were, they were in such a rush to reach the highway.

The crowd thinned as Japheth and Hannah made their way deeper into the base. When they reached the bunker sector of the base, they began looking for numbers on the concrete buildings with rounded roofs that were built half aboveground and half belowground. All of the gray, concrete bunkers in this sector were unguarded and that was encouraging. All they needed to do was get in, find the Book, and get off the base as quickly as possible. They turned the corner to see a row of bunkers on each side of a service road.

"404-B, 404-A, 402-D . . . So, 400-C must be on this side with the even numbers," calculated Hannah.

"Sure, the only one with guards in front and a razor wire fence around it?" Japheth observed. He concluded that the heavily protected building must be the one with the empire's most dangerous material inside; these must be the most elite guards sworn to protect its contents with their lives. Their comrades guarding bunkers of lesser importance were long gone. The two remaining guards in front of 400-C were debating whether they should stay.

Japheth and Hannah paused and made a quick plan for getting inside past the guards. Their plan was bold and risky, but by now they had little choice.

Walking toward to the guards, they noticed that they were heavily armed and immediately tensed as the two young people approached them. They brought their weapons to ready and held their fingers on safety. Alert, but not yet in their firing positions, this was the best that Japheth could expect. It would only take a second for them to release safeties and fire. One of the guards had his aim on Hannah and the other pointed his weapon directly at Japheth with a professional glare.

The couple came within five or six feet of the guards and stopped when ordered to halt.

"What are you doing here?" one guard challenged. "This is a restricted area. You need to leave now."

"We don't want to be here either. Can you tell us how to get off the base?" Japheth had a confused look on his face and his hands were concealed under Methuselah's cloak. He positioned himself equidistant between the two guards, while Hannah moved two or three steps behind and to Japheth's right with eyes lowered, but alert to Japheth's every move.

The first guard eased just slightly when he sensed that the young man was not a threat, and that was Japheth's cue to raise both hands from under the cloak and turn them toward each guard. A silent jet of synthetic spider venom vapor shot from the canisters in his hands directly into their faces. The closest guard raised his hand too late to stop the vapor from instantly dropping him to the ground. Unfortunately, the second guard had his finger on the trigger, and he was able to fire one burst from his automatic weapon before he too slumped to the ground in a heap.

"Are you all right?" Japheth asked, stepping away from the dispersing cloud and turning to Hannah. The spray of bullets from the guard's automatic weapon had hit the ground between them and ricocheted across the street.

"I'm fine," she replied as she stepped back to avoid inhaling the vapor as it drifted away.

They waited upwind a few seconds and then approached the guards. Hannah picked up their weapons, expertly removed the clips, cleared the rounds in the chambers, and threw the weapons and ammo in opposite directions. Wow, she knew all about weapons, too! The guards were incapacitated, and Japheth checked their pockets for keys to the gate. Not finding any, he examined the gate and the lock that secured it.

"Great. It's a combination lock; no wonder they didn't have a key."

"They wouldn't have a key or a combination, anyway," commented Hannah. "This is a top security bunker and guards don't have access. Whatever is kept inside this one is so valuable that it was still guarded while the others were abandoned. I don't suppose you have some fancy mechanical gadget hidden in Methuselah's cape that can automatically figure out the combination, do you?" she asked.

"No. I have something even better," replied Japheth with a grin. "This is a piece of putty made of powdered magnesium that will open the gate in a flash, literally."

He removed the gray substance from a pocket in the pouch, molded it around the lock, and then took out a match. He ignited the match and stuck the wooden end into the putty while the flame moved slowly along the wooden stem acting like a fuse.

"Don't look!" he said as he took Hannah's arm and they ran. With a bright flash and a loud bang, the lock disintegrated and fell in two pieces on the ground.

They ran back to the gate and kicked it open with ease. Glad that they didn't have to climb over the razor wire, they entered the bunker door and found themselves faced with a small entranceway that led to another door. This door had a key lock. Japheth picked it in less than a minute with his pocket knife. When the door finally opened, they noticed a musty chemical smell.

"Whatever they keep in here stinks," remarked Japheth as he waited for his eyes to adjust to the gloom inside. He found a light valve on the wall, similar to the one in Methuselah's lab, but nothing happened when he turned it. He reached into the cloak and searched for another of Methuselah's inventions.

Japheth took out a small chem light and shook the vial to break the inner capsule. A green glow gradually filled the bunker. They descended some steps into the cool interior and eventually became accustomed to the slight chemical odor as they walked along a central corridor, which was about a hundred feet long with aisles on either side extending away into the dark recesses of the bunker. Along each aisle were heavy industrial shelves holding cylindrical canisters emblazoned with ominous markings.

"This one says, 'Danger: Instant Death if Opened Without Protection.' And this one, 'Poison: Do Not Touch or Breathe Contents.' Like I would ever do that," remarked Hannah.

They walked down every aisle in the entire bunker and read the warnings on each canister. Nothing seemed unusual or out of place for a chemical bunker to indicate where the Book might be hidden. This was where the empire kept its most dangerous weapons. Obviously, hiding the Book here made sure nobody would stumble across it by accident. This was probably the most secure bunker in the entire world. If not for the chaos on the base, they would never have been able to get near the bunker. With the sky literally falling outside, this bunker now hardly concerned the imperial accountants.

"We've looked in all the shelves and found nothing. I think we should go around the walls and see if there is some sort of hidden compartment or other hiding place where the Book could be," said Japheth.

"Wait, didn't Eli say it was in the back of the bunker?" recalled Hannah, leading Japheth by the hand while he held up the glowing vial in his other hand. Just as she expected, Hannah came to a wooden door in the wall at the far end of the bunker. The concrete wall was covered in grit and spider webs. There was no handle on the door, and, from the sound it made when she kicked it, the door was made of solid wood and was several inches thick. Japheth worked on the lock with this knife for longer than he would have liked and still couldn't find any way to open it.

"I don't suppose you have any more of those flashy, melty things?" Hannah asked hopefully.

"Sorry, I'm out of those. I'm certain the Book is on the other side of this door. But I can't figure out any other way to get inside."

As he spoke those words, the ground trembled briefly and dirt fell on their heads. Japheth shined his light up above them and noticed the cracked ceiling.

"Whatever we're going to do, we better do it quickly. Another ground tremor like that and we'll be buried."

Just then, there was another shake, and more dirt fell. They heard some canisters roll off shelves in the distance, and the doorframe in front of them cracked.

"It looks like that quake broke the door frame," cried Japheth. "Let's give it some help and see if we can break it away from the latch."

They began kicking the frame next to the lock, and it gave way enough for them to pry it opened slightly with their fingers. They leaned their weight on the door, and the frame pulled away slightly from the wall. After a few more tugs on the frame, there was enough space between the door and the frame to finally pry the door open. It groaned inward, and the two stumbled into a small room containing a desk and a single file cabinet. It was apparently an administrative room, and the file drawers probably contained ledgers of canister inventories. This was where they must have regularly accounted for the empire's most lethal chemicals.

Hannah knew what the Book looked like, and she quickly rifled through the contents of each file drawer, throwing aside the bound hardcover ledgers. When she came to the last drawer, her hands touched a leather-bound book and her heart raced.

"Here it is!" Hannah exclaimed in a breaking voice as she turned toward Japheth. He shined the light on the dirty square, twelve inches on each side and four inches thick. He cradled it reverently in his hands until another shake dropped dirt on them again and a piece of the concrete ceiling knocked the light from his hands.

"That was too close. Let's get out of here!" Japheth grabbed a leather courier pouch hanging from a hook on the wall, put the Book in it, and snapped the cover closed. He threw the pouch over his shoulder, grabbed Hannah's hand, picked up the light in his other hand, and they ran toward the bunker entrance into what was left of daylight.

Exiting the bunker, they found the guards still immobilized, and they retraced their route back to the main gate to leave the base. The crowds on the base had thinned somewhat, and the two joined one of the last waves of people hastening along the highway that passed the front gate of the base. For now, they would mingle in the flow of people, not caring about their destination, only interested in distancing themselves from the city and the base.

The ground continued to rumble at intervals, and the expanse of the sky was an eerie, incandescent, pale green. Whatever was happening high in the sky behind the clouds was only dimly shrouded, as if it meant to part the cloudy veil and reveal itself. The air seemed alive with movement and sound. The threatening sky and the unpredictable shaking of the ground continued to provoke terror in the evacuating civilian and military crowd.

Japheth and Hannah walked briskly, thinking that their mission was almost complete. The sooner they reached the ark, the better, as they looked at the sky and wondered how much longer it would be before the torrent of water behind the bright, violent fireworks was unleashed.

CHAPTER 51

Eden's Promise, Ark Compound

That Evening: Seven Days Before the Flood

Noah rested in his lawn chair after dinner and looked at the protective, illuminating Presence overhead. The distant, steadily shining pillar of fire above him had never moved. It was the brightest object in the heavens and could even be seen glowing faintly during the day. In spite of the vivid colors in the sky and the rumbling of the ground, the pillar remained a reassuring reminder of God's faithfulness, and protection, while the rest of the world was spinning out of control into chaos and violence. Noah would never know of all the attacks that had been stopped, and all the plots against him and his family that had been quashed, because God's Presence protected them from harm.

With this meditation in his mind, and his supper settling in his stomach, he drifted calmly in and out of sleep. While drowsily nodding off, he did not notice the flame silently descend from the sky and settle above the entrance door to the ark. No one else in the house saw it either, while it held motionless above the ark. When Noah opened his eyes again slightly, he saw the bright light illuminating the ark and the compound. He knew it was not a fire burning in the ark as before. He looked at the pillar of fire and felt at peace.

It is time, Noah thought to himself. *Everything is ready, and the stage is set for the next event in God's program. All that He foretold will come to pass, just as Lamech assured me before he died. No cause for frustration or worry.* Noah thought of Japheth, and calm from God filled his heart. Japheth would be here in time. Noah didn't know how this was possible.

His son was far away with Methuselah, and Noah had had no tangible indication that he was even alive. But God had said that Noah's three sons and their wives would be with him and Miriam in the ark when the flood came. He would continue to believe God and consider the matter settled.

Whether he actually saw this, or only dreamed it, he wasn't sure. The shining flame rose back quickly into the sky and resumed its location high over the ark. But something more was happening. He beheld the pale colored lights, waving like gossamer banners in the breeze; like giant feathers that reached from horizon to horizon. In the North, the lights dimmed and brightened in slow motion. Some changed colors and shapes and lit the ground with the brightness of a full moon. The flaming Presence of God shined even brighter with the colorful sight as a backdrop. Noah had lost all track of time looking at the beauty of the lights, and he failed to notice that Shem and Ham had joined him and were also staring up into the sky in amazement.

Unbeknownst to Noah and his two sons, what they were seeing was an atmospheric disturbance brought on by a combination of changes in the earth's magnetic field and the descending vapor canopy. Never since creation had there been a shift or disturbance in the planet's magnetic field; dramatic changes were taking place deep in the earth's core, which also shook the surface. Meanwhile, invisible rays from the sun, which had before been entirely absorbed by the vapor canopy, were now bouncing off Earth's magnetic field unimpeded, and a new layer of luminescent, charged particles—an "aurora"—formed in the thin atmosphere above the vapor canopy. Within a few days, the thick layer of water would descend further and obscure the aurora with a dark, opaque cloud.

When Noah finally noticed his sons standing nearby, he blinked from his partial sleep and turned to them. He knew then that it had not been a dream, but the first communication from God since the pillar of fire appeared over the compound. Noah had counted down the years from God's first revelation to this final year. Now God revealed that they had exactly seven days before the deluge.

"Come here, Shem and Ham. We must now move into the ark and load the animals." He was energized by what God had briefly revealed this time, and he was comforted by the certainty that the years of waiting were finally over. The next seven days would be a time of nonstop activity.

They would take all the caged animals and the family's belongings into the ark. They would empty the supplies from the compound buildings and make the ark their home from now on; all their time would be occupied with settling the animals. Any remaining human provisions and animal feed must be brought on board. Noah was also reminded that the rain would last forty days and nights. He assumed that it would rain continuously for those forty days, and he was heartened that it would not last longer. Those would be long days, but they would eventually come to an end. He didn't know exactly how long they would have to wait for the waters to subside, but he was certain the ark would eventually come to rest somewhere on solid ground. In the meantime, there was work to do.

"But what about Japheth?" asked Shem.

"Will he be with us soon?" chimed Ham.

"I'm certain of it," replied Noah. "Sometime in the next seven days. I do not fully understand how it will happen, but I believe all three of you, and your wives, will be with your mother and me when the time comes. My anxiety over his safe return is something I have finally come to terms with."

"Does that mean he'll show up with a wife?" asked Ham.

"Of course, he will. Who she is, I have no idea, but she will be the girl God wants for him, and I am certain she will be wonderful." Noah was more confident than ever.

"Look above us; the turmoil in the sky only confirms that we are in the last days. Dramatic changes are taking place, and we will see things in the next seven days that have never happened before. This is only the beginning.

"So," Noah exclaimed, rising from his chair and stretching his legs, "let us get to work rounding up the farm animals from the pens and gathering up the others from the cages in the barns. While we do that, the women can begin moving our few remaining provisions into our living spaces on the ark."

They began working on their checklist of chores before settling in to spend their first night in the ark. From that day forward, they prepared all their meals on the ark and slept in the bedrooms built around the central kitchen area. They only left the ark to continue loading animals and provisions. They brought the ceremonially clean, sacrificial animals in groups of seven and the non-sacrificial animals in pairs—one male and one female. Insects, birds, and small creatures were carried in their cages, and the farm animals were led up the dirt ramp, across the lowered door, into the ark, and settled into their stalls. Things went surprisingly smoothly and they managed to have all their animals loaded by the end of the first day.

"That was a lot easier than I thought," remarked Ham as he dropped onto a nearby bench just inside the door of the ark. "Even with all those animals inside, the place feels empty. Are we done? I need a nap."

"Not by a long shot, you lazy bum," chided his brother, who stood in the doorway looking out on the compound. "This place will be packed with animals in the next few days. Our work has just begun. In fact, I can safely predict that you'll not be getting a nap for a long time to come."

"And how can you be so sure?" his brother inquired as he reclined on the bench.

"Because I know something you don't," Shem retorted. "You'll be so busy you'll hardly even have time to eat. I know that's hard for someone like you to imagine, but it's true. Come here and see."

Ham lifted his lanky frame off the bench with a groan and joined Shem, standing at the top of the dirt ramp leading from the compound up to the door of the ark. From this vantage point, they looked across the compound toward the distant entrance gate and the driveway beyond. Stretching as far as they could see, an orderly line of evenly spaced animals wove its way silently toward the ark. Pairs of identical animals, of every shape imaginable, and apparently all juveniles from their sizes, made their way slowly across the now-deserted compound, toward the ramp, and into the ark. The first pair, small dinos about four feet tall, with three horns and cute little spike-studded tails, stopped at the door and looked at Ham.

"I think you'd better show them to their room," his brother joked.

"What is this, an animal hotel?" Ham laughed.

"I guess so. There must be a 'Vacancy' sign out front. We'd better get them checked in right away. You take these dinos, and I'll take the next pair. Hurry now, the line extends to the horizon and they aren't going to wait for you. Better get Mom, Dad, and the girls too. Looks like the fun has started!"

The family would run back and forth with little rest for the next five days. As peaceful as the parade of animals was in the beginning, the beasts immediately vocalized their restlessness as soon as they were secured in their pens. Like hotel occupants incessantly demanding room service, the new residents bellowed, chirped, cried, and howled in their new lodgings. Only after a few days did they begin to habituate and settle down. But the line of new animals seemed unending. And as soon as someone put them in their pens, the new arrivals hollered until they were fed and bedded down. The family was exhausted, yet the animal parade continued nonstop.

CHAPTER 52

Outside Rephaim Military Base

Same Night

If U'ungu, the Imperial Secretary of Fatherland Protection, had thought their travel to the ark would be easy, he was dissuaded when he surveyed the chaos outside the military base as night approached. Since the descent of the vapor canopy, there was only the changing color above to tell day from night. Daytime sky was mostly a pale yellow, dominated by a hazy sun and scattered dark clouds. Intermittent flashes of blue-white lightening were followed quickly by a rumble of thunder. Lightening would occasionally strike a tree or building and elicit shrieks of terror from humans and animals alike. The sky at night exhibited a red glow as background for the blue-green aurora that still shifted shapes back and forth above the panicking crowds that sought shelter from the coming judgment.

The core team of imperial police troops was ready to implement GOLDEN DAWN and head south to the ark, but the emperor was late in arriving with his consorts and palace staff. Secretary U'ungu, seething with anger, walked briskly over to Chief Inspector Baaki.

"What is the problem now, you imbecile?" U'ungu swept his arm toward the hundreds of armed men awaiting their orders.

"Mr. Secretary, our plan has always been to depart one day before our emperor arrives from the palace to clear the way ahead for him. We will wait here until he gets closer." Baaki was growing tired of his superior's incessant complaining, which only added to the chaos of tens of thousands of evacuating civilians streaming slowly past the road outside the base on their way south.

"What do you intend to do if he is further delayed?" the secretary demanded.

"I intend to implement our prearranged plan." Baaki knew that any large-scale military operation must hold to its operational plan unless change became unavoidable. U'ungu was raising trivial objections. "My men will form a lead party," Baaki explained, "to clear the road ahead of the main palace contingent, protect the emperor's harem with additional troops, and provide cover behind the civilians. It will take longer than we planned, but that is how we will move ahead. We will, of course, have to stop for rest from time to time, and we will stay overnight at the sites where we have pre-positioned food and supplies. It is all in the plan, and we must stick with it."

"What if things don't go as planned? Have you thought of that?" U'ungu was obviously not satisfied with Baaki's explanation, and it seemed he might be on the verge of taking over the operation—a formula for further catastrophe.

"There are numerous contingencies which we have gone over dozens of times, Mr. Secretary. I believe we have thought of everything." Baaki stood firm.

No sooner had he finished, than a messenger arrived out of breath and stood at attention, waiting for Baaki to recognize him.

"What is it? Is it from the emperor?"

"Sir, the emperor and his party are moving toward the marshaling area, but are being hindered by the crowds. Other Anakim have joined him, and they are cutting down all who obstruct the emperor. Meanwhile, his consorts and staff fall further behind. He ordered troops to keep up with him, but he has left the rest of his contingent behind. The crowds are stealing all they can from the palace staff's valuables and supplies. It is a mess, sir." Fearful of his superior's reaction to the bad news, the messenger took two steps back and remained at attention.

Before anyone could speak, another messenger entered their midst from the opposite direction. He, too, was out of breath and had to pause for a minute before he could speak.

"With your permission, sir," the messenger announced.

"Go ahead. What is it?" Baaki responded curtly.

"Sir, the overnight supply caches along the highway to the south have been overrun by the crowds. Food and provisions stored for GOLDEN DAWN are gone. Our troops have either been killed or fled their posts."

"Are these part of your anticipated 'contingencies,' Baaki?" the secretary taunted.

"No, but I am not surprised," he responded with resignation. "The emperor will do all he can to save himself, and for now we must focus our energies on helping him reach the ark. The rest of his party can fend for themselves." He thought for a few moments before summoning his sergeant.

"Sergeant Bata!"

"Yes, sir!"

"Form up a dozen of your top men, and bring them here. There will be a change of plans."

"There better be a change of plans," mumbled Sergeant Bata as he walked back to the soldiers sitting on their packs waiting for orders, "This is a complete disaster." When he overheard the report that the emperor was thrashing his way toward them, he felt a self-preserving urge to get out of the Anakim's way. Bata returned in a few minutes with a grim squad of young commandos, who arranged themselves in an orderly formation in front of Chief Inspector Baaki.

"Sir, the formation is ready!" the sergeant reported as the squad stood at attention.

"Men, we will be departing from our original plan for GOLDEN DAWN and splitting into two groups. Bata, you are squad leader of these men, who will escort me and Secretary U'ungu to the ark through the Great Forest and avoid the clogged highway. We should be able to move faster through the woods than on the highway."

"Wait, what about the emperor?" U'ungu interrupted.

"Allow me to finish, and I will explain!" Baaki's glare silenced the secretary.

"Sergeant Bata's squad will form an advance party with us to reach the ark compound ahead of the emperor, subdue those in Noah's compound, and open the front gates for his arrival. The remaining several hundred troops from GOLDEN DAWN will make contact with the emperor's approaching force and support him in moving along the highway to the ark. Judging from the massive crowds, movement along the highway will be very slow, but I have every confidence that our emperor will allow nothing to stand in his way."

Baaki turned to his sergeant and gave him instructions for bringing additional supplies and weapons for their trek through the woods to enter the ark compound. Before the sergeant departed, Baaki took him aside quietly.

"Bata, send me another soldier—your best scout for fast travel through the forest—for a special mission. I want him to quickly reach the ark compound ahead of us to fetch my informant and meet back up with us en route. My informant will guide us to a secret entrance into the compound."

CHAPTER 53

Weather Outpost #22

Dawn the Next Day

"That's our last measurement pod," observed Akmed as he gazed into the sky and watched the floating speck disappear from sight a few minutes later. The sky had been filled with lights and ominous sounds for the past week. The sun was sometimes visible, but was often obscured by high-level, opaque clouds. The three students had made pressure profile measurements almost every day since Mr. Tuuki had departed for headquarters with evidence that the water vapor canopy was moving downward. Now, the layer was dangerously unstable. The measurements were indisputable: The layer was not only moving toward the ground, but it was doing so at a faster rate than when they had first measured it. Their free-flying balloon probes were becoming more difficult to recover as the winds aloft increased and their directions became erratic. The few probes they managed to recover yielded alarming data that they forwarded to their central office. Of course, no response came in return. So, after their last probe was released, they sat in the break room to ponder their next step.

"Why do we bother sending up probes if we already know what they'll tell us?" asked Karaa. "Spending our time making measurements isn't doing any good. I think we should abandon the station."

"And do what?" asked Akmed bitterly. "I hate staying here as much as you, but where can we go? When the water vapor hits the surface of the earth, it'll burst its contents in a phenomenon like nothing anyone has ever witnessed before. You've seen the data. The observation balloons bounce off the layer like it's a solid wall. In the beginning, they floated gently against the air-vapor boundary, and we could only see the gradual shift in pressure. Now, the balloons bounce off and record some of the coldest temperatures we've ever seen. We probably won't be able to recover the pod from this last balloon, if the winds continue swirling in every direction."

"When Mr. Tuuki left, he said we should leave the station for higher ground if he didn't come back," Mobi spoke more assertively than usual. "I'm with Karaa. I think we should leave and find someplace higher—the higher the better. We should be safe if we can make it to Mount Karkom. It's almost two thousand feet high—a thousand feet higher than here. Water won't reach that high, will it?" Mobi's eyes pleaded for agreement, but he didn't get it from either of his friends.

"If the rough calculations of the amount of water in the canopy were correct, it won't matter where we are," replied Akmed. "We'll try to recover the last measurement pod, and then we'll decide what to do. It may not make any difference anyway, but at least we will have served the empire as best we could."

"Not that the empire can do anything for us now," groaned Karaa as she turned away with tears in her eyes.

CHAPTER 54

Outside Rephaim Military Base

That Morning

Japheth and Hannah were exhausted after waiting all night in the evacuating crowd that hardly moved forward. Japheth gripped Hannah's hand tightly when they saw an imperial policeman, who was trying to direct a throng of refugees to the side with their carts piled with furniture and other belongings to keep them from hindering the dino-drawn military vehicles. He picked them out from the crowd in the dim dawn light and called them over as they neared.

"You! Sethians!" he shouted. "Come here, and show me your papers." The bored officer motioned them to the edge of the road while he continued to wave people on.

Japheth and Hannah approached the man warily, and Japheth whispered, "I saw Methuselah handle his kind before. Let me try talking to him."

They walked up to him on the side of the road while the mobs of people and carts continued rumbling slowly past. With eyes downcast to avoid the policeman's glare, heads of families hurried along the road and kept their families close, so they wouldn't be separated.

Japheth stopped about a foot from the man, while Hannah stayed a few paces to Japheth's right. She listened attentively as he spoke in a calm voice with the officer, who stood officiously with his hands on hips.

"Look into my eyes, and listen to me carefully," Japheth spoke in a soothing voice as he withdrew a paper from his cloak and looked unblinking into the man's tired eyes. "I will show you our ID and you will concentrate on it until I speak again. Nod if you agree."

The man gave an almost imperceptible nod without blinking.

"Very good. Here is our imperial ID."

Japheth brought the paper up from his side and held it a few inches from the man's face. The officer stared blankly without focusing. After a few seconds, Japheth lowered it and said softly, "All is in order. Let us go."

The man rubbed his eyes, looked at Japheth and said, "All is in order Sethian. Move along now." He stepped back into the middle of the road and resumed waving on traffic. "Let's keep it moving, people. Everyone keep moving!"

They rejoined the escaping throng, and Hannah looked at Japheth with wonder. "What on earth happened? Where did you come up with an imperial ID?"

"Oh, that? It was just some paper I found in the cloak this morning." Japheth retrieved it from his pocket. He handed it to Hannah and she puzzled at it.

"It looks like a list scribbled on a rumpled piece of paper. How could the policeman take this for an ID?"

"Methuselah once told me that people could be persuaded to believe anything when a suggestion they are already inclined to accept is given in a soothing tone. It's a mind trick that doesn't always work on people with strong convictions, or people who are alert to it. That policeman was tired and bored from directing traffic all night and didn't really want to arrest us. I figured he wanted to avoid the hassle of arresting us and having to guard us until his relief arrived. So, I told him what he already wanted to do, and he did it."

The couple continued walking for a few minutes, until Japheth led Hannah to the side of the road. The carts and refugees were bunched up ahead at another intersection, where more police were directing them off to a side road.

"This isn't going to work," Japheth observed. "That mind trick will only work one-on-one, and those officers ahead look more intent on their job and have partners nearby. If nobody was on the road, we could reach the vicinity of the ark in five or six days. At this rate, it will take weeks to reach the ark, and we'll get stopped at every intersection. We need to get off the road and make our way through the forest."

"But once we're in the forest, how will we know where to go?" Hannah asked. "I'm a city girl, remember. I've been with the Resistance all my life and know my way around Cainite thugs and imperial soldiers in the city streets. But the thought of cutting through the forest gives me the creeps. Flesh-eating dinos, poisonous plants, snakes, swamps—that kind of stuff can kill you."

"That's true, but my brothers and I grew up playing in the forest. We thought nothing of building camps and spending nights out in the high-canopy jungle. We'd play games of escape and evasion just to see how long we could stay 'lost' before we found each other. Don't worry. We'll make it. Besides, I've still got some handy gadgets left."

Everyone on the road was preoccupied with escaping from the city toward higher ground. They paid no attention to Japheth and Hannah when they separated themselves from the crowd and entered the woods beside the highway. The mass of refugees knew that something terrible was brewing, but they didn't know what. If they had focused more on the ever-shifting colored lights in the sky and counted the almost continuous mild tremors under their feet, they might have rightly concluded that escape was futile.

Japheth and Hannah made their way slowly through the dense underbrush between the road and the tall trees of the forest. It was dusk and it would be even darker under the shade of the trees. They moved quickly when the brush thinned, trying to put as much distance between themselves and the road as possible before stopping for the night. After an hour of walking in the growing darkness, Japheth stopped at a large tree whose narrow aboveground roots extended in all directions, forming cubbyholes and crevices where they could rest safely for the night. Japheth gathered soft moss and piled it in one of the larger openings between the roots. When they settled under Methuselah's cloak for the night, using the backpack with the Book safely inside for a pillow, Hannah commented on how warm it was.

"Methuselah put a very thin sheet of metallic silver between layers of the cloak's fabric," Japheth said. "He said it would retain body heat comfortably on the coldest nights. It makes the cloak heavy, but we could even use it for currency, if we ever needed the money."

"I didn't want a technical lecture, silly," Hannah teased, wrapping her arms around her new husband.

The Great Forest

Next Day

Hannah awoke with a start the next morning and smelled smoke. She turned to see Japheth sitting by a fire. "Did you make breakfast?" she called as she crawled out from under the heavy cape.

"I didn't make it as much as pick it." Japheth pointed to fruit in a basket and stood to greet Hannah with a kiss.

"All I can offer my bride this morning is fruit and water." Hannah sat on the ground in front of the basket that he had woven and filled with fruit. He gave her a hollow gourd of water.

"Aren't you the busy survivalist now," she said admiring the carved cup before she took a drink. "Cold and fresh. This is a pleasant surprise." Hannah took a bite of something red and juicy, while Japheth tended to the fire.

"I started reading the Book of Adam this morning while you slept. It's amazing," Japheth began, sitting down next to Hannah and biting into a piece of fruit. "It's everything Methuselah told me and more. I get goose bumps reading Adam relate what God told him more than sixteen hundred years ago. To think that Enoch interviewed him and wrote down only brief portions of all God told him. It's a divine, written record of what we've only had before in verbal tradition."

Japheth opened the Book and pointed to a thinning, well-worn page. "We've been told through Sethian generations that God placed an innate hatred between the Evil One—Satan—and Eve, and between his 'seed' and Eve's 'seed.' In the future, Eve's seed will bruise the head of the serpent, and the serpent will bruise her seed's heel. I'd always been taught that Eve's 'seed' referred to the Promised One who would come some day. But beyond that, nobody was sure who He was or what that meant. And the references to bruising a heel were very cryptic.

"But this explains it all very clearly," Japheth exclaimed. "The first half is about the Son of Man, born of a woman descended from Eve, who will be conceived miraculously by the Spirit of God without the seed of a human man. He is the promised God-Man who will one day be called Savior, Redeemer, and King. God will, in fact, become a human being—literally the Son of God—but He will be hated by most people and loved by only a few. Men influenced by the Evil One will reject all His offers of blessing and kill Him, thinking they've beaten God at last. In a demonstration of God's omnipotence, the murdered Son of God will be raised from the dead after three days. He will have given His life as a payment for all of our sins—past, present, and future—and His resurrection will demonstrate that the price He paid was sufficient to satisfy God the Father."

Japheth stared into the fire, pondering what he had read. "I'm only part way through the Book, but it's clear we must do everything in our power to bring it with us onto the ark. The Evil One would like to keep the message of this book from future generations. It's up to us to take it to them."

Japheth stood abruptly and extinguished the fire. He and Hannah placed some gourds of water with the fruit in the basket, made sure the fire was out, and headed out on a trail Japheth had discovered earlier that morning.

"We'll take this trail for now, until we can find a clearing. I have no idea where we are or even if we are heading in the right direction. But if I can get to a clearing with a view of the sun overhead, I can figure out how to get to Methuselah's lab."

Hannah wondered how he planned to do that, but, by now, though she had met Japheth three days ago and been married to him for two days, she was confident that he could do almost anything.

Within an hour of carefully following the path, which Japheth said was an animal track, they noticed dim sunlight ahead, and they came out of the high trees into a small meadow of tall grass and sparse bush. Japheth stopped in the center of the clearing and trampled the grass to form a matted space ten feet across. He located some large flat rocks and piled them in the center of the clearing to form a platform about two feet high. Then he removed a shiny object from his pocket and presented it to Hannah.

"What's this?" she asked, turning it over in her hands and admiring its shape and smooth metallic surfaces. Whatever it was, she was sure Japheth would tell her all about it.

"This is a solar geolocator or astrolabe. Think of it as a pocket-sized, self-locating and homing analog mechanism," he announced proudly. "I call it a 'computer,' but Methuselah said it's too small. He called it a 'mere calculator,' but I think he was jealous he didn't have one this portable."

"Right. That tells me a lot. Explain it to me in language I can understand." Hannah gave it back and waited for him to explain.

"Here, let me show you." Japheth unfolded the compact device and set it on the flat rock pedestal. He took the miniature lens from its indentation, attached it to its hinge, and aimed it toward the sun. He then carefully turned the lens until the bright, focused beam was centered on a gridded target at the base of the fold. He pressed a button and waited, while the mechanism buzzed quietly.

"It's calculating sun angles, grabbing the time from the chronometer, and comparing computed angles and times to the solar tables it has stored in its memory. We'll wait about ten minutes for it to stop, and then I'll press the button again so it can come up with a second location."

He did so, and the calculator's buzz resumed. When the sound ceased, he lifted the mechanism carefully and folded the lens back into its compact home. He turned it over in his palm and showed her the numbers on black and white dials flush with the cover.

"Methuselah's lab is fifty-two miles from here in that direction," he said, pointing into the distance. "It also tells us our location on the earth, but that isn't important to us now. This dial shows the bearing to the lab, and on the other side is the compass that we'll use to navigate through the forest. Approximating a straight line through the forest won't be easy, but we should reach the lab in three or four days, assuming we don't stray off our course or run into problems along the way."

Japheth handed the calculator to Hannah and picked up the basket of food and water.

"You navigate, while I make our new path through the forest undergrowth. Hold the compass as flat as you can, like this. The red mark on the outer ring of the compass is our desired direction of travel, while the compass arrow should always stay on this mark showing North. You'll need to keep track of our direction while we walk along, but you'll get the hang of it. Stop periodically and let the arrow settle down if we make quick turns. You tell me 'right' or 'left' to correct my path, and we'll be fine."

Hannah wondered how Japheth knew all this, but was glad to have something to do while they walked through the forest. They didn't go fast, which was fine with her, and it kept her mind off snakes and things she knew were lurking in the bushes. Walking behind Japheth and telling him what to do was a welcome change, too.

Within ten minutes, she called for him to stop. "This compass is jumping all over the place," she exclaimed. "I'm holding it as level as I can, but come here and see what I mean."

She passed the device to Japheth, and he examined it before agreeing. "Looks like the compass has gone haywire. Either the geolocator is wrong, or some natural phenomena is causing it to be this erratic." He recalled the disturbances in the atmosphere and the shaking in the earth. "Instability in the earth's magnetic field could be causing this. We'll have to make do for now." He pocketed the shiny device and they began walking together through the brush.

"We'll try walking in the direction I first calculated and hope we can stop at least once a day to measure new angles. Let's hope the sun remains visible some of the time."

In all, things went well enough during the day, and they stopped to eat fruit and drink water several times. Japheth estimated they had walked almost twelve miles since they had started walking that day. Hannah wondered how he knew that, but by now she had complete confidence in her amazing husband.

He found a sheltered spot for them to spend the night in what might have once been an animal den among large boulders, and then went out to find fruit and water, while she gathered wood for a fire. He came back with the basket and set it down next to a pile of twigs she had set out.

"I thought you said you had never camped out in the woods before."

"I haven't, but you're not the only smart one in the family," she replied playfully.

"Well, I'm blessed," he retorted as he kissed her on the lips. "You've constructed a beautiful pyramid of twigs, and now I want to see if you can start it with one match." He gave her one chemical stick from his cloak. "We'll need a big fire tonight to keep warm. You look real tired from walking all day and you'll need to sleep well," he observed with concern.

Hannah was about to strike the match, when she stopped abruptly.

"Wait. I hear voices . . ."

CHAPTER 55

The Great Forest

That Night

Immediately, Japheth also smelled smoke. He carefully removed the unused match from Hannah's hand, concealed it in a cloak pouch, and listened.

"People talking," Hannah whispered. They silently gathered the pyramid of twigs and put them out of sight in the bushes. They used branches to carefully sweep the clearing of evidence that would reveal their presence and then crept out of the clearing into the dense brush.

After several minutes, they determined the direction of the sound and discerned that it was the voices of several men. They couldn't tell how many were in the group, but they appeared to be making a camp for the night. From the aroma of roasting meat, they were obviously preparing dinner.

"We should try to distance ourselves from them in the dark, but I'm afraid of making noise that would alert them to our presence," Japheth cautioned.

Hannah made a suggestion. "Maybe we could get closer and see who they are. Figure out if they're a threat to us or not. It they're refugees leaving the city who've gotten lost, we shouldn't have to worry."

"That's a good idea. Let's move closer." Japheth agreed.

Japheth and Hannah took their time stepping carefully in the darkness in the direction of the voices. Their footsteps made almost no sound in the lush, moist moss and undergrowth between the trees on the forest floor. When the flame of the campfire and men's silhouettes came into view, they inched closer to listen in on their conversation. The smell of cooking meat was tantalizing. As the group ate around the fire, there was an obvious argument building. One man sat across the fire in full view of Japheth and Hannah. Apparently, he was the leader, for he was dressed in some type of formal attire while the others were in camouflage military dress. He spoke loud enough to be heard over the crackling fire.

"This is the worst meat I've ever been served," he complained to nobody in particular.

When there was no reply, he directed his address to a man on the other side of the fire, whose back was to the two observers. "Baaki, you should have made better provision for this expedition and brought more suitable food." He threw his piece of meat into the fire.

"Mr. Secretary, we had little time to prepare when we split from the main movement to cut through the forest," replied the chief inspector tiredly. He had been listening to this complaining for two days now, and he'd had almost as much as he could take.

"That is no excuse. You and your people should have been prepared for this obvious eventuality. GOLDEN DAWN underwent years of planning under your supervision. With these new developments in the atmosphere, it would not have taken much intelligence to figure that we would want to attack the ark as quickly as possible."

"I remind you, Mr. Secretary, that you echoed the emperor's words when you told us that so-called prophet was a madman whose warnings about changes in the atmosphere were untrue. We all thought this could never actually happen. Apparently, we were all mistaken, and now the empire is reaping what it has sown."

"When we meet up with the emperor at the ark in the next few days, your impertinent tongue will be silenced. I will have no more insolence from you. Am I understood?" U'ungu remained defiant.

"We shall see . . . sir." Baaki resigned himself to being regularly berated by the secretary of Fatherland Protection until they reached the ark. When they successfully delivered him and met up with the emperor's brigades at the ark, Baaki would see to it that he perished in the attack. He was not about to be stuck in the ark with that pompous fool.

Their original mission, carefully planned for an orderly movement of the imperial court and the palace staff, had been changed at the last minute so that their small troop could reach the ark in advance of Emperor Anak and they could open the compound gates from the inside. Plans for GOLDEN DAWN had not been realistically based on a natural catastrophe actually happening or for the simultaneous evacuation of the city of Enoch and its surrounding towns along their intended route. Their original timetable had assumed quick travel on the highway—a plan doomed from the start. Panic in the city clogged every road as the masses fled blindly in the direction of the ark. The volume of people and their many belongings meant moving at a fraction of the pace planned. In a rage, Anak had ordered dinos to trample anyone in their path and soldiers to kill anyone who wouldn't move out of his way. He took all available troops for himself and moved ahead, leaving his consorts and underlings behind. GOLDEN DAWN had been an overly optimistic contingency in the unlikely event there was local flooding from a vapor canopy collapse. This was labeled a simple "continuity of command exercise," so the emperor would not appear to be fleeing like the rest of Cainite civilization to preserve himself.

Chief Inspector Baaki had had his doubts that the earth tremors and disturbances in the skies were simply local phenomena, as the emperor and his officials had continued to insist. This was serious, and he'd been thinking about Noah's message ever since ominous weather observations began pouring in from around the world. Getting into that ark seemed like a good survival objective, and he was determined to be on that ship when the catastrophe finally came. He didn't know how much time they had, but he suspected it was not much.

After a long silence, talk among the soldiers turned to how they would get into the ark compound to open the gates for the emperor from the inside. Japheth was stunned by what he heard and didn't want to miss overhearing a single detail of their plan, so he and Hannah crawled closer.

"Secretary U'ungu, I would like to review our plan for getting inside the ark compound," began Chief Inspector Baaki. "My source from the inside will be joining us later tonight to lead us to the place in the wall where we can enter by stealth so that we can open the main gate from the inside for the emperor to come in with his brigades. I don't want to go into more detail until my source arrives, but suffice it to say that this approach will be more successful than our previous attempts to attack the compound with heavily armed soldiers. Prior attack units were inexplicably annihilated before completing their missions, but we believe this was because they used frontal attack tactics, where an unknown force automatically repelled them. This time, we will be guided by an inside source to a vulnerable entry point, where we will go in covertly and unopposed."

"And who is this unknown source that we are staking our lives upon?" asked the secretary skeptically.

At that moment, a soldier entered the illuminated circle and whispered something to the chief inspector. Baaki acknowledged him and said, "Sergeant Bata, bring her here. Mr. Secretary," the inspector announced formally, "our inside source is here, and you will now have your answer."

The sergeant reappeared in seconds leading a young woman by the arm and pushed her toward the chief inspector. Japheth was only twenty feet away, but she was turned away from him and he couldn't see her face.

"She's a girl!" sneered U'ungu. "Is this some sort of joke?" The official glared at the chief inspector and his sergeant.

"Not at all, Mr. Secretary," Baaki replied proudly. "This girl has fed us highly detailed inside information on the progress of the ark construction and the movements of Noah's family and his hired workmen for years. I vouch for her reliability," he commented without looking at her.

Immediately, Japheth knew who she was. His stomach tightened, and his heart ached when he thought how many times she had talked of marriage and he had resisted her advances.

Deva turned to face the chief inspector, and when Japheth saw her profile silhouetted in the fire she was no longer beautiful. The harsh bitterness of betrayal was all Japheth saw.

"I've held my part of the bargain, and now I want to be paid," she demanded as she walked boldly up to the chief inspector. "You promised to pay me for information and said the family wouldn't be hurt. I want to be paid now, or you can find your own way in." She defiantly stood her ground.

"Well, things don't always work out the way you want, do they? You'll get paid as soon as you get us into the compound, and then you're welcome to spend your money any way you wish. You can go to the city, if there's anything still left of it, and enjoy yourself to your heart's content." With that, he laughed, and the other soldiers joined in.

"Listen," Baaki threatened her, "you *will* lead us to the compound, and you *will* show us how to enter without opposition. If you do not, my men will have their way with you, and you'll regret your second betrayal more than your first."

Deva's shoulders slumped in defeat. She began to sob quietly.

"I think I will turn in for the night," the secretary announced. "I want to leave at daybreak and reach our destination as soon as possible. Your source is a kitchen girl! Unbelievable!" He walked out of the campfire circle into the darkness.

The soldiers stood and prepared to settle in for the night. Sergeant Bata gave orders for relieving the sentries and tending the fire overnight. "Tie the girl up and make sure she doesn't leave. She stays with us now until we get inside the ark compound." He turned to retire, while the soldier tightly trussed the girl's hands and feet, and she lay sobbing on the ground.

Japheth moved away as quietly as he could. Hannah crawled backwards until the guard's campfire was only faintly visible through the foliage.

"We need to get away from here as quickly as possible," Japheth whispered. "We'll walk in the general direction of the lab and put some distance between us and them before daybreak. The last thing we want is for our paths to cross during daylight tomorrow."

Hannah put her arm under Japheth's and move closer for warmth while they made their way silently through the forest. She could feel the tension in his body, and she sensed it was from more than the danger of being so close to imperial troops.

"Was she your girlfriend?" she asked when they found an untraceable path.

Japheth knew his unease was obvious, and he told her that his parents had suggested Deva for his wife, but he had rebuffed her.

"I wasn't ready for marriage, but since she worked and lived in the compound I saw her every day. She insisted we 'escape' together to see the attractions in the city of Enoch and settle there. Marriage to her was only a convenience to satisfy my parents. She wanted to shake off the 'backward country ways' of my family and join in the so-called 'vibrant culture' of the city. Taking in the arts and entertainment of the city had been her dream ever since she was a small child. She saw me as her ticket out, so she could live her life unhindered by family traditions."

"But you didn't go along with that?"

"No, that's not how I was brought up. Our goals and ideals were totally different. I felt no attraction to city life, and, having seen it in the last few days, I don't regret it one bit."

"So, why did your parents try to set up your engagement to her in the first place?"

"That's always been a puzzle to me. I figured they were in a hurry to get me married so God's program for me to enter the ark with my wife would be settled according to my parents' timing. I prayed about the type of woman God would have for my wife, and Deva fell short in every category on my list."

Hannah gave a short laugh. "So, let me guess. You listed characteristics of your future wife in categories and rank ordered them?" she chided as she clung to his arm.

"Of course," replied Japheth with a serious face. "How else would I do it?"

She poked him in the ribs playfully, and they moved faster through the woods away from the military patrol.

"What did I say? Am I in trouble now?" Japheth pleaded.

"You need to tell me where I fit into your carefully tabulated categories," she said as she squeezed his arm in the darkness. "That should give us some entertaining moments," she mused.

The couple walked in silence for a while before they found a suitable place to spend the night.

"We can't risk making a fire, so I'll pull some branches together for shelter overhead to keep the moisture off of us and put down moss for bedding. We'll sleep under the cloak again." Japheth was tired and still shaken from the betrayal he had witnessed by the soldier's campfire hours earlier.

They huddled under the cloak for a second night, content to be in each other's arms. They whispered about their uncertain future.

Japheth thought of the Book that formed the pillow under his head and wondered if he would have time to read more tomorrow of God's plan for the human race. Hannah was content knowing that the God of the Universe had a wonderful plan ahead for them as a couple, as well as for all humanity.

CHAPTER 56

Weather Outpost #22

Next Day

"I found it!" shouted Mobi from deep in an overgrown thicket. "Over here!"

Akmed and Karaa walked toward the sound of his voice and found him pointing up at a tree where the orange parachute of the probe had become tangled.

"Good job," replied Akmed. "Now, climb up and get it. And be careful," he laughed.

Mobi grumbled about always being the one sent to bring back dangling probes. The truth was, he liked climbing tall trees. The vantage point gave him a chance to enjoy a view of the countryside that nobody else could see. But not today. The sun had dimmed further, and the darkness seemed to almost touch the tops of the distant hills.

When the three returned to the station, they went about extracting and transcribing the profile data wordlessly by rote. They feared what the data would reveal, and they were not surprised when the layer was shown to be below ten thousand feet and that, again, the probe was unable to penetrate it. After they prepared their final message to headquarters and sent the courier bird off, they gathered around the break room table.

Akmed smoothed out a large topographic map with his hands, and the others put coffee cups and cereal bowls around its edges to hold it down. They carefully searched terrain around the station for higher mountains. As Mobi had surmised, Mount Karkom appeared to be their best choice, and it was only a one- or two-day hike away. They packed as much food and as many supplies as they could carry. They donned all their protective clothing to ward off the increasing cold and hefted their loaded backpacks. When they gathered a few minutes later at the door of the station, their faces were drained of any hope or expectation that their hike to Mount Karkom would put them in a safer position. But they had to do something.

The three stood in front of the station that had been the site of their work and study for years. What had five days ago been a blue hemisphere sky above with a bright halo-shrouded sun was now obscured by multi-colored pastel curtains of light—the product of high-altitude electromagnetic disturbances—floating from horizon to horizon. The illuminated sheets were punctuated by flashes of static electricity embedded in the cloud-shrouded background. Under any other circumstances, it would have been a beautiful display of lights in the sky.

"That's all the incentive I need," observed Akmed as he turned his back on the spectacle and glanced at his two friends. "Let's get going."

The three students began at a steady pace toward their mountaintop destination with outward determination, but with an empty, resigned inner hope. None of them thought that their flight would save their lives, but they had to try. Each was alone with their thoughts as they hiked toward whatever future remained for them on Mount Karkom.

CHAPTER 57

The Great Forest

That Morning

Japheth and Hannah began their fourth day in a thick mist that they found strangely comforting. The lights in the sky were obscured that morning by a refreshing, cool fog, and they felt entirely alone as they progressed through the quiet forest, following as best they could the last course the astrolabe had calculated the day before. Japheth wanted to take a new measurement, but he had to wait until the sun became visible to help them find a clearing away from the dense foliage where they could take a useful reading.

They were making good time; they had agreed that they were now out of sight and sound of the imperial troops heading for the ark, so they took fewer precautions in their travel. It was doubtful they would run into any other groups that might threaten their safety. Nonetheless, if they heard anyone coming they would avoid them to be on the safe side.

As the mist began thinning late in the morning, Japheth stopped to take stock of their situation. They had found fruit and water after joining a worn trail earlier and, they had more fruit left over in their basket for the evening.

"We'll take a new bearing with the astrolabe in the next clearing," Japheth said. "We've been navigating by dead reckoning for two days, and I'm concerned we will have gradually gone off course. Even small errors in bearing accumulate over time and result in large discrepancies, never mind our natural tendency to veer off. I should have taken a sun shot yesterday, but the fog was too dense. Now, we don't know where we are and how far we are from the lab. If I could navigate directly to the ark using a compass, I would gladly have taken that route. But the astrolabe memory has only one destination programmed into it—Methuselah's underground complex—and we couldn't have risked following the same path as that imperial force. They could have sent out patrols ahead of them, and if we ran into them we'd be done for."

"Don't feel you have to justify your decision to me, dear. I think you made the right choice under the circumstances. I know we'll get to the ark in time," Hannah reassured him.

"I wish I was more certain of our distance from the lab. When we get there, I want to send a message to my father warning him about the approaching patrol and Deva's betrayal. If she gets there before us, she might give him some excuse to open the gate for the soldiers. I still can't get over her betrayal!" Japheth groaned.

They finally found a clearing in the early afternoon, and Japheth quickly set up the astrolabe for a sun sighting. In less than an hour, the shiny brass instrument had whirled through its calculations and produced a new range and bearing to the lab.

"The good news is that we should be able to reach the lab by tomorrow. The bad news is we did drift off course somewhat, so now we'll have to retrace some of our steps. Given the remaining distance we have to travel, we should be in the vicinity of Methuselah's underground lab before noon."

They resumed their journey as Japheth cleared the way through heavy brush, and Hannah tried to make sure he walked in a straight line. As they went along, Hannah asked what they would do when they arrived at their destination.

"What if you can't get into the underground lab?" she inquired. "We've had almost continuous earth shakes for the past four or five days. Will the cavern still be accessible? What if it's collapsed?"

"Those are good questions," Japheth replied. "They've been nagging me, too. If the entrance in the hillside is blocked or the door won't open, we'll have to skip the message to my father. But if possible, I'd like to pick up some tools from the lab that might help us reach the ark quicker. I'm counting on being able to get to the ark before the patrol, but our options are dwindling."

They kept their spirits up for the remainder of the afternoon by talking about what they would do when they finally got onto the ark and Hannah met his family. So much had happened in the past days: their capture and imprisonment; their marriage; the loss of her adoptive father, friend and Japheth's great-grandfather; the recovery of the Book; and nonstop travel through the dense forest. They'd had little time to fully appreciate how their lives had changed.

That night, they sat near the fire after eating dinner and building their shelter. Japheth pulled the Book from his backpack and opened it to where he had left off a couple of days before.

Before he began reading, Hannah shivered and put her hands in his. "Do you think it's colder tonight? I don't remember it being this cold at night—ever."

"It is. Must have something to do with changes in the atmosphere. It was very foggy this morning, too. I don't remember that ever happening before. It just means things are changing more rapidly, and we need to hurry to the ark."

He began reading aloud, holding the Book nearer to the fire and moving closer to Hannah under the cloak for warmth. They read late into the night, until they finished the last page.

"This is so exciting! No wonder Methuselah believed it was worth his life to preserve it for future generations. We absolutely *must* take this with us on the ark." Japheth was thrilled by what he read, yet humbly challenged that he was the last one on earth responsible for preserving it.

"What I find so astounding is that God, in His infinite wisdom, knew the history of mankind before the beginning of time. His Son created the world and sustains it even now. God knew when He created Adam that he and Eve would sin, yet He granted them free will to choose to follow God or not. Everything bad we see around us—evil, corruption, violence, and death—is the result of Adam's sin. No wonder he was so saddened as he grew older. He could still recall what it was like to walk with God in the Garden without a sinful nature, yet he had lost all of that.

"The one thing that heartened Adam that we know from the Book," Japheth went on, "was God's promise to take care of sin. God saw down the corridor of history and planned for our redemption in

His perfect time. Now, we look forward to that day—whenever it will be—when our sins will be put away 'as far as the east is from the west.' I look forward to that day when the Promised One comes to make the crooked ways straight for ever!"

Japheth's joy in reading about God's plan for the future was contagious, and he and Hannah spoke about it into the night. They read details of future events that Noah, Lamech, and Methuselah could only summarize because, apart from the writing in the Book, the original, detailed revelation through Adam had been passed down verbally from faded memories. The oral revelation was accurate, but not complete. Japheth held in his hands a firsthand record of Adam's personal conversations with Almighty God, the Creator of the Universe. He cradled the Book in his hands and peered into the campfire. Knowing about events from creation to redemption, and ultimately to a new creation, sent chills through him, and it wasn't because the air had turned unusually chilly.

God would repeatedly give mankind stewardship of truth and responsibilities in the form of covenants, and each time mankind would fail God. But man would repent after being chastened; God would honor His gracious promises and forgive man, and give him another opportunity to demonstrate his faithfulness. A remnant of those who trusted God would be preserved through millennia, and God would bless them. At the end of history, God will have demonstrated to men and angels mankind's need for God's infinite grace. God's triumph over evil, sin, and death in the end of time will bring all those who trust in Him to worship Him forever in a newly created universe. Quite a lot to pack into such a small book!

Japheth was thrilled and troubled at the same time. From what he read, he had an outline of the future. Even the generations that immediately followed his own would fail God. They would depart from His ways and become no better than the Cainites that Japheth and his family left behind. This disappointment was there amid the background of God's faithfulness and tender loving care. Japheth and Hannah purposed to live their lives for Him in the new world, no matter what happened around them, and to teach their children the importance of knowing God.

When they drifted to sleep that night, they rejoiced in what God was going to do and could hardly believe the part they would soon play in God's eternal program for the world.

The next morning, they quickly broke camp and began their final hike to Methuselah's underground lab, which they would reach in a few short hours.

They trampled through brush that alternated between thick, lush bushes—parted by repeated thrashing with Japheth's hiking stick—and waist-high ferns in semi-darkness among widely spaced trees. Japheth sensed that the vegetation was familiar and he stopped, motionless, with his head cocked to one side. He looked up at the fir trees that rose above them.

"What is it?" Hannah asked quietly as she stepped next to him. "Do you hear something?"

"No, I don't hear . . ." Japheth hesitated for a few seconds, and then relaxed to pull Hannah close to him. "I *smell* something. What do you smell?"

She wrinkled her nose and thought for a few seconds to place the smell.

"Is that citrus?"

CHAPTER 58

Methuselah's Underground Laboratory

It didn't take Japheth long to find the entrance to the lab—or at least what was left of it. The earthshakes had caved in the roof of part of the lab, and trees and debris had fallen down in a jumble that obscured the entrance. The couple dug to where Japheth recalled that the entrance should be and found the coded locking mechanism crushed. But the stone door had twisted off its hinges enough to allow them to squeeze through. The dim interior was partially blocked by tree roots and large boulders. Crushed instruments, overturned storage cabinets, and broken water pipes made the room a maze of obstructions. Their eyes gradually adjusted to the dim light that filtered through openings in the ceiling.

"I didn't expect this much damage," observed Japheth. "I thought Methuselah had reinforced the ceiling and walls enough. It would seem that these earthshakes have a lot of power behind them. Look, those support columns have been snapped like twigs."

Hannah was careful to avoid jagged metal jutting out from flattened machinery and parts strewn about. She stepped over mounds of books spilled from their shelves into the water that coated the floor. The smell of chemicals came from the far end of what had once been a large cavern, and was now a maze of rocks, dirt, and debris that had fallen onto twisted metal and splintered wood. And the ground still trembled at random intervals.

"Japheth," she called out, "are you looking for something in particular?" She was getting nervous because she heard him moving nearby, but couldn't see him clearly.

"I'm looking for tools that were stored in this area of the lab," he replied.

"Every time the ground shakes, more dirt falls on us. Don't you think we should get out of here?"

"Just a few more minutes, and I'll have the tools I need. I want to climb up to the opening in the roof to see if the birds are still there."

"Oh, hurry! I'm creeped out in the dark with the floor shaking like this. I need sunlight and fresh air." Hannah was close to panicking and wanted to get out.

"Tell you what, why don't you start climbing up to the ceiling, or roof, or whatever is left, and see if you can find the bird cages. Look for a stairway or ladder. It has probably fallen down, but it will be your indication that the birds are just above you."

"If I had some idea which direction to start in, that would help, too," she exclaimed. "Is there a way to get more light?"

She heard a muffled pop in Japheth's direction, and a green glow illuminated his hand and face.

"How about this?" he asked triumphantly as he held a jar above his head. "I found the toolbox and some more chem lights. Here, use this to find whatever is left of the stairway." He lobbed the glowing jar over to Hannah.

Hannah saw the lighted object coming in her direction and instinctively caught it before it hit her. "Hey, give a girl a little more warning than that, will you?" she scolded him.

"Sorry! But that was a good catch."

Hannah held the light above her head to illuminate the area around her, allowing her to move faster among the shambles. Soon she found what remained of a demolished stairway and started climbing a tree that had dropped straight down from above into the open lab space. She called out to Japheth, "I'm climbing up to the light above and will let you know what I find. I need the fresh air before I have an anxiety attack. You're on your own."

She made her way up the tree, until she heard the sound of birds. Sunlight filled the top of a tree that was lodged inside the cavern of the lab. Just before she reached the roof, she saw wire cages of birds piled on a large branch extending out under the ceiling. Crawling out onto the branch, she reached a small cage with the word 'Noah' written on a piece of paper affixed to the door. *These must be birds trained to fly to the ark compound*, she thought. *Makes sense to label them like that.* Hannah dragged the small cage closer and noticed that it contained one bird.

Soon, Japheth climbed up the tree and joined Hannah on the fractured ground above the lab. They moved away from the opening and sat on the grass with the bird cage and a bag Japheth carried over his shoulder, along with the satchel containing the Book. They discussed what to do next.

"I'll write a short message on this paper and tie it to the bird's foot with thread from my shirt. If my father receives it in time—and we have no idea if he will even be looking for a message—he'll have some warning about the coming attack. He'll know we are making our way to the ark, and he'll be waiting for us. That's all we can do for now."

Japheth removed a pencil from his bag and wrote:

FATHER,

TROOPS ARE COMING TO ATTACK THE ARK. DEVA IS A TRAITOR—BEWARE.

WE WILL BE THERE SOON.

JAPHETH

He tied the note to the bird's leg and released it into the air. They watched it circle their clearing for several minutes. "It's probably confused because of the lights in the sky and the cold wind. I hope it can find its way to Eden's Promise in spite of the changes. But we can't stay here.

"I just had a brilliant idea!" Japheth exclaimed. "We must hurry to the Farm and get ready for the next part of our trip."

The Farm

The complex of buildings had fared no better than the lab. Most of the buildings, especially the large barns, had collapsed. Japheth showed Hannah where he had trained his animals, but none of the structures remained intact. Of course, the animals were gone; he and Methuselah had released them before they left for the city of Enoch. That was less than two weeks ago. He couldn't believe all that had happened to them in that time. It was as if his entire lifetime had been packed into a small box. He felt overwhelmed.

Moving through the broken timbers in a storehouse, Japheth filled a feedbag with grain and slung it over his shoulder. With Hannah carrying the Book and Japheth carrying the bag of tools and the bag of grain, they walked slowly away from the complex of buildings toward the tall redwood trees in the distance.

"I hope you still have some energy left," Japheth commented as they walked through the grass field and gazed up at the towering redwoods before them.

"Why?" Hannah asked. "What do you have in mind?"

"We have a climb ahead of us," he replied as he stopped at the base of a tree trunk as wide across as a house. He peered straight up and shielded his eyes with his hand from the lights in the sky. He walked around the tree until he found the heavy climbing rope that led to the platform high in the distance.

"Climb that?" Hannah exclaimed incredulously.

"I'll help you after I reach the top. It isn't that hard a climb."

"Easy for you to say, jungle boy. I have to keep reminding you that I'm a city girl. Why do you keep forgetting that?" Hannah joked.

"Trust me. I'll make it as easy for you as I can." Japheth made a loop in the rope about three feet from the ground and showed her how the loop fit around her and under her arms. He tied the bags of tools and grain to the end of the rope. "I'll pull the bags up first, and then drop the rope down. You put this loop under your arms and I'll pull you up. If I stop, it's because I need to rest a moment. Place your feet on pieces of bark or branches to take some weight off the rope and wait for me to continue. Oh, and don't look down."

Japheth climbed hand over hand up into the mist. He nimbly put his feet into crevices in the heavy bark and pulled himself up with his muscled forearms. In less than five minutes, he was on the platform and out of breath. *Better not collapse now*, he thought.

After raising the bags of tools and grain, he called down for her to slip into the loop, and he began the slow process of hoisting her to the platform. She helped considerably by holding on to the rope and bracing her feet on the bark. When she stepped onto the platform high above the ground, Japheth finally collapsed in exhaustion.

"What a view from up here," Hannah exclaimed after she set the Book next to the tools. She walked to the edge of the platform and leaned over the railing to look at the ground below. "The farm buildings look tiny from here."

She turned to Japheth to find him gawking.

"You walked right up to the edge and looked down!" He sounded surprised.

"So? It's a nice view from up here."

"'Just a city girl, you keep telling me? You have no fear of heights. You're not the least bit nervous standing five hundred feet in the air, leaning out over the edge with nothing between you and the ground below." Japheth was clearly annoyed.

"What do you mean? You climbed up that rope like it was nothing." She looked at him quizzically. "Oh, I see. Jungle boy is afraid of heights, is he?" She pulled him toward the edge of the platform. "Hold on to me, and we can enjoy the sights together."

"I think I'll look for some supplies," he said as he disentangled his arm from hers and backed away from the railing. "You've never been afraid of heights in your life? Just a city girl? Right."

"Well, I'll hold on to you if you get too scared," she said playfully.

"Can we change the subject? We have work to do."

Japheth unpacked his tool bag. He produced two sharp knives along with pieces of rope, leather straps, and wire. He pulled out an armload of pouches made of metallic foil and a half dozen glass bottles of a colored liquid. He set those aside and disappeared around the trunk of the tree. Hannah followed him to where he had opened the cover of a large storage box and removed an odd shaped leather contraption. Unlike saddles she had seen for horses, this one had six straps over ten feet long with buckles placed at the ends and loops at various places.

"Is that a saddle?" she asked.

"Yes, neat, huh? I'll explain what it's for later, after we have dinner."

"Dinner? Where are you going to find dinner up here?"

"Ah, your brilliant husband can produce dinner in a snap. Come with me."

Japheth was careful to sit away from the platform railing as he and Hannah opened two foil pouches. "This, my dear, is dinner prepared by an engineer. Methuselah packaged food in these containers so they would last a long time. Unfortunately, we have to eat them cold. But they're nutritious and somewhat tasty. This looks like macaroni and cheese. That is chicken casserole. Any preference? Oh, and these are bottles of fruit juice."

They ate their dinner, admiring the variety of colors across the sky as the earth's magnetic field intensified and diminished at random intervals. When the sun set, only the aura illuminated their perch in the tree, and Hannah noticed something even more unusual.

"What's that just above the trees across the way?" She pointed in the direction and said, "It looks like a bright star almost on the horizon."

Japheth stared at it for a few moments, before holding Hannah close to keep her warm. "That's the Shekinah—the Presence of God—that's been standing guard over our compound for many years. We'll head straight for it as soon as our transportation arrives."

Japheth removed a metal object from his tool bag and blew into one end. It made no audible sound, but Hannah watched him as he continued to blow into it repeatedly for a minute. "This is a whistle to call our ride to the ark. It's tuned to a frequency that can only be heard by the giant Quetza. I hope the one I trained will come here when she hears it. I hesitated to tell you my plan, because I didn't want you to be afraid here in the treetop. Apparently, my concern was unfounded, since you're not bothered by heights. So, I'll tell you my complete plan, and we can go forth from there. I hope we'll be at the ark within a few hours after my baby arrives."

"Wait a minute, your 'baby'?"

"I call her my 'baby' because I raised her from an egg. She thinks I'm her mother. Doesn't know any differently. You'll like her. She's very friendly and will do anything I ask her to do. Her name is 'Brave Baby,' but I call her 'BB' for short."

"Sounds very strange to me. I've seen Quetzas high in the sky above the city and have always been afraid of their size and grotesque appearance. That boney head and leathery skin—Yuk!"

"But BB has such a sweet disposition. And her skeletal appearance is the way God made her. And she's big—really big; more than forty feet wingtip-to-wingtip. I hope she can carry both of us to the ark. Besides, we'll have the Shekinah to guide us, and the flight should cut days off our journey. We'll land in the compound at the foot of the incline that leads up to the door of the ark and take her in with us. She walks a bit funny, but she should make it up. What do you think?"

"Just because I'm not afraid of heights doesn't mean I'm eager to strap myself to a bird and fly through the air," Hannah replied.

"First of all, she's not a bird," Japheth corrected. "She's technically a reptile. That aside, I've flown on her many times before, and she's quite tame with someone in the saddle on her back. Like I said, she'll do whatever I tell her to do. It'll be a piece of cake."

"Has she ever flown with two people?"

"Well . . . no. But it's only a short flight to the ark for her, and I'm sure she can make it. I brought material to modify the saddle to carry two people."

"How about the Book? And Methuselah's cloak, the astrolabe, and all the other goodies in the cloak pockets? Can she carry both of us and all these things, too?" Hannah was concerned that their weight would be too much for the ungainly reptile. "Anything else you plan on bringing along with us?"

"You're right, we'll have to take only the essentials with us. I hate to leave these other things behind, but if we have to then we will. When she gets here, we'll see how she handles our combined weight and decide then."

"I hate to bring up so many questions," Hannah injected, "but what if BB doesn't come? Suppose something has happened to her? She could have migrated away with all these disturbances happening, or she may have forgotten what to do when she hears the whistle. Any number of things could have happened. Can we make it by land from here?"

"As the bird flies, pardon the expression, it's only about forty miles. But on foot we'd also have to cross the Euphrates River. There's a bridge downstream, but getting there would take us out of our way by at least another day or two, and that is the route the emperor and his forces will be taking to the ark. I don't want to run into a patrol or, worse, the imperial entourage. I figured we'd avoid any hindrance if we flew directly to the ark."

"But if BB doesn't come, taking the bridge will probably be our best alternative," Hannah mused.

"I don't know. The strong current of the river will make it dangerous to swim across. But let's see what happens between now and tomorrow, and then decide what to do. I'll stay up and blow the whistle during the night. You can get some sleep," Japheth suggested.

Hannah curled up under the cloak and Japheth sat beside her, rubbing her back. "We're going to make it, you know. I can't predict all that will happen, but we'll make it."

He looked at Hannah smiling in a deep sleep. Japheth blew on the whistle at intervals as he paced across the platform and studied the sky in fascination at what was happening all around them. Not only was the sky bright with colors, but, from his vantage high in the giant redwood, it seemed like he could reach up and touch the curved dome of the sky. The water canopy above the atmosphere was lowering hourly, and he guessed they had only a day or two before it could no longer sustain itself in the air. How it could stay suspended this low for so long, without collapsing, was beyond him. The pillar of fire in the distance radiated its fiery beams, like a sentinel calling him home. He sat next to Hannah, watched her sleeping peacefully, and dozed off.

He awoke with a start, thinking in his half-sleep that a shadow had passed over him. He listened for movement in the tree canopy above him, but heard nothing. His eyes blinked open again when he realized that what he heard was . . . nothing. No birds chirped. There was not even a slight breeze. What had awakened him? Had it been a dream?

When he walked toward the edge of the platform, a Quetza with a wingspan almost as wide as the platform itself, descended from above and landed clumsily on the railing in front of him.

CHAPTER 59

The Farm, Quetza's Perch

Next Morning

"Wake up, Hannah," Japheth announced. "Our ride is here!"

Hannah turned over, and then started with a jolt. Her eyes widened as she sat upright and exclaimed, "So that's your baby!"

"This is BB," he replied proudly. "Say hello to Hannah. Say hello!"

The winged monster gave a croak and a caw in response. She nodded her head up and down until Japheth rewarded her by throwing a handful of grain into her gaping mouth. She remained awkwardly balanced on the railing, which Hannah now concluded was her perch after she noticed how scratched it was. At Japheth's command, BB hopped off the railing to the floor of the platform, and the entire tree and platform shook.

"I haven't seen her in months, but she looks well-fed and healthy. Maybe she's put on weight, too." Japheth walked around, examining her wings folded around her body, and made sure she had no injuries. She obediently lifted each foot at Japheth's command. He told her to spread her wings, and Hannah had to jump back to avoid being knocked over. Japheth had said her wingspan was forty feet, but it looked even bigger to her. In spite of her enormous size, she looked like a skeleton wrapped in dark brown leather; each bone was visible. She moved with the quickness and agility of a much smaller animal.

When Japheth finished looking her over, he stood next to Hannah, with a concerned expression.

"Do you think she can carry both of us?" she asked.

Japheth examined BB more before answering. "I don't know. We may have a problem." He walked around her again and stopped in front to look at her body closely.

"I think BB may be a mother soon."

"You mean she's pregnant?"

"She looks heavier than when I saw her last, and she has this bulge in her midsection that wasn't there before. I think she's carrying at least one egg. I estimate that Quetza eggs can weigh fifty to seventy-five pounds each, so she might not have enough reserve strength to carry two people. Other than that, she looks healthy enough and glad to see us. Let's put the saddle on her and see if she is willing to fly."

Japheth retrieved the leather saddle and wrapped the straps around her neck and under her wings. The bridle went around her neck and the reins rested on the saddle. The saddle was high on her back, but far enough away from her head, so when she lifted it the rider wouldn't be poked in the face by her protruding head bone. Loops around where her wings joined her body kept the rider and saddle tight against her back. Fortunately, the straps didn't pass over the bulge in her belly. Japheth added a new strap to the saddle for a second rider and cinched it snug. When he finished, he appraised the fit and proclaimed it adequate.

"She made no fuss with the saddle and bridle, so I think she's willing to fly with at least one passenger. The question is what will she do when two of us climb on?"

"We should make ourselves as light as possible, don't you think?" asked Hannah.

"Yes. Unfortunately, we'll have to leave everything behind except the Book. We should take our shoes off and empty our pockets, too. Just wear shirts and pants."

When the two had reduced their weight as much as possible, Japheth spoke the command, "Mount!" and BB assumed her rider mounting position. She obediently bent forward, so her beak touched the floor and her head bone was out of the rider's way. She spread her wings slightly and hunched forward, so her leading wing joint touched the floor. Japheth showed Hannah how to step up onto the back of the animal's left knee and then into the stirrup. Swinging her leg over, Hannah settled into the saddle, put both feet in the stirrups, and grabbed the reins.

The Quetza suddenly stood upright, and Hannah clutched the reins and leaned in the saddle to avoid getting hit by the steed's head. "Whoa there!" she yelled.

"She thinks you're ready to fly. Hold on, and I'll see if she'll let me get on, too."

"Well, whatever you do, don't let her take off with me solo. I want you holding me when I take my first flight."

Japheth gave the command, "Mount!" a second time, and the brown-winged reptile swiveled her head toward him, as if to ask, *"What?"*

"Mount!" he repeated firmly.

With a sigh, the winged reptile assumed her mounting position. Japheth gingerly stepped up and settled in the saddle behind Hannah. He wrapped a strap around his waist and cinched it tight to hold him against the back of the saddle. Making sure the backpack containing the Book was firmly on his back, he reached around Hannah, took hold of the reins, and leaned to the side just as BB's head bone came down almost to her back and she gave a shudder. She stood upright with some effort and took two tentative steps toward the railing.

"If she jumps up on the railing, we'll know she's ready to fly. Hold on. When she does that, it's only a few seconds until she makes her commitment to take off."

BB shuddered a few more times as she stood in front of the platform edge and eyed her takeoff perch. She was flatfooted and stable standing on the floor of the platform. Up on the railing she might be unbalanced with two riders on her back and could tip immediately over the edge. She continued to stare ahead, shifting her weight from one foot to the other, trying to decide if she wanted to fly or not.

Without warning, BB took one step forward and hopped onto the railing. Japheth and Hannah redoubled their grip on each other and the saddle. The Quetza unfolded her wings, extended them out as far as possible, and, leaning gracefully forward, fell in a slow motion arc toward the ground. Both riders closed their eyes and prayed.

Immediately, they felt the animal's wings thrust down again and again until they were no longer falling. Japheth opened his eyes first and was startled to see the ground only a few feet below them. They had cleared the ground, but BB was laboring mightily to gain altitude and rise above the trees. She circled in the large clearing beside the farm buildings, gradually gaining height with each turn, but she was struggling to stay in the air. Time and again Japheth thought they were high enough to clear the trees, but then the mighty animal flew in another circle to gain more altitude.

"She can barely make it above the trees," Japheth said. "How will she cover the distance to the ark?"

When they rose above the trees, Japheth turned the Quetza toward the Shekinah flame on the distant horizon. BB obligingly made the turn, but then fell lower toward the treetops several times before recovering and resuming her flight to the ark. She repeated the cycle of struggling higher, flying for a few minutes, and then losing altitude before trying to climb again. Her heavy breathing became a labored wheeze. She bravely attempted to do what Japheth asked, but was exhausted. She had covered more than half the distance to the river, and from their height he could see the outline of the ark in the distance. Japheth feared that if BB landed in a tree to rest she would not be able to take off again, and they would wind up stuck high in a tree. He looked for someplace to land on the ground, but there were only high trees close under them. The uneven thrashing of BB's wings slowed, and one wing and then the other dipped toward the ground. Unable to fly level, she turned left and then right with each beat of her wings. Each breath became a moan, and Japheth knew she was finished.

In mid-stroke, the mighty reptile gave a loud cry and headed down into the trees. She hit the top branches, and for a moment Japheth feared that she might become lodged there. But her weight, combined with that of the two riders and their downward momentum, was enough to cause her to fall through the top branches and plummet into the lower boughs with even greater velocity. Though the branches slowed them, they hit the ground with a bone-jarring thud. The leather saddle strap broke, and Japheth and Hannah were thrown a short distance from the tree as BB rolled several times to stop on her side in a twisted jumble of wings and legs.

"Are you hurt?" Japheth asked his wife, who lay motionless on her face in a pile of leaves. He turned her over and checked her breathing. She probably had the wind knocked out of her when she hit the ground, but she seemed otherwise unhurt. He sat her up against a tree, where she began to move and mumble something about being punched in the stomach. When she opened her eyes and smiled at him, he knew she would be all right.

The Quetza flew in another circle to gain more altitude.

Japheth was sore, but not hurt. He left Hannah and turned his attention to BB, who had not moved since she fell in a small clearing a short distance away. As he bent next to her head she opened her eyes slightly. Her breathing was shallow and labored, and she didn't resist when Japheth tried to lift her head. He checked her for broken bones and found nothing amiss, except for scrapes and cuts from the branches that slowed their fall. The traumatic fall had taken its toll on her skin, and he wondered what it must have done to her internally. He tried to feel her pulse and could hardly find one. With barely any pulse and shallow breathing, Japheth feared the worst.

"How is she?" asked Hannah, crawling over to Japheth, who was cradling BB's head.

"I'm afraid the exertion of carrying the weight of both of us and then the fall through the trees was too much for her. She had such a strong spirit and gave it her all. Just like Methuselah gave his life for us back there, BB took us more than half way to the ark and gave her life for us. I'll miss her." Hannah held Japheth quietly in her arms.

After a few minutes, Hannah looked into Japheth's tired face. "What do we do now?"

"I wish we could stay here longer, but we need to move on. We have a few more hours through the forest to reach the river before dark. I know exactly the direction, and we should emerge from the forest on the riverbank just across from the sawmill. The ark should be in sight, and we will be inside by tomorrow morning. And none too soon, judging from the dark layer of clouds that is descending." Dense clouds now obscured the colored lights higher in the sky, and occasional flashes of white lightening and rumbles of thunder punctuated the frigid atmosphere.

Japheth laid his hand on BB's head and whispered a goodbye. He couldn't tell if she was breathing and felt it best to leave now before he broke down with emotion. He and Hannah walked out of the forest into a clearing from which they saw the Shekinah star over the treetops. There was no question they were very close to their destination, and, if they could reach the river by dark, they could plan their crossing.

Hannah wondered if this was a good time to tell Japheth that she couldn't swim. Probably not. She could sense that her husband had enough on his mind after losing BB. They walked hand-in-hand with growing excitement through the darkening forest toward the steady, distant light near the horizon. Tomorrow would be their last day on the old earth.

Mount Karkom

Early Evening

When Akmed, Mobi, and Karaa reached Mount Karkom, they found they were not the only ones seeking shelter there. Several dozen people had gathered already at the rocky summit and clustered in small groups. Families with children had made the long climb and huddled together for warmth. Others tried to hide from the wind between large rocks.

As the three students gathered behind a rock outcropping, Akmed lowered his voice. "We seem to be the only ones who thought of bringing extra food and clothing. How long do you think it will be before we're approached to share what we have?"

"Not long," Karaa commented as she looked around the rock. "All eyes are on us and they seem to be arguing amongst themselves."

Akmed looked around. "There's a deeper crevice over there that we might all be able to fit into. We could defend ourselves from there if they come at us." They moved their position and crawled into the larger opening with their backs to the rock and their food bags behind their bended legs. No sooner had they settled when a figure reached through the opening.

"Give me your food," the man demanded forcefully. "If you refuse, I'll take it from you myself."

Suddenly, there was a brilliant flash of white light followed by a loud bang that hurt their ears. A bolt of lightning bounced off a nearby rock, formed itself into a ball about two feet in diameter, and spun on the ground for a few seconds before it disappeared with a loud "Bang!" as suddenly as it appeared. Nobody had ever seen this kind of lightning before.

The man ran off when a crack of lightning came from above, and another incandescent ball floated past the opening of the crevice, setting a nearby patch of grass on fire. "I'm scared!" whimpered Karaa softly. The trio was paralyzed in fascination by the glowing display of lightning on the rocks around them. The barren mountaintop and the rotating cloud layer exchanged bursts of charged electricity that danced with white and blue sparks around the rocky summit. The discharges were blinding flashes and deafening claps of thunder, followed by silent floating balls of pale blue lightning that made their skin tingle and hair stand on end. The three students wedged between the rocks were somewhat protected, but other clusters of people who had not sought cover did not survive the electrical onslaught.

When the sound finally ceased and the brilliant display diminished, the three carefully gazed out of their shelter to view the charred landscape. The only sounds they heard were a howling wind among the sharp rocks and a soft rumble of thunder as the electrical storm retreated, temporarily, into the distance.

When they squeezed back into their meager shelter between the rocks, they knew this was a foretaste of more to come.

"We're going to die here. I know it." Karaa cried.

"Karaa, don't talk that way," chastened Akmed. "We're all scared, but we can't panic. As long as we stay in here, we're relatively safe."

"I heard somewhere that an old prophet was taken into heaven from the top of a mountain in a chariot of flames surrounded by balls of fire," Mobi said in a daze.

"Why in the world would you bring that up?" Karaa sobbed.

"Maybe he thinks we'll be taken up into heaven and saved from destruction," Akmed laughed.

"This is what Noah warned about," Karaa said between gasps for air. "The flood will cover this mountain. We're sitting here waiting to die."

Akmed wasn't laughing anymore. The three huddled in their tiny crevice trying not to think about death.

Inside the Ark

Same Night

Noah fell into bed, exhausted from guiding, feeding, watering, and quieting animals nonstop for the past six days. The trail of animal pairs had thinned and then finally ceased, Noah instructed Shem and Ham to lock the compound's front gates. He was tempted to leave them open during the night to allow Japheth to enter, but he concluded that the family would be more secure if they were closed. Strange things were happening in the sky above, and who knew how the population would be reacting. For the past six days, darkness was a relative term. At first, there was a noticeable distinction between ribbons of pastel light that flew high across the starry sky for what now passed for night and the dull copper-colored overcast that marked daytime. Yesterday, the sky had turned into a thick, dark gray blanket studded with ink-black clouds and continuous lightning and thunder. This display was itself terrifying, and Noah wondered what it would be like when the waters above finally broke loose.

He turned to see Miriam looking at him. "Can't sleep?" he asked.

"I'm thinking about Japheth and where he is right now. I know he's alive and must be doing all he can to get here."

Noah held her close and listened to the muted rumble outside and the random noises coming from thousands of animals still settling in throughout the ark.

"When the three boys were born, we committed them to the Lord," Noah whispered. "I thought that was the extent of trusting them into God's care. Raising them took more faith still, especially for you when they were little, but they all grew into fine young men. And, as long as they stayed with us, it was easy to trust God because we could see them each day and guide them along in life. Shem and Ham married well, and that was God's doing. I worried, too, when Japheth didn't marry. We thought we did the right thing trying to arrange his marriage to Deva, but now I see we took matters into our own hands rather than trusting in God's providence. Japheth left with Methuselah to further his education. That was less difficult, because I knew my grandfather would guide him in the things of the Lord. But we haven't heard from them in almost a year, and my faith in God's promise is being stretched to its limit."

Noah turned over to face his wife. "What if we lose him forever?" he asked with a catch in his voice.

"We won't. He'll be here in God's perfect time. Hasn't God brought us this far by His grace and mercy? Didn't He send Methuselah to help build this ark? Didn't He send His Presence to shine over us and protect us? Didn't He send all the animals to us when He knew we couldn't possibly gather them all together ourselves?" Miriam was reassuring in her questions, and Noah knew "Yes" was the answer to each.

"Since we can't sleep, let's pray for Japheth's safety, wherever he is. God knows everything going on now—especially in these final hours. His hand is in all of this, and He will do what is best."

They prayed into the night. When they finally drifted to sleep, it was good that they could not hear the sound of thousands of screaming voices still miles away.

CHAPTER 60

Euphrates River and Eden's Promise

The Last Day

Japheth and Hannah were awoken in the dark by sounds coming from the river just beyond the brush lining the bank. They had walked through the night and arrived only a few hours earlier. Their sleep was fitful, huddling under a pile of leaves to ward off the chill that had settled during the night, without Methuselah's cloak to warm them. They listened to the sounds from the river.

"Boatloads of people are floating down the river. Dozens of boats. Where are they all going?" Japheth wondered. "The water is warm compared to the air and that accounts for the dense fog. I've never felt the air this cold before."

Having rested what little they could, the sounds from passing boats now spurred them to continue on. The two walked carefully to avoid falling into the river. Soft light came from the pillar of fire less than a mile away. Its indistinct golden glow was diffused by the fog, giving the bushes and river's surface an eerie radiance. They stood on the river bank and listened intently. Sounds seemed to come from everywhere, but it was clear they were all moving in the same direction, which Japheth said was down stream toward the sea. None of the boats were visible, so that meant that people in the boats could not see the couple standing on the shore. The boat traffic would complicate crossing the river; the last thing they wanted was to be "rescued" from the water and have to explain themselves. As Japheth pondered their next move, Hannah moved closer to him for warmth.

"Can we cross the river without getting wet?" she asked.

"If I could find a small boat that may be possible, but I don't recall this part of the river being inhabited, so I doubt we'll come across any. I don't have the tools to build anything large enough to carry us. We're getting short on time, too. We'll have to swim across, but I can tie some pieces of wood together with vines to float the Book above the water and keep it dry. We can swim alongside it and push it to the other side. Should take us less than an hour. What do you think about that?"

"Sounds like a great idea except for one small detail. This city girl never learned how to swim. I didn't tell you when you first mentioned swimming across because I hoped we'd find an abandoned boat or something." Hannah's eyes pleaded with him, and he held her closer. "I'm sorry to spring this on you now."

"We'll get across if I have to carry you there," Japheth reassured her.

"If I can make a small raft with enough floatation, could you hold on to it while I push us across?"

"I think so, if you promise to stay next to me and not let me go." Hannah held him and showed the first sign of fear that Japheth had ever seen in her.

"I'll be holding you all the way. My wife will be with me in the ark, and that's a promise from God. Let me look for materials and see what kind of a raft I can put together. But I wish I had a chem light to see my way around in this murk."

It took Japheth several hours to find the things he was looking for along the bank of the river and in the forest adjoining it. He piled everything in the sand, where the bank sloped gently to the water's edge, and began sorting through it.

"What I have in mind isn't very large, but I hope it will be enough for you to hold on to and keep the Book dry."

Japheth laid pieces of driftwood side-by-side in a square about four feet on a side. He then wove vines between the pieces to tie the driftwood together. He attached dried gourds around the edge of the small raft.

"This driftwood is soggy, and I don't know how much it will keep afloat. The gourds should add enough to the buoyancy to keep it from sinking, as long as it stays together long enough to get to the other side."

Japheth pulled the wooden raft to the edge of the water and securely tied the backpack containing the Book in the middle. He tied more vines around Hannah's waist.

"This should keep you from floating away, if for some reason you briefly loose your hold on the raft." He tied four large gourds to the vine harness that crossed over her shoulders and back to her waist several times. "I know this isn't comfortable, but it's a precaution only until we get to the other side."

"How are we going to get past the boats in the river?" Hannah asked.

"That's only one of our two problems. I'm counting on the fog and darkness to keep us from being spotted. Nobody will be looking in the water for swimmers in the dark. Just in case though, I'll pile some branches on the raft so it looks like a clump of floating vegetation."

"Speaking of the darkness, shouldn't we see the sun coming up soon?"

"I don't think we're going to see the sun again for a while," Japheth speculated as he looked up into the fog. "This darkness is more than dense fog. I think the canopy layer has condensed enough to completely obscure the sun. We have a little light from the Shekinah across the river, but I believe the sun is blocked everywhere else. My hunch is that the Lord's Shekinah is all that's keeping the layer from collapsing. That means we need to hurry."

"Was that the other thing bothering you?" Hannah asked as she clung to him for warmth.

"No. I'm concerned about the cold after we've been in the water for a while. You're shivering already, and we aren't even wet yet. The cold air will sap our strength further when we come out of the water on the other side in our wet clothes. We have only light shirts and pants, and they will be soaked. That's another reason for us to get to the other side as quickly as we can."

Japheth finished tying the raft and Hannah's flotation device. They stepped into the river and pushed the raft out until the water reached their shoulders. Japheth made sure Hannah had a good grip on the raft and he pushed them into deeper water. He encouraged her to float and let him kick to push them into the main current of the river. It was only then that he noticed how strong the current was and that it would surely carry them past their sawmill destination, which lay directly across the river from them. He compensated for the current by aiming the raft upriver somewhat and kicking harder. They heard some boats pass nearby, but the fog was so dense that they couldn't see them. Near mid-river, they heard voices in the fog heading straight for them.

"Quiet," Japheth whispered to Hannah. "Hold on tight and pray they don't hit the raft. Keep your head under the branches. I'll hold on to you and dip underwater for a minute."

As he feared, the approaching boat was heading straight for them. When he saw the bow wave a few feet from them, he held Hannah tight and put his head underwater. The boat hit the raft and pushed it aside sharply, almost overturning it. It spun around and bumped against the side of the craft a few times as it went past.

"We hit something!" someone in the boat shouted.

More voices cried out, and, even from underwater, Japheth could hear terrified screams.

"It's nothing," shouted a commanding voice. "Just some floating wood. Everyone be quiet and settle down. As soon as we reach the open sea, we'll be safe."

When the wake of the passing boat subsided, Japheth raised his head to breath. "Are you okay?" he whispered while they bobbed in the middle of the river.

"Other than being freezing cold, close to drowning, and afraid of losing you in the dark, I'm fine."

"The Lord will get us through," Japheth replied. "Hang on, and we'll be on the other side of the river in a little while."

But they had drifted downstream past the sawmill, and Japheth had to push the raft upstream against the current along the shore for another hour. On this side of the river, the bank was steep and dense with undergrowth. Japheth calculated that, even swimming against the current, they would make better time in the water and be warmer than if they tried to walk through the dense brush on the bank, soaking wet.

When he finally saw the outline of the mill emerge through the mist, he was taken aback by its towering height when seen from water level. Getting in would be difficult, especially after their tiring journey across the river, which he guessed had taken over two hours. They were both shaking with cold and exhausted.

Japheth brought the raft nearer to the mill's paddle wheel that measured thirty feet in diameter. Only a few feet of its bottom section was in the water, while the rest above was shielded with heavy planks to prevent anyone from accidentally falling into the movement of the wheel. When they built it, Methuselah had said that the wheel was the weak link in the fortified barrier that circled the compound. He shielded the wheel as much as he could, fortifying the walls around the mill as he had the rest of the compound. The stone walls of the mill itself rose high above the wheel and extended in both directions to solidly meet the twenty-foot high compound walls. But Japheth figured that they could get in from river level by climbing on the wheel behind the shield and entering the building through a small hatch. From there they could walk to the ark in less than thirty minutes.

The wheel was a hybrid design that could be pushed by the river current at its base—undershot—or aided by water diverted from upstream through a channel that spilled over the wheel—overshot. The mill had been abandoned when they completed the ark and hadn't been used in years. Flow in the upper channel had been blocked off, and Japheth hoped the wheel was locked in place, so that it wouldn't rotate as they climbed it. He could envision them being crushed if the wheel turned while they were climbing inside. He quickly put that thought away and pushed Hannah and the raft over to a partly submerged paddle of the wheel.

"The water here is deep, so you'll have to let go of the raft and hold on to the paddle until I can untie the backpack from the raft and join you. We'll climb the wheel together and be inside in no time." Japheth hoped he sounded optimistic through his chattering teeth.

Hannah hesitated at the wide wooden paddle and reluctantly let go of the raft. She still wore her web of floating gourds and wasn't about to take it off until she was out of the water. While she held on to the paddle, Japheth untied the backpack from the raft and slung it over his shoulder. He let the raft drift away, since they no longer needed it. He swam next to Hannah and rested for a minute, gripping the slippery paddle. He looked up into the darkness inside the wheel casing, but he couldn't see anything.

"Can you climb onto the paddle?" Japheth asked his shivering wife. The paddle was more than eight feet across, but they could climb between the paddles and the casing near the axel, which had a narrow clearance.

"Not with this clunky bunch of gourds tied around me," she complained. "As much as I hate to part with them in the water, I think they need to come off."

"You're right," Japheth replied as he untied them and cast them into the flowing water. "How's that? Can you climb now?"

"I guess so. Think we'll find warm, dry clothes inside?" she asked hopefully.

"Not likely. Keep moving though. I'll look for something when we get inside."

When they both put their full weight on the paddle, they heard the wheel creak and felt it move a few inches. They stood on the sloping surface that was half in the water and looked for a handhold to climb higher inside the wheel. While they moved to either side, the wheel moved again sending them down into the water.

"This isn't going to work if it keeps moving. You stay here with the Book while I go back into the water to find something to block the wheel." Japheth dropped into the water and swam away, leaving Hannah shaking and gripping one of the paddles.

He returned, pulling something in the water.

"I found our raft! It got caught in some brush sticking out of the bank a little way down. It's big enough to wedge between the wheel and the covering. All we need is for it to hold until we've climbed the twenty feet or so to the maintenance hatch."

Japheth maneuvered the soggy clump of driftwood against the wheel and jammed it as tight as he could between the wheel and the stone wall. He climbed back onto the paddle next to Hannah.

"We'll try this again and find you some dry clothes."

"And how about a cup of hot cocoa?"

"Now you're pushing it, sweetie."

"Thought I'd ask. Maybe they have room service in this sawmill," she said jokingly as she peered up into the darkness.

"For the next few feet, it's all by feel. Let's hope the wheel is wedged tightly enough," he prayed.

Japheth led the way as he put his foot onto another paddle and pulled himself up between the wheel and the stone foundation of the mill house. The wheel creaked, but it held steadily while they climbed the angled spokes, which were slippery from moisture and who knew what else from the river. Hannah was glad it was dark so she couldn't see the mushy river slime that she knew clung to everything she touched. The smell of decaying vegetation was also making her nauseous. Glad for the dark, she continued climbing behind her husband.

They passed the wheel axel and the tight angles of the spokes made the footing increasingly difficult. Finally, the spokes were nearly vertical, so they knew they were near the top of the wheel. Japheth stopped and felt for the small access hatch that led into the building.

"It has to be here somewhere," he mumbled.

"What if it's locked from the inside?"

"There's no lock, but there is a latch. If I can find the door, I can slip something through an opening and lift the latch. There it is!" Japheth exclaimed. "The door is only two feet square for access to the wheel from the inside for maintenance. Now, I need something flat and rigid to put through the opening near the latch."

"We don't have anything but our clothes. What can you use?"

"Let me think," he pondered. "Of course! I can use the cover of the Book. It should be thin enough to fit through the crack." Japheth removed his backpack and held the Book in the darkness. He unclasped the two leather straps binding it.

"Don't drop it," his wife cautioned.

"That would set us back, wouldn't it? Don't worry. He held the Book in both hands, opened it carefully, and put the edge of the stiff leather cover through the crack and lifted up. With a muted double click, the latch raised and then dropped to release the small door.

Dim light from the nearby pillar of fire and fresh air entered the damp enclosure and it was a welcome relief. Hannah crawled through the opening and was glad to be out of the damp, confined space of the wheel. Her entire body, especially her hands, knees, and feet, were covered in a greenish-brown muck. Japheth joined her and latched the door behind them.

"We wouldn't want anyone else climbing up and using our entrance, would we?" he joked. "Let's try to clean off some of this gunk and find something warm. We're more cold than tired after being soaking wet for hours."

They were on the second level of the mill, about ten feet above the main floor where logs were cut into planks for the ark. Another level above them was an outside platform facing the ark in the distance. A lift, or freight elevator, driven by the water wheel and attached to a block and tackle system inside the mill walls, slowly raised finished timbers from the main floor level up to the top level, where they were moved to waiting carts that used gravity to roll down a narrow railway inclined steadily toward the ark a half mile away.

When they explored the second level of the mill, they found some dusty cloth bags used for ground grain. The mill could be converted from sawing wood to be used for grinding grain, and they had done this numerous times during the construction of the ark. They used the bags to dry themselves off and wipe most of the grime from their arms and legs. They found rags that workers used to clean the machinery, and among them were tattered shirts and pants. Soon, they had them on instead of their filthy wet clothes.

"Not exactly a fashion statement," Hannah declared as she turned before Japheth to show off her ragged outfit. "They smell dusty and itch like crazy. But the itching will keep us warm, right?" Hannah said optimistically.

They rested in the darkness for a moment and were ready to begin walking toward the ark, when Japheth heard something.

"Listen, do you hear voices?"

"Probably just more people going down the river on boats," suggested Hannah.

"No, these sound like they're right below us." Japheth went to a narrow gap in the outside wall at the side of the building and looked to the ground at the narrow riverbank below them.

He returned quickly and whispered: "It's the imperial troopers with Deva. They're trying to get into the mill."

Japheth and Hannah peered through cracks in the wall from their perch on the second level and observed a half dozen soldiers below them in dark camouflage uniforms, carrying weapons and making their way along the narrow space between the high compound wall and the river's edge. A few steps behind them came Deva, pushed forward by Chief Inspector Baaki. The girl slowed, and he shoved her forward. "Keep moving!" he growled impatiently. "Once you show us your secret entrance, we'll let you go. I've had enough of your constant whimpering!"

The girl was weeping softly as she stumbled in front of the official, and he pushed her to keep up with the squad of soldiers.

"There it is," she said, pointing to the wall.

The armed commandos continued their cautious movement along the wall and kept their weapons at the ready behind and in front of their path. Their training demanded peak alertness as they scanned the area for any possible threat. With all they had been through in the past six days, they had little patience left for their sniveling informant. The sooner they entered the compound, the sooner they could be rid of her.

Deva stood before a plank in the heavily reinforced wall and ran her hands up the edge of a section marred with deep cuts and gouges. She found a spot four feet above the ground and pushed on the board with both hands. The plank swung in and up to reveal an opening barely twelve inches wide and three feet high. She squeezed through the small opening and stood on the other side.

Japheth watched from above and stared at the opening in the wall. He had had no idea it was there. How had he missed that all these years? Hannah leaned over him and felt him wince as Deva spoke to the chief inspector from inside the compound.

"This was made by Wazim when the wall was first built, so he could come and go at night to report to your courier in town. He showed it to me when he left and I took over. Nobody else knows it's here." She disappeared into the brush inside the compound and walked toward the sawmill building.

One of the soldiers observed in a low voice that the opening was not large enough to allow them to pass. "Sir, we can't fit through that opening with our equipment. My men are too big even without our gear, and I suspect you can't fit through either."

"Then I suggest you use something to make the opening bigger!" he shouted. "And stop whispering. You don't actually believe anyone will overhear us out here, do you? We're still a half mile from the gate. Do whatever you need to do to get inside. Now!"

CHAPTER 61

Eden's Promise, The Ark's Entrance

While Shem and Ham guarded the door of the ark, they talked about what would happen next.

"I'm worried about Japheth as much as Mom and Dad are," said Ham. "I know they have strong faith that God will bring him to us before the rain comes, but, with only hours left, it seems like an impossibility."

"That's not how I see it," replied Shem. "Like Mom always says, 'God brought us this far—He'll bring us the rest of the way.'"

"That's what she says, all right. I just wish it would be over. This waiting is killing me."

The two sat silently on their bench just inside the large entry door, wrapped in their thoughts and staring at the empty compound yard before them. The line of the fence surrounding the compound was unseen in the dark, but they knew they had bolted the front gate securely. As soon as Japheth appeared, they would start raising the door to the ark. They could see nothing but the dirt ramp leading to the door and the ground around it for about a hundred yards, lit by the towering Shekinah directly above their heads.

"Do you hear something?" asked Shem.

"Sounds like a crowd of people—a large crowd. Maybe it's some of the town's people who've finally come to their senses and decided to believe what Dad's been saying for more than one hundred years."

"Sounds like more than just some of the town's people. Sounds more like an entire army."

As the sound steadily intensified, they could discern the shadow of the fence outlined in the distance. At first, only the gate was backlit, but then they saw lights through spaces between boards in each direction from the gate along the outside of the wall. Though they couldn't see the lights directly, they saw the top of the wall silhouetted by torches against the black sky.

"They definitely want to get in. I hope the gate and walls hold. But if there are that many people out there, and they really want to get in, I doubt the gate will hold very long," Ham speculated.

"Wake up Mom, Dad, and the girls, and get back here to me right away," commanded Shem as he stood on the threshold and squinted to see better. "If they do get in, we'll have to raise the door and that will take both of us. I'll get the winches ready."

Ham ran off while Shem untied the cords for the winches that raised the door like a drawbridge. The screams and wails of the large crowd became a roar that almost drowned the rumbling thunder.

The Sawmill

The soldiers used the ends of their weapons and bayonets to pound on adjacent panels of the opening. While they did that, Japheth and Hannah moved to the other side of the room. "They'll be inside in a few minutes," Japheth whispered. "I don't want to run into them between here and the ark and take on that squad of soldiers. Let's see if we can find a cart on the rail platform."

Japheth led the way up a shaky ladder to the top level of the sawmill where the finished planks had been loaded onto carts to be rolled down to the ark. They had built the rail platform more than fifty feet above the ground, so that loaded carts could roll by gravity to the ark and stop at the ramp. Empty carts were returned to the sawmill with a rope pull driven by a drum, using power from the turning water wheel. The entire process could be operated by two people—one person at the sawmill and one at the ark. Japheth's hope was that they would find an empty cart on the platform and could ride it down to the ark. The entire ride would take less than five minutes, if all went well.

Hannah reached the top of the ladder following Japheth, but, stepping off the top rung, her foot slipped, tipping the ladder backwards. The two watched it fall in slow motion. It hit the floor with a loud crash.

"There's someone inside the sawmill," cried Secretary U'ungu. "It must be someone from the ark. Now they know we're here. Hurry, we need to stop them from warning the others."

The soldiers increased their attack on the planks and tried prying the boards off with renewed urgency. They levered against the hard wood with their bayonets and were in danger of cutting each other, they were so close together around the small opening. Deva, still inside the fence, ran to the front entrance of the sawmill. She opened the door on the ground floor, ran across the main cutting room, heading for the stairs to the second level.

Deva called up for someone to help her. Japheth and Hannah didn't hear her as they stepped onto the elevated platform and looked for a lumber cart. "Nothing," exclaimed Japheth. "They must have left all the carts at the ark when they finished milling."

"Wait. Here's something . . . if it still works," Hannah said doubtfully.

Japheth ran to the far side of the platform and recognized a machine covered with a tarp.

"This is a hand cart. My brothers and I built this to run up and down the tracks without using the rope tow from the mill. Help me put it on the tracks."

He and Hannah dragged what looked like a wooden door with four wheels on its corners and a wood and iron contraption on top of it in the shape of an "H." They managed to lift one set of wheels onto the tracks, and then the other.

"The H-shaped handle pivots up and down to move a linkage under the cart that drives the wheels forward or backward. We spent days racing this thing up and down the track. It was fun back then—but just what we need now," Japheth grinned.

They stood on either side of the handle and lifted and pushed. Nothing.

"It must be rusted. Keep pushing," Japheth urged. The wheels that were once well greased now resisted noisily, but they began to loosen. When the cart barely crept to the edge of the incline, they heard the ladder from below bump against the rail platform and shake as someone climbed up to their level.

"Push harder and get us over the edge," shouted Japheth. They both put all their might into the pumping action, and as the front wheels of the cart reached the crest of the track and gravity began to add to their efforts, the rear wheels followed. Japheth looked back as their roll accelerated.

"Wait!" Deva screamed, standing on the platform with her arms held out in desperation.

Japheth held her eyes for a full five seconds while the cart gained speed down the sloping rail, and then he turned away to concentrate on their destination in the distance.

The Sawmill Railway

The soldiers had split into two groups; one followed Deva to the top level of the mill to apprehend whomever she had run after, and the other headed toward the front gate to let the emperor and his troops into the compound. The soldiers following Deva saw Japheth and Hannah descend the rail line and immediately turned back to descend to the ground floor and pursue them.

During this time, the sky was completely black, except for the bright light of the Shekinah. It was no longer a giant flickering flame, but now a blinding white light that lit the immediate area of the ark and the compound as bright as sunlight. It moved directly over the entrance gate to the compound and, in its bright light, Japheth and Hannah could see the end of the railway about five hundred yards away. Their cart aimed for the railhead at the base of the ramp to the ark, while the first group of soldiers raced for the front gate. The paths of the cart and the soldiers were steadily separating as they both neared their objectives.

Looking to his right, Japheth could see armed men through the trees, running toward the front gate of the compound. He doubted they could make the hand cart go faster without causing it to jump off the tracks. But Japheth figured he and Hannah would reach the bottom of the railway at about the same time the soldiers reached the gate. If he was right, only two hundred yards would separate them. Once the gate was opened, they would face thousands of invaders, probably led by Anak, who would be insanely intent on getting into the ark to avoid the catastrophe he now realized was only minutes away.

It was one of those strange moments when time seems to slow down. Japheth felt a calm wash over him in spite of all the danger and chaos. They had been running against the clock for the past week. The vapor canopy had descended by the hour to almost touch the hilltops. Signs of impending doom terrified the Cainites outside to the point of mass hysteria. He could hear the distant roar of angry voices, clamoring to get into the compound. Once unleashed into the compound, they would all rush straight for the ark. *Why hadn't they listened before? Why had they mocked his father when he told them their violence and evil would be judged some day? Why had only a handful of true believers survived to this day?*

These thoughts passed through his mind in an instant, until he switched his focus onto something more immediate than their race to get into the ark—*how will we stop the speeding cart when we reach the end of the railway?* As he remembered, he and his brothers ran the cart up and down the rails in friendly competition, but never had to deal with the abrupt end at the bottom. Slowing to a gradual safe stop now would mean losing valuable time in their race against the relentless force determined to open the gates and reach the ark before the door closed. The alternative seemed obvious to him now: they would have to continue at top speed and jump from the handcart just before it left the track at the end and crashed. In his mind, Japheth did a quick calculation of the risks of speed versus possible injury. He remembered that the ground in front of the ramp was heavily compacted and not the best landing spot.

"We'll have to jump at the last second before the cart crashes," Japheth yelled to Hannah, who continued to move her handle up and down to propel them onward. Their arms were numb with exhaustion, but they were fired with adrenalin. "Roll when you hit the ground, and make for the ramp as soon as you get to your feet."

Outside the Front Gate

Even Anak's seemingly limitless energy was beginning to diminish, as he stood at the gate of the ark compound and bellowed at the pillar of flame above him. He was unaccustomed to being thwarted, and he had spent the past six days fighting against the mass of people, carts, and animals that congested all available roads and pathways. His attempts to go around the jammed exodus through the swamps had been further hindered, so he and his men had used brute force to trample upon those in their way. Thousands had died by his sword or were crushed under his dino's feet as he and his troops had made their slow, but steady, progress. They had finally reached the gates of the compound and, in exhaustion, found them to be impenetrable. Methuselah had constructed the gates from iron-hard wood, reinforced with metal bands that proved to be resistant to the battering ram that Anak's escort had hastily fashioned from a fifty-foot tree. The emperor's reaction to frustration was to curse the sky above and lash out at everyone around him. Meanwhile, thousands of his subjects pressed against the rear troops, ready to spill like a tidal wave into the compound when the gates finally opened.

The crowd gave a cheer when they saw the gates yield slightly to the repeated battering. The troops renewed their efforts as men, women, and children added their hands to slam the improvised ram against the compound gates.

Thousands of eyes looked up as the column of fire slowly descended between them and the outside of the gates. The troops dropped their battering ram and stumbled back against the bodies piled behind them. Those nearest to the flame were burnt in a flash and a puff of smoke, and the gates behind the flame were blackened. The battering had weakened the wooden slabs, and a visible gap had formed between the double doors that offered an invitation to the troops to press forward. Some of the men rushed the opening, but they were incinerated before they reached it.

The Ark's Entrance

When Shem turned and peered toward the gate, he noticed that the Shekinah had grown more brilliant than before and was behind the gate. From his vantage point in the doorway of the ark, all he could tell was that something large had stopped pounding on the gate. From the corner of his eye, he noticed movement inside the compound.

First, he saw dark shapes in the distance obviously intent on reaching the front gate. At the same time, he saw a handcart racing at top speed toward the end of the tracks at the foot of the ark and more dark shapes in pursuit of them far behind. If it was a race between what he could now tell was a half-dozen camouflaged, armed soldiers and the runaway handcart, it looked like they would reach their respective goals at the same time. The handcart was obviously out of control, and the two riders were bracing for the impact. He blinked when he noticed they were dressed in rags. *What . . .* ? he thought.

Near the Ark's Entrance

Fifty yards from the end of the track, Japheth looked to see the commandoes inside the compound nearing the heavy crossbars securing the gate. Seconds before their impact, he yelled, "Jump!" and he and Hannah leapt from the cart. When they hit the ground, the cart flew from the tracks, hit a pile of rail ties, and tumbled forward. It landed in pieces with a splintering crash at the edge of the dirt ramp leading up to the ark's entrance.

The couple's fall was barely cushioned by clumps of grass near the ramp, and they fell hard, but rolled several times before stopping in the dust. Japheth called out, "Hannah, are you all right?"

"I'm in one piece, if that's what you mean," she replied, standing unsteadily.

"Where's my backpack with the Book?" Japheth cried as he looked around them. He saw it halfway between him and the soldiers who had reached the front gate.

Without warning, the Shekinah flame moved purposefully as if it were alive, leaping over the front gates, and descending inside the compound above the backpack with the Book halfway between the compound gates and the ark. Anak pressed his massive body against the charred doors to widen the opening. Other Anakim moved ahead of him and wedged through the massive gates, but in their rush to reach the ark their momentum carried them toward the fiery pillar, and the nearest were consumed. Anak avoided a similar fate by stopping suddenly and looking for a way around the incandescent obstacle. The few Anakim who dared to force their way around the pillar of fire were also felled by flames that reached out to each side to form a wall of fire. Anak, dressed in his blood-splattered armor and with his back against the compound wall, considered his next move in a focused determination to enter the ark regardless of what others did.

Finally, the gate flew open to a deafening roar of voices. Like a dam breached by the overwhelming force of built up pressure, thousands of soldiers and ragged civilians poured into the compound. Clamoring over each other, they ran into the fire and were incinerated.

To retrieve the Book of Adam, Japheth had to run toward the Shekinah that blazed between him and the approaching throng of invaders. He stood paralyzed with fear at the thought of having to go *toward* the crackling inferno to recover the Book. His hesitation seemed like an eternity, as he watched the next wave of humanity reduced to a pile of ashes.

The flaming Presence of God stood immovable above the Book and blocked the onrushing mass of Cainites and Anakim. Japheth finally responded, ran toward the flame, grabbed the backpack and returned to Hannah. He had been *under* the Presence of God and was not harmed!

"This is it! Only another hundred feet and we'll be safely inside." They ran with all their might up the slope without looking back.

Those invaders who still couldn't stop in time continued to be propelled into the pillar of fire. Others were pushed forward by those behind them, and the torrent seemed unending. Everyone who came near the Shekinah disappeared in a flash of smoke. The Emperor Anak was nowhere to be seen now. The couple clamored up the ramp, and the divine pillar of glowing heat shifted smoothly to a position at the top of the ark above its entrance. The thousands who had halted behind the charred bodies rushed forward again now that the pillar no longer impeded them. Anak emerged from their flank to lead the charge, waving his sword over his head and adding his inhuman voice to the waterfall of sound.

Japheth and Hannah blocked out the sound to focus on running as fast as they could up the ramp. Before them, they saw the door to the ark, like a wide drawbridge between the ark's entrance and the dirt ramp, already closing.

CHAPTER 62

Mount Karkom

During the night, thousands had fled from villages and towns hoping to find safety on Mount Karkom. Some men had violently snatched the three students' supplies from them that morning, and then fought over them among themselves, only to rip the clothing into pieces and scatter the food on the ground. The stronger stepped over the packed bodies huddling together, searching for anything they could take for themselves.

Electrical storms continued to pass over them, unleashing lightning and thunder. The three closed their eyes and covered their ears to block out the screams and cries of those who did not die immediately; nothing could remove the smell of burning flesh left behind in the lull when the electrical storms moved on. Shaking from the cold and the thought of yet another passing storm had left them numb. They were overwhelmed with thoughts of complete hopelessness. They looked up at a suspended ceiling of murky water, rippling in the wind like an inverted seascape, illuminated from within by brief flashes of lightning. By now it was almost close enough to touch. In the blackness between flashes, they longed for death to relieve them of torment.

The invisible blanket of water vapor that had hovered peacefully and silently over their world, protecting them for centuries, was now within a few feet of the rocks at the mountain peak.

Akmed's last thought flashed through his brain: *Noah was right!*

CHAPTER 63

The Ark's Entrance

"Japheth!" shouted Shem from the door of the ark. "Run faster!"

When Japheth looked up at his brother in the doorway, he could see that the gap between the rising ark door and the top of the dirt ramp had widened. They would have to climb onto the raising door and get inside. Hannah noticed the same thing and quickened her pace up the ramp. It might have only taken ten seconds to reach the door, but they were winded from their fall from the hand cart, hadn't slept in two days, and had all but run out of adrenaline. What should have taken seconds felt like forever.

The door was now three feet above the ramp and slowly but steadily rising. Shem reached down and lifted Hannah up to the edge of the door. He pushed her toward the entrance, where Ham had just arrived to pull her inside. Shem grabbed Japheth and pulled him up and onto the ramp. As they stumbled into the ark, the silent, glowing Presence of God remained above the ark. This gave the onrushing torrent of people a small shred of hope that they might reach the door unimpeded before it closed.

When the four hesitated in the half-closed entrance, they sensed another presence, and Japheth looked up.

"Watch out!" he shouted to the others. Japheth shoved them to one side as a giant, dark object flew through the opening of the door to the ark. Everyone fell against each other into a pile and sat stunned.

"Way to go, girl!" Japheth exclaimed. "You made it!"

"What is that thing?" asked Shem as he rose to his feet, lurching back as its squawking filled the interior.

"That's 'BB.' She's the Quetza I raised. She saved our lives, and now she's safe," Japheth exclaimed as he hugged the leathery creature.

"She's safe in here for now. But let's get that door closed all the way," Ham said.

"That's being taken care of for us," observed Shem above the din of the mob running up the ramp. The door by now was almost closed, and the others realized for the first time that the winches were turning by themselves to seal them safely inside. Anak was a mere twenty feet away, running over bodies piled five deep, and screaming for the door to open.

The door slammed shut with a solid thud. Shem and Ham ran to engage the locking mechanism. They could hear muffled shouting and pounding on the outside of the door.

"Let's get you to Mom and Dad. They've been praying nonstop that you'd get here in time. Nothing like cutting it close, brother," Shem said as he hugged his younger sibling.

"We have quite a story to tell," said Japheth as he led Hannah along the passageway into the interior.

Inside the Ark

The reunion with Noah and Miriam was tearful, as Japheth expected, but they were tears of gladness and relief. God was good, and everything had worked out as He said it would.

"This is Hannah, my wife," Japheth said proudly, when he finally extricated himself from his mother's tight embrace. "We met a few days ago, and that's a tale in itself. Great-grandfather married us just before we escaped from the Cainite prison, and we've been on the run ever since. You'll love her."

"I know we will," his mother exclaimed as she hugged Hannah in another tearful embrace.

They all hugged and laughed as Japheth went through the introductions of his brothers and their wives. The almost festive atmosphere was suddenly dampened when the ark shook violently.

"What was that?" asked Noah. "It felt like the ark dropped."

"It probably did," observed Japheth. "The deck feels tilted, too. The people outside may have moved one of the support blocks. If they knock too many out, the ark may roll over."

"There are people outside?" asked Noah incredulously.

"I'd guess ten thousand, maybe more," said Shem. "They're trying to get into the ark. But as soon as Japheth and Hannah made it inside, God closed the door."

"Just as God foretold from the beginning," lamented Noah. "They heard the message and rejected it each time. What more could He have done? God offered the gift of free salvation repeatedly. How many times I said it was only by faith you can enter through the door. But they would not listen. It is a joyous day for our family, but a very sad and bitter day for the rest of civilization." Noah's understatement dampened everyone's conversations when they thought of what would happen in the next few hours.

As the family gathered around the dimly lit dining room table for a cup of hot tea, they listened to the distant muffled sounds that penetrated the thick hull. The indistinct noise of voices was soon replaced by a steady rushing, roaring sound like a waterfall building in strength.

"That must be the rain," observed Noah. "Forty days and forty nights, God said. And we don't know how much time we will be afloat after that. When we next walk on dry ground in the sunshine, it will be a different world."

They sat silently thinking about what lay ahead for their family. They noticed a soft glow filling the room as if the walls radiated light. Japheth hurried out of the family quarters into the animal area, where he could look up the open center space to the upper deck.

"Amazing!" he shouted with excitement when he returned to the dining room. The family was talking about all that had happened minutes before God closed the ark door.

"Look around!" he exclaimed. "*God's Presence is filling the ark with light*!"

ABOUT THE AUTHOR

Michael Vetter spent his childhood and teen years in Latin America and the Caribbean before he attended college in Massachusetts. He received degrees in Mechanical Engineering (Lowell Technological Institute, now UMass Lowell) and Ocean Engineering (Massachusetts Institute of Technology) before being commissioned an officer in the U.S. Air Force. His service in the air force included tours as a scientific and technical intelligence officer for airborne reconnaissance operations and a threat assessment intelligence analyst. During an assignment with the air force, he trusted Christ as his Savior and was active in the Officers' Christian Fellowship.

After nine years in the air force, he enjoyed a twenty-five year career in the civilian defense sector as an analyst, program manager, and department head in the fields of intelligence, surveillance, and reconnaissance.

He is active in the teaching ministry at Salem Bible Church in Salem, NH. He edits a newsletter for Grace Dental and Medical Missions and serves as a Spanish translator in short-term dental and medical field evangelism clinics in Latin America.

Run Before the Rain is his first novel in a series of Christian adventures for youth and young adults with high-technology plots set in ancient civilizations. He enjoys kayaking, downhill skiing, and international travel. Michael and his wife Mary live in Salem, NH. He may be reached at mfvetter@yahoo.com.